D0269740

CP/

000000731712

Until the Sea Shall Give Up Her Dead

Until the Sea Shall Give Up Her Dead

SEAN THOMAS RUSSELL

MICHAEL JOSEPH
an imprint of
PENGUIN BOOKS

MICHAEL JOSEPH

Published by the Penguin Group
Penguin Books Ltd, 80 Strand, London WC2R ORL, England
Penguin Group (USA) Inc., 375 Hudson Street, New York, New York 10014, USA
Penguin Group (Canada), 90 Eglinton Avenue East, Suite 700, Toronto, Ontario, Canada M4P 2YR
(a division of Pearson Penguin Canada Inc.)
Penguin Ireland, 25 St Stephen's Green, Dublin 2, Ireland (a division of Penguin Books Ltd)
Penguin Group (Australia), 707 Collins Street, Melbourne, Victoria 3008, Australia
(a division of Pearson Australia Group Pty Ltd)
Penguin Books India Pvt Ltd, 11 Community Centre,
Panchsheel Park, New Delhi – 110 017, India
Penguin Group (NZ), 67 Apollo Drive, Rosedale, Auckland 0632, New Zealand
(a division of Pearson New Zealand Ltd)
Penguin Books (South Africa) (Pty) Ltd, Block D, Rosebank Office Park, 181 Jan Smuts Avenue,
Parktown North, Gauteng 2193, South Africa

Penguin Books Ltd, Registered Offices: 80 Strand, London WC2R ORL, England

www.penguin.com

First published 2014
001

Copyright © Sean Thomas Russell, 2014

The moral right of the author has been asserted

Set in 13.5/16 pt Garamond MT
Typeset by Palimpsest Book Production Ltd, Falkirk, Stirlingshire
Printed in Great Britain by Clays Ltd, St Ives plc

A CIP catalogue record for this book is available from the British Library

HARDBACK ISBN: 978-0-718-15751-7
TRADE PAPERBACK ISBN: 978-0-718-15752-4

This book is dedicated to the memory of my mother, Shirley Russell, who taught all of her children a love of books.

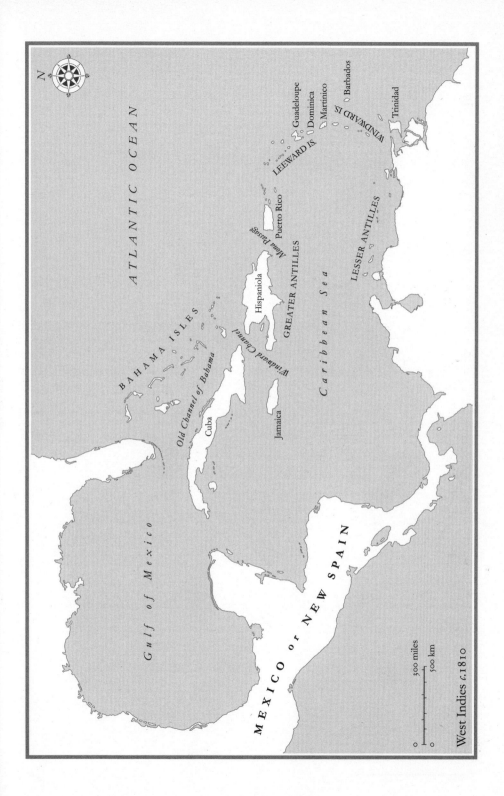

N

ATLANTIC OCEAN

BAHAMA ISLES

Old Channel of Bahama

Cuba

Jamaica

Windward Channel

Hispaniola

Mona Passage

Puerto Rico

GREATER ANTILLES

LEEWARD IS.

Guadeloupe
Dominica
Martinico
Barbados

Trinidad

WINDWARD IS.

LESSER ANTILLES

Caribbean Sea

Gulf of Mexico

MEXICO or NEW SPAIN

300 miles
500 km

West Indies c.1810

One

Lady Hattingale, accompanied by the physician, descended the great stair a few steps at a time, paused, her
head inclined and nodding at the doctor's words, and then
undertook the next three steps. The butler awaited them at
the bottom, a near-statue of discretion and deferment.
When the physician and the noblewoman came near he
whispered a few words and both physician and lady turned
their attention to Charles Hayden, who waited ten paces
distant.

'Captain Hayden,' she said, crossing toward him.

Hayden made a leg. 'Lady Hattingale.'

'Dr Goodwin, our physician.'

'Sir.'

'You have come to enquire of Lord Arthur,' she said – it
was not a question.

'And to speak with him if it is possible.'

Lady Hattingale glanced at the physician, who seemed to
consider this request most seriously.

'I do not think it would do any great harm,' the doctor
decreed. 'Ten minutes, though, no more. Do not speak on
any subject that might cause him distress.'

'Is he yet so fragile?' Hayden asked.

'He lost a great deal of blood. I am still somewhat surprised that he survived. But the young are full of surprises.'

'And his arm?'

'We will see. I think he will keep it, but he may never have full use of it again.'

'Thank you, Dr Goodwin,' Hayden said, 'for all you have done.'

The man made a modest nod. 'Who is your surgeon?'

'Obadiah Griffiths.'

'Carry him my compliments. I do not think Lord Arthur would have survived without his timely ministrations.'

'I will very gladly do so,' Hayden replied.

Lady Hattingale saw the doctor to the door and the butler took Hayden up to Lord Arthur. He was let into a large, sun-flooded room, where he found Wickham buried under a sea of white coverlets. The midshipman's face beamed like a lighthouse upon seeing his shipmate.

'Captain Hayden, sir . . .'

'This is a cosy little cabin they have given you, Wickham. You must be an admiral now to have such a cot.' Hayden sat down upon a bedside chair. 'You are pale as a cloud. I have seen fish bellies not half so white as you.'

'I am told I left half my allotment of blood upon the deck of our ship, sir.'

'Someone is always cleaning up after you reefers.'

Wickham smiled.

'Did you speak to Dr Goodwin, sir? Did he say when I might be allowed on my feet again?'

'He did not. All he said was that you are recovering apace and that you should be playing the fiddle again in a fortnight.'

'My mother will be most happy to hear it. I was a terrible disappointment as a musical prodigy.'

'Well, there, you see, one advantage already – a happy mother.'

Both fell silent a moment.

'Did we lose many men, sir?'

'We took losses, yes. But all our *Themis*es came through unharmed, you excepted. Did I never tell you not to stand in the way of a musket ball?'

'You did, sir, but I forgot myself in all the excitement.'

'That is why you should listen to your elders, for I am four and twenty and you are but six and ten.'

Again a silence settled around them.

'I am told there is to be a medal, sir?'

'That is the rumour. All the captains Lord Howe saw fit to mention in his missives to the Admiralty are to receive a medal for their part in the battle on 1 June.'

'You must have been mentioned, sir.'

'By some miracle, I was. I did not think the admiral knew my name. He did not, however, mention a number of captains who I am certain shall feel they have been slighted. I expect there will be a great deal of resultant ill will.'

Wickham nodded, as there was nothing new in this; admirals always had their favourites. 'Have you any news, sir? Are we given orders?'

'*I* have been given orders. *You* are to rest and recover.'

Wickham nodded and glanced away, blinking.

'Where is *Raisonnable* bound, if a mere landsman may ask?'

'You are no landsman, Wickham, but only temporarily aground. The spring tide will float you off. I am the captain of *Raisonnable* no more but have been given a new ship. One you are more than a little familiar with. *Themis* is her name – a fine frigate with a black character.'

'*Themis*, sir!'

'Indeed, and we are sent on convoy duty into the Baltic, with most of your old shipmates aboard.'

'Why, sir, when away? Mayhap I will be recovered enough to take ship with you.'

'We sail within the week but I expect you to buckle down and recover so you will be ship shape when we return. Mr Stephens has informed me that it is likely we will be sent to the West Indies after the hurricane season has passed.'

'November, sir?'

'Not before December, I should think. That gives you some goodly amount of time to complete your refit and resume your station aboard.'

'I shall set the dockyard hands to work on my ailing limb immediately, sir.'

'I am happy to hear it. The midshipmen's berth has become a nursery, full of children who do not know which end is which – and I am talking about their person, not the ship. I need you back to instruct these boys in the finer points of being an officer in His Majesty's Navy.'

Wickham grinned. 'I remember, sir, when I first set foot aboard in my new rig with gleaming buttons and snow-white breaches.'

'Yes, I remember my first days as well. I could hardly comprehend a thing that went on around me.'

'I was the same, sir. And then a new, young lieutenant came aboard and taught us all what service meant.'

'You know those new lieutenants, all brash and thinking they know all.'

'I hope to be one myself, some day.'

'You were an excellent acting lieutenant, Wickham, and not in the least brash or all-knowing. Why, I should recommend you to any theatre company, you were so convincing.'

This almost put a hint of colour into the midshipman's face, and he appeared to search for something to say.

'I have been reading the papers,' Wickham offered, 'one-handed.' He tried to smile. 'Do you think that Robespierre can survive the summer?'

'I do not know,' Hayden said, feeling his spirits sink. He had had no news of his family in France for many months. 'The Committee is sending anyone to the guillotine, almost without trial – a mere accusation is enough to take a man's head. It is a frightening time to be French. There must be a backlash against this – there must be a return to reason.'

The door opened then and Lady Hattingale entered. Immediately, Hayden rose to his feet.

'Please sit, Captain Hayden,' she said. 'I am but a nursing sister here.'

'Your ministrations have worked a small miracle,' Hayden observed. 'This midshipman appears well on his way to a full recovery.'

'He is doing splendidly, but forcing him to rest is my greatest contribution ... which he resists at all times. Perhaps, Captain, you might order him to stay abed until the doctor allows him to quit it?'

'Mr Wickham, I hereby order you to rest until this good nurse and the physician allow you to rise. In fact, you are to follow their instructions in every detail. Do you comprehend what I am saying?'

Wickham nodded submissively. 'Aye, sir. I shall do all within my power to be a better invalid ... but it is not in my nature.'

'No,' Hayden responded, 'it is not, but you will be back aboard ship the sooner for a little patience, I am certain.'

'Is it three o'clock already?' Lady Hattingale enquired as the mantle clock chimed. 'You see, Lord Arthur, how quickly time speeds? You shall be on your feet in no time at all.'

Hayden took the hint and rose.

'I must bid you adieu, Lady Hattingale, and thank you again for all you have done for Lord Arthur. We all believe he will be an admiral one day, if he does not want to be Prime Minister.'

'He will make a better admiral, I think,' she answered, and rose as well. 'Let me walk you out, Captain.' Then, to Wickham, 'You have your orders, Lord Arthur. Rest. I shall find you another book to read.'

Hayden gave a nod to Wickham, who touched an invisible hat with his good hand.

'Thank you for coming, sir. Remember me to the others.'

'I do not think they have forgotten; they ask about you hourly. We will be back from our convoy in a few weeks and I will look in on you at that time. Be well.'

Wickham gave a nod, appearing suddenly unable to speak.

Hayden and Lady Hattingale went into the hallway beyond, and toward the stair. She was a very tall woman of perhaps fifty years, though she carried these lightly. She was elegantly but simply dressed and wore no jewellery – not even a ring. To Hayden she seemed a practical and steady woman – just the sort he would choose to nurse his unlucky midshipman.

'He appears thin as a whip,' Hayden observed.

'Yes, he very nearly did not survive,' Lady Hattingale replied, shaking her head but a little. 'I thank God that he is on the mend and hope he does not take a sudden turn. Lord and Lady Sanstable will arrive presently.'

'I expected them here.'

'They were visiting in the north but I am certain set out the very instant they had word.'

'I am sorry not to have met them. Lord Sanstable has been a good friend to both me and my ship.'

'And well he should be,' she said, and smiled. 'Lord Arthur worships the ground you walk upon – or perhaps I should say "deck".'

'I cannot imagine that is true.'

'Lord Sanstable is convinced you have been a great and good influence upon his son.'

'I wonder if his lordship will feel the same after he has seen his son so gravely hurt?'

'You could protect him only at the cost of his honour,' Lady Hattingale very wisely observed. 'Lord Sanstable comprehends this.'

The final stair was reached and in a moment they arrived at the great entrance.

Hayden paused. 'Thank you again, Lady Hattingale, for all you have done for Lord Arthur.'

'I have known him since the day his mother brought him into this world, Captain Hayden. I could not have done less and wish I might do more.'

Hayden was out of the door, where a groom stood waiting with his hired horse. Portsmouth was but a short ride, and all the way there Hayden found himself overcome with the most morbid feelings and such tides of emotion that he could hardly keep his saddle. All of the midshipmen were his charges, given into his safekeeping by apprehensive parents. But the truth was he could not keep them safe. He could try to make them good sea officers, but they would ever face mortal danger. Wickham, he realized, had become something of a protégé – more like a nephew than a young gentleman. Of course, it flattered Hayden to think of himself somehow part of such a distinguished family – for he was of more modest stock. But musket balls did not care what colour blood they spilled – blue or red, it was all the same to them. That was the harsh truth of the sea officer's life. Anyone who stood upon a quarterdeck was a target for enemy fire. Hayden, Archer, Wickham – they could all easily end their lives sewn up in a hammock, slipped over the side into a dark, watery grave . . . there to wait until the sea shall give up her dead.

Two

It began as an uneventful crossing – if crossing a vast and volatile ocean in the dead of winter could ever be construed as uneventful. A three-day gale in mid-December, however, changed all that and set in chain a series of 'events' unlike any Hayden had ever known or even imagined.

To begin, three men were thrown down from aloft; two broke on the deck and departed this life upon that instant but the third, beyond all odds, landed upon one of his fellows, who had not heard the cries, and now it appeared to be a question of which would live, for both lay in the sick-berth sorely hurt.

The next event was less dramatic but infinitely more sensitive. Hayden had been prevailed upon by Admiral Caldwell, the commander-in-chief of the Barbados station, to carry the admiral's secretary out with him. The man, who was also a cousin to the admiral's wife, was presently installed in a cabin in the *Themis*'s gunroom. And it was in regard to this particular gentleman that Lieutenant Benjamin Archer had approached his captain.

Beyond the gallery windows, night's sullen tide gathered on the eastern horizon. Across the sky, however, quickly fading shades of pale purple, rose and gold appeared to have been pastelled upon the clouds. Shortly, a servant would slip in to light the lamps. The frigate's cabin, which had once seemed as grand as a ballroom to Hayden, now appeared cramped and dreary compared to the great cabin he had so recently vacated upon the 64-gun ship *Raisonnable*. He had been too junior a captain to retain such a command and now he was back on the ship no other officer wanted, his rise and fall so rapid he had barely a moment to register either. At least, he reminded himself, he had retained his post. *And* he was not headed north into the Baltic on convoy duty, where he had so recently spent several cold, wet months, often fog bound and land-blind. Instead, he shaped his ship's course toward the West Indies, and the warmth of those verdant islands had reached out to the crew of the *Themis* the previous week.

Archer stood in his usual post-somnolent state, uniform not quite dishevelled enough to provoke comment. In his hand he held a small square of cream-coloured paper, neatly folded. The young lieutenant was struggling to find some way to begin and looked sheepish or, perhaps, embarrassed, Hayden could not say which.

'And what is it, exactly, that Mr Percival has done to distress you so, Mr Archer?'

'Well, sir . . . he has given a poem to Mr Maxwell.'

'The cherub?'

'Yes, sir.'

Midshipman Maxwell had been dubbed 'the cherub' the instant he had set foot on the deck, for no one aboard had ever seen a youngster who so resembled a seraph, from his curly, yellow locks and rosy cheeks to his rather angelic smile.

'That hardly seems a capital offence – unless it is a particularly bad poem.'

'It is rather good, sir, but then his claim to have written it is somewhat exaggerated, as I believe a player by the name of Shakespeare wrote a very similar poem some years past.' He held the poem out to the somewhat mystified Hayden.

Hayden unfolded the paper, and there, in a very beautiful hand, was written:

> Shall I compare thee to a summer's day?
> Thou art more lovely and more temperate.
> Rough winds do shake the darling buds of May,
> And summer's lease hath all too short a date.
> Sometime too hot the eye of heaven shines,
> And often is his gold complexion dimmed
> And every fair from fair sometime declines,
> By chance or nature's changing course untrimmed;
> But thy eternal summer shall not fade
> Nor lose possession of that fair though ow'st.
> Nor shall Death brag thou wander'st in his shade
> When in eternal lines to time thou grow'st.
> So long as men can breathe or eyes can see,
> So long lives this, and this gives life to thee.

'So Mr Percival gave this poem to Mr Maxwell, claiming it to be of his own making . . . to impress our young midshipman with his poetic skills?'

Archer shifted uncomfortably and then said in a very low voice, 'I believe it was to impress him with his ardour, sir.'

'Ahh . . .' Hayden felt suddenly as though he had been thrown into a part of the ocean he had not swum before. 'And how is it you are certain of that?'

'It is a love poem written by Shakespeare to a young man, sir.'

Hayden glanced at the poem. 'I see no indication here that this poem was written to a man rather than a woman.'

'I believe it was dedicated to and first presented to the Earl of Southampton.'

'By Shakespeare . . .'

'Yes, sir.'

'Shakespeare the playwright.'

'The very one, Captain.'

'I am . . . somewhat . . . dumbfounded.' Hayden looked at Archer again. 'Our Shakespeare?'

'Yes, sir.'

'The things they neglected to teach me in school . . .'

'I can say the same, Captain.'

'How did you learn of this, then?'

'My brother, sir.'

'The barrister?'

'The very one, sir. He belongs to a Shakespeare society.'

'I did not know such a thing existed.'

'It would appear there is at least one.'

Hayden glanced at the scrap of paper again. 'He is quite certain this sonnet was written to a young man?'

'Quite, sir. It is but one of many, a fact apparently well known among scholars, sir.'

'Well, they have kept it rather a secret from the rest of us.' Hayden glanced again at the poem he still held. 'I shall never view Shakespeare's plays in the same way again.'

'It does give them a certain slant, sir.'

'Yes. But to the matter at hand . . . How has Maxwell taken all of this?'

'He came to me rather embarrassed, sir. In fact, I should say he felt somewhat ashamed. He asked my advice on how best to proceed, not wishing to offend a cousin of the admiral's wife.'

'Hmm. Does anyone else know of this?'

'Mr Wickham, sir; he sent Maxwell to me.'

'Let us try to keep it among the four of us.'

'I agree, sir, but I am not quite certain how to deal with it.

I suppose I could give Mr Percival a copy of the Articles of War . . . ?'

'But he is a civilian and only governed by them at the extreme. When does the midshipmen's reading society next meet?'

'Tomorrow, sir.'

'Do you still attend?'

'Whenever duty allows, Captain. I intend to be at the next meeting.'

Hayden passed the poem back to Archer. 'Excellent. Invite Mr Percival to your meeting, then produce this poem, saying that he has brought it to the attention of the group, read it aloud and discuss it. Be certain to inform everyone who Mr Shakespeare wrote it for. Mr Maxwell will have no more troubles with Mr Percival after that, I trust.'

Archer looked immensely relieved. 'Thank you, sir. I believe that is an excellent plan.'

Hayden hoped he was right. Best to save everyone embarrassment in this matter — not least the captain. 'How is Mr Wickham getting on?' Hayden asked, as much to change the subject as anything.

'I do not believe he has gained any more use of his hand since he came back aboard, sir. He remains one-and-a-half-handed, though I believe he is determined to make the best of it, all the same.'

'He would not let anyone know any different, no matter how he felt.'

'I believe that is true, sir.'

'Do keep your eye on him, Mr Archer, and inform me immediately if you see signs of melancholy. The young . . . they never imagine that they will not heal, but when they discover they have injuries that will stay with them all their days . . . Well, I have seen more than one youth struggle with this realization.'

'I will observe him most carefully, sir. You may rely on me entirely.'

'I already do, Mr Archer. Is there anything else?'

'The small cutter has a touch of rot in the transom, sir. Mr Hale is seeing to it.'

'Are you happy with your new carpenter?'

'I am, sir. I shall miss Mr Chettle, but the new carpenter seems a good sort, if you can overlook his bawdy humour.'

'I have overlooked greater things.' Hayden nodded to his first lieutenant. 'Mr Archer.'

'Captain.' Archer touched his hat and let himself out, allowing Hayden to return to his accounts.

'Shakespeare,' he muttered. 'Who would have thought it?'

Over the sounds of sea and breeze Hayden heard a cry and turned away from his paperwork. By the time he had risen to his feet and pulled on a coat there was a knock on his door. He opened it to find his marine guard and one of the younger hands standing just beyond – the sailor out of breath.

'The lookouts have spotted a boat, sir,' the boy said, making a knuckle. 'Mr Ransome has sent me, sir, requesting your presence on deck.'

'You do mean a boat, Jackson, not a ship?'

'Most definitely a ship's boat, sir. Appears to be only a handful in it, Captain.'

By the time Hayden emerged into the damp evening, dusk had darkened the sea and only a dim glow remained in the west, the sunset retreating rapidly.

'Where away, Mr Ransome?'

The lieutenant pointed.

It took Hayden a moment to find it, but there, upon the breathing back of the sea, a ship's boat rose and then dropped out of sight.

'Heave-to, Mr Ransome, if you please. We will take them aboard.'

Hayden put his hands on the rail cap. Wickham appeared at his side with a glass, which he fixed on the boat, distant perhaps a hundred yards. Most would hardly take notice, but the midshipman had an awkward grip with one hand – the result of the injury sustained on 1 June. He hid it well, but his friends took secret notice.

'How many, Mr Wickham?'

'I can make out only two, sir.' Wickham peered into the tube a moment more. 'It would almost appear to be a Navy boat, Captain, but the men are not in uniform.'

'Well, we shall soon know their story.'

The occupants of the boat quickly revealed that the lack of uniform was not an accident. Although one shipped oars, he had only the vaguest idea of how they should be employed. He did manage, after a time, to lumber, stem first, into the *Themis*, causing every seaman aboard to wince noticeably. The castaways required aid to board and then collapsed on the deck, both of them an almost unhuman colour and clearly horribly ill.

'Hoist in the boat, Mr Ransome,' Hayden ordered, and then turned his attention to the castaways.

'You are English,' one managed, slumped down against the hammock-netting. 'Thank God,' he said with feeling. 'We feared you were French.'

'Only in the smallest degree,' Hayden replied, and then in Spanish, for that was, by their accent, clearly their mother tongue, 'How long have you been adrift?'

Hayden half expected, by the looks on their faces, that they might not answer and instead begin to weep, but the same young man spoke.

'One day only,' he replied in English, 'but we were made terribly ill by the storm and have had almost no water or food. I am Don Miguel Campillo, Captain.' He put a hand on the shoulder of his companion. 'My brother, Don Angel. We prayed and the Lord sent you. You are the hand of God, sir.'

'I have been called many things, but that is by far the kindest. Charles Hayden, Captain of His Majesty's Ship *Themis*.' He turned to one of the hands. 'Water . . . and pass the word for the doctor, if you please.'

A moment later the castaways were draining the dipper and then draining it again. Hayden thought the younger, Angel, might begin to sob and was controlling this up-welling of feeling with difficulty.

'Will you come down to my cabin?' Hayden asked when they had drunk their fill. 'I have called for the doctor.'

Miguel struggled to his feet and balanced himself against the hammock-netting. 'Thank you, Captain.' His voice was noticeably less hoarse. 'We have no need of a doctor. We are just ill from the sea. It will pass. You will excuse our show of feeling, I hope, but we feared we would never be found and would perish on this great desert of water. God has delivered us; He must have some purpose for us yet.'

'At the very least, I think you should speak with the doctor. May I help you?' Hayden enquired of Angel, who remained slumped on the deck.

'We can manage, Captain, thank you.' With some difficulty, Miguel pulled his brother to his feet and they set off along the gangway, brother supporting brother and hammock-netting supporting both.

Hayden thought them to be perhaps twenty years and sixteen or seventeen. They were not Spanish peasants, as the elder made very clear by his use of 'Don'. Their dress was plain, but Miguel's manner, though polite, showed not the least deference. His English was polished. The two were obviously related, though the older had progressed further into manhood and his face and form showed it. Dark, well made, not overly tall, serious, perhaps even wary, but then they were with strangers and had just felt the cold presence of Death lurking among the high-running seas.

The ladder was negotiated with difficulty and on the gun-deck they found Dr Griffiths waiting outside the door to Hayden's cabin, a grey presence a bit more undertaker-like than Hayden believed was ideal in a surgeon. Inviting everyone to enter, Hayden introduced the doctor and then excused himself. When he emerged on to the darkened deck, the oceanic night had settled upon a restive sea.

Ransome spotted Hayden and came over, touching his hat. 'Did you learn how they came to be adrift, sir?'

'Not yet. I thought it best Dr Griffiths see them before I made such an enquiry. I suppose it might also be polite to offer them sustenance before subjecting them to the Inquisition.'

'Well, at least they should be familiar with inquisitions and know how to conduct themselves.' Ransome looked out over the sea. 'I do not know if God preserved them, but half an hour later I doubt the lookouts would have made them out in the dark – they would have been left adrift.'

'I agree. They are fortunate beyond anything one might have a right to expect.'

'Such is the fickle lady, sir,' Ransome observed.

'Lady Luck, you mean?'

'Yes, sir. It is best to leave as little as possible to chance, I have come to think.'

'Really, Mr Ransome? You have chosen a damned odd profession for anyone wishing to leave little to chance.' Not to mention, and Hayden didn't, that Ransome had a reputation as something of a gamester.

Ransome laughed. 'I chose it before I grew philosophical, sir.'

'Did not we all . . .'

Ransome nodded toward the companionway. 'The doctor, sir.'

'If you will excuse us, Mr Ransome?'

Hayden motioned for the doctor to accompany him back to the taffrail, where they might find some privacy. The ship lifted and settled on the long-running seas, working up into the wind and falling off again.

'I do hope it is seasickness and not some pestilence?' Hayden began.

'I believe it is nothing more, though neither gentleman would allow me to examine him more closely. They assured me there was no illness aboard their ship other than the common varieties.'

'Did they tell you how they came to be adrift in the middle of a rather large ocean?'

'They did not volunteer any information, Captain, and I felt I should leave all such enquiries to you.' Griffiths looked at Hayden. 'What shall we do with them?'

'Carry them to Barbados. I suppose I shall have to hang cots for them in my cabin, though it will be a bloody nuisance.'

'Is there not some other arrangement could be made?'

'The midshipmen's berth, I suppose, but my impression is that they are rather above such rough and tumble.'

'Yes, I quite agree.'

'I will go down and have an explanation with them. Should I offer them any specific foods, Doctor?'

'Nothing salted – I fear they drank a little seawater.'

'Nothing salted?' Hayden replied, incredulous. 'Are we not on a ship at sea? Salt is the major portion of our diet.'

'Well, do the best you can,' the doctor called after him.

Miguel Campillo rose from his seat when Hayden entered and then Angel took note and followed suit.

'Please, sit,' Hayden said, 'by all means. How fare you now?'

Neither looked in the least recovered from their ordeal and they slumped back down on the bench that ran beneath the gallery windows, side by side, elbows on knees. Before each stood a bucket, no doubt called for by the doctor.

'Excuse us, Captain Hayden,' Miguel said hoarsely. 'It was the motion of the small boat. We were forced to bail for our lives during the height of the storm and that exhausted our reserves.'

Angel looked up at Hayden and whispered, 'If I could but lie down . . . ?'

'I have ordered cots for you both. They should be carried up immediately. I hope you do not mind sharing my cabin? There really is no other place at the moment.'

Angel glanced at his brother, who nodded. 'Thank you, Captain. Wherever you choose to quarter us . . .'

A quiet knock on the door and Hayden called for it to be opened. The marine sentry's face appeared. 'Your cots, sir,' he said.

'Bring them in, if you please,' Hayden ordered.

There were eye-bolts in the beams in various places throughout the cabin where cots had been slung at different times and in different weathers, or simply away from occasional leaks in the deck-head.

'I shall let you rest and recover,' Hayden told them, 'but first, I must know if we should be searching for other survivors. Can you tell me quickly from what ship you were cast adrift and what happened?'

Miguel shook his head sadly. 'I doubt very much there are others, Captain. We sailed from Cádiz aboard a Spanish frigate, the *Medea*. The captain was a friend of my late father's. He carried us to Vera Cruz, to our uncle. Last night, our ship was running under reduced sail. In that state it was struck by another ship, staving in her stern. The two ships clung together for an instant and then were wrenched apart by the seas. There was no saving the ship; it began to sink immediately. The captain put us, with a sailor, in the first boat to be launched. Others were then to climb down and join us, but the boat was torn free of the ship and the sailor cast into the sea. We could not save him nor had we strength enough to row back to the ship. I do not know if other boats were launched. I pray Captain Andreu survived, for he was dear to us.'

Hayden nodded. 'You were driven then by the waves and wind without recourse to sail or oar?'

'That is correct.'

'And at what time did the collision take place?'

'After the supper hour. We had gone forward for the evening prayer or would have been in the captain's cabin and certainly swept out to sea.'

'I will heave-to until morning and make a search at dawn.'

'We will pray for the others, Captain.'

'Rest. Use the leeward quarter gallery.' Hayden pointed to be sure there would be no misunderstanding. 'My servant will slip in later to hang my cot and I will come to sleep not so long after.'

Hayden bid them goodnight and returned to the deck.

Ransome was still officer of the watch and Hayden sent for him immediately. Mr Barthe, the sailing master, appeared at Ransome's side at the same instant.

'We will remain hove-to and attempt to hold station as best we can until dawn. It appears, Mr Barthe,' Hayden said, 'that they escaped a Spanish frigate sunk by collision. Their boat was torn free of the ship with only one other aboard and he was lost over the side at the same instant. Come daylight, we will make what search we can.' Hayden turned his attention to the sailing master. 'If their boat was blown dead downwind from sometime around ten last night, where do you think the ship would have sunk?'

Barthe pressed his lips into a sour line. 'Difficult to say, Captain. We have had strong winds and have been making twenty miles of current a day. If I might consult my charts and ponder it a moment, sir?' He looked up at his captain, round face barely visible in the dark. 'What of the other ship?'

'I do not know. It would appear she stove in the transom of the frigate and then the two ships were torn apart.'

'At the very least, she would have lost her bowsprit, and perhaps her foremast as well. Even if her hull remained undamaged, it might have been some time before she could sort that out.' Barthe touched his brow as though in sudden pain. 'A stove in transom . . . She would not swim long, sir. Perhaps only minutes.'

'I agree. We all saw how long the *Syren* floated when not nearly so grievously wounded,' Hayden reminded them, referring to a ship sunk by collision on convoy duty not a year past.

'Perhaps we shall find the other ship, sir, and have an explanation,' Ransome suggested. 'We might hope they saved the crew, Captain.'

'If they did not founder as well. Alert the lookouts, Mr Ransome. I doubt they will see anything on this dark a night, but we must do all we can.'

'Aye, sir.'

Hayden stood with the sailing master a moment more.

'Peculiar, is it not, Captain,' Barthe said, lowering his voice, 'to find a boat from a sinking ship with only two aboard?'

'I agree, but more peculiar things have occurred, as we both know.'

Barthe nodded then touched his hat. 'That is true, sir, but this . . . Well, I've never heard of such a thing before. If you have no more need of me, Captain . . . ?'

'We are hove-to in the middle of a deep ocean, Mr Barthe; I believe Mr Dryden can keep us safe until daylight. Goodnight, Mr Barthe.'

'Goodnight, sir.' Mr Barthe waddled off into the night.

Hayden stood looking out over the sea, which still rolled heavily from the recent gale, though the wind had taken off considerably. Tattered cloud flew ever swiftly by but, high above, the stars spread densely across the heavens. He expected a clear day next, with fickle winds. It would make his search difficult, but there might be seamen out there yet, clinging to flotsam if not in boats.

A throat cleared behind and Hayden turned to find the surgeon's mate standing a few paces off.

'Somehow, Mr Ariss, I doubt you come bearing good news.'

'Dr Griffiths sent me to tell you that MacDonald has departed this life, sir.'

'The unfortunate whom the top-man fell upon?' There were new men in the crew and Hayden did not yet know all their names.

'That is correct, sir.'

'God rest his soul. His luck was as bad as the two Spaniards' was good.'

'So it would seem, sir. Luck can be like that.'

'Indeed it can. Thank you, Mr Ariss.'

'Goodnight, sir.'

This news left Hayden very low; he was not sure why. Perhaps it was the entirely arbitrary nature of ill luck; the idea that it could fall upon one in forms never conceived of and against which it was impossible to defend oneself. As though being struck by lightning became suddenly common.

In this foul temper, Hayden retreated to his cabin. The carpenter or his mates had fitted a canvas panel fore and aft to provide some privacy to both Hayden and his unlooked-for guests. By a dim light Hayden made his nightly toilet and, creeping about to make as little noise as possible, rolled expertly into his swaying cot, where sleep would not come no matter how he attempted to entice it. He closed his eyes and listened to the common sounds of a ship at sea: creaking cordage and the sound of men moving about the deck. Hove-to as they were, the motion was very comfortable – an almost gentle lifting and falling. Through the screen he could hear the Spanish brothers breathing softly and he could not think of them as anything but intruders stealing away the little privacy he had.

Spain, Hayden knew, was being hard pressed by French

armies in the Pyrenees and, after its initial successes, was beginning to take losses. The British government feared that Spain's resolve would weaken if further losses were incurred. The question then would be, would Spain turn against her former allies, or try to remain neutral? Hayden's own belief was that, if sufficiently threatened by France, Spain would rather fight a distant island nation than a great power with her even greater armies. The brothers asleep beyond the screen might be enemies and he would not even know.

The world was in tumult. Robespierre had fallen in July, but the chaos in France continued. The war had been carried to almost all the oceans of the world, and the West Indies, toward which he sailed, was no exception. The valuable sugar islands were being traded back and forth and, on some, the slaves were in revolt. The guillotine had crossed the Atlantic, carried by fanatical Jacobins bent on purifying their revolution. It was a time of fear and constant change – unsettling to everyone, as the outcome was as yet uncertain.

As almost every night of his life since he had gone to sea, Hayden woke several times. Commonly, he stirred to listen and sense the motion of the ship – to be certain all was well – but this night, each time he woke it was from a dream of a woman coming to his cot. In the darkness he could not make out her face but only a wave of hair tumbling about her shoulders, her graceful movement, the pale silk of a nightgown, perhaps, and the sweet scent of her skin. Each time he awoke with such longing that it was almost a physical pain – a fever.

Three

Soft whispering in a strange tongue. Hayden came fully awake . . . and then he realized the sound came from beyond the newly erected panel. Spanish.

Hayden spoke Spanish well enough – not so well as Italian or French – and he comprehended a good deal more, but this whispering was too low for him to catch more than a few words.

The Spanish were allies, of course, and these brothers were likely nothing more than the castaways they claimed, but there was something – as Mr Barthe had said – *peculiar* about finding only the two of them in a boat. Two from a complement of some two hundred. He wished now that he had not revealed his knowledge of the Spanish tongue. It would have been less than gentlemanly, but he might have learned something of what had happened to them – assuming it was something other than what they claimed.

The younger brother made a hissing sound and whispered, 'Listen . . . I believe he is awake.'

The conversation ceased forthwith.

Hayden realized his breathing must have changed as he woke, giving him away. As there was no more advantage to be gained, and this was commonly his hour to rise, he rolled out of his cot and commenced his morning toilet. Breakfast arrived, lamps lit.

Rustling behind the screen preceded the arrival of Miguel and, soon after, Angel.

Hayden rose. 'I do apologize for the noise,' Hayden offered. 'I rise before the sun, but you, of course, may sleep as long as you wish.' He motioned to chairs. 'Please, join me.'

'We are happy to rise when you do, Captain,' Miguel replied, sliding into a chair. 'And please, it is your cabin. We well understand that the captain of a ship must come and go whenever his ship has need of him. Do not spend a moment in concern for us.'

Hayden's steward and servant were quickly offering food.

'I tend to eat simply at sea,' Hayden informed them – half an apology. 'I hope you won't mind?'

'One grows so tired of elaborate meals,' Angel replied quickly. 'And I find simple meals produce the best conversation.'

'I fear I might be a disappointment to you, Don Angel. Before I have had coffee I can barely mumble a few words.'

'Then you must have coffee, Captain,' he said, and motioned Hayden's servant with such confidence that the man filled Hayden's cup before he thought, and then turned red as a marine's coat. Hayden let it pass, not wishing to embarrass his guest.

'We will begin a search today to see if there are any other survivors from your ship. Can you tell me, now, what occurred?'

Angel glanced at his brother, clearly deferring to him.

'We set off,' Miguel began, his face darkening, 'three frig-ates from Cádiz, sailing for Vera Cruz. We were guests of Captain Andreu, who, as I said, was a friend of our late father. All went well until the gale. Captain Andreu told us to not be alarmed, for his ship had been through many much worse.' His voice lowered noticeably. 'But that evening a mass was held for all the officers and men who were not on watch to pray for our deliverance. I could tell that the men were frightened and dismayed. Some appeared unnerved. Many of these men had spent their lives at sea. I assumed from this that the storm was much worse than Captain Andreu had told us.'

Hayden nodded. 'Yes, we went through it as well. A hard gale – not a storm – but the seas were confused and steep and greater than the wind warranted.'

Miguel glanced at his brother as if Hayden had confirmed their own thoughts. 'As we prayed, there was a thunderous, great crash and we were all thrown down upon the deck. Immediately, water began to rush in. Some men were orderly but others made a rush for the ladders and in the panic trampled their crew mates. I was knocked down myself and, if some man, I know not whom, had not hauled me up by my collar, I should have been killed. Captain Andreu got us to the deck and established order there. The men were frightened for their lives but Captain Andreu had their respect. The ship was already down by the stern and sinking more rapidly than I would have thought possible. There was no saving it. We were told by the officers on deck that there had been a collision, but the other ship was not then to be seen.

'Captain Andreu put us in the first boat launched with a single crewman – I think you say a coxswain – and we were hoisted out and into the terrible seas. Men were to climb down into the boat then, but the ship suddenly rolled away from us and our boat was torn free. We were thrown down and the boat half filled. When I rose to my knees the coxswain was gone and the ship had rolled on its side. The seas drove us away from the ship. We bailed for our lives.

'I did not know how to manage a boat in such seas, but it hardly mattered; we became ill with the motion and could barely move. We bailed enough to stay afloat – fear being greater than our sickness. After a very long time the winds grew small and the seas less angered. The whole day we lay in the boat and prayed to be saved. And then, as night found us, Angel see your ship far off on the horizon. The rest you know, Captain Hayden.'

Hayden took a fortifying sip of his coffee. 'You were beyond lucky to have survived the sinking, and then to have been discovered at sea . . . Well, it is a vast ocean . . .'

Angel appeared moved, his eyes glistening. 'God preserved us. There can be no other explanation.'

Hayden, who was less convinced that God intervened in the affairs of men, said nothing. 'Don Angel, you have a bloodstain on your shirt and jacket,' Hayden noted. 'Are you injured?'

Looking confused, Angel opened his coat, revealing a shirt stained a muddy red. 'No. It is some other's blood – from the melee, I think – but I do not know who.'

'Well, you were fortunate not to be injured.'

Angel fixed his gaze on Hayden. 'You place a great deal of faith in luck, Captain.'

'It is the sailor's superstition, Don Angel,' Hayden responded. 'When I was a young midshipman a ship fired grape at our quarterdeck from barely thirty yards off. Four of us stood together – three abreast and one behind me. We were, all of us, thrown down on the deck; the men to either side were wounded and the man directly behind me was killed. It was impossible. The shot would have had to pass through me to strike him, yet he was killed instantly. When he was examined by the surgeon, it was found that the shot had struck him in the chest and severed both a major artery and his spine. A miracle – or perhaps divine intervention –

was the offered explanation for my survival. But then, we realized the ship's bell had been struck at the same instant – struck at such an angle as to have deflected the grape shot, killing my friend but missing me.'

Angel reached out and touched Hayden's arm. 'But you do not know that it was not a miracle or divine intervention, Captain. God might have preserved you for some other purpose.'

Hayden shrugged. 'Perhaps. Perhaps it was to find you and your brother, adrift in a great ocean, just as you said. You must excuse me. I am called to the deck. We shall begin our search for survivors. It has only been a day. There is always flotsam; some men might yet be alive.'

Miguel rose as Hayden did and touched his brother on the shoulder. Angel appeared confused a moment and then came to his feet as well. Hayden went out.

Dawn was summoning its energies beyond the eastern horizon. The last remnants of the gale had blown clear and the stars glittered against the lightless sky.

'Captain on deck,' Hayden heard from nearby, and there was a rustling in the dark as men shifted or stood. Out of habit, Hayden went to the binnacle, but the ship was hove-to and did not really have a heading – and he could easily have told it from the stars on such a night.

'Captain . . .'

Hayden turned to find Archer approaching.

'Mr Archer,' Hayden replied. 'All is well, I trust?'

'Perfectly well, sir. We have a fair topsail breeze, sir, and the sea has gone back down.'

'It is a fair breeze for Barbados, Mr Archer, but not necessarily so for our purposes.'

'I take your point, sir. I have detailed men to go aloft as lookouts and I shall station men around the deck as well.'

'Have a boat cleared away and ready to launch, Mr Archer, in the chance that we find anyone.'

'Aye, sir. And how shall we proceed?'

'I shall confer with Mr Barthe, who I am certain has been consulting his charts, estimating the winds and currents, and has come to a conclusion. Even so, it is a needle in a haystack, Mr Archer, a bloody needle in a vast haystack.'

Hayden took a turn around the deck, as was his habit, and spoke here and there with the hands and officers. Many men were new and Hayden was only now learning their names and character. A few had been fishermen or had sailed in merchant ships but too many were landsmen snared by the press. These men were rather wide-eyed and silent; they had never experienced the ocean in its anger and were still shaken by it. Another day would see them begin to recover, Hayden thought. Then the relief would appear and they would start to breathe again and even laugh. The first bad gale at sea was always unnerving.

Upon his return to the quarterdeck, Hayden found Mr Barthe and Archer huddled in conversation.

'Mr Barthe,' Hayden addressed the older sailor, 'I have confidence that you have given our pending search your most careful consideration?'

'I have spent some energies on it, Captain,' Barthe admitted. 'Shall we look at a chart, sir?'

Mr Barthe had a temporary table set up under the upper deck just outside Hayden's cabin, for charts were at once costly and invaluable. Without them, a ship wandered lost among unknown perils.

Hayden, Archer and Barthe were joined by Wickham, the only midshipman senior enough to be included in such a gathering – indeed, Wickham had recently been acting-lieutenant. Hayden allowed him certain privileges to soften the blow of being reduced to a mere reefer again.

In the glow of a lamp, Barthe indicated a pencilled circle.

'It is my best guess, Captain, that the Spanish frigate went down here. Allowing for wind, current and seas, any boats would have been driven downwind . . .' Barthe put the point of his compass in the centre of the circle and drew a few degrees of arc dead downwind. 'I do not believe a boat would have passed beyond this point in so short a time.' He tapped a little triangle between the arc and the circle. 'We are here, sir. We have not held our position perfectly all night but have been carried by the current and lost some to the wind as well. Even so, any boats or wreckage should be downwind of us. I believe we should sweep here, sir, forth and back perhaps two leagues either side of our present position.'

'Twelve miles, Mr Barthe,' Hayden observed. 'That is a great area of ocean.'

'So it is, sir, but the winds varied somewhat in direction during the gale and even more so after.' Barthe met his eye. 'To be safe, Captain.'

Hayden considered a moment then turned to his first lieu-tenant. 'Mr Archer, we will wear at the end of each sweep and keep the wind ahead of our quarter. If there are survivors we must not miss them.'

'Aye, sir. When shall I begin, sir?'

'An hour after the sun is up, Mr Archer. And Mr Archer? Launch a cutter, if you please. In these seas I believe we can safely stream it manned.'

'Aye, Captain.'

Barthe and Hayden were left alone over the chart and Hayden related what the Spaniards had told him of the frigate's sinking. Barthe shook his head and looked very grave.

'I do not hold out much hope of finding anyone else, sir.'

'No, but I for one will sleep better if I feel we have scoured the sea as best we can.'

'I agree entirely, Captain Hayden. To lie awake wondering if there was a man out there clinging to some bit of flotsam . . .' He tapped his chart. 'If only for our own peace of mind we must make the most thorough search we can manage.' Barthe looked up at him. 'And how fare our survivors, sir?'

'Better this morning. They ate, which I take as a very good sign.'

'Indeed it is. If they are the only two survivors . . . Well, maybe there is something to this Papism, sir.'

Hayden laughed. 'Mr Barthe, I am the only man aboard you should ever say that to.'

'It was but a momentary lapse, sir. It shall not be repeated.'

'Let us repair to the deck.'

'Aye, sir.'

Dawn had not yet chosen to make itself known, but the wind blowing from the north-east felt suddenly warmer. There was often a light squall of rain at sunrise but this morning the horizon appeared devoid of low, dark cloud. The men who had gathered over Mr Barthe's chart now stood in the stern of the ship, looking off to the east.

'How did Homer describe the fingers of dawn?' Hayden asked suddenly.

'"Wine dark", was it not?' Barthe answered innocently.

'I believe it was "the wine-dark sea", Mr Barthe,' Archer said softly.

'And "rosy fingers of dawn",' Wickham added.

'Ah, well, the fingers of dawn might well be "rosy",' the sailing master asserted, 'but I have never seen a "wine-dark sea".'

'You lack a poetic soul, Mr Barthe,' came the voice of Lieutenant of Marines Hawthorne. 'It often appears "wine-dark" in my experience.'

'I am certain it is, if you look through a fully charged claret glass, Mr Hawthorne,' Barthe replied, mock-testily.

Hawthorne appeared among them, tall and erect. 'Ah, that is the explanation. Homer must have done the same, I should think.' Hawthorne glanced from one to the other. 'And why are we all staring off at the horizon?'

'We are awaiting the sun, Mr Hawthorne,' Archer told him, 'so that we might begin our search for survivors.'

'The sun will arrive at its usual hour. All your staring will not change that. But by all means, do not let me discourage you. I am certain that Homer would approve.'

Eastern grey turned to crimson and then a rather spectacular gold. Archer sent lookouts aloft and all the midshipmen appeared with their glasses. Those not on watch went aloft as well. Hayden had often noted that anything that broke the monotony of a ship's routine – especially on passage – was taken up by the men with great zeal. There were soon men all about the ship, scrutinizing the sea at every point of the compass.

Hayden ordered the ship underway and the morning trades quickly bellied the sails. Miguel and Angel appeared then, and Hayden invited them to the windward side of the quarterdeck, along with Mr Percival, the admiral's poet-secretary. The sea, however, was uniformly empty of anything but water, though admittedly they did see petrels and a very fine specimen of the bosun bird.

The watch below soon tired of this and wandered off, a few at a time. They had all seen an empty ocean before. Hayden quizzed the sea with his glass, not so much because he thought he would find anything but because the lookouts would not want their captain to spot something from the deck before they saw it from aloft. The first lieutenant, Mr Archer, would quickly find a suitable punishment for such a failing.

The first sweep revealed nothing, but upon wearing and beginning their second sweep flotsam began to appear – a grating, a gun carriage without its gun, a broken barrel. Standing on, they found a capsized boat, but a subsequent investigation revealed the larboard side had been stove in. All this did give Hayden some hope, however.

Just before noon, a lookout on the forward tops sang out: '*On deck!* Flotsam, two points off the larboard bow!'

Archer, who was forward, called up, 'What is it, Higgins?'

'Don't know, sir,' came the reply. 'Mayhap the stump of a yard, Mr Archer. Might be men, sir, but they ain't moving.'

Hayden and most of the guests went quickly forward. It took Hayden a moment to find this object in his glass but, finally, he did.

Angel approached and stood beside him. 'Are there men, Captain Hayden?' he asked softly.

'I cannot be certain.' Hayden handed the young man his glass.

After a moment of futile effort Angel returned the glass to Hayden with a shrug. 'I could find nothing.'

'There is a bit of a trick to it,' Hayden said. 'Stare intently at the object and raise the glass to your eye without removing your gaze, even in the smallest degree. Easier said than done on a moving deck. It is one of those odd skills that, once learned, is never lost.'

Angel nodded, but Hayden could not help but think he looked unsettled, almost apprehensive.

The ship was hove-to and the cutter quickly surging over the waves, white sweeps catching the sunlight as they broke the surface then disappeared briefly into the sea, over and over. The little boat covered the hundred yards of heaving blue in record time and brought up smartly alongside the flotsam.

Hayden turned his gaze aloft. 'Mr Wickham? Can you see what they do?'

Wickham's head appeared from the tops. 'I cannot, sir.' There was a murmur above, the head withdrew and then reappeared. 'They appear to have taken aboard a man, sir.'

'Alive?'

The midshipman shrugged. 'I cannot say, Captain.'

Hayden beckoned one of the hands. 'Pass the word for the doctor, if you please.' And the man ran off, bare feet padding along the gangway.

The cutter was soon making its steady way back to the *Themis*, Hayden's own coxswain, Childers, at the tiller. Hands, officers and guests gathered at the rail, staring at the boat, which was laid expertly alongside. A hammock was lowered. A moment later it came up the side, bearing the body of a young man, bits of seagrass tangled in his hair and streaming from his limbs. He was laid out on the planks, eyes closed, a stain of glittering seawater overspreading the deck about him.

'There is no need for me to examine this man,' came the doctor's voice. He had appeared at Hayden's side. 'Drowned.'

'Did you know him?' Hayden asked Miguel and Angel, both of whom looked terribly grim. They stared at their own fate, lying before them, evaded by the smallest margin.

'I did not, Captain,' Miguel replied, 'but the names of the crewmen were unknown to me.'

'Pedro,' Angel whispered. 'His name was Pedro. His family name I did not know. He was well liked.' He turned to Hayden. 'What will you do with him?'

'We have no choice but to bury him at sea. I will consult our parson as to how this should best be done. We realize, of course, that he is of your church and not ours.'

Angel nodded and turned his attention back to the man lying on the deck. 'So many died without last rites. I believe God will not mind.'

In the end the man was sewn into the hammock used to lift him to the deck and slipped over the side, after Mr Smosh had intoned some suitably neutral words. The search continued, but the excitement and novelty had been extinguished by the discovery of the dead sailor. Two hundred men had almost certainly gone down into the dark depths, and it was a sobering realization for every man aboard.

By mid-afternoon the search was abandoned and Hayden ordered the *Themis* back on her course for Barbados. The north-east trade had returned and sped the ship along, her sails full and drawing. She rolled heavily in these conditions, but there was nothing for it.

Over supper Hayden could not help but feel his Spanish guests looked both haunted and relieved and, though the former was easily understood, the latter was not, causing him to wonder if he was not, somehow, mistaken about their feelings.

Later, Hayden ascended to the deck, where he stood by the taffrail, admiring the stars and small moon. It was a close night, for they had entered the zone of equatorial summer; soon, no doubt, they would be cursing the heat, after longing for it the previous weeks. It was as fine a night at sea as Hayden could remember. The trades had eased a little after sunset and the motion of the ship was more civilized, yet she still hurried on her way.

Hayden set out on a circuit of the deck, to stretch his legs and settle his supper. He made his way along the starboard gangway to the forecastle, where Archer intercepted him, coming the other way.

'Have you come to take a turn of the deck, Mr Archer?'

'I have come, sir, from the midshipmen's reading society.'

'Have you? And how went your meeting this evening?'

'Most instructive, Captain. Mr Maxwell produced a poem by Shakespeare which provoked the most lively discussion.'

'And was Mr Percival in attendance?'

'He was, sir, and uncommonly silent on the matter of our interest. He retreated to his cabin the moment we drew to a close. I confess, I felt a little sorry for him.'

Hayden nodded. 'Have you experienced a more lovely evening at sea, Mr Archer?'

'Hardly, sir. I can almost imagine I smell the perfume of the island flowers already.'

'You have an acute sense of smell – they are more than a sennight off yet.'

Archer accompanied Hayden back up the larboard gang-way, where Hayden's eye ran over every little detail of his ship that could be made out in the dim light. It was well known among his crew that nothing amiss escaped his notice. For most of the crew it was a matter of pride that the captain would find nothing to trouble his eye. For the rest, it was a matter of angering the bosun, who was a large man, and, though Hayden believed him kindly by nature, he was not averse to doing his duty and inflicting as severe a punishment as he believed a given transgression required.

Hayden and Archer parted at the quarterdeck gangway, Archer going below and Hayden returning for a moment to the taffrail. He stood there, admiring the night, listening to the sounds of his ship speeding across the vast ocean. A whisper reached him, coming up through the open skylight. Feeling rather ignoble, he crept silently nearer.

'No one but the English know we are alive,' Miguel said in Spanish. 'To everyone else, we are dead. We may claim to be anyone we wish. Anyone at all.'

'But the English will not keep our existence a secret,' Angel replied, just as softly.

'No, but we will have time to find a ship in Barbados – to slip away.'

'And how will we pay for our passage, Miguel? Everything we possessed has gone to the bottom of the sea.'

'There will be a way. I will find it.'

'I still believe we can confide in Captain Hayden. He is a good man; I feel it.'

'No doubt you are right, but he is, above all things, dutiful. A typical Englishman.'

'Captain . . . ?' The man at the helm spoke quietly. 'I believe I saw a light, sir.' He gestured to starboard.

At the sound of a voice the Spaniards went silent and

Hayden crept away as stealthily as he could. When he was a dozen feet off he said clearly, 'Where away?'

And damned if it was not a light! Hayden called up to the lookouts, who spotted it almost immediately. Ransome came hurrying along the deck, whence he had been overseeing the renewal of some chafing gear.

'I will deal with the lookouts, Captain . . .' he said as he mounted the quarterdeck '. . . suitably.'

'I have no doubt of it, Mr Ransome, but what of this light?'

'On deck!' the lookout on the maintop called down. 'Light a league off our starboard beam, Mr Ransome. Appears to be moving north, sir.'

'Away from us,' the lieutenant said. 'I wonder if she is one of the Spaniards?'

'It would seem unlikely. They were headed for Vera Cruz.'

'Shall we alter course, sir, to close with them at first light?'

'I think we have lost enough time on this crossing, Mr Ransome. Let us continue on our way.'

'Aye, sir.' He touched his hat and turned away, calling out, 'Mr Hobson? Replace the lookout on the maintop, if you please.'

'Aye, sir.'

And so Hayden was left standing at the starboard rail, watching a mysterious light rise and disappear, growing ever smaller.

No one but the English know we are alive.

We may claim to be anyone we wish. Anyone at all.

It would appear that Mr Barthe would be proven right; there was something peculiar about these two brothers. And Hayden thought it best he find out what – perhaps also typical of an Englishman.

Four

There were, aboard his ship, a number of men Hayden trusted utterly. Indeed, he had trusted them with his very life on more than one occasion. However, it was not merely a question of trust that caused Hayden to choose Dr Griffiths, Lord Arthur Wickham and Lieutenant of Marines Hawthorne as his confidants. The certainty that they would not betray a confidence was every bit as important. Finding a place to speak privately, however, on so small a ship was almost a greater difficulty than deciding who should be included in the conversation.

Normally, Hayden would have arranged such meetings in his cabin but as he now had two guests, and they were the subject he wished to discuss, he had been forced to look elsewhere. The foretops would have been ideal for his purpose – send the lookout down and they would have all the privacy one could ask for – but the good doctor did not like climbing to heights. In the end, Hayden led his companions down to the orlop, where, outside the door to the forward powder magazine, they held their discussion, standing but a spark away from utter destruction. As quietly as he was able, Hayden related what he had overheard the previous night while lingering by the skylight.

Immediately Griffiths asked, 'If they are not who they claim to be, then who are they?'

Hayden shook his head. 'I do not know.'

'It does sound like they are running from something,' Wickham observed. 'I wonder what it might be?'

'The law?' Dr Griffiths suggested.

'They do not seem like criminals to me,' Hawthorne replied thoughtfully. He crouched between the beams, steadying himself with one hand.

'True, Mr Hawthorne,' the surgeon said, 'but that is the business of certain criminals – appearing *not* to be what they are.'

'They seem rather young for that game,' Hawthorne replied, a little defensively.

'I am certain we could speculate until we reach our old age,' Hayden told them, 'and conclude nothing. I am asking your aid in discovering who our guests might be and what their intentions are. Mr Wickham, you are near the age of Angel, so perhaps you could make some effort to befriend him. He might have need of a confidant. Your particular charm, Mr Hawthorne, could be put to good use in our cause.'

'Ah, if only these Spaniards were señoritas,' Griffiths said, and grinned. 'They would soon be telling our good lieutenant their most intimate secrets.'

'And of course, you, Doctor,' Hayden continued, 'who knows what they might let slip in conversation – for who does not trust their doctor?'

Griffiths gave a small shrug.

'And I am sharing my cabin with them and so might glean a fact or two. We shall see. If they are lying about their identity, what else might they be hiding? Did their ship really founder after collision? Why was there blood on Angel's clothing?'

'I should keep a close eye on my valuables, Captain,' Griffiths cautioned. 'They sound desperate for money.'

'I have so few valuables. Turning me over would hardly be worth the effort.'

Wickham looked thoughtfully at Hayden. 'I do not suppose, sir, it would be possible simply to confront these brothers with your doubts about their story?'

'Only if one is prepared to fight a duel,' Hawthorne replied cheerfully. 'These Spaniards . . . they do not take anyone traducing their honour very kindly.'

'Perhaps not a good idea, then,' Wickham allowed quietly.

'It would seem to me,' Griffiths offered, 'that young Angel believes that you, Captain, can be trusted with their secret – whatever it might be. I suggest our best hope of finding out who these young men are lies with you.'

'I will do all I can,' Hayden assured him.

'I am not certain why we care,' Hawthorne observed. 'What is it to us? Undoubtedly, the Spanish authorities might want to know who these two gentlemen are, but unless there is a reward offered for their apprehension I cannot see why it should matter to us in the least.'

Hayden was rather taken aback by this 'The Spanish Navy will certainly want to speak to what appear to be the only two survivors from a crew of some two hundred souls – and that is if only one ship sank. It was a collision; we do not know what became of the other ship. They are keeping back some information – I do not know what.'

This caused a moment of silence, but Hawthorne's objection had taken root; Hayden felt it as well. What was this matter to them? Why did he care if the Spaniards were lying?

'It seems to me,' Wickham offered quietly, 'that if Angel

was suggesting they confide in you, Captain, they can hardly be criminals. No, there is some other reason they do not want it known that they have survived. Perhaps we might learn their story by offering them our aid?'

'A difficult bargain to make until you know what it is they are hiding,' Griffiths stated.

'Nor is time our ally in this matter. We are but a week out from Barbados.'

It was on this uncertain note that their gathering adjourned.

Five

Sleep was a difficult proposition for Angel Campillo. He moaned and muttered and woke often from nightmare. Being cast adrift in a small boat in a strong gale and coming so near to death was enough to give a hardened sea officer nightmares, Hayden thought; he could not imagine what such an experience would be like for a landsman. The muttering, though almost loud enough to be clear, was in Spanish, and largely indecipherable to him.

He did, to the best of his abilities, make himself amiable and approachable, spending considerable energies to win the trust of the Spaniards. The more he spoke with them, the more he found them congenial company, good-hearted and kind. Miguel was undoubtedly more guarded and wary, but Angel seemed more troubled. This manifested itself in brooding and a kind of pained distraction, his attention focussed on things not present.

Perhaps four days after their discovery, Hayden found himself alone at the breakfast table with Angel for the first time; the two brothers were ordinarily almost inseparable.

'And where is your brother?' Hayden enquired.

'Off with Mr Hawthorne, for what purpose I cannot say.'

Well, Hayden thought, the marine lieutenant was apparently doing his part.

'You slept well, I trust?'

Angel made a face – almost a grimace. 'As well as I do commonly.'

'If I may be permitted to observe, Angel, you appear to be much affected by your recent misfortune.'

'Misfortune, Captain Hayden? My brother and I were delivered from certain death . . . when so many others were lost. That is not misfortune . . . at least not for us.'

Hayden nodded. 'That is true, but do not suffer any guilt over your good luck. It was beyond your control . . . everything that occurred.'

Angel looked away, thoughtful a moment. 'Do I appear to be suffering guilt, Captain?'

'I do not know, Angel, but many do. I have seen it. A single member of a gun crew will survive a battle and then be tormented by some species of guilt that he alone lived when all the others perished. Often, they feel it undeserved.'

Angel nodded. 'I do feel . . . great distress that so many others died while my brother and I were spared. I do not understand why . . . why us and not the others? And, yes, it does not feel deserved, though it is not my place to question the purpose of God.' He looked at Hayden then. 'But I am not the only resident of this cabin who appears troubled, Captain Hayden. I imagine at times that you suffer some regret or sorrow.'

Hayden had been at pains to hide this . . . but apparently was not as successful as he believed. He wondered if it was obvious to all or if only Angel had seen it because he shared Hayden's cabin.

'Disappointed hopes, Angel. A common affliction for sea officers, I fear. It is no small thing for a woman to marry a man who will spend his life at sea.'

'And often in danger,' Angel added.

'And that, as well. The cure for me shall be employment,

which I hope to have plenty of once we reach Barbados. There is nothing worse than a long sea passage with little or nothing to break the monotony. One has far too much time to contemplate one's troubles – an unhealthy state, to be sure.'

'There are many ways to avoid one's troubles, Captain – wine, gambling . . . brothels. Sometimes the enemy must be faced head on. As an officer, I am quite certain you know this to be true.'

'I do, but some enemies are not so easily vanquished and there is no choice but to fly from them . . . until one has time to gather one's resources.'

'That is true as well, Captain Hayden.' He raised his coffee cup as though to offer a toast. 'To the enemies we flee – may we turn to vanquish them one day very soon.'

'Hear,' Hayden responded, lifting his cup.

As Hayden made his way to the deck not long after, he had the strange feeling that Angel had learned more of Hayden's secrets than he had of the Spaniard's. For some reason, he found this very slightly amusing – he did not know why.

The day dawned and the sun burned down, its unrelenting fire relieved only by the constant cooling trades, sifting down skylights and scuttles and through the open gallery windows in Hayden's cabin. On such days Hayden thought there was no better place to be in all the world, sails full and drawing, the crew busy about the ship, the broad-backed waves of the trades stretching off to the far horizon, a vast depth of blue both above and below. Mother Carey's Chickens scuttled across a surface broken now and then by porpoises or a distant whale. Below, in the shadow of the passing ship, a small population of fish – dorados, striped pilot fish and others

Hayden did not know – had taken up residence and remained on station day after day. During the dark hours, schools of flying fish would smack into the topsides and occasionally one or two would make it on to the deck, where the ship's cats patrolled in hopes of finding a fresh supper.

The great enemy on such crossings, where the sails were set and sometimes their sheets not touched for days at a time, was chafe, and the bosun and his mates were seemingly always at work aloft, renewing thrummed mats and scotchmen, the slush bucket in steady employ. It was a happy ship, Hayden thought, which gave him a small sense of pride.

There was, however, a pall hanging over his vessel – a palpable anxiety, if not a bridled fear. Its source was no secret: they were sailing toward the breeding ground of the Yellow Jack – the fever that killed without distinction of age, vigour or rank. It was well known among hands and officers alike that, once contracted, recovery was beyond rare. This disturbing knowledge was a weight balanced against the very real prospect of rich prizes, for the seas to which they sailed were a cruiser's dream – provided one survived to collect. Hayden often heard the men whispering – stories of crew mates who had caught the Yellow Jack – the stories almost always ending the same. There was, however, one man aboard who it was claimed – and he did not deny it – had come down with the dreaded fever and, against all odds, survived. His name was Jimmy Walker, though he was known as 'Yellow Jack' among his mates – or just 'Jack'.

'Ask Jack about the fever,' one of the men would say, and he would saunter over and regale them with his gruesome tale – how a dozen men in the sick-berth all perished while he lived – a miracle he attributed to an overly regular intake of sauerkraut, which was sometimes carried aboard ships as an antiscorbutic. As a result, the ship's allotment of sauerkraut was diminishing at a rapid rate and the men continued to request it at almost every meal. Dr Griffiths was of the opinion it had no effect in warding off either the scurvy or Yellow Fever, but Hayden allowed it to be served regularly because it eased the fears of some of the men and he well knew that the men feared disease even above the dangers of battle.

The forenoon was a bustle of work about the ship, and Hayden found himself often in consultation with his lieutenants, who were yet unseasoned, and Mr Barthe, whose experience outstripped Hayden's by more than two decades but who never acted beyond his station. The activity about the ship continued into the first dog-watch.

When the sun had made its way into the west, Hayden found himself alone upon his sacred stretch of quarterdeck, and was drawn to the stern by the sparkling wake and some flicker on the distant horizon – likely a crest caught by the sun. He stood with his legs braced against the roll of the ship – for with a quartering sea she did roll terribly – hands upon the taffrail, almost too hot to touch in the sun.

It was then that the voice drifted up to him – speaking ever so softly in Spanish. 'Heavenly Father,' Angel whispered, 'I thank you for delivering Miguel and me from certain destruction. I ask your forgiveness for the terrible sin I have committed and for which I shall do penance all of my days. I do not know, Heavenly Father, why you preserved my earthly life. I pray it is to allow me to erase this dreadful stain. If it is your will, I shall offer my life in your service. But if it is your will, Heavenly Father, that I shall endure punishment for my sin, I will accept it without complaint as your obedient servant. Your will be done. Amen.'

Hayden heard a rustling below as Angel rose from where he knelt by the gallery window. It was only then that Hayden realized his shadow was very starkly cast down upon the sea astern.

Not a moment later Angel emerged at the head of the aft companionway, clearly hurrying. Hayden had not seen any point in rushing off or trying to conceal where he had been – his silhouette, with its distinctive hat, was unlikely to be mistaken for that of anyone else.

Angel came quickly aft and Hayden beckoned him on to the windward side of the deck – the small area reserved for the captain. He leaned over the taffrail, as though assuring himself of the distance to the open gallery windows.

As a commander in numerous actions, Hayden had learned it was best not to wait but to seize the initiative. In this case, however, he felt it best to 'boldly' retreat.

'I do apologize, Angel,' Hayden offered contritely. 'I came to the rail just as you completed your prayer. It was not my intention to eavesdrop upon your conversation with God.'

'You heard me, then?' A wary look, sidelong.

'Only at the very last.'

Angel stood, staring out to sea for a long moment, perhaps unable to find words or uncertain how he felt. Then he nodded.

'When we were cast adrift,' he began, his voice tight, 'there were three of us: my brother, myself and a seaman. He was an uncouth, brutal man but he kept us all alive through the storm when my brother and I were too ill even to bail. When the storm passed we all understood our true peril. We had no food and only a small amount of rainwater we had collected in a bucket.' Angel stopped again, taking hold of the rail, as if the memories crept over him, too real to bear. 'This seaman, he would not share the water but threatened us with a knife and let us go thirsty. I had, secreted in my jacket, a small package wrapped in oilskin. When this man realized it, he thought I was hiding food, or perhaps valuables. He demanded it and when I refused he attempted to wrest it from me by force. He and Miguel fought but the sailor was a large, strong man, and he threw Miguel into the sea and then turned on me. What I had hidden in my jacket was not food – it was a pocket pistol, carefully wrapped and still dry. I could not let him take it, so I . . .' He closed his eyes and steadied himself. 'I shot him . . . through the heart . . . and he collapsed upon me. That is why my shirt was soaked in blood. I helped Miguel back into the boat.' Angel paused for a second. 'Less than an hour passed before the seaman departed this life; we rolled him over the side. That is my sin, Captain Hayden. I killed a man.'

Hayden felt himself nod, trying to hide his utter surprise – he had been expecting a much more innocent sin from the likes of Angel Campillo. 'Clearly, you acted in self-defence,' Hayden assured him. 'You and your brother might not be alive otherwise.'

Angel appeared to take no comfort from Hayden's assertion. 'It was proven to me, Captain, by the appearance of your ship that I was under the protection of God. Killing the man was not necessary. It was a moment of weakness . . . weakness of faith.'

Hayden did not quite know what to say to that. Having had men attempt to kill him on more occasions than he cared to remember, he had never waited for the intercession of divine forces. He acted to preserve his own life.

'Sometimes, Angel, we must act on our own behalf rather than await the hand of God. To stand passively, expecting your enemy to be felled by lightning or to be struck down in some other manner when he threatens your very life – that might not be lack of faith but imprudence, if not outright foolishness. God does not intervene in all of men's affairs, no matter how great the faith of those involved. Too often we must draw upon our own resources.'

Angel appeared to consider this.

'Then you do not think I have committed a cardinal sin?'

'The man threw your brother into the sea – to certain death. He likely intended the same for you. Your actions saved your brother's life and almost assuredly your own. No court would blame you – not even a heavenly one, I am sure.'

Angel appeared to struggle to master his emotions. 'Thank you, Captain Hayden. Your words give me comfort. There is no priest to hear my confession and to counsel me in this matter.'

'There is the Reverend Smosh . . .' Hayden suggested.

Angel looked at him and almost smiled. 'Do you not know, Captain, that I should burn in hell for all eternity for consulting a heretic?'

'It had slipped my mind,' Hayden replied. 'Do forgive me.'

'I do not require the aid of Mr Smosh when I can speak with you, Captain. Was your mother not a Catholic? I am informed she was.'

'She still is, to the best of my knowledge, but, like all sea officers in the Royal Navy, I am a member of the Church of England.'

'Of course,' Angel said. He was silent a moment but then glanced obliquely at Hayden. 'Must you report what I have told you to your commander when you reach Barbados?' he asked softly.

'It would be my duty to do so . . .' Hayden replied.

Angel nodded. 'Will there be a trial?'

'An incident between Spanish citizens upon a Spanish vessel . . . I do not believe there would be. However, my commander would be obliged to report what occurred to the Spanish authorities.'

Angel nodded again. 'I see.' He made an awkward bow and took his leave then, thanking Hayden once more for his counsel.

As Hayden had been eavesdropping upon the young man's private conversation with God, he felt a small pang of guilt at being thanked.

Well, he thought, what do I make of this? Certainly he was under an obligation to report the incident. No court would find Angel guilty of any crime. The only witness was his brother. There would be stigma, perhaps, but then being exonerated by a court might relieve the young man's obvious burden of guilt.

It occurred to Hayden that this death did not explain why Angel and his brother appeared to be lying about their identities. There was, for that, some other explanation.

Hayden found the doctor in the cockpit. Griffiths sat at a work table in a little stain of light cast by a single lamp, honing surgical blades upon a fine whetstone. Why he did not do this upon the deck in the brightness of day, Hayden could not comprehend, but the doctor displayed several small peculiarities of this nature – all speaking of a desire for privacy.

Hayden repeated to Griffiths what he had overheard and the subsequent revelation that Angel had made.

Griffiths removed his spectacles and examined them for some malignant mote that grew large in his vision and asked, rather bluntly, 'And what if Angel was lying?'

'What do you mean?' Hayden wondered, somewhat stupidly, he realized.

Griffiths held his spectacles up to the dull light and squinted. 'What if he was lying about killing the man – or about the reason he killed him?'

The very idea took Hayden by surprise. The confession had seemed so very genuine, so heart-rendingly difficult for Angel to own to. Even so, Hayden felt a little foolish. It certainly could have been a lie and he should have considered this possibility himself.

'I doubt anyone would confess to killing another and have it be a lie. It seems rather more likely that you would lie to cover over such a murder.'

'Yes, unless what you actually did was worse . . .'

'Such as . . . ?'

'Cut the ropes holding the boat to the ship and then shot the man or men you must share your food and water with. We all saw what happened on *Les Droits de l'Homme* when men panicked and swamped the boat.'

Hayden sat down upon a stool. 'Do you think this is possible? That Miguel and Angel are capable of such . . . treachery?'

'We are, most of us, capable of more villainy than we suppose if we believe such villainy will preserve our precious lives.'

Hayden felt as though he had suddenly wakened from a rather pleasant dream into a less than pleasant world.

'Miguel,' Griffiths went on, 'is a very amiable young man, Captain, but Angel . . . Angel has a kind of disingenuous charm that is difficult to resist. It is akin to the charm Mr Hawthorne displays, though of a much different nature. Mr Hawthorne's charm serves very definite ends – at least when it comes to the female sex. I wonder if Angel's charm, Captain, is not employed to some purpose as well . . . ?'

He took up a rag lying on his small table and rubbed at the lenses of his spectacles.

'You remain fast in your belief that our guests are criminals or frauds of some nature?'

'We know they are frauds, Captain. You overheard them admit it.'

'That is true, but it is possible they are hiding their identities in some cause that is not criminal. After all, not so long ago I was pretending to be a French sea captain named Gil Mercier.'

'You were attempting to confuse our enemies, Captain,' Griffiths stated, replacing his spectacles upon the bridge of his nose and moving his head from side to side to see if he had expunged whatever smudge had offended his vision. 'As Angel and Miguel are lying to us, perhaps they are attempting to do the same.'

'Confuse their enemies . . . ?'

Griffiths nodded.

'French spies . . . ?' Hayden said with some wonder.

'Spaniards in the employ of the French.'

'Do you truly think that is possible, Doctor?'

'If they are not criminals? Yes.' Griffiths reached up and

stripped off his spectacles again, clearly frustrated that *something* still impaired his sight. 'I should be careful what I told them, Captain. We do not know to whom they might repeat your conversations.'

Six

ayden woke early and slipped out of his cabin and to the upper deck. He was avoiding his guests that morning, and he was not certain why. Unquestionably, it had to do with his conversations – first with Angel, and next with Griffiths.

His steward, Winston, brought his breakfast to the quarterdeck and Hayden ate it perched upon a small bench. He busied himself about the deck then, while the sweltering sun floated up out of the eastern sea.

Hayden climbed to the maintop, ostensibly to examine a check in the topgallant mast but largely to get up into the clear air and push back his horizon, as though doing so would allow him to see beyond the doubts and questions that troubled him.

He examined the sea at all points with a glass – a desert of watery dunes all moving in train toward the south-west. He heard a laugh below and looked down to find Angel climbing tentatively up the ratlines with Midshipman Gould and a top-man as escort. Upon the rolling ship this was an unnerving exercise for a landsman, and it became even more so as he climbed, for the roll became more pronounced with each rung. Still, the young Spaniard bore up and climbed on, clinging, white-knuckled, to the ropes, face flushed. His hat had been left below and his hair escaped its ribbon to stream in the wind and whip about his sun-browned face. With some instruction, he made his way around the futtock shrouds, and then his head appeared in the lubber's hole. Hayden offered him a hand.

'Captain Hayden!' he cried. 'I did not realize you were here. Am I imposing?'

Hayden shook his head. 'In no way, Angel. I am merely taking in the view. Clap on there. You do not want to be thrown out of the maintop.'

Gould and the top-man retreated, mortified that they had led Angel up into the tops when the captain was there.

'You might find it best to sit,' Hayden said. 'Loop an arm around a futtock, there.'

When the young Spaniard was settled and safe to Hayden's eye, he sat down by the aftmost futtock and looped an arm around this.

Angel gazed out over the wind-driven blue and smiled broadly, exhilarated, if a little frightened.

'You never climbed aloft on the Spanish frigate?' Hayden asked.

'I did not, Captain Hayden.'

'When I went into my first ship as a midshipman I was aloft at any excuse. The poor lieutenants – they could hardly keep me out of the tops.'

'You take pleasure from danger, Captain,' Angel said. 'Is that why you would not give up the service for the woman you spoke of . . . the one who disappointed you so?'

The question caught Hayden by surprise. 'The thought of giving up the service never entered my mind.'

'But if you had – this woman you cared for – would she have accepted your suit?'

The ship rolled to starboard so that Hayden was all but

staring down into the sea racing by, inducing a moment of vertigo. 'I do not know. I . . . I do not.'

'Perhaps she was waiting for you to make such an offer – to give up the sea and make a life safely ashore with her.'

At the end of the roll, as the ship lurched slowly back to larboard, Hayden's shoulder was pressed hard against the shroud and he thought, how easy it would be to slip off the maintop and plummet into the cold, fathomless sea. 'Perhaps . . . I cannot say.'

He closed his eyes. Maybe she was waiting for just that . . . and he had been obtuse and not seen.

Henri, Henri, he thought. *Is that what you stood waiting to hear?*

For a long moment he stared off toward the veiled horizon, his last meeting with Henrietta perfectly recalled – a play he had attended a thousand times. She had been waiting for him to say something, he thought, but he had never understood what. Nor had it occurred to him that the ending could have been altered had one player but spoken a different line.

'Have I said the wrong thing, Captain?' Angel asked gently.

'I fear you have said exactly the right thing, but I never saw it myself – the more fool I.'

Hayden might have said more, but there was a call from below.

'May I join you, Captain?'

It was Mr Percival, the admiral's secretary, his foot already upon the ratlines. Hayden beckoned him on. 'Indeed, Mr Percival, climb up – but take a strong hold upon the shrouds. We do not want you swimming to Barbados.'

One of the hands standing near beseeched the secretary to leave his hat in his care, lest it blow into the sea, and the hat was duly passed down. It took some little time for Percival to climb into the tops. Each time the ship rolled so as to throw him out over the sea, he would stop and thrust his arms through the shrouds, pressing himself to the tarred ropes as though to a long-absent love.

Finally, though, he managed to squeeze himself through the lubber's hole and emerge on to the platform, out of breath and crimson-faced.

He took a seat between Angel and Hayden, clinging to the futtock shrouds like a man staring out of a gaol. As soon as he caught his breath and looked around at the great expanse of straining canvas, he said, "'We have laughed to see the sails conceive/And grow big-bellied with the wanton wind . . .'"

'Is it Shakespeare?' Hayden asked, his conversation with Archer coming to mind.

'*A Midsummer Night's Dream*,' Percival replied. 'One of my favourite speeches. Do you know Shakespeare, Angel?' he asked of the young Spaniard.

'Only a little. *Romeo and Juliet*, of course; *As You Like It*, and the one with the magician . . . Prospero, I think.'

'*The Tempest*,' Percival declared.

'That one was very difficult for my English.'

'When you see the plays on the stage it seems that all is made clear. Is that not so, Captain?'

'It does make a great difference.'

Without a hat, it was revealed that Percival's hair on top consisted of lank little strands shot through with grey. Hayden did not know the man's age – past sixty, he thought – and though the secretary was still moderately vigorous, his skin was dry-dull and his carriage leaning toward stooped.

He was, however, a man of great erudition, an amiable

dinner companion and well informed on diverse subjects from literature to the production of cotton and sugar. He spoke several languages more than passably (though not so well as Hayden), and was widely travelled in his capacity of secretary to the admiral. He was not an unpleasant person to have aboard and, but for the recent awkwardness with one of the new midshipmen, Hayden considered him an excellent shipmate.

Hayden thought himself to be somewhat imperceptive in certain matters, but he was quite confident in this particular case that Percival had not climbed up to the maintop for Hayden's company. It was the young Spaniard who had drawn him there, which made Hayden wonder if Angel had not made the ascent to escape the attentions of the admiral's secretary. Angel, however, gave no indication of finding Percival an aggravation. Quite the opposite, in truth. The two chatted away amiably in both Spanish and English until a call from below caught their attention.

It was a rather distressed Miguel, who stood on the quarterdeck, staring up, hands planted on hips.

'Come up!' Percival called down.

Miguel, however, shook his head, appearing both angry and agitated.

'Why will he not come up?' Percival enquired of Angel.

The young Spaniard laughed. 'He is fearful of . . . high up . . . like this.'

'Afraid of heights?' the secretary prompted.

'Yes. That is it. He is afraid of heights. I must go down.'

'Well,' Percival replied, and appeared about to protest, 'if you must.'

Angel scurried, crab-like, to the lubber's hole and slowly

lowered himself, his head disappearing with a last, tight smile, perhaps a little apprehensive about the climb down.

Ransome sent one of the topmen aloft to see that Angel reached the deck safely. Hayden and Percival watched the young Spaniard's progress for a moment and then Percival looked at Hayden and smiled.

'She is a very charming young woman, do you not agree, Captain?'

'I do beg your pardon, Mr Percival . . . Do you refer to the young Spanish gentleman who just departed our company?'

Percival laughed pleasantly, and shook his head. 'I do, Captain, but, for my money, she is no gentleman. I have seen many a comely young woman arrayed in the clothing of men – costume balls, you know – and she is not even one of the more convincing *faux* males.' His brow wrinkled. 'You did not know?'

'I confess, I doubt it yet.'

Percival suppressed a smile.

'You jest, Mr Percival, surely?'

'I do not. Don Angel is a young lady dressed in the clothing of a man. I have not said a word of it to any other because I wanted to observe her and Miguel without them realizing I comprehended their deception. I did not know if you were aware of it.'

Hayden almost laughed, though he did not quite know why. 'You have left me somewhat speechless. I will admit to difficulty crediting what you suggest.'

'Do take a close look at Angel's hands when next you can. They are very fine-boned and small, the skin both soft and femininely smooth. She has perfect little ears; hips, though hardly broad, broader than a young boy's; and her shoulders are comparatively narrow. She blushes modestly, and slips away at any bawdy jest, laughs like a well-bred young woman, walks as young noblewomen are trained to, has a wonderfully full and sensuous mouth and eyes like no man. Her bosom has been wrapped to hide its swell, and – at the risk of sounding crude – her breeches are not quite as full as they should be. In sum, a handsome young woman in the clothing of a man. I believe she has deceived whomever she has because she is a Spaniard and the ship's company does not quite know what to expect of a young Spanish nobleman and are not the least surprised to find him somewhat effeminate, as you must agree Angel is.'

Hayden did not know what to say. Much of what Percival catalogued, upon even the briefest reflection he knew to be true, but given that it had become the fashion among young men to display their finer feelings in public – weeping in the public theatre and at musical recitals – he would not have been in the least surprised to find a young man who blushed at the sailors' bawdy humour. He did realize, however, that Angel never displayed his feelings in such a way that they would be noticed and admired for their intensity and purity, as the fashionable young men did. Angel's refinement of feeling seemed quite natural and neither exaggerated nor affected.

'Have you not noticed, Captain Hayden,' Percival said, interrupting Hayden's thoughts, 'that Angel is often in your company? I have seen her lingering on the deck, waiting until you have concluded some business with your crew, only to feign surprise when she finds herself in your presence. She does hang upon your every word, and catches herself when she believes her feelings too transparent. You saved her life, and I am of the opinion that, given her beliefs, she thinks you were sent to be her rescuer and she sent to rescue you.'

'I do not believe I am in need of rescue, Mr Percival,' Hayden informed the secretary, trying not to sound scornful.

'Are you not? Have you not suffered recently from romantic disappointment? Who better to rescue you than a young woman, who, I might add, has a great deal to offer? If one looks past her dress, she is comely and vivacious, her manner is both cultivated yet somehow simple and genuine, she is educated in the way of women of her class, she plays the pianoforte quite well, according to her brother, is a masterful conversationalist, charming in the extreme, and eminently sensible. All the men aboard value her company, even if they do not realize quite why, for most, like you, do not comprehend that she is a woman, and it is to her femininity that they respond.' Percival paused a moment to look down upon Angel, who had reached the deck and was pulling back his hair to tie it with a ribbon. Suddenly, this seemed an utterly feminine motion to Hayden.

'Do you know the story, Captain Hayden, of the natural philosopher who took aboard ship with him a "boy" who nightly shared his cabin? Upon arrival at their first South Pacific isle the natives immediately recognized this boy as a young vahine, though no one aboard ship had ever suspected. I wonder what it says about the English that we are so obtuse?'

Hayden felt some irritation at this, as clearly he was one of the obtuse Englishmen – unless, of course, Percival was wrong.

The admiral's secretary appeared to read his thoughts, or perhaps his face. 'Do not be embarrassed at this, Captain. No one else aboard has noticed that Angel is, in fact, a young woman. Any attraction they might feel to Angel would be a source of embarrassment and would be both suppressed and denied.'

Below, Angel put a hand lightly on the shoulder of his brother, who was clearly still angered and distressed that Angel had climbed aloft. But why should he be? Young men habitually sought thrills of one sort or another. The gesture, the hand so lightly on the shoulder, was at once familiar and appeared, suddenly, feminine.

'Do you see?' Percival asked quietly, his eyes drawn to the same scene. 'She mollifies her elder brother. In a moment she will set her charm to work and very soon she will make him smile – even laugh. He is no more able to resist her charm than I am . . . or you are, if I may say it.'

Percival rolled up on to his knees from where he sat and went on hands and feet to the lubber's hole. He lowered himself over the edge and said, 'It has been a pleasure speaking with you, Captain.' He was about to disappear when his eyes narrowed and he pointed. 'What is that speck . . . far off?' he asked. 'Or do my eyes deceive me?'

Hayden followed the secretary's gaze, and there, just on the horizon, was an amber-brown smudge, so small it was almost undetectable. Standing, Hayden looped an arm around a shroud and raised his glass.

'Mr Archer!' Hayden called down to his first lieutenant.

'Sir?' Archer shaded his eyes and looked up.

'Sail, off the larboard bow, just on the horizon.'

Hayden raised his glass again. The lookout, whom Hayden had sent down to give himself a moment of privacy aloft, came scrambling up.

'Lambert!' Hayden called to him as he climbed.

'Sir!'

'See our guest reaches the deck safely, if you please.'

'Aye, Captain. That I will.'

Hayden lifted his glass and quizzed the distant sail once more.

'Can you tell anything of her, sir?' Archer called up.

But Hayden could not . . . A ship, nothing more, so distant as to be invisible from the deck. 'I cannot, Mr Archer. We will alter our course to intercept. Call the sail handlers, if you please.'

'Aye, sir,' came up from the deck.

Hayden lingered a few moments more, his mind torn in two directions at once – wanting to consider the remarkable conversation he had just held with Percival, and drawn to this strange sail.

He forced his mind to his duty and went down the backstay, hand over hand.

Archer stood waiting for him.

'Shall we beat to quarters, Captain?'

'The moment we have altered course, Mr Archer. Where is Mr Wickham? Send him aloft. Let us see if he can make out this ship.'

The sail handlers hurried to their stations, but there was no panic, no pushing, despite the palpable excitement. Mr Wickham appeared and went up the mainmast, a gaggle of off-duty midshipmen tailing behind, their shiny new glasses slung over their shoulders in imitation of Lord Arthur.

Wickham did not stop at the maintops but climbed on until he sat astride the topgallant yard. The ship was put on her new course, picked up her skirts and went surging over the trade-driven seas, which now struck the *Themis* abeam, sending heavy spray sometimes high into the rigging. The gun crews went to their places, but before they had cast off their guns a call came from aloft.

'*On deck!*' Wickham twisted about to find his captain. 'She appears to be under jury rig, Captain. Only a stump of one mast standing.'

Barthe had come, and stood by his captain at the rail, where they had a view of Wickham. 'Is she a Navy ship, Mr Wickham?'

'I cannot be certain, Captain, but I do not believe she is. Transport, more like. No flag that I can see.'

'Keep your glass on her, if you please,' Hayden called up. 'And be alert for any sign that she is not alone.'

'Aye, sir.'

Gould stood a few feet off. 'Sir? Shall I send aloft our colours?'

'Not yet, Mr Gould. Have the French colours ready as well. We shall quiz this ship before we draw within range of her guns – has she any to speak of?'

'Aye, Captain.'

'Is she the other Spanish frigate, do you think, Captain?' Barthe asked. The master stood, hands on the rail, squinting off to the sector of sea that hid this mysterious vessel.

'I cannot answer that, Mr Barthe. Where is Miguel? Mr Gould, find one of our Spanish guests, if you please.'

Gould left his flags in the care of the cherub and scurried off. A moment later he returned, herding both Angel and Miguel before him.

'The ship that struck the *Medea*,' Hayden began, trying not to stare quizzically at Angel, 'was she a transport or a frigate?'

Angel looked to Miguel. 'We sailed in company with other frigates, Captain, but we did not see the ship that sank us.'

'Well, we have a heavily damaged ship in the offing. I would like to know what she might be before I draw within range of her guns.'

Miguel and Angel glanced at each other again, and Angel shrugged. 'I do wish we could offer more, Captain Hayden.'

'We shall discover her origin soon enough,' he replied.

It was, however, almost two hours before they could make her out. Hayden went forward, the only place from which this ship could be seen clearly on their point of sail.

Having beat to quarters, almost every hand aboard had a station, but those few who had no duties gathered on the forecastle. The doctor was there, as was Hawthorne, who might range about the ship as he was needed once he had his orders from Hayden. Smosh was there as well, minus his clerical collar, as he would aid the doctor in the cockpit, should that be required, and there was terrible superstition about priests in the sick-berth. Both the Spaniards were here, as was Mr Percival, chatting with Angel in Spanish.

The ship was not a mile distant, and Hayden could plainly see that she had only thirty feet of her foremast standing and had used spare spars or recovered yards to jury rig a mast that crossed but one yard.

'On deck!' came the call from Wickham. 'I can make her out, Captain . . . She's a slaver.'

Seven

It was not just caution that had the *Themis* hove to a hundred yards to windward – the horrifying stench of slavers was notorious. Even the brisk trade could not carry this odour away. Hayden had sent Archer across to the slave ship, and now he returned with the ship's master in his cutter.

All along the deck the men stared at the drifting ship, which was stuffed to the gunnels with a cargo of Africans – men, women and children. The slavers had allowed a few of these poor creatures out on to the deck to stand upright and take the ocean air – not from compassion, Hayden guessed, but in an attempt to bring a greater portion of their cargo to market alive and in a condition to be sold. These dusky men, all but naked, stared back at the crew of the Navy ship, perhaps uncertain if they were saviours or presented an even greater danger.

'Poor buggers,' Barthe pronounced by Hayden's elbow, though whether he meant the men being carried into slavery or the crew of the stricken ship he could not say.

Smosh was positioned at the rail beside the master. 'These men trade in souls,' he declared.

Percival glanced at him. 'You do not believe, Mr Smosh, that the inferior races were put here to serve men?'

'I do not believe any race was put upon this earth to be worked and sold like cattle.'

The cutter came alongside at that moment and the master

68

of the slaver – a ship out of Bristol – clattered up the side, Archer at his heels.

Archer touched his hat. 'Richard LeClerc, Captain Hayden, Master of the *Orion*.'

Hayden shook the man's hand. 'Are you the owner, Captain LeClerc?'

'No, sir. She's owned by a syndicate. All Bristol men of good standing.' The man looked over at Archer, clearly unsettled. 'We lost our masts in the gale, Captain. No doubt you went through it yourselves . . . though you fared better than we. I can likely make port under jury, sir – not Port Royal, where I was bound, but some port – the problem is I won't have half a cargo when I arrive, for I didn't set out with water or victuals for such a slow crossing.'

'I can tow you into Barbados, to which port I am bound,' Hayden offered. 'It will not be fast, but quicker than you are sailing now and you shall not end up on a reef – I will see to that. Have you stores for a fortnight?'

The master shifted from one foot to the other, creases wrinkling up his forehead and appearing around his eyes.

'A fortnight . . . Mayhap. We will be on tight rations, though. I cannot grant you salvage rights – not when there is the least chance I can make port on my own. I *can* offer you a portion of the profits, sir.'

'There are seldom "profits" when such arrangements are entered into, Captain LeClerc.'

'A portion of the sale of my cargo, then. Five per cent,' the master said. 'We have seven hundred alive yet, and I expect to have nearly that many when we arrive.'

Hayden wished he were anywhere but on his deck having this discussion, for he wanted nothing to do with this man's trade, but he could not leave a ship to sail on under her scrap of canvas, all but unmanageable, a sea of reefs and islands before her, not to mention her shortage of victuals and water. The human suffering would be beyond comprehension.

Behind the slaver, Barthe was making small motions with his head and half gestures with limp hands.

'Allow me to consult with my officers, Captain LeClerc.'

Barthe and Hayden immediately retreated to a place where they could speak privately.

'That man is offering half what we should be due,' Barthe whispered. 'He is in a fix, Captain, for he could lose half his cargo, even if he did bring his ship into a port – which we both know would be a feat of seamanship that would see the man a legend.'

'We are talking about a large number of lives, Mr Barthe. And I do not mind saying that the entire business . . . unsettles me.'

'I do realize we are speaking of lives, and I am of the same opinion as you, sir: trade in human souls is revolting, but . . . There is right and wrong, sir, and 5 per cent of the sale of his slaves is an insult, sir. We should not take less than 10 per cent, and half that again would not be unfair, sir.'

Hayden could feel the eyes of his officers upon him, for they would all share, should the ship be considered salvage. Even if they settled on a commission to tow the slaver into port, they would certainly expect – and deserve – a portion of the moneys.

The Reverend Smosh came and hovered two yards distant, his doughy face drawn and dark.

'Mr Smosh,' Hayden addressed him, 'do you have a question, sir?'

'I do apologize, Captain, but as the guardian of human

souls, sir, I feel I must intercede on behalf of the hundreds entombed upon that ship.' He shook his hand in the slaver's direction. 'I believe that to profit from the sale of these poor people will put a stain upon your ledger that can never be erased. It is a base evil, sir – and you know I am not prone to making such pronouncements.'

'It is a legal trade, Mr Smosh,' Barthe reminded him, 'no matter how reprehensible one feels it might be.'

Smosh turned readily upon the sailing master. 'Legal at this time. I pray that will soon change, for it is a blot upon the character of our people.'

'What am I to do, Mr Smosh?' Hayden asked the parson. 'I cannot leave this ship to drift on toward the reefs and dangers that lie ahead.'

'No, Captain, you cannot. You must not, but—'

But Barthe interrupted. 'If her cargo were wool, Mr Smosh, or any other commodity you care to name, we would be entitled to a portion of her profits if we towed her into port. That is the custom of the sea. You might not approve of the theft of the poor sheep's wool, but should we then leave the ship carrying that wool to drift? Or are you suggesting we must carry it into port for no profit at all?'

'That is precisely what I am suggesting – nay, urging – Mr Barthe.'

'Well, you have not spent your life at sea, Mr Smosh,' Barthe replied testily, 'and are not yet fully versed in the practices and customs. If we save this master and his cargo, we are entitled to be paid for it, and paid handsomely, no matter if he carries wool or men . . . and you will receive a portion of that money.'

Smosh drew himself both up and back half a step. 'I

should not take it were it a fortune, Mr Barthe. I should not allow a single piece of such lucre to cross my palm.'

'The officers shall be glad to hear of it,' Barthe informed him, 'for we will happily divide up your share. Thank you.'

In truth, Hayden was largely in sympathy with Mr Smosh in this matter, but he had his officers to think of, and they – even those who bore strong feelings against the trade of slaves – would expect their share of any moneys which derived from the rescue of this stricken ship.

'I cannot leave this vessel to drift and I cannot refuse the master's offer without provoking all my officers and crew, who will feel sorely cheated – cheated by me. I will not have my own men hold such feelings against me, Mr Smosh. There is little enough profit in this life as it is.'

Smosh made a little bow. 'Captain, I beg you reconsider. Profiting from the sale of these poor souls – it is damnable, sir. Damnable.'

'I have little choice, Mr Smosh. It is a legal trade – though we are of one mind in this; I disapprove of it heartily.'

Smosh said nothing, but neither did he make any sign that he accepted his captain's decision. There was no doubt in Hayden's mind, though – he would rather an unhappy parson than an unhappy ship.

'Ten per cent, Mr Barthe?'

The master nodded once.

Hayden crossed the deck to the slaver's master.

'Ten per cent, Captain LeClerc, and we have an arrangement. Shall I have my clerk draw up an agreement?'

LeClerc hesitated, but then nodded and offered his hand to Hayden.

Hayden turned to Barthe and Archer. 'Arrange gear to take this ship in tow, if you please. And Mr Archer, we no longer need to be at quarters.'

Guns were boused up against bulwarks and the crew set to arranging gear to tow. It was a common enough task, for prizes were often too damaged to sail, and after actions British ships sometimes had to be towed back to port.

Cables were arranged and a messenger line rowed over to the slaver so that a larger cable could be carried across. As well as the business was managed, it still took a good part of the forenoon. When the *Themis* was put on course again, her speed was not half what it had been.

'Barbados recedes before us, Captain,' Wickham offered as he stood by the taffrail beside Hayden, watching the slaver set her scrap of canvas to aid their efforts.

'So it would appear, Mr Wickham. I have not asked in some time, but how fares your hurt?'

'Well enough, sir. I have one finger that does not obey my commands, but the physician said I was lucky not to lose half my limb, sir. I am but four-fingered on that hand but I count myself lucky, even so.'

'You were luckier not to bleed away your life. Griffiths preserved more than your arm.'

'So he did, sir, and I shall never forget it.'

The two stood awkwardly a moment. Hayden realized that Wickham now bore a reminder of his mortality with him – into every action, every cutting-out expedition, into every storm even. He would never be free of it. The service did this to the young gentlemen – brought them to maturity before their time.

Wickham went off about his business, leaving Hayden

at the taffrail watching their tow, gauging the skill of her helmsmen, for if she were not steered well she would sheer and part the tow cable – and anyone upon Hayden's quarterdeck would be in mortal danger should the cable whip back before it fell into the smothering sea. He decided that the master of the ship must know his business, for the men at the helm were keeping her steady before the seas.

'Did you expect to enter the slave trade on this voyage, Captain?' It was Angel, appearing at his elbow, and his conversation with Mr Percival on the maintop came back to Hayden.

Have you not noticed, Captain Hayden, that Angel is often in your company?

'I did not, but then neither did I expect to be dressed as a French captain, upon a French ship, chasing English mutineers . . . but that occurred, as well.'

'You seem always to be somewhat at war with yourself, Captain,' Angel observed. 'Your French side at odds with your English. Your feelings about slavery at odds with your desire to save the lives of these unfortunates – not to mention keeping your avaricious crew happy.'

'I should not call them avaricious,' Hayden answered firmly. 'Do you know how few opportunities these men will have *in their lives* to possess more money than they require to but meet their daily needs? Prize money can mean the difference between their children going hungry or having food upon their table. Do not judge them for this desire.'

'I do not judge them,' Angel said with emotion. 'I lost everything I possessed when the *Medea* went down. I understand their situation better than most might imagine.'

Hayden turned to regard the young Spaniard. 'But surely you have family, Angel. The uncle you go to . . . ?'

Angel seemed to hesitate, but then nodded. 'Yes, my situation is not the same as your sailors'. I did not mean to compare my lot to theirs.' He said nothing a moment, and Hayden found himself gazing at the young Spaniard's face. Was he indeed a woman in disguise? Or could Percival have merely decided to create some mischief by telling Hayden this story?

'I have been thinking, Captain Hayden,' Angel said, so no other might hear, 'that I overstepped the boundaries of . . . politeness. I should never have suggested that you failed in some way to speak as you should with the woman you courted. I could not know what was in her mind and it was not my place to speak as I did. I apologize.'

'You have no need of doing so,' Hayden replied. 'I fear your insight was entirely correct but came too late. I should have spoken but did not comprehend my situation. If only I had known to say, "I shall give up the sea and make my way ashore, for a life without you shall be but half a life." Perhaps that would have won her heart.'

'It would win the heart of many a woman, Captain,' Angel said with surprising feeling, and then turned, hurried to the companionway and disappeared below without so much as a nod or a 'by your leave'.

Hayden stared at the deck opening down which the Spaniard had retreated. He could not have been more astonished or confused had Angel slapped his face.

Either Percival is correct, he thought, or Angel is of the same persuasion as Percival himself. Certainly Angel's response to the declaration Hayden *should* have made to Henrietta would never have been expected of a young man with the common desire for women. Hayden shook his head, his thoughts in a tangle of confusion.

Was it possible that Percival had seen something that no other man aboard could see? Hayden turned to stare aft. He was beginning to feel Percival was not wrong. There was a young woman living in his cabin and he seemed to have attached her feelings without even being aware of her sex!

Inexplicably, thoughts of Henrietta came to mind – Henrietta, who was, by now, married; Henrietta, who had chosen another over him.

Hayden shook his head. Somehow, he had secretly hoped she would undergo a change of heart. And so, here he was, yearning for her yet.

I am the captain of a machine of war, he thought – not some love-sick youth. If she can make a life without me, I can do the same without her. *Pining* is overly romantic, if not puerile.

He gazed at the confused wake trailing along behind and, at the distant end of the long tow rope, the slaver.

Too many regrets trailed behind him and would not release their grip.

He wondered again at Angel's response to his words. What had he said? '*I shall give up the sea and make my way ashore, for a life without you shall be but half a life.*'

'*It would win the heart of many a woman, Captain,*' Angel had replied, before colouring and hurrying below.

I should stopper my mouth, Hayden thought. When I do speak, my words always land me in trouble.

A foul odour assaulted his senses then, carried to him on the pure ocean trade, the smell of men lying in their own filth, entombed in excrement and transported to a life of confinement and endless toil.

Perhaps I spoke wrongly in this matter as well, Hayden thought. Mr Smosh counselled me otherwise, but I did not heed his words. Perhaps he did speak for a higher power and I turned my back.

Eight

The calculation of each man's share of the profits from the delivery of the slaver became the sole diversion – perhaps the compulsion – of the *Themis*'s people. Debts were both paid and entered into on the basis of this, as yet, unearned capital. The estimates of the moneys coming to the *Themis* varied; in the majority of cases, according to the character of those doing the valuing. The older and more cynical tended to talk in terms of a few pounds and cautioned others not to squander moneys that were not yet in their purse. The optimists, the young and the generally feckless, however, reckoned themselves as wealthy as lords – and not all of these were uneducated hands. This rule, however, did not hold in all cases. A few who by experience or years should have known better began to see, if not mountains, at least hills of gold. Mr Barthe, to Hayden's utter surprise, was one of these. His appraisal of the slaves' value increased several times each day and his plans for these moneys became more grandiose each hour. This had become an object of general amusement among the other officers – that is, among those who were not daydreaming of coaches and manor houses of their own.

Hayden thought there was much to be learned from observing the manner in which each man, sometimes in opposition to his humour, responded to this impending wealth. Barthe, commonly the most bitter and cynical of his officers, was now revealing himself to be the most prone to wishfulness.

Others, however, were deeply unsettled by the whole business and found the dark shadow of the slaver trailing behind as distressing as the discovery of a lump growing in the guts, its existence half denied and utterly dismaying. Smosh spoke openly of the evil in their wake and he had a good number of followers, these not always the most devout among his flock. Wickham had informed Hayden that he did not wish to receive any profit from the sale of slaves, and Griffiths, who could much less afford such nobility, had joined this same camp. Lieutenant Ransome, who, like Hayden, was perennially in need of money, was tortured by this matter for several days but finally decided that his hopes for a match with one of Wickham's unmarried sisters were more critical to his future (or so Hayden assumed), for he reluctantly informed his captain that his share could be divided among those wishing to profit from such a foul enterprise. Hayden thought the young man might break down and weep when he made this pronouncement, but the young lieutenant mastered his feelings.

There was yet another faction among his crew, and it was, in Hayden's view, the most fascinating of all. The ideas of this group were being expounded on the quarterdeck within Hayden's hearing as he worked at his table.

'Well, let me ask you, Doctor,' Mr Barthe's voice came down the skylight, 'if we had not discovered this slaver, would not many – perhaps hundreds – of her unfortunate Africans have died for want of food and water?'

'Most assuredly they would, Mr Barthe,' the doctor replied.

'And would you not agree that it is better to be a live slave working some plantation than to die at sea?'

'I suppose I must agree that slavery is a small improvement over that particular alternative, but—'

But Barthe was not finished. 'Then more good has come of our efforts than evil, one must admit . . . ?'

'Mr Barthe,' the doctor argued, 'all this rationalization and extenuation does not excuse an institution that takes free men from their homes, reduces them to the state of *property* and forces them to labour for the good and profit of others.'

'I agree, Doctor. You could not be more right, but, as we have saved their poor lives, and by the traditions and laws of the sea we are entitled to an agreed upon share of the profits, there is but one thing any man of conscience might do . . . I, and many others, intend to give a portion of our legal earnings – legal, mind you – to an anti-slaving society.'

'Let me see if I comprehend what you have proposed, Mr Barthe,' the doctor answered. 'Though you disagree vehemently with the institution of slavery, you are about to profit from the sale of slaves? To somehow purify this profit, and to absolve yourself of your involvement, you intend to give a portion of your money to men who are fighting to make slavery illegal in Britain and her colonies?'

'You miss my point, Doctor. I am about to profit from the preservation of hundreds of lives.'

'But you preserve those lives so that they might be sold into slavery – and your profits will come from that sale, Mr Barthe. You are, in effect, no different from an investor in a slaving expedition. Do you not see a contradiction, Mr Barthe, in making profit from selling free men into slavery and then taking some part of that profit and giving it to those who fight that terrible practice?'

'But if I do not take my rightful share, Doctor, it will be

divided up among others who do not share my beliefs. No part of it will then go to the cause of abolition. How is slavery to be abolished if the anti-slavers are not supported? Printing pamphlets and renting halls for speakers costs money, sir, money that comes to the societies by donation.'

'Mr Barthe, I doubt that the abolitionists would accept money from the sale of slaves. Their principles are not so . . . *pliant* as yours.'

'Well, then I shall keep all the profits from salvaging this ship and give the anti-slaving society moneys earned from my profession, Dr Griffiths. Will that satisfy them, do you think?'

'A society with the purpose of combatting prostitution will not, Mr Barthe, accept money from the owner of a brothel, no matter how it is earned!'

'You misconstrue my point, Doctor . . . Ah, here is Mr Hawthorne. Let us present our cases before him.'

'Abolitionists should not be frequenting brothels,' Hawthorne immediately offered, forcing Hayden to suppress a laugh.

'Mr Barthe is just explaining,' the doctor informed the marine, 'how he will give a portion of the moneys he earns from the selling of free men into slavery to the anti-slaving societies.'

'Very kind of him,' Hawthorne could be heard to reply, 'but I regret to inform you, Mr Barthe, that to profit from stealing away men's freedom and allowing them to be bought and sold like cattle is, well . . . reprehensible.'

'Then I should do as you both have done and refuse my share of the profits?' There was no audible reply to this, and Mr Barthe went on. 'If I do this, the anti-slaving societies will receive no advantage, and I can assure you that such a decision will not aid these poor unfortunates (Hayden could only assume Barthe waved a hand toward the slave ship) in the least. I shall, by donating some of my profits, be doing more to abolish slavery than either of you. Good day to you, sirs.'

Hayden heard the sailing master stomp off.

'Is it possible he is right?' Hawthorne wondered aloud.

'Mr Hawthorne!' the surgeon chastised.

'But you do comprehend his position, Dr Griffiths?'

'Mr Hawthorne, if we were to accept Mr Barthe's argument, then why should we not finance expeditions to Africa to buy slaves, sell them across the Atlantic and give all the profits to the anti-slaving societies? That would do much to further the cause of abolition, would it not?'

'But there is a great difference, Doctor. These slaves have already been taken from their homes and are destined for the slave markets. Unless we act to free them, which would make us all criminals and mutineers, then these poor souls will soon be plantation slaves. Their destiny cannot be changed. We could, however, do something that is within our power – give all the profit we are to make to the abolitionists. Or perhaps we could do something more substantive and buy some men – or some families – from this very ship with our profits. Buy these people and grant them their freedom?'

'Buy slaves with the profits from the sale of slaves?'

'Buy them and free them.'

'Leave it to you, Mr Hawthorne, to take a clear moral issue and find some way to cloud it.'

The discussion came to an end at that moment, as Dr Griffiths was called away.

The ink had dried upon Hayden's quill as he listened, so he swirled it in his inkwell. He had not realized that finding this stricken ship would have such an effect. Men who had never thought much – and cared less – about the institution of slavery were suddenly forced to make decisions about it. Hayden glanced out of the gallery window at the slaver bobbing in their wake, dragged bodily along as she reached the trough of each wave . . . as though the two ships were shackled together and their fates somehow commingled.

Nine

At sunset the sky darkened with low, fraying cloud and, though rain spattered down upon the waters all around and the seas got up, the wind made only a little. The ground-swell, however, was enough to strain the tow cable so that it parted and the slaver dropped quickly astern. To keep the lights of their tow in sight, the *Themis* was hove-to and every few hours set briefly before the wind to keep near the drifting slave ship.

Once he was assured that his lieutenants understood what was required of them, Hayden retired below to the warmth and cheer of the gunroom, for he and the ship's guests had been invited to dine that evening.

Mr Percival and the two Spaniards sat among the regular officers and warrant officers who made up the gunroom's complement. Mr Smosh, Dr Griffiths, Hawthorne and Archer were all scrubbed and buttons polished. Ransome, who also had a cabin letting on to this small rectangle, was officer of the watch and therefore on deck.

Mr Archer was the official host of this meal, as he was the senior officer in the gunroom, and he took up this duty with a will. Plying guests with food and drink appeared to be his principal responsibility and, at this task, he proved to be efficiency itself. All off-duty officers and guests were sufficiently jolly, Hayden observed.

Conversation had ranged widely and presently settled on the proper character for a sailor's wife.

'A large dowry, above all,' Mr Hawthorne joked.

'Nay, nay – she must be comely, so her husband shall never be tempted to stray,' Mr Smosh argued.

'What say you, Captain?' Archer enquired.

'I am the last man here to ask, Mr Archer,' Hayden replied, with a surreptitious glance at Angel. 'I have been love's fool more often than I have shown wisdom in this particular matter.'

Hawthorne waved a finger in the air. 'Any man who has not been a fool in love has never known the rapture and frenzy that overthrows reason. A man *reasonable* in love is but imbibing bread and water to slake his meagre appetite. He has not the devouring yearning that casts aside all pride to fill that unendurable void that has grown within.'

'Hear! To fools in love,' others echoed. Glasses were raised and a toast enthusiastically drunk.

Into the small moment of silence that followed, Mr Percival said softly, 'I pity women; their passion can never be the equal of a man's.'

'Why, I should take the opposite side in such an argument, sir,' Hawthorne informed the admiral's secretary. 'Women are but forced to conceal their passion, for such madness is thought unseemly in a woman.'

'Mr Hawthorne is very correct,' Angel interjected. His colour was high with wine and his words very carefully enunciated. 'Why else do women flock to see *Romeo and Juliet*? It is to see a young woman's passion unleashed without fear of censure. In their secret hearts they are all Juliets who dream one day of a marriage wherein their passion might be given its head—'

'Like a wild mount between smooth thighs,' Smosh added drunkenly, and all laughed that this had come from the mouth of a parson.

When this laughter died away, Percival turned to the young Spaniard, who was seated beside him. 'Why, Angel, it would appear you are let into the secret thoughts of the fairer sex. How is it that you became their confidant?'

Angel looked somewhat uncomfortable at this question but then replied, 'Unlike many men, Mr Percival, when women talk, I attend to their words rather than merely pretend to do so.'

The admiral's secretary raised his brows a little, then turned to Hayden. 'What think you, Captain?' he asked. 'Who has the greater passion? Young Romeos or their Juliets?'

'I am not the pilot to have sounded the hearts of women, Mr Percival, nor do I have charts for those foreign waters. When I venture there I am but a poor sailor on a moonless night, the sea fathomless, shoals unmarked, storms and squalls unpredictable – in a few words, entirely out of my depth.'

Hawthorne turned suddenly serious. 'It would appear you have more wisdom in these matters than you claim, Captain,' the marine lieutenant observed.

'The passion of Juliets is the greater,' Angel asserted.

'Even than your own manly young passion, Angel?' Percival asked, his smile not well hidden.

Angel coloured. 'I have not the experience to answer that yet.'

Archer waved a hand at the young Spaniard. 'He knows so much of women though he has not *known* a woman.'

Hawthorne turned to Angel's brother. 'How is it, Don Miguel, that this slip of a youth claims such knowledge of a woman's heart when he has not tasted the bitter wine that is love?'

'He has observed my follies in this matter, Mr Hawthorne,' Miguel replied. Of all present, he was clearly the farthest into his cup.

'Ah.' Hawthorne turned to Hayden. 'Captain, you are playing the politician in this matter. Give us your uncensored opinion: has Angel still a girlish heart not yet grown to manhood? Is that his secret?'

Hayden turned his goblet slowly on the table, staring into its crimson depths. How to phrase it? 'I do not think this is some affliction of youth, Mr Hawthorne. No, I think Angel is a Rosalind, with the wise, knowing heart of a woman secreted within the form of a young man.'

'A woman's heart wrapped in a tiger's hide,' Griffiths pronounced, and a toast was drunk to their young tiger.

Mr Percival yet maintained that the passion of men was greater but, in the way of conversations made slippery with wine, this one slid on to matters less serious.

It was late in the middle watch when Angel and Hayden helped a drunken and sleepy Miguel back to their shared cabin. The rolling of the ship on the long groundswell initiated a three-man trip-and-stagger that began Angel laughing and then Hayden as well. Several times Angel brushed against Hayden and, once, when the ship rolled, fell against him and lingered in that position just an instant longer than strictly necessary, pulling away with what Hayden imagined was reluctance.

Was this a young woman made bold by claret and the belief that her secret desire was hidden beneath a man's clothing? Or was it a young man? Had Hayden imagined that Angel had pressed himself to him, for a second?

His own brain was a little addled by drink and the need for

sleep, so his thoughts and feelings seemed to run in all directions at once.

They managed to get Miguel up the ladder by Angel pulling and Hayden pushing from behind.

At the door to Hayden's cabin, the marine sentry let them in, poorly hiding a smirk. Because of the swell, the cots swung forth and back to an uncommon extreme – though in fact it was the ship that moved and the cot which stayed nearly stationary. Even so, getting the limp Miguel into his cot was all but an impossibility. He was both dead weight and lolling, so that he constantly slipped through one's fingers. Twice they tried to manhandle him into his cot as it swung near but failed, all but dropping him to the floor. They then bent double with laughter and were forced to recover a little before a third attempt saw the job done.

With some difficulty they removed Miguel's shoes and decided that he must sleep in his clothes, for undressing him in a swinging hammock was both exhausting and dangerous.

Angel put a hand on Hayden's arm.

'Thank you,' he whispered, as though not wanting to disturb his brother. 'I could never have managed alone.'

'It was nothing. Sleep well, Angel.'

Hayden retreated beyond the partition and into his own half of the cabin, his heart beating from the effort of manhandling the limp Miguel, or from his growing hope that Angel was in fact a young woman.

Percival had put this thought in his head, and now Hayden could not force it out. With some effort, he mastered himself and went about his nightly preparations, though sounds that he took to be Angel undressing did try to draw his thoughts on to other paths.

It took but a few moments to perform his toilet and, when he emerged from the quarter gallery, he found Angel standing by his swinging hammock, holding the ropes that suspended one end. His hair was down and neckcloth gone.

'Does everyone know my secret?' Angel whispered.

For a few seconds Hayden did not know what to say.

'Mr Percival and myself. No one else . . .' he replied just as quietly; there was a sentry stationed outside his cabin door. He walked closer, reaching up and taking hold of a beam so that Angel was not two feet distant.

'Will he reveal it?' Angel asked.

'I do not believe he will.'

'And you . . . ?'

'Your secrets are safe with me.'

But what was Angel's secret? That he was a woman dressed as a man, or that he preferred men?

'Rosalind, you called me . . .'

'Because I have wondered if Angel was your real name – the name you were given at birth.'

A shake of the head. 'No . . . I was christened Angelita but, like Rosalind, hid my true sex away, though she called herself Ganymede, not Angel.'

The two stood, face to face, hardly knowing what to say – Hayden uncertain if he could believe what he had heard.

'If I had known that Mr Percival and yourself both knew my secret . . . I should have been more discreet about the passions of women.'

'That secret is safe with me as well.'

'Do you remember that Rosalind, dressed as Ganymede, helped Orlando fall out of love with another?'

'Yes, but her intention was the opposite.'

'That is so, but perhaps I might perform this same service, for I cannot bear to see you suffering.'

'Has that been your intention?'

'I – I do not know. I have been so confused. For all this time I am to be acting a man, yet I have so wanted to be a woman. To speak to you as a woman.'

'I think you have been doing just that, but I have been too obtuse to know.'

The ship rolled and Angelita lost her footing, and just as Hayden put out a hand to steady her, she put a hand against his chest. And then she pressed her face into the hollow of his neck, her breath very short.

'Does this feel strange?' she asked.

'To be honest, yes. A moment ago I was not absolutely certain you were a woman, and for a long time after you came aboard ship I believed you a young man. I confess I do not know quite what to think . . . or what to feel.'

Angelita stepped away from him now, and looked up into his face. 'I hope you will be able to learn to see me as I am – a woman – though no one else must ever know.'

'I swear, Angel, I will not tell a soul.'

'I am Angelita . . . but you must never say it where any other can hear. Even my brother – for he must not know that I have revealed my secret to you. He would be very angry.' She appeared to search for words, and did not meet his eye.

Outside, the wind moaned in the rigging and the seas hissed as they passed beneath.

'Charles . . . ?' Angelita whispered. 'I have lied to you – more than one.'

Hayden felt a certain dread run through him.

She appeared to gather her thoughts, or perhaps to decide if she should tell him this. 'My father died a few years ago and, in time, my mother remarried. I tell you most honestly that my father was very wealthy. His estates, of course, would go to my brother, but not until he comes of age. This man my mother married, he has a son about Miguel's age, but that family's estates are small compared to my father's. One night, my brother was out with his dearest and oldest friend, who was like a brother to him. They had been drinking and, on a lark, exchanged coats. As they walked home they were set upon by . . . I don't know how you say . . . by bad men. His friend was killed, but Miguel was only thrown aside and left unharmed. It was Miguel's belief that these men meant to murder him but, because of the darkness and the exchanged coats, killed his friend by mistake. They were not robbers, because they took nothing.' She closed her eyes as though she could block out the very idea of someone attempting to murder her brother. 'This man, my stepfather, worked upon my mother to have her agree to marry me to his son. If Miguel was dead – *were* dead – the way would be clear to have my father's estates given to my husband. My mother would never believe that this man she married was so false, but Miguel and me . . . we had no doubt. We believed his life was in danger – Miguel's life – and I was to be married to someone I despised. So we fled . . . upon the ship of a friend of my father's, as I told you. We planned to go to our uncle – my father's brother – who we believed would protect us until Miguel came into his inheritance; once the lands were his, they would be out of the grasp of my stepfather and his son.

We believed we were safe once we were at sea . . .' Her voice had become dry and small so that he strained to hear the words. 'But during a calm – not long after we sailed – the captains of the other frigates and some officials travelling to Vera Cruz came aboard our ship to dine. One of these officials we knew – he was an associate of my stepfather. He had been to our home many times and knew Miguel and me by sight. We thought he would reveal our identities immediately, but instead he said nothing. This we found confusing. If he did not intend to reveal who we were and have us returned to Spain, what did he intend? Would he demand money? Was he not such a good friend of our stepfather as we thought? Was it a coincidence that he was on that ship? Miguel believed that it was not and that he planned to have us murdered when we reached Vera Cruz. Once we both were dead, then my stepbrother could inherit my father's estates. All that would be necessary would be for my mother to adopt him as her heir.

'We dreaded our arrival in Vera Cruz, but we did not comprehend the true danger. One evening we went forward to the . . . where the injured sleep . . .'

'The sick-berth?'

'Yes. We went there to visit a young officer who had befriended us and had the bad luck to be injured in a fall. The collision occurred while we were there. Lamps were thrown down upon the deck and shattered so that all was dark. There was a great panic, for the ship began immediately to sink. The few men in the sick-berth were borne out. Two crewmen who appeared to be helping told us to stay out of the way and wait but then, as soon as the sick-berth was empty, they turned on us with knives. We were taken by surprise, but I had a pocket pistol secreted in my jacket and shot one as he attacked me. That was his blood on my clothing. The second ran off. We made our way to the deck. There the captain put us into the boat, but Miguel was frantic with fear. You must understand – there had now been two times of men trying to kill him. There was no way to know who aboard had been sent to murder us or how many they might be. Every man aboard seemed like a threat, so Miguel . . . he forced this man to cling to the ropes and cut us free, setting our boat adrift with only we two in it. The coxswain was hauled back aboard.' She covered her eyes and Hayden saw tears slip between her fingers.

'Men might have made it into the boat and been saved if not for us . . . What Miguel did was very wrong.' Her voice disappeared then and Hayden could hear her attempting to find it again. 'Miguel keeps saying we might have been murdered or the boat swamped by frightened sailors . . .' A long, shuddering breath. 'I think he will do anything to live – to keep us alive. He is so frightened.' She turned a little and looked up at Hayden, her eyes glistening. 'Would a court convict him? Has he broken a law?'

'I do not know Spanish law. If he were a sailor, certainly he would be court-martialled and found guilty . . . But he is not a sailor so I do not know what would be done . . .'

'If no one survived the wreck, then no one knows but Miguel and me . . . and now you.'

'I wish you had not told me,' Hayden whispered.

'I did not want there to be lies between us. I wanted only truth.'

'That truth might force me to tell lies . . . to those to whom I am duty bound to tell the truth.'

'I – I am sorry if I have put you in a difficult place.'

'Do not apologize. You were right – better we have truth

between us.' Hayden's thoughts seemed to be mired in fog. 'How long until Miguel comes of age?'

'One year and one half.'

'Not so long . . . You do have an uncle in Vera Cruz?'

'Yes, of course. The brother of my father.'

'And you trust him?'

'With our lives . . . As I do you, Charles.'

The words of Mr Hawthorne came to him then: '*the male romantic myth is rescuing the damsel in distress*'. Madame Adair, who lived in fear of the guillotine, Madame Bourdage and the exquisite Heloise. And now Angelita. He did not think of himself as having this tendency, but his recent history would seem to prove otherwise.

What is the difference between a hero and a fool? A fool wears motley . . .

Hayden could not help but wonder if he was being taken for a fool again.

The ship's bell tolled somewhere deep in the wind.

'I fear I am becoming a terrible burden to you . . .' Angelita whispered.

'No. You have suffered terrible misfortune, but luck is like that, I have found. It will run bad for a time and then all will be well. We must weather the gales and make the most of fair winds.'

'I fear that God has turned against me . . .'

Hayden did not say that he thought all the gods were unaware of her existence, and his as well. 'I do not believe that God could turn against someone such as you.'

Hayden paused a moment. 'You have done a very brave thing to escape this situation, to cross an ocean.'

'It did not seem brave . . . it was desperate. But here we are and now I have told you all my secrets.' Angelita touched his arm. 'Sleep well, Charles.'

And with that she retreated quickly behind her screen.

For a long time Hayden stood, his hand upon a deck beam, the ship rolling beneath him and his mind reeling. Percival had not been lying. There was a woman living in his cabin – a comely and charming young lady!

Ever since Angel and Miguel had stepped aboard he had been dreaming that a woman came to him in the night, as though somehow his senses had known but his waking mind did not believe it.

Hayden undressed and rolled into his cot, where he lay, bemused. But then his thoughts turned to Henrietta, whom he had been missing all these long months.

Dear, dear Henri, he thought. I believed we would marry, have children and grow old together. Instead you joined your life with another's, and here am I, between continents – so very far from solid ground – the sea ever and always moving beneath me. I believe, because of your fine and generous heart, you would wish me both love and happiness. But what would you say of this young señorita, who Percival believes is enamoured of me? Perhaps you would be amused by my predicament? I do believe you would say, 'Do not look to me, Charles Hayden, for I belong to another.' You have released me . . . but my heart has not yet let go of you.

Ten

A tapping within his dream, discreet, distant; a pause; and then again, more insistently. Of a sudden, Hayden was started awake from a very pleasant dream.

'What is it?' he muttered.

Muffled, from beyond the door.

'Your breakfast, sir.'

'Ah. I have overslept. Give me a moment, Winston.' Hayden rolled out of bed, strangely buoyant, and hummed a tune as he shaved by deadly dim lamplight. His steward laid out his breakfast and, as soon as he was gone, Hayden turned to his servant.

'There is some little pricker in my dress coat, Baines. Will you take it forward to some light and see if you can find it?'

'Shall I not do it here, sir?'

'I can pour my own coffee, Baines.'

'As you wish, sir, but where in the coat shall I search?'

'Lodged in the lining, somewhere in the back. You will find it if you put it on, I should think.'

'Aye, sir.' He fetched his captain's coat and went out.

As soon as the servants had left, a fully dressed Angelita appeared, and took a seat at his table.

'You look rather like a girl dressed for a masquerade,' he whispered.

She put a finger to her lips. 'Shh! You must not even say such a thing in private.' She tilted her head toward the door, where a marine stood guard outside.

'Well then, Don Angel,' Hayden said aloud, 'you slept well, I trust?'

'I had very odd dreams,' Angelita replied, pouring coffee for two. 'I dreamed I was a common player – in, perhaps, one of Senior Shakespeare's plays – and I was, if you can credit it, a woman dressed as a man.'

'That is very odd. What was the gist of this play?'

'It is something of a jumble in my mind, but I believe there was also a man – a knight, I seem to remember – and I became his page . . .'

'Like Sancho Panza?'

'Oh, nothing like him! But we travelled the land searching for a necklace, I think – a magical necklace that had the power to reverse enchantments. I remember . . . it was to reverse the enchantment on a princess who had been turned into an ass! The knight was in love with this princess, but she was bespelled by another – that is why he searched for the necklace – to break the spell and win her regard.'

'I wonder if I have not seen this play . . . ?'

'Only if you were in my dream. So the knight and the page – who was a woman disguised as a man – travelled, and had many adventures, until finally they came at last to the cave of an ogre. The knight and the ogre fought a terrible battle, but finally the knight prevailed and took the necklace from the ogre's cave. For safekeeping he put it around his own neck, but when he did so the strangest thing occurred – an enchantment, of which he was unaware, was lifted from him . . .' Angelita appeared to run out of words and, embarrassed, shrugged and threw up her hands.

'But you must finish. What was the nature of the spell that was lifted?'

Angelita coloured a little. 'I do not know; at that moment I awaked.'

'Well, that is a strange dream. And the page who had dressed as a man – what became of her?'

'The dream ended before I could know.'

'Ah . . . Well, it is a very incomplete story.'

'Maybe tonight I will dream the ending.'

'But what of the princess who was turned into an ass . . . ?'

Angelita shrugged. 'She must have so remained. But she was very foolish not to return the knight's love, so I feel very little pity for her.'

Hayden arrived on the deck as the pervasive grey of early morning overspread the world. All but a few of the brightest stars had been absorbed into this watery sky, which Hayden well knew could prove blue and cloudless in but half an hour.

His mind still whirled at the revelations of the night – and the morning. Angelita's 'dream' left little in doubt – she believed he was still under the spell of Henrietta and must somehow have that spell lifted.

'*Maybe tonight I will dream the ending,*' she had said. Maybe Hayden himself would have that dream.

Archer spotted him and came striding over the deck, shaking him out of one course of thought.

'Have we our tow in sight, Mr Archer?'

'She is a mile off, sir, north-east by east.' The lieutenant pointed toward a dim point of light. 'Our wind has taken off, Captain, and comes from all points. We are slatting about, but I would venture we shall have the trade again by noon. If this lump would only go down, sir, our sails and gear would be the better for it.'

Hayden put a hand on the binnacle to steady himself as a train of larger seas rolled the ship. There was not wind enough to keep the sails full and, as Archer had said, they slatted and thrashed about in their gear.

'How I hate it when the wind leaves and the sea stays on like an unwanted guest.' Archer's tone was bitter and his look resentful.

'Like a mother-in-law who you cannot possibly ask to leave.' This observation came from the marine lieutenant, who appeared out of the murk.

'What would you know of mothers-in-law, Mr Hawthorne?' This was Barthe, who had emerged but an instant before from the companionway.

'Enough to know that they are largely to be avoided, Mr Barthe. Have you reason to complain of your wife's begetter?'

'She is a saint, in truth, perhaps the sweetest-tempered creature ever produced by the fair month of June.'

'Given the foul nature of her son-in-law, she would either be a saint or a scold. No one else would survive,' Hawthorne parried.

'Well, I cannot argue that,' Barthe replied.

Hayden directed his gaze to the slaver, but the growing light had swallowed its dim lamps.

'There is no advantage to taking up our tow until this sea goes down a little and the trade is re-established, but let us shift nearer as soon as we may. I should like to hail her master and be certain all is well.'

The sky continued to brighten and then the eastern horizon announced the coming of the sun. There was still some cloud, but all of a pure, benign nature.

'*On deck!*' came the call from above. 'Sail on the starboard quarter and hull down.'

No one on the deck could make out this ship for some time and then the sun lifted clear of the sea and illuminated the distant sail.

'See the men fed, Mr Archer, and then we shall beat to quarters.'

'Aye, sir.' Archer was off at a run.

Angelita appeared on deck and began searching the ocean anxiously. Hayden beckoned her near and held out his glass.

'Is this one of the frigates you sailed with?'

She took the glass awkwardly but with the sea running could not keep the distant ship in its small circle. She passed it back to Hayden and shrugged. He could not help but note that the morning's glow had gone; she appeared pale and drawn now.

Miguel emerged from below and lumbered over to the rail near Hayden and his sister. He too had a look through Hayden's glass but after a few seconds thrust it back toward Hayden; then he leaned over the rail and was horribly ill. He slipped down on to the deck then, with his back against the bulwark, and Hayden had a hand fetch him some water.

Within half an hour the drum called the men to their stations and the guns were cast free.

'Do not open ports, Mr Archer. With this damned sea running we shall take water over the sills.' Hayden walked a few paces forward and found the lookout on the maintops. 'Does she have wind, Price?'

'Her sails will fill a moment, sir, and then 'tis all thrown out again. I get a glimpse of her now and then, sir, and imagine she might be a frigate, Captain.'

'Pass the word for Mr Wickham,' Hayden ordered Maxwell, one of the new reefers.

A moment later Lord Arthur appeared, his glass in hand.

'I believe you will have guessed my orders, Mr Wickham?'

'Up to the tops, sir, on the double.'

Hayden nodded. 'I should like to know if she is one of ours, or if we are in for a fight.'

He watched Wickham go hand over hand up the ratlines, his useless finger more in the way than not.

Just as Wickham hauled himself on to the maintop, seas reached them, originating in the north-east, and these collided with the leftover slop from the gale, producing a sea that tossed their ship around so that she corkscrewed and shied and all but rolled her rails under.

Everyone aboard took hold of something solid lest they be thrown across the deck, such was the violence of the motion. Poor Miguel was sick again – into a bucket this time, for he could not rise to lean over the rail. His sister crouched by him, speaking softly to him in Spanish.

'We shall have these last sails in, Captain,' Mr Barthe called out, 'or they will be rags in five minutes.' He clung to the mainmast shrouds for all he was worth.

Although Hayden agreed entirely with the sailing master, he was reluctant to send men aloft at that moment, for they would be able to do nothing but hold on for their lives.

But then, a little breath of wind whispered across the deck, sighed and died away.

'Is it the trade . . . filling in?' one of the new middies asked.

'Hush! D'you want to put a curse on't?' one of the hands hissed at him.

Again, a little breeze bellied the sails and, again, they fell slack and began to thrash.

And then a little wind, a little more, the smallest gust. The ship heeled, steadied and began to make way.

'She answers her helm, Mr Archer,' the man at the wheel called out.

Just then came a call from above.

'*On deck!*' It was Wickham. 'I am in agreement with Price, sir, I believe we have a frigate in the offing. She appears to be flying a Spanish flag, sir.'

'Well, well,' Barthe muttered, but he glanced at the Spaniards and did not say more.

Angelita rose and came to Hayden immediately.

'This will be the ship upon which the friend of my step-father sails,' she whispered, her voice quavering.

'You and Miguel had best go below . . . down to the cockpit with the doctor. But, Angelita . . . we cannot know what ship this is; the flag might be a ruse.'

Hayden had one of the hands help Angelita get Miguel below.

'Set a course to meet this ship, Mr Archer, and pass the word for my officers and young gentlemen.'

When the officers had all gathered aft, Hayden brought them into a circle. 'Not a word of our castaways to this ship.' Hayden watched surprise register upon their faces.

'But will Miguel and Angel not want to join their own people, Captain?' the sailing master wondered.

'I have no time to explain, Mr Barthe, but you must trust that I know what I do in this. Not a word.'

'Aye, sir.'

Hayden sent them all back to their stations, no doubt with questions in their minds, but he trusted that more pressing matters would soon drive those out.

The real question at that moment was whether this ship wore her true colours, or was trying to draw Hayden near. He did not have his own ensign flying and did not plan to send it aloft until he was more certain this ship was a friend.

Nagging at the back of his mind was the matter of his two castaways . . . overlain by recollections of Madame Bourdage and her beautiful daughter. How grateful they had seemed for his assistance, how genuine-seeming their thanks. Was he falling prey to this same device – rescuing a beautiful young woman? Suddenly it seemed possible that everything Angelita had told him was calculated, each different truth a carefully constructed lie. An evil stepfather, after all. An attempt on her brother's life – a forced marriage, even the reputed wealth. Was it not convenient that all their property – their money – was lost in the sinking of the ship? He was certain, upon reflection, that he had read that novel. And who had offered to aid these unfortunate siblings? The same gull who had offered to aid Madame Bourdage. At just the right moment Angelita had revealed her true sex and all but confessed her feelings for him. What honourable man would betray a woman so enamoured of him, especially one so sweet and handsome? Had she held back the queen of hearts for the very last trick?

'*On deck!* Captain, she is altering course to run from us.'

Hayden moved to where he could make out Wickham. 'Climb up, Mr Wickham, and see if there is another ship just over the horizon.'

'Aye, sir.'

Archer came and stood a few yards distant.

'Do you think she might be a Frenchman, sir?'

'She might well be Spanish, Mr Archer, but that does not

mean she is still an ally. There is much speculation in the Admiralty that Spain will not be on our side much longer.'

'Then our guests might not be guests, sir . . .'

'Yes, though I am quite certain they are civilians, all the same.'

The idea that he felt a growing attachment to an enemy was distressing. Hayden considered a moment.

'Send our colours aloft, Mr Archer, if you please. We will see if that has any effect.'

'I do not think they will be able to make out our colours on this point of sail, sir.'

'I believe you are correct. Run them up the foremast to leeward – damn flag etiquette!'

The folded ensign was carried forward and sent aloft. Luckily, there were halyards in numerous places about the ship for sending aloft signals that were to be seen from one direction but obscured from another.

The red ensign fluttered aloft and streamed to the wind. Hayden trained his glass on the distant ship, but there was no sign that she was altering course. And then the shadows among the sails began to change shape.

'She turns, Captain,' Wickham called from above. 'I believe she is coming toward us . . .' Wickham lowered his glass and looked down at his captain. 'She has altered course to meet us, sir.'

'Stay aloft, Mr Wickham, and see if you can make her out as she draws near. Even if she is a Spaniard, she might not be a friend.'

'Aye, sir.'

'Mr Archer?'

'Sir?'

'Let us work our ship below this frigate. I would like to heave-to as she approaches so that we have a broadside trained upon her.'

'You will give her the weather gage, sir?'

'Yes, with this damn sea running we shall be able to open our gunports, and she will almost certainly be taking water over the sills if she tries to do the same.'

The two ships approached each other with the wariness of pugilists meeting for the first time. Hayden was able to force his opponent up to weather and, in the running sea and filling trade, the opposing ship heeled with her deck exposed and her gunports above water only as each crest passed. By the time they were in that position, though, Hayden was quite certain she was exactly what her flag claimed – a Spanish frigate. All along her rail the crew gathered, staring silently at the British ship, which was clearly in a superior position. It occurred to Hayden that the Spanish might be in the same predicament as he – wondering if their two countries were at war and if Hayden was in possession of that knowledge before them. Upon the quarterdeck the officers were arrayed, and Hayden could see several well-dressed gentlemen among them – not in uniform.

Speaking trumpets were brought forth and pleasantries exchanged. It appeared that neither captain believed its nation to be at war with the other, and this caused a lessening of anxiety all around.

'Two of our small fleet collided in the gale,' the captain called in Spanish. 'One was damaged and has limped on for Vera Cruz. We believe the other foundered. We have been searching for survivors. Have you found any – or any boats?'

Hayden cursed himself for a fool. The boat Angelita and

her brother had escaped in was on his deck. 'We found a dead man tangled in some flotsam, Captain, and an empty boat floating up to her gunwales . . .' He pointed at the Spanish boat. 'We buried the man at sea with all our prayers.' Hayden described the drowned sailor on the off chance that someone aboard that ship might know him, but no one seemed to.

The Spanish captain nodded. 'No one else then?'

'I am sorry to say, no. Would you like us to send this boat over to you?'

'It is yours by custom of the sea . . . and I have all the boats I wish to carry.' He pointed off toward the distant slaver. 'Is she one of your ships, Captain Hayden?'

'A British transport dismasted in the gale. We have taken her in tow.'

'Has this ship found any survivors, Captain?'

'I can assure you they have not.'

The man nodded as though he had not expected to hear otherwise. 'Where is it you are bound, Captain?' the Spaniard asked.

Hayden made a gesture with his free hand and shouted into the trumpet. 'I am under orders from the Admiralty, Captain, and may not reveal them even to our most trusted friends.'

'I understand. Good luck to you, Captain.'

'Good luck to you in your search.'

Hayden ordered his ship underway, then wore to return to their tow. He had Wickham watch the Spanish frigate closely; she did nothing but resume her course. In an hour she was on the horizon, then gone.

About that time, Dr Griffiths emerged from below.

'I have left two frightened Spaniards down in the cockpit. I assume it is safe for them to return to the deck?'

'It is. I shall send someone down to release them.'

Griffiths looked off in the direction of the Spanish ship – the tops of her sails just visible. 'So, we did not turn them over to the Spanish ship. I am quite certain there is an excellent reason for doing so . . .'

'I believe there is.' Hayden did not offer an explanation and knew Griffiths would not enquire further.

The surgeon nodded. For a moment, however, Hayden thought he *would* ask, for he seemed about to speak. Instead he said, 'This might sound a little mad, Captain . . . but do you think it possible that young Angel is . . . well . . . is he not too elegantly beautiful to be a man? Could he be a young woman in disguise? You share their cabin . . .'

Hayden suddenly found himself unable to decide if he should confide in Griffiths or deny the obvious – for it was obvious . . . to him, at least.

'I can assure you, Doctor, that Angel is a young man. There is no doubt on that score.'

'Ah. Then I have sounded rather foolish, I fear.'

'Not in the least, Doctor. I am quite certain others have entertained the same thought.'

The doctor nodded and excused himself, appearing somewhat out of sorts or embarrassed. Hayden regretted lying to him but felt he had no choice – he had given his word, after all.

The *Themis* soon met the drifting slaver, but was forced to wait two hours before it was felt the seas had become regular enough and the trade constant. The tedious journey toward Barbados resumed.

When all the gear had been arranged to his satisfaction Hayden repaired below to eat a late dinner. His cabin had been dismantled when the ship was cleared, but now it looked much as it had when he left it that morning, all of his belongings replaced exactly as he preferred. He had ordered his steward to feed his guests at the regular hour – noon – not wishing them to go hungry when he was otherwise engaged. As he finished his meal, Angel appeared – he still had trouble thinking of her as 'Angelita', having called her 'Angel' for so long.

Hayden had his servant clear away the moment coffee appeared and, as the man retreated out of the door, Angelita leaned near and whispered, 'Thank you, Charles, for not turning my brother and me over to our people . . . and for trusting me.'

'I could do no less. There were a number of Spanish civilians aboard that frigate; I saw them upon the deck.'

'Yes, they are officials being carried out to Vera Cruz. The man we distrust is very tall – half a head taller than you and certainly the tallest man among the civilians.'

'I marked him, then. Round-faced and quietly dressed. At one point he whispered something to the captain, who then asked if the slave ship had found any survivors. I assured them that she had not.'

'Do you think they believe you?'

'I do hope so. Like a fool, I forgot that we had taken aboard your boat. I told the captain we found it drifting, all but filled with water, though empty of any people. In such a gale a boat could easily be rolled over and everyone aboard lost.'

'And we – Miguel and me – we did not know the management of a boat in such weathers. I have said it before, but it could only have been the hand of God that preserved us.'

Hayden let this pass without comment.

'They must have asked themselves if there could be any reason I would not tell them the truth ...' This was not explicitly a question, but he did let it hang in the air.

Angelita considered this a moment and then shook her head. 'They would know no reason for you not to tell them the truth. So I think they believe you.'

Hayden nodded – it was what he had hoped she would say. 'There is one other matter ... Dr Griffiths asked me if I thought it possible that you were a woman disguised.'

Angelita drew back, both hands limp upon the table. 'He knows, then?'

'I assured him you were most definitely a man.'

She put a hand to her heart and let out a long breath. 'No one must know,' she whispered, rather breathless of a sudden.

'I wonder if I should tell him the truth and charge him not to reveal it? Griffiths would never repeat anything I asked him not to. The man is discretion dressed and walking.'

Angelita squeezed his wrist. 'I think it is better if you say nothing ...'

'Perhaps, but as it stands he might ask the same question of others. This could set people to wondering.'

'I will endeavour to be more manly. Say nothing, Charles, I beg you. It must never be known. Miguel's life would be in danger. My life, too, might be endangerous.'

'If that is your wish.'

'How long now, until Barbados?'

'A few days, if the weather stays as it is. Three or four, perhaps.'

Angelita took this in. 'I will spend less time where others might observe me. It cannot be known that I am a woman. It cannot.'

'Then we will keep up the ruse. But, Angelita, what will you do when you reach Barbados?'

She shook her head, the smallest motion, her lovely mouth turning down. 'I cannot say. Barbados . . . was never in our intention.'

Eleven

The long journey to Barbados resumed, the trades carrying them along, the slaver following behind like a bad deed that could never be forgotten. Angel and Miguel were guests of the midshipman's berth that evening and took their supper there, where it had been decided that only Spanish would be spoken, which sounded very much like a language lesson to Hayden, for only Wickham had enough Spanish to ask for the salt to be passed.

Hayden ate his dinner alone, read for an hour, then took a turn around the deck. Finding everything to his satisfaction, he descended the ladder to the gundeck. Passing the skylight to the gunroom, he heard laughter and then the distinctive, accented English of Miguel Campillo proclaiming the superiority of Spanish wine.

Nodding to his marine sentry, Hayden entered his cabin. A lamp glowed from beyond the sail-cloth partition, but Hayden could not tell if Angelita was there or if the lamp had merely been lit by his steward. In case his guest was sleeping, Hayden made his toilet as quietly as he could.

Emerging from his quarter gallery, he doused his own lamp and immediately saw the lovely silhouette of Angelita cast upon the partition.

'Are you there?' came her whisper from beyond the canvas.

Hayden drew nearer so that his voice would not carry to the sentry or up the skylight.

'Yes,' he whispered.

The shadowy Angelita reached out a hand and pressed it flat to the softened old cloth. For a second Hayden hesitated and then he touched his hand to hers. The cloth was drawn taut enough that they could not grasp hands, but he could feel the heat of her palm against his.

She moved nearer and they leaned gently forward until their foreheads met. He could hear her now; jagged little gasps for breath. His own lungs had grown tight. They pressed their cheeks together.

'I do not think my mother would approve of this,' Angelita whispered.

'We are in separate rooms,' Hayden said, just as softly. 'Even a priest could not complain of that.'

Without another word they both moved forward so that Angelita's face pressed against his chest and their bodies leaned into one another.

'I cannot find my breath,' she whispered.

'Nor I,' he replied.

He swore he could feel her heart pounding – though perhaps it was his own.

'There is so little between us,' she breathed, 'from a different people, a different life, your language I speak but poorly . . . yet there is only this scrap of sail keeping us apart. Or is there something more . . . ?'

Hayden attempted to control his breathing and then said ever so softly, 'Foolish of me, is it not, to cling to hope when the woman in question has married another?'

'You are loyal, Charles Hayden, and you loved her deeply. It speaks well of your heart that you have not been able to let her go.' Angelita tried to gather her breath. 'Is it really hope you cling to, or is it that you do not want to let go of this . . . *feeling*? Love is a precious thing, after all.'

'I want to let it go . . . and I do not. I want to feel anger toward her . . . and I cannot. I do not want to speak more of her, because I am here with you . . . and yet I do. Am I not a sad, love-sick youth?'

'We are both young in these matters. I do not know how to banish this ghostly woman from your heart, but I do not know if you can love another until she is gone.'

Reluctantly – Hayden could feel it – Angelita stepped back, though her hand lingered a second longer on his chest, as though she were sounding the depths of his heart.

'Sleep well, Captain Hayden,' she whispered, and then she extinguished her lamp and was gone in that instant.

A moment more Hayden stood by the partition, and then he went to his cot, where he lay, attempting to calm his racing heart. Beyond the partition he could hear Angelita, so near that he could tell, by the sound of her breathing, that she did not sleep. He imagined he could feel the warmth and sense the soft scent of her body.

Even more than that, he thought he could perceive her suffering, which caused him to feel more than a little ignoble. He wondered at her apparent attachment to him. How did one distinguish fleeting infatuation from deeper, lasting feelings? It was difficult enough to tell them apart in one's own heart, let alone the heart of another.

Did I not feel strongly about Henrietta when first we met? he asked himself. Certainly he had. And what had he done? He had dithered and been 'reasonable', and she had slipped away.

It occurred to Hayden that, once they reached Barbados, Angelita and her brother would be off to Vera Cruz at the first opportunity. He knew, once that occurred, he would never see her again. It would be as though she had died. Here, aboard ship, he could speak with her and seek her company at his pleasure, but once she was back with her family they would never allow such a connection to continue. He was only a sea officer, after all, and not a suitable match for such a woman.

The idea, however, that she would be gone caused him more distress than he could have imagined. What, exactly, did that mean?

His usual breakfast was laid out and, as he prepared to eat, rustling sounds emanated from beyond the partition. Angelita emerged a moment later, looking wan and tired. It was now so very obvious to Hayden that she was a woman that he could not comprehend how anyone could not see it.

'I hesitate to ask if you slept well . . .' Hayden said.

'Very poorly, I fear.'

Hayden's steward served breakfast to her and, as had become her habit, she poured coffee for them both.

'I did not hear your brother return . . . ?'

'No doubt he became insensible with drink and spent the night lying in some corner of the ship.'

'Mmm.'

The rest of the meal passed in silence. When the servants had cleared away, Hayden asked that the coffee be left and released them to other duties.

'I am sorry you slept poorly,' Hayden offered, for lack of something better to start the conversation.

Angelita shrugged. A second of awkwardness, and then she

whispered, 'I have exposed my feelings before I should – before I knew that you shared them – because I hoped . . .' but she fell silent and wiped a sleeve across her eyes, which glistened.

'I am the one who is foolish, clinging to feelings for a woman who has chosen another.'

She reached out and put a hand on his wrist. 'But you are mourning. You comprehend this, do you not? You grieve for the person you have lost. Wounds to the heart take much longer to heal than wounds to the body.'

'I fear you will be gone to Vera Cruz before I have come out of mourning. I seem to be healing more slowly than I would like.'

Angelita squeezed his wrist and met his gaze suddenly. 'I should like very much to be patient and very proper and to give you all the time you need, but I fear the same. We have so little time to find if we can be content in one another. Not enough time, perhaps . . .'

'Then we must make use of the time we have.'

There was no hesitation on either part. Each leaned forward and they kissed, turned in their chairs and embraced, only a section of table holding them apart.

The door handle rattled at that instant and they flew apart, just as Don Miguel was let into the cabin. He was a disaster of red eyes, unkempt hair and dull skin.

'What goes on here?' he enquired, and stopped.

Angelita, who was blushing, picked up her coffee cup and raised it to her brother. 'The English call it breakfast, brother. Would you care to join us, or are you yet too ill from drink?'

'I shall break my fast later,' he said coldly, and retreated beyond the screen.

'And I should be about my duties,' Hayden said, draining his cup and rising to his feet.

Angelita glanced back once to be certain her brother could not see and then squeezed Hayden's hand before he left.

Twelve

The trade blew across the decks like a warm caress. Hayden emerged from the companionway and stood a moment, feeling the touch of the air upon his skin – he had escaped the English winter and come to a part of the world where perfect summer days followed one after another in endless succession.

Archer spotted his captain and immediately set out to intercept him, his face, Hayden could see, tightened from some concern.

'I think our wind is making a little, Captain,' he said, after quickly exchanging pleasantries. 'Our tow is sheering about more than I like.'

'Let us have a look, Mr Archer.' The two men made their way quickly along the gangway and were on the quarterdeck headed for the stern when an angry swarm of Spanish invective spewed out of the skylight. Hayden did not quite catch the meaning, though it was clearly Miguel, and in a rage, too.

'Who are you that I should answer such a question?' came an equally angry reply from the Spaniard's sister. 'You are not my father. You do not make choices for me.'

Archer glanced at Hayden, and they both hurried past the skylight. When they reached the transom, the argument, if anything, was louder. Archer cleared his throat and the voices fell to hissed whispers.

The first lieutenant pointed at the ship following in their

wake, the long tow rope sawing down into the waves that lay between the two ships. Even at that distance Hayden could see the helmsmen of the slaver fighting the wheel.

'What is your opinion, Captain?'

'I am in complete agreement with you, Mr Archer; we must reduce sail.'

'Aye, sir.' Archer went off at a brisk pace, calling out orders.

A moment more Hayden stood, watching the trailing ship, and then he heard footsteps behind and turned to find Miguel Campillo bearing down on him, all signs of a barely controlled rage in his carriage and manner. He came to Hayden and stood directly in front of him, shoulders squared, and looked Hayden in the eye, even though the naval officer stood a number of inches taller.

'Sir,' he said, his accent thickened by emotion, 'you have wronged me and my family. And I had thought you an honourable gentleman.'

'Officers of the British Navy do not take such accusations lightly, sir.'

Miguel leaned close and whispered to Hayden in Spanish, though the words were not less threatening for their reduced volume. 'I will not withdraw what I have said, sir. You have discovered my sister's secret and taken advantage of her innocence and trust.'

Hayden drew himself up. 'I have done no such thing! My conduct toward your sister has been beyond reproach.'

'Then why does she believe you have intentions to ask for her hand? Why does she hold such hopes if you have not led her to believe so? You, sir, do not know your place. Our family would never consider you a match for her.'

Miguel glanced over his shoulder. All around the quarterdeck men were staring, but they looked quickly away. The Spaniard put Hayden between himself and the rest of the crew, and whispered, 'If keeping our secret were not of the utmost importance, and you had not saved our lives, I would demand satisfaction. That, sir, is what I think of your actions. If it were within my power, I would remove my sister and myself from your ship this instant, but that is not possible so I demand that you break off this affair with . . . That you break off this affair immediately. It cannot continue.'

The two men stood face to face, neither giving way. There was the muffled sound of tearing, like tissue, and then a black snake whipped out of the sea toward them.

'*Down!*' Hayden hollered, so loud it hurt his throat. He grasped Miguel by his lapels and threw him upon the deck, landing half atop him.

The tow rope whirred over them like a giant scythe, struck something fleshy with a horrifying smack then slammed into the larboard bulwark like a bar of steel.

For a second neither man moved. Miguel looked around in confusion.

'The tow rope parted,' Hayden heard himself say, and he shifted to rise. As he did, so Miguel's head snapped around.

'*Angelita!*' He was on his feet, pushing past Hayden.

There, on the deck, lay his sister, unmoving, curled up as though she slept, her unbound hair in a wave over her face. Miguel was bending down beside her only an instant before Hayden.

'Do not move her!' Hayden warned the Spaniard. 'Pass the word for the doctor!' he called out. And then more urgently. '*The doctor!*'

Her coat was ripped open along her right side, and her shirt beneath that. Both were stained with new blood.

Miguel stretched out his hands to his sister, his dispute with Hayden forgotten.

'She is not breathing . . . !' he said.

Hayden put his fingers before her nose and mouth. 'She is. I can feel her breath – though too faint.' He glanced around and called out testily, '*Where is the doctor?*'

She lay still, the stain on her side growing.

'I have seen this before,' Hayden told Miguel, without taking his eyes from Angelita. 'In Corsica . . . Much worse than this. The man lived.'

Hayden was vaguely aware that Archer was standing over him.

'Permission to heave-to, sir . . . Captain?'

'Yes, Mr Archer, by all means. Heave-to.'

The doctor came running up the nearby ladder.

'The tow rope,' Hayden replied when the doctor raised a single eyebrow. 'It parted and scythed across the deck . . .' He made a helpless gesture toward the girl lying on the hard planks.

'Don Miguel,' Griffiths said gently, 'if you will allow me . . . ?'

The Spaniard rose to his feet and made room for the doctor, whom Hayden was certain wanted out of the way any individual whose emotions might get the better of his reason. But Hayden himself was fighting an impulse to take Angelita in his arms. His throat had tightened to such a degree that he was afraid to speak, lest he reveal his feelings.

For a moment the doctor bent over her, feeling for a pulse at her throat.

'Who saw this?' the doctor asked of the men gathered around.

'I did, Dr Griffiths,' one of the hands answered. 'Just out the corner of me eye, sir. Rope came in like a serpent, sir, and the end caught the young gentleman without warning. Like 'e'd been flogged by a Titan, sir. Don't know 'ow it didn't tear 'im in 'alf.'

Two hands appeared with a cot at that moment, and the surgeon, and Miguel and Hayden slid the still-limp girl on to the stretched canvas. Four seamen took it up, but Hayden knew she was light as a feather and one of them could easily have borne her.

He followed down the ladder and forward. As they reached the entrance to the sick-berth, the doctor leaned near to Hayden. 'Keep his brother out here if you can, Captain.'

Hayden nodded.

'Don Miguel?' he said to the Spaniard. 'We must remain out of the doctor's way . . .'

Miguel nodded and, as the door to the sick-berth closed, set immediately to pacing across the deck like an expectant father awaiting the birth of a child. He did not look at Hayden, who was torn between his duty to his ship and his desire to stay near Angelita. Men were killed by ropes whipping back – strong men.

The motion of the ship changed as Archer ordered her hove-to. They would need to run another cable to the slaver, which was now adrift, but that could wait a little while. The two men paced the deck back and forth, the tension between them palpable, as though they awaited the doctor's verdict as to which of them was the newborn's father.

The doctor did not emerge for half of an hour and, when he did, he appeared very grave, if not indignant.

'Angel has regained consciousness,' the doctor told them, speaking quietly. 'The ribs are terribly bruised and may be cracked. I cannot say. They are not displaced and I do not think they are broken. On top of this – despite the fact that I was assured otherwise – Angel has been revealed to be a young woman.'

'I was sworn to secrecy, Doctor,' Hayden explained quickly, 'and dared not break my trust.'

Griffiths nodded. 'No one owes me an explanation, but the men in the sick-berth are now sensible of it and you well know that they will not keep it dark.'

Hayden nodded.

'I do not think the sick-berth the best place for a young woman, Captain,' Griffiths went on.

'Can she be moved to my cabin?'

'With care, yes.'

'May I see her, Doctor?' Miguel asked.

'You *are* her brother ... ?' Griffiths sounded suddenly uncertain that anything he had been told about these castaways was true.

'Yes. Yes, of course I am.'

The doctor nodded to Hayden. 'She has asked to see the Captain first, and then you, sir.'

There was an awkward moment, and then Hayden let himself into the sick-berth. The men lying in their cots regarded him with uncommon interest, he thought. A blanket had been hung to give the sole female patient privacy, and Hayden found Angelita there, behind the screen, lying beneath a coverlet, her bare shoulders and arms exposed. Her face, blanched and bloodless, was drawn tight with pain, tiny lines appearing at the corners of her eyes and upon her usually smooth brow.

Hayden took the chair beside her cot, which swung gently back and forth.

'The doctor tells me you will make a full recovery . . .' he told her in Spanish, uncertain what to say.

She nodded and reached out. Hayden gently took her hand.

'Do not listen to my brother,' she managed. Hayden could see that each word was like a little knife in her side. 'I am not a child and I will make my own choices, now. He is not my father, nor has he reached his majority – we were born the same hour . . . and I was born first. He has no say over my life.'

Hayden was not quite certain how to answer this, and instead observed, 'It hurts you to speak?'

She nodded. 'But I do not want you to break off with me . . . because of my brother.' A tear squeezed out from the corner of her eye and ran crookedly down her cheek.

'Miguel and I will have to reach an understanding, then.'

She pressed his hand. 'Do not give in to him.'

'I am more concerned, at this moment, about you and your recovery. That is the most important thing.'

'I am young. My body will heal . . . but young hearts . . . they are fragile.'

'I know,' Hayden replied, with more feeling than he intended. 'We are going to remove you to my cabin. I fear it will cause pain, but this is a sailors' sick-berth and no place for a woman.'

'I do not care about the pain – I want to be in your cabin.'

'Then we will move you as soon as the doctor allows. Your brother awaits outside.'

'Send him in.' She gave Hayden's hand a squeeze and tried to smile.

Hayden went out, ignoring the stares. Beyond the door, Miguel hovered, his anger replaced by anxiety.

'She is asking for you, Don Miguel.'

He went in without a word, or even a nod.

The surgeon waited there, looking askance at Hayden.

'I do apologize, Doctor,' Hayden declared, 'it was, as I said, a matter of keeping my word.'

'It is your prerogative as captain to reveal or not to reveal whatever you wish to your officers. We are all, however, going to feel a little foolish, having been taken in by Angel's act.'

'You were the only one who suspected . . . you and one other.'

'A small compensation. You are quite certain, then, that their story is true and they are to be trusted?'

'Miguel . . . ? I cannot say. Angelita, yes, I trust her.'

The doctor looked at him, a little cynically, perhaps. 'Then she had a reasonable explanation for disguising herself as a man?'

'I believe so.'

The doctor considered this. 'Well,' he said, 'I cannot think how we shall keep it secret now.'

Hayden agreed, but only nodded.

'I should see to my patient, Captain . . .' Griffiths cocked his head toward the sick-berth.

'And I to my ship.'

In a moment Hayden was back on deck, where Archer had the hands in a long line, passing a new rope up from the cable tier on to the quarterdeck. The slaver drifted downwind and this meant moving the *Themis* to a position where a messenger line could be carried over by cutter. Archer appeared to have everything well in hand and Hayden stood by, quietly observing, and largely approving the manner in which this was all managed.

While he watched, Miguel appeared a few yards distant and made his way on to the captain's private few yards of deck.

'Don Miguel,' Hayden greeted him solemnly.

'Captain.' For a moment Miguel stood silently. 'I must thank you, Captain Hayden, for saving me from injury, if not worse. I wish, however, that you had saved my sister in my place.'

'Had I only known she was there . . .'

'Or had I known . . . This is your ship, Captain, and I am in your debt. But I appeal to your sense of honour and to the genuine affection I believe you hold for my sister. She was born and has lived in the highest society in my country. Every-one expects her to make a brilliant marriage, to a man from one of the best families. I understand that you are an excep-tional officer with a very promising future, but . . . do you really think it fair to take her from her family and friends, from her country, to dwell where? In England? – a sea cap-tain's wife, left always waiting and wondering, and suffering near-constant anxiety? Will this be a happy life for her? She is very young and has not carefully considered what that future would mean. All she sees is a handsome and charming captain – a man who saved her life and to whom she is utterly grateful. And I must remind you, Captain, that my sister and I belong to the Church of Rome, and you do not. Will you change your religion for her?'

'An officer in His Majesty's Navy must belong to the Church of England,' Hayden said quickly.

'Then you would ask her to convert to your religion – at risk of her mortal soul? Think of all these things. You are more experienced than she, Captain Hayden. Ask yourself if this is really what is best for my sister? That is all I ask of you.' Miguel gave a curt bow, and went quickly below, leaving Hayden standing upon the quarterdeck, feeling as though he had somehow made commitments without ever meaning to do so, and yet the thought of Miguel taking Angelita away from him filled him with a terrible dismay. Above all things, he could not allow that.

Thirteen

Gould and Wickham found Hayden using the gunroom table to prosecute the war on his most hated enemy – paperwork. He had commandeered this space while his own cabin had been turned into a hospital chamber.

'We have books for Angel . . . Doña Angelita,' Wickham began, proffering a small stack of volumes.

'That is very kind of you. Leave them on the table and I will see she receives them . . . and promise not to forget to inform her who it was that sent them.'

The books were stacked carefully, clear of Hayden's papers. Angelita had become the ship's 'pet' since her true sex had been revealed – not that Angel had not been before. Archer would not allow the deck over the captain's cabin to be holystoned in the morning when it might disturb her rest; the hands on the quarterdeck and the helmsmen were constantly hushed. Even the poor lookouts were required to call down to the deck as quietly as possible while still being heard. Little 'treats' were provided by the cook (who apparently had some foods squirrelled away that no one knew about). The gunroom officers sent both food and drink and yet more reading material.

Angelita was the talk of the ship, and at least half the men aboard assured everyone who would listen that they had suspected – or even known – from the day she had come aboard but had said nothing for fear of ridicule. The reason that everyone had sought out Angel's company now seemed perfectly obvious and her charm easily explained. Angel Campillo was a comely young woman!

Neither of the midshipmen showed any sign of leaving, so Hayden put down his quill.

'Is there something more?' he enquired.

Gould glanced at Wickham, silently electing him spokesman. 'We were wondering, sir, if you would like to join our syndicate?'

'And what syndicate would this be, Mr Wickham?'

'A group of us, sir, have decided to put our profits – or, in some cases, a portion of the profits – from the slaver toward buying the freedom of some of the slaves, sir – preferably a family, if one exists.'

'I see. And what will become of this family once you have purchased their freedom?'

'Well, sir –' Gould took up the case – 'we have discussed it at some length, sir, and decided that sending them back to their homes in Africa would likely see them again fall into the hands of slavers. We do not want that, sir, so we thought it best that we write to the abolitionists in England and America and ask if they would find a position for them in either country.'

'What kind of "position", Mr Gould, if I may ask?'

'I am quite certain they could be taught a trade, sir, or they might go into service. I do not really know, sir. We thought the abolitionist societies would be best able to make such a decision.'

'It is a noble idea, Mr Gould, and I am for it in principle, with the slight reservation that I fear what will become of them, cast ashore in a foreign land where they speak no English. But as I do not wish to profit from the sale of slaves myself, and have no better design for what to do with my money, you may count me in . . . for my full share.'

'That is very handsome of you, sir!'

'It is a small good set against a very great evil, but it is all I can do without becoming a criminal, which I am not prepared to do.'

Hayden went back to his paperwork for yet another hour but, as the ship's bell signalled eight bells – ship's noon – he scribbled some instructions for his writer and collected all his stores lists, mess lists and so on into a box and tucked it under his arm.

Very quickly he made his way up to his cabin, where Angelita rested. The cabin had been divided into three by canvas screens – Angelita to larboard, Miguel on the centre line and Hayden to starboard.

As it was now rather impossible for them to pursue their affair, due to Angelita's injuries, a kind of peace had settled between the three – Miguel and Hayden both more concerned for Angelita's well-being than for their disagreement.

Miguel perched on the long bench beneath the open gallery windows, through which the trade came freely in. He looked up as Hayden entered, nodded and went back to his book. He was happy to chaperone from beyond the screen, it seemed.

Angelita lay in her cot, eyes closed, an open book pressed, pages down, upon her breast. Hayden was about to attempt a silent retreat when her eyes opened and she smiled. Her colour was better that day, he thought – perhaps a little too high – and her forehead was thinly glossed with sweat.

'Are you fevered, my dear?' he enquired, and took the chair beside her.

'No. It is just this oppressive heat. The doctor assures me that my injuries heal as they should and have not gone septic, for which I thank God hourly.' She had refused tincture of opium after one encounter with it, assuring the surgeon that she would rather endure the pain than feel *that* way again.

'Griffiths knows what he is about and, of course, faith is the physic of the gods.'

She reached out and put her hand on Hayden's arm in the most familiar way, as though they had a perfect understanding, an understanding that had grown up between them over some months rather than mere days. Although he thought he should find this disquieting, in fact he instead found it rather comforting. He was well aware that some of his officers worried that they were about to witness another scenario, such as had occurred with the Bourdages, but Hayden did not believe Angelita to be scheming. She and her brother were penniless and very far from family or any connexions who might offer them aid, and in that situation a convenient marriage or even a betrothal that could later be broken off would be most useful but, despite this, Hayden felt certain this was not in her mind, even in the smallest degree.

It had always been his belief that bad marriages came from couples rushing into nuptials before they had come to know each other's character – of course, this desire to wait had cost him Henrietta, so clearly circumspection in such matters could also lead to things going horribly wrong.

He felt, therefore, utterly in conflict with himself; his hopes pitted against his natural reticence in such matters. One hour he would think he was acting foolishly and he should make Angelita aware that he thought they were moving too quickly, and then he would think, no, there is always risk in matters of the heart. There is ever the chance that things will not come out well, no matter how cautiously one approaches such matters.

'You look trouble?' Angelita said.

'"Troubled", do you mean?'

'Yes. Troubled, my poor Charles.' She grimaced then, holding her breath tightly. And the spasm passed.

'It is just the slave ship . . . It follows me about like a difficult decision that I wish not to make.'

'The law, the expectations of your crew . . . these are at odds with your own feelings about slavery.'

'Yes. I feel I can do nothing, that, in fact, I am being forced to support an institution which I detest.'

'You must make your peace with this, Charles. It is beyond your strength to make it different. To reprimand yourself constantly . . . this will change nothing.'

'You are right, but it is so much easier said than accomplished – at least, in my case.'

She squeezed his arm. 'It is because you have such a good heart. That is what I thought from the moment we met. You have a good, pure heart.'

But I am such a coward, Hayden thought. I would more readily face cannon fire than risk bruising a girl's feelings.

They were silent a moment. And then Angelita said softly, 'Are you having some regrets about what has occurred between us? Tell me if that is so . . .' Her eyes glistened suddenly, and the smallest tear trembled in the corner of one eye.

'Regrets? No. I have none. I do worry that it has all happened quickly and we have not thought it through. Your brother has pointed out, correctly, that we are of different religions.'

'But I do not care,' she whispered. 'I do not believe that God judges us by the church in which we worship but by our deeds. I will become a member of any church you name if it will allow us to marry.'

The very words 'to marry' struck him like a spark in the pan. At once he felt utter apprehension and . . . *joy*. How could that be?

'I think I have frightened you, my dear Charles, with this word. I shall never say it again or broach this subject. It is now to you. If you do not speak of it again, then neither shall I. And I will understand. I do not wish you to enter into such a covenant with me if you have any doubts.'

'*On deck!*' came the call down through the open skylight. '*Land, Mr Ransome! Land ho!*'

Hayden rose quickly and kissed Angelita on the cheek. 'You are my mermaid, discovered in the deep sea, sent to me by Poseidon. When the gods send you a mermaid . . .' He smiled at her, and shrugged

Squeezing her hand, he hurried out, feeling small and cowardly and, at the same instant, an almost serene happiness.

Fourteen

The island of Barbados was not blessed with a natural harbour or all-weather anchorage of any description. There was only the open roadstead off Bridgetown, which was both crowded and busy with the commerce of this small but prosperous island. This exposed anchorage had but two benefits – that of being in the lee of the island, the trades blowing from the opposite side, and of being so utterly open to the sea that sailing out, if the winds suddenly demanded it, would not be impeded by headlands or off-lying reefs.

Hayden sat upon a chair in the official room of the station's commander-in-chief – the recently installed Admiral Benjamin Caldwell – a man Hayden had met on one or two previous occasions.

The very well turned out and bewigged admiral sat reading Hayden's report of his Atlantic crossing through the glinting lenses of a pince-nez suspended by hand several inches before his face. He was half obscured behind a large desk of French manufacture, no doubt recently liberated from one of several French possessions the British had taken. When the admiral finished reading he lowered both the sheaves of paper and pince-nez, and turned toward Hayden.

'A woman . . . ?' he said, rather astonished.

'Yes, sir.'

'And no one realized?'

'Two men mentioned their suspicions to me, but no one else.'

'You were aware of her ruse, though . . .'

'I was sharing my cabin with the guests, sir.' Hayden waved a hand at the door, beyond which lay an antechamber. 'I have brought the brother here in the event that you might wish to speak with him.'

'Mmm.' The admiral demurred. His left eye appeared to twitch. 'It is a matter for the Spanish, I think. It is the oddest thing that they were adrift in a boat alone, though, is it not?'

'The explanation they gave—'

'I read your report, Captain.'

'Of course, sir.'

'And they lost everything?'

'Everything but the clothes on their backs . . . and their lives.'

Caldwell gave a distracted little shake of the head – almost a tremor. 'There is a merchant here, a Spaniard; not an official envoy – more of a commissioner, I suppose – but he sees to the interests of the Spanish government whenever necessary. I will bring the matter of the castaways to his attention. Perhaps he can aid them on their way to Vera Cruz.' He shifted the pages of Hayden's report, as though shuffling the matter of the Spanish castaways to the bottom of the pile. He then rested his hands upon the table and leaned a little forward. 'You were at the battle of the First, Hayden – in command of *Raisonnable* – were you not?'

'I was, sir.'

'But you were not in Portsmouth when the King graced the fleet with his presence?'

'No, sir. Lord Howe had dispatched me to follow the French fleet, to be certain it returned to Brest.'

'Yes . . . the *fleet* . . . Well put. The almost intact French fleet that returned to the unassailable harbour of Brest.' He rose to his feet, his colour suddenly high. 'And were we recognized for our parts in this battle, Hayden?'

Hayden was uncertain how to respond, so he made a small gesture that could be interpreted in any number of ways.

'No,' Caldwell asserted, 'we were not.' He paced toward the open window then turned back to face Hayden. 'Did you see the state of my ship when the battle was done? My sails and rig cut to ribbons, masts still standing only because the hand of God held them so. Thirty-one dead and many more wounded. How many men did Lord Howe lose? And you, Hayden, I saw you in *Raisonnable* come to Lord Howe's aid when he was beset by two ships, and I saw you lay your ship alongside a Frenchman with treble your weight of broadside, and did you receive a knighthood or silver plate? Or even a commemorative medal?'

Hayden made no answer – he had received such a medal but thought this an inopportune moment to mention it.

'No! Medals were reserved for his lordship's ...' he searched for words '... *fart catchers*!' The admiral resumed pacing. 'All my dead men, dead to no purpose. And what of the grain convoy? Never intercepted! The greater part of the French fleet escaped to be repaired. *Seven prizes* we had to show for our efforts! Seven! We should have had *twenty*! The truth is, and no one will say it aloud, the lord admiral's nerve failed him at the end and the French were allowed to escape. There it is. The harsh truth, but I have said it and will not withdraw it. They are calling it "the *Glorious* First of June". It should be known for all time as "the Infamous and Shameful First of June". But *Howe* –' he pronounced the name with utter disdain – 'has connexions in the Admiralty and is a hero. I have few, and it would seem I was not even present at the *glorious* battle. None of my men was killed or wounded, it seems, my ship untouched.' He stopped and looked over at Hayden, suddenly abashed, even embarrassed by his out-burst. 'Well, we are far from the Admiralty and their bumbling here, thank God,' he said more mildly. 'We can prosecute our own war. And there is prize money to be had – a fortune if one is lucky and not shy . . . *and* if you can avoid the Yellow Jack. Spend as little time in port as you are able, Hayden. That is the secret. The healthful sea air will soon cleanse your ship of the putrid diseases that are carried off from the shore.'

'I shall keep the sea as much as I am able, then, sir.'

Caldwell returned to his chair, and for a moment it appeared as though exhaustion had swept over him. His eyes – his entire being – seemed to lose focus. And then an almost imperceptible shiver ran through him and his con-centration returned. 'You are no doubt aware that we have suffered reverses as of late? Guadeloupe taken and then lost . . . The Saints, the same. The army, God bless them, have not been as stalwart as I might wish. Though it must be said that the French have had numbers everywhere. If we had only intercepted the convoy transporting their army . . . but our intelligence failed us. We were not so well informed then as presently.' He considered a moment. 'I awake each morn-ing wondering if the Spanish remain allies and praying that I might learn of their betrayal before the news reaches Havana. In these waters only the French are our enemies – but if the Dons betray us . . .' He paused a moment, considering. 'We take these islands at great cost, Hayden, and what does our government do? Uses them at the bargaining table when treaties are written. Who in their right mind would trade an island rich in sugar for Quebec and the surrounding French possessions? One might as well trade a few rocks and trees for silver! Yet that is what our government did.' He shook his head, shrugged and looked up at Hayden. 'I might have need of you to transport soldiers, Hayden, but I will employ you as a cruiser as often as I am able. It is a rich hunting ground, and I am informed that you are a very capable captain.'

'I do not know who informed you, sir, but I thank them.'

There was at that moment a bustle in the office beyond. A loud voice, speaking in a heavy French accent, came reverberating through the massive doors. Caldwell glanced up at the doors and then back to Hayden. The voice rumbled on, more quietly, so that Hayden could not make out the words.

'Do you know the other captains here? Jones, Oxford and Crowley?'

'Sir William I know by reputation,' Hayden said, referring to Captain Jones.

'Who does not . . . ?' the admiral replied, and smiled.

'Oxford not at all, but Crowley I have had the pleasure of meeting on more than one occasion.'

'You shall get on with them splendidly, I am quite certain. Not one of them is the least shy. Sir William is the senior officer and prosecutes his war with the usual zeal.'

'I shall look forward to sailing alongside them, sir.'

The admiral looked suddenly more serious, his brows drawing up so that a cleft appeared between them. 'Now, Hayden, am I correct in remembering that you were recently mistaken for a French officer . . . by the French themselves?'

'That is correct, sir. When we were wrecked aboard *Les Droits de l'Homme.*'

'So your French is very good?'

'I speak it as well as I speak the King's English, sir.'

'Excellent. Would you stay a few moments longer? I have the Comte de Letandresse waiting beyond the door, and his English is only a little better than my abysmal French.'

'I am at your service, sir, if I may be of assistance in any way.'

'Thank you.'

The admiral went to the great doors and opened one, revealing Miguel and a large, moustached man seated beyond. A word with his secretary and the moustached gentleman was brought in.

Caldwell gestured to Hayden as he rose from his chair. 'I have asked Captain Hayden to remain with us. His French is excellent.'

'Where did you learn to speak French, Capitaine?' the man enquired.

'My mother was French. I spent much time in Brittany and Bordeaux when I was young.'

'Ah, my own family had estates in Burgundy – also great wine country. And how is it you have come to be in the King's Navy, if I may ask?'

'My father was an English sea captain. I grew up in England.'

'Ah, that is the explanation.'

'I was acquainted with Captain Hayden's father,' Caldwell informed the Frenchman.

'I did not know that, sir,' Hayden said.

'I cannot claim to have known him well, but we were acquainted. He was a respected sea officer.'

Hayden felt a little softening toward the admiral at this admission.

'You may speak freely before Captain Hayden,' Caldwell assured de Latendresse. 'Nothing said here will be repeated.'

They all took chairs. The Frenchman perched upon his skittishly, as though he might jump up and leap out of the window at any instant.

'I have just, as you know,' de Latendresse began, 'returned from a dangerous fortnight on Guadeloupe. The Jacobin forces are there in greater numbers than I previously believed – at least fifteen hundred-strong, I am told, perhaps more. It was very dangerous for me to move about the island. Many of my old friends had been discovered or taken away merely because their sympathies had fallen under suspicion.' He shook his head unhappily. 'It was very brave of them to stay . . . though even more it was foolish.' He looked up, his eyes infinitely sad. 'But some of us must take such risks if this Jacobin madness is to be defeated and a rightful monarch restored.'

'Is there not some vulnerable point,' Caldwell asked in English, 'some point where we might land our troops?'

The Frenchman looked rather confused by this and Hayden quickly translated the question. De Latendresse puffed out his lips and considered a moment before answering.

'These revolutionaries . . . they are not so foolish. They know best where their enemies might land, and these places they have invested with cannon, and, nearby, troops have made camps. You might land a force, but to carry the island . . . it would take many men, I think, for getting ashore would be very costly.'

'And what of our own islands?' the admiral asked. 'Will the Jacobins attempt them, or no?'

The Frenchman shook his head slowly. 'The French have

no plans for further attacks this season,' he assured them. 'They have not got the ships for such adventures.'

'Will they not be reinforced from France?' Caldwell asked him.

'Not this season, Admiral.'

Even this news did not cheer Caldwell; he appeared to sink a little lower in his chair with each bit of the comte's intelligence. The conversation moved away from the strategic position of the British in that area of the Caribbean Sea and on to mundane matters, the admiral and the French noblemen enquiring about the well-being of family and friends. It seemed that the comte lived with his comtesse and several children in a large house provided by the Navy. They were without a country – castaways of a different sort – and no doubt living in fear that the French might invade Barbados.

Finally, the interview came to an end and Hayden departed, leaving Caldwell and the comte discussing who among the French exiles living in Barbados might be trusted and who might be a spy planted among them.

Hayden gathered up Miguel and the two went out into the streets of Bridgetown. The day was warm, the wind fragrant with the spicy perfume of flowers. The city itself was a-hum, tradesmen's carts and barrows passing by, planters in their carriages and gigs, dusky-skinned slaves and freemen going about their business, and then the Creoles with their nutmeg skin and striking features – to Hayden's eye, more handsome than either of the races that spawned them. In among these walked smiling sailors who made knuckles to Hayden as they passed. There was little danger of desertion on such a small island and the hands were commonly given leave to go ashore, to their great delight and the profit of local inns and bawdy houses.

It was but a short walk to the beach off of which the *Themis* lay at anchor, the stricken slave ship nearby. Hayden could see his crew at work about the ship setting aright all the wear of a long sea crossing.

Hayden explained to Miguel that the admiral would send a letter to the Spanish merchant who acted as commissioner for his government when required, and he hoped this gentleman would aid them on their way.

Miguel took this in, watching all the while where he put his feet. This news did nothing to cheer him or put his mind at rest, Hayden thought. Indeed, it almost appeared to increase his anxiety.

'This news does not appear to have cheered you, Miguel?' Hayden ventured.

'My sister told you that two members of the crew on the Spanish frigate attempted to murder us?'

'Yes.'

'I fear that this commissioner you speak of will send word to the wrong people, revealing that we are alive, and we will be in danger again.'

'And who would the wrong people be?'

'I wish I knew. Our stepfather has many allies . . . more than I realized.'

Hayden wondered how much of this fear was real and how much imagined. He did believe that there had been an attempt on Miguel and Angelita's lives by sailors on the frigate. That would be enough to make anyone distrustful, certainly.

'The offer of my aid still stands . . .' Hayden informed the Spaniard.

Miguel stopped abruptly. 'Captain Hayden,' he said curtly, his voice shaking with suppressed anger, 'you do not seem to comprehend what has happened. I cannot demand you walk out with me, as you have saved my life and the life of my sister, but do not think for a moment that I approve of your actions. No, sir, I believe you have betrayed my trust and acted as a . . . a *bounder*. The sooner I might prise my sister from your clutches, the better. I do not want your money, sir. I want nothing to do with you at all!'

With that the Spaniard turned and set off down the beach. How he intended to get out to the ship when he had not a penny to pay a boatman, Hayden did not know.

Hayden's own cutter waited, drawn up on the beach, the crew lounging in the shade of a nearby tree. The coxswain soon had them up and launching the boat.

'Where is the Spanish gentleman, Captain?' the coxswain asked.

'He was detained, Childers. You may return for him in one hour.'

'Aye, sir.'

As he was rowed out to his boat over water so clear he felt he sailed through the air, Hayden realized that the slaver was sending its human cargo ashore in lighters, some of the poor people so weakened and ill that they had to be helped down into the boats. The sight so distressed him that he had to turn away.

What else could I do? he thought. I could not leave them to drift in the Atlantic.

Yet the sight of them being carried ashore to be sold made it very clear that he had participated in this shameful trade. He had towed these poor creatures to Barbados and to a life of slavery. The truth that he could do nothing else without breaking the law was of little comfort.

Hayden clambered up the side of his ship, spoke briefly with the lieutenant who was officer of the watch and then went below to his cabin, where he found Angelita sitting in a chair near the open gallery windows, her head bent over an open book. She looked up as Hayden came in and a joyous smile set her cheeks aglow.

'Charles!'

'My dear, you are up. Has the doctor allowed it?'

'Yes. I am following his very orders.' She rose from her chair, stiffly and slowly for one so young. Her page was marked with a ribbon and the book placed gently on the seat, then, pushing on the back of the chair, she stood more or less erect, a grimace then a smile of determined triumph crossing her face.

Hayden began toward her, but she held up a hand to stay his progress.

'Let me cross to you. I am to walk about the cabin a little today.' Moving more like a puppet than a supple young woman, she made her way slowly across the six or seven paces that divided them and nearly collapsed against him.

Hayden put his arms about her lightly, so as to apply no pressure to her injured side. The feeling of her in his embrace, pressed against him, was intoxicating and he breathed in the scent of her hair as though it were the finest perfume. The idea that she would soon be gone caused him such a feeling of loss that he could hardly bear it.

'The instant your brother believes you can be taken safely ashore he will have it done,' Hayden whispered.

'Then I should be back in my cot . . . immediately.'

Hayden told her that Miguel remained ashore for an hour and then relayed to her their conversation.

'He is trying to act in the place of my father but I would rather he remained a brother,' she said quietly. 'If we do not accept help from you, Charles, then who will it come from, and at what price?'

'The admiral tells me there is a Spanish merchant here who acts on behalf of the Spanish government when required. Admiral Caldwell promised he would write this man a letter. And certainly you could write to your uncle and ask him for aid?'

She pulled away from him so quickly that she was wracked by a spasm of pain. Finally, it faded enough that she was able to look up at him. 'This merchant, he would write to my mother; I have no doubt of it. And then our whereabouts would become known to my stepfather. We cannot have this happen, Charles. I believe we would be in danger again – mortal danger. As to our uncle – he does not know we are fleeing to him. We planned to come to his house unannounced and plead our case before him. If he believed us, and we think he should, then he would not betray us to my mother. We dare not write to him lest he misunderstand and alert my stepfather where we are.'

Hayden nodded as she nestled into him again.

'Will you send me away, then?' she asked in a small voice.

Hayden took a long deep breath and leapt. 'Not if I can prevent it by any means short of a duel. But your brother will never consent to us marrying.' There ... it had been said. There was no other way to keep her near without compromising her honour, and he would not let her go. That much was clear to him.

She pressed closer at these words. 'Did I hear you ask for my hand, Captain Hayden?'

'I must get down on one knee to ask for your hand, officially.'

'Is that how it is done in England?'

'Yes. Is it not so in Spain?'

'In my country it is all arranged between families.'

'I do not believe our families, such as they are, will agree, so we must find another way . . . Are you weeping?'

'With happiness . . .' She did then bury her face in his chest and wept silently a moment.

'You should be back in your cot,' Hayden said when she appeared to recover from this excess of emotion. 'You have been up and about enough for one day.'

Hayden aided her in every way and, not without considerable pain, she was settled again in her cot.

'Do we need my brother's consent, here?' she asked. 'I do not know the laws.'

'Your brother's consent . . . ? I am not certain. You cannot marry without your parents' consent until you are one and twenty. And you are but twenty, you tell me?'

'Yes, until six months.'

'I will investigate. There might be a Presbyterian church here, and the Scots are more lenient in these matters.'

Hayden sat and held her hand awhile, talking of small things: the town, his meeting with the admiral. There was something odd about the meeting that he had not been able to comprehend until he began to speak of it aloud.

'The Royalist who came in – this comte – he told me his family estates were in Burgundy, but his accent, though very faint, was not quite right. It was the way he said "*dangereux*".

I have only heard it pronounced so in the south – in parts of Languedoc.'

'Why would he not tell the truth?'

'Perhaps he is not who he claims, my dear.'

'If that is so, then perhaps he is neither noble nor a Royalist,' she said softly.

'That is my fear, especially as he appeared to have the admiral's complete trust.' Hayden considered a moment. 'Ask your brother his impression of this man; he sat and conversed with him in the antechamber for some time.'

'The accent, you would know better than Miguel, but manners . . . We are both very familiar with the manners and attitudes of the French aristocrats, as so many fled to our country. I will ask him.'

Angelita began then to nod and muttered an apology for this before she fell asleep. Hayden went to his table and began looking over his stores lists. The ship would need to be victualled and watered before she could go to sea, and he wanted to be ready the moment he received orders.

However, even though he tried to fix his mind upon his stores lists it would not be so confined. He had entered into an understanding with a young Spanish woman he knew hardly at all. Had he gone mad? He did not feel the least mad but only a growing excitement and deepening affection. Her family, of course, would never approve. He was not certain his own mother would think it wise. But he felt so . . . at peace with her. He felt as though the sun had miraculously risen on a perpetual twilight and he was only now becoming aware that he had been living in near-darkness. It was the intimacy, the growing trust, the shared secrets that charmed him. Just the knowledge that she was sleeping nearby filled him with delight.

Well, Hayden thought, I am not the first man to be a fool in love.

When he had been at his paperwork an hour, Miguel returned, opening the door quietly.

Hayden indicated, silently, that Angelita slept. Miguel nodded. It was an odd association that had grown up between the two men; they were utterly divided over the connection between Hayden and Angelita but united in their concern for her. This led to a strange and uncomfortable alliance, not so much of convenience as concern. Given that Miguel had informed Hayden several times that he wished to shoot him – and he meant this in its most literal sense – it seemed strange that they could cooperate in any way, but, when it came to Angelita's recuperation, they did.

Hayden forced himself to attend to his paperwork a little longer but then came to a decision and slipped out in search of Midshipman Lord Arthur Wickham, whom he found teaching spherical geometry to the cherub in the midshipman's berth.

'Mr Maxwell,' Hayden addressed the new middy. 'I need to have a word with Mr Wickham, if you please.'

The midshipman retreated quickly, leaving captain and protégé alone.

Wickham awaited whatever was to come with his usual uncanny focus.

'Mr Wickham, I should like to send you ashore on an errand of some delicacy . . .'

'Aye, sir.'

'I wish to know if there is a Scots Presbyterian church or priest of that faith on this island.'

'Certainly, sir,' Wickham replied, without blinking. 'When should I begin?'

'Immediately, Wickham.'

'Aye, sir. I shall go ashore this instant.'

'And Wickham . . . ?'

'Sir?'

'Not a word of this to anyone. Anyone at all.'

'You may count on my utter discretion, sir.'

'That is why I have asked you.'

'Thank you, sir.'

Without another word or a single question, the young man hurried off.

Hayden then went in search of Reverend Smosh, whom he found instructing the ship's boys – a task he had taken on with great relish. Hayden thought that if there were any among them with the least academic inclination they would be prepared to go up to Oxford in but a few short years.

'Mr Smosh, might I interrupt your dissertation for but a moment?'

'Certainly, Captain,' the chaplain replied, then turned to his students. 'Read on – one paragraph each, aloud – then pass the book to the next.'

Hayden and Smosh spent a moment finding a place to speak privately, and there the corpulent little minister stood, awaiting the captain's pleasure.

'Mr Smosh, I might have need of your services – to perform a marriage ceremony.'

'Which service I should do most happily. Who, might I enquire, are the happy couple?'

'Myself, Mr Smosh, and Doña Angelita.'

Smosh hid any surprise he might have felt. 'Ah. Is it possible, Captain, given this young lady's nationality, that Doña Angelita is a member of the Church of Rome?'

'She is prepared to become a member of the Church of England.'

'Which of course is not something that can be accomplished overnight. Is there any reason to hasten such a union?'

'Not the usual reason but, in this case, a disapproving brother.'

'I see. So she would have to become a member of our church in some haste?'

'Mere minutes, I suspect.'

'Ah . . . Well . . . I might enquire if she is a member of the Church of England and, if she were to answer in the affirmative, I would have no way of discovering if that were the truth or no.'

Hayden nodded. Smosh was not given to making decisions by the book – any book.

'Doña Angelita is of age?' he then asked. 'That is to say, one and twenty or older?'

'I only have her word on this matter. Her brother, who opposes the marriage, would likely claim she was not.'

'I believe in this case that I would accept the lady's word if my captain were to assure me it were true.'

'She is one and twenty, I am quite certain. Do we require a licence?'

'I can provide the licence. When would these nuptials take place, if I may ask?'

'Soon, but I must get her brother ashore first.'

Smosh nodded, and looked down at the deck a moment. 'I wonder if this gentleman's propensity to drink himself senseless might provide an opportunity?'

'Reverend Smosh, whatever are you suggesting?'

'It is merely an observation, Captain, that in the brief time he has been aboard this Spanish gentleman has drunk himself into a stupor on more than one occasion. I suspect a man of such dissolute habits might find himself in a similar state again, given half an opportunity. If he were to fall into properly convivial company . . .' His eyes lost focus and he appeared to consider. 'A certain officer of marines comes to mind . . .' The priest shrugged his heavy shoulders.

Hayden thanked the priest and went in search of Hawthorne.

'I thought you would be ashore, Mr Hawthorne,' Hayden said, when he found the marine officer in the gunroom with a disassembled pistol lock laid out on a square of linen.

'I have been ashore and plan to return there on the morrow, if my captain will give me leave.'

'I believe he might be prevailed upon to allow that.' Hayden made a gesture to the cabins that lined both sides of the gunroom.

'We are alone,' Hawthorne informed him.

Hayden took a seat and leaned over the table to speak quietly.

'I wonder if it might be possible to get Don Miguel senseless with drink this evening?'

'I wonder if it is possible to stop him, given that wine is provided; the man has not a sou to his name.' Hawthorne regarded his commander. 'Does the reason for this proposed drunkenness involve a young lady?'

'Indeed. Smosh would marry Doña Angelita and myself, but her brother will not allow it.'

'Ah. It is likely not my place to question my captain, but is this a somewhat precipitous marriage?'

'Entirely . . . and I do not care. Neither does she.'

Hawthorne nodded, his face very serious. He considered only a moment. 'I might have need of involving others. Mr Archer, Barthe, perhaps Wickham ... Ransome, possibly.'

'Involve who you will, but word must not reach Miguel or our opportunity will be lost.'

'I shall exercise all care. We must have a supper in the gunroom to celebrate our successful crossing – an ancient tradition of His Majesty's Navy.'

'Ancient traditions are to be upheld at all costs.'

'I agree. Leave this matter to me, Captain. Give it not another thought.'

Hayden rose to his feet. 'Mr Hawthorne, were it within my power, I would make you captain of marines.'

'If it were within my power, sir, I should make you Admiral of the Blue. But only because I have grown rather tired of red.' He glanced at his coat.

Both men laughed, and it was not at their wit.

In a few moments Hayden was pacing back and forth across the quarterdeck by the transom, his excitement barely contained. Was he really about to marry? That very evening? Given how long he had known the prospective bride, he thought he should feel some trepidation, some doubts. He felt neither. And that seemed almost as remarkable as the fact that he was about to become a husband.

Henrietta came to mind at that moment. Was this headlong rush into matrimony a result of his failed suit for Henrietta Carthew? Had he hesitated because he had doubts about marriage to Henrietta, as his friend Robert Hertle always believed? Or had he shown wisdom then and was acting the fool now? He did not know. He was not about to let Angelita escape. He knew, somehow, that he would regret it the rest of his days if he did so. The rest of his days.

'As I regret the loss of Henrietta,' he whispered, as he stopped to look over the side. 'I shall not make the same mistake a second time.'

Miguel accepted the gunroom's invitation, though Angelita deemed herself not recovered enough to attend. The gunroom's occupants were all present, as were Hayden and the senior midshipmen. It was a convivial atmosphere, though close, with only a little breath of air whispering down the gunroom skylight, which was itself under the cover of the quarterdeck.

'A toast to our crossing, gentlemen,' Mr Hawthorne proposed, holding aloft his claret glass. The marine was sitting next to Miguel and had taken on the duty of keeping the Spaniard's glass fully charged.

The toast was drunk, and it was not the first. The King's health had been toasted earlier, sitting, as was the custom in the gunroom, with its low deck-head. The health of wives and sweethearts had been drunk to, with only a few half-hidden smiles showing. The successful passing through the gale was toasted, as was Miguel and his sister's miraculous survival.

'We have not drunk to the health of our steadfast ally, the King of Spain,' Barthe offered.

That ruler's health was toasted. And then that of his Queen.

However, despite these quantities of claret, Miguel seemed terribly and inconveniently sober, as though he had sworn that very day to curb his drunkenness. Hayden was of the opinion that several of his officers were further into their cups than the Spaniard.

Griffiths glanced his way and made a small shrug with his narrow shoulders. He rose to stoop beneath the beams. 'I beg your indulgence, gentlemen, but I must take advantage of this momentary pause between courses to look in briefly on a patient.' The doctor stooped out, leaving the chair to one side of Miguel empty.

The atmosphere in the gunroom was certainly jolly, as Hayden had hoped, but it seemed to him to have a forced quality to it, an edge of anxiety, perhaps. He could not say whom Hawthorne had taken into his confidence, other than Barthe and Archer. Several others had concocted 'toasts' that would not normally have been heard in the gunroom, so perhaps his secret was concealed from no one present.

The evening wore on, wine flowing with a liberality which, even safely at anchor, one seldom saw in the *Themis*'s gunroom – or perhaps any other gunroom. Miguel, however, was hardly more than mildly inebriated, and nowhere near drunk enough to pass into unconsciousness, as he had more than once since being discovered drifting in the Atlantic.

Hayden's emotions swung wildly from trepidation to almost unendurable excitement and then to worry that his marriage could not take place because Miguel remained stubbornly sober.

The doctor returned, the next course served, glasses filled, conversation engaged in. A song was proposed and sung as the servants cleared away. Hayden noted the doctor filling

Miguel's glass, after which Griffiths nodded to Hayden, for what reason the captain could not say.

Yet another course, after which Hayden thought Miguel looked distinctly groggy, his eyes fluttering closed and then snapping open. He slumped lower in his chair and, finally, if not for Hawthorne and the surgeon, would literally have slipped under the table.

The doctor took the Spaniard's pulse, nodded, apparently satisfied. He then pointed long fingers at Miguel's glass. 'This must be disposed of, and not drunk by anyone,' he instructed.

'I will see to that, Dr Griffiths,' Wickham offered, taking up the glass with some care.

'Whatever did you put in it?' Hawthorne asked the surgeon.

'A mild soporific. He will wake in the morning refreshed and without any ill feelings.'

'Lest they be toward his new brother-in-law.' The marine turned to Hayden. 'How shall we proceed?'

Hayden rose to his feet. 'First I must up to my cabin to wake Angelita, if she sleeps, and then ask for her hand.'

Hawthorne almost reeled back, and everyone else froze where they stood. 'You have not asked for the maiden's hand?'

'Her brother was always hanging about.'

Hawthorne glanced around at the others. 'Well, what if her answer is no?'

Hayden shrugged. 'Then I suppose the wedding must be called off.'

'My God, sir, I do hope you are confident of her answer.' Barthe was as incredulous as Hawthorne.

'Is one ever perfectly confident, Mr Barthe?'

Barthe shrugged, lumbered into his cabin and quickly

reappeared, bearing a package wrapped in plain paper, which he proffered to Hayden. 'In the event that she accepts you . . .' he said.

'What is it?' Hayden asked, as he reached out to take the offering.

'A dress. It was meant for one of my daughters, but I think she will give it up in this cause. If it is not a proper fit, tell me; I have daughters of all heights and proportions.'

As Hayden began for the door, Hawthorne barred his way. The marine held out his hand, and upon his palm lay a plain gold ring.

'Where did you find this?'

'Some gold coins were donated – the blacksmith forged it on short notice.'

Hayden could hardly believe what he was seeing.

'You should keep it in your pocket, Mr Hawthorne. And thank you. Thank you all.'

Up the ladder to the gundeck, past the marine and into his cabin. He deposited the package on a chair and found Angelita in her cot, reading by lamplight.

'Captain Hayden!' she said, as always delighted to see him appear. 'But where is my brother?'

'Asleep, and not likely to wake before morning. I have come to ask you a question, but I fear you must rise from your sick-bed to hear it.'

She laid her book aside with such haste it almost tumbled to the cabin sole. 'If you will steady my cot and give me your hand . . .' Gingerly, but without hesitation, she swung her legs over the side and lowered herself to her feet. For a night-gown she wore one of Hayden's shirts, with the sleeves severely reefed. It fell to her knees.

'There, I am on my feet. What is this question?' she asked, and looked suddenly as frightened as a child.

Hayden took her hand and went down on one knee. Her other hand went to her mouth.

Hayden took a calming breath. 'Doña Angelita, will you do me the honour of becoming my wife?'

The tiniest little gasp, and then tears. A whispered, breathless, '*Yes.* Above all things, *yes* . . .'

Hayden rose to his feet, and she favoured him with the sweetest kiss he had ever known.

'But when?' she asked, drawing far enough away to bring his face into focus. 'My brother will never allow it.'

'This very night. Mr Smosh has agreed to perform the ceremony. He will ask you two questions. Are you one and twenty or older, and are you a member of the Church of England. You must answer yes to both. Can you do that?'

'To be your wife I would tell a thousand lies. But where? Is there a church nearby?'

Hayden waved a hand around his cabin. 'This will be our church. I know it is very modest, and we do not have a special licence, but we do have a licence and, within the hour, we can be man and wife.'

She looked around. 'It will be a perfect church. It lacks only my family and all who are dear to me.' She turned back to Hayden. 'But you will be here, and you will be my family now.'

They embraced, though with care to her injured side.

'I have something for you . . . a gift from the sailing master, Mr Barthe.'

Hayden took up the package and put it into her hands. The ribbon was quickly untied and, inside was a lovely, pale cream dress; simple yet beautiful, Hayden thought.

She held it up in the lamplight.

'Perhaps not the wedding gown of which you have always dreamed?' Hayden said softly.

'As long as you are the groom, I would wear a sack. It matters not at all. Tell Mr Barthe it is a most beautiful gown.' She grinned at Hayden. 'The most beautiful I presently possess.'

She retreated to dress and put up her hair. Hayden, already in clean linen and dress coat, took up a brush and swept away any dinner crumbs. He examined himself nervously in a mirror and concluded he would do.

Angelita was not half of an hour but reappeared with her hair held up in the ribbon that had closed Mr Barthe's package. A knock sounded at his door and Hayden opened it a crack to find Hawthorne and, hanging back behind him in the dim light, his steward, several midshipmen and hands, all bearing burdens hardly discernible in the dim light.

'What is the verdict, sir?'

Hayden suspected his marine guard had overheard and the news was already known.

'The best possible, Mr Hawthorne; guilty of aspiring to matrimony and sentenced to a lifetime of it.'

The marine broke into a grin. 'May I be the first to say "Congratulations", sir.'

'Thank you, Mr Hawthorne.' Hayden waved at the men lingering behind. 'What is all this, then?'

'Whenever it is convenient, Captain,' Hawthorne said, 'we have come to ready your cabin for a wedding.'

Angelita had crept up, and peered around Hayden's shoulder.

'Are you ready for our guests?' Hayden asked of her.

She looked rather confused. 'If it is the English way . . .'

Hayden beckoned the men in. In a blink, the screens were taken down, cots and furniture removed, lanterns hung and lit, flowers arranged, a simple altar created. Mr Smosh gave directions here, and Mr Hawthorne there. A constant stream of men went in and out and beyond, on the gundeck, Hayden could see the hands gathering and talking quietly among themselves.

'It would appear word has got out, sir.' Archer nodded to the crew collecting along the deck. 'The gunroom servants must have let it slip, sir.'

Wickham came in the door at that moment. 'Sir, the hands have learned you are to marry this very hour and they have charged me to ask if they will be allowed to attend the ceremony?'

'Where did they ever get such an idea?' Ransome answered, before Hayden could speak. 'You may inform them that they may not!'

There was a moment of awkward silence, and then Angelita said softly, 'But they have all been so kind to me . . . Is it not acceptable . . . ?'

'It simply is not done,' Hayden replied, 'but then we are far from the shores of both England and Spain . . .' He hesitated a moment and then turned to his first lieutenant. 'Let us take down this bulkhead, Mr Archer.'

Mr Hale and his mates had the bulkhead down in a trice, and the cabin now opened on to the gundeck, where the men all stood, grinning and speaking quietly among themselves. Mr Smosh had a brief, whispered conversation with Angelita, which concluded happily, Hayden assumed, by the looks upon their faces. A few more moments of buzzing about, and then Mr Smosh called out for order and the hands quickly removed their hats and stood silent as penitents at the final judgement.

Smosh stood before the opened gallery windows with the starlit waters beyond. He glanced once at Hayden, who gave a small nod, and the parson began.

'Dearly beloved, we are gathered together here in the sight of God, and in the face of this congregation, to join together this man and this woman in holy Matrimony; which is an honourable estate, instituted of God . . .'

The words, which Hayden knew almost by heart from his attendance at weddings, flowed over him like an incoming tide and bore him onward. He glanced at his bride, standing not two feet distant, almost a-tremble with suppressed excitement, and he felt a peace descend upon his heart and his mind, as though all doubt and conflict and worry had been washed away by the words of the chaplain, and he stood there, made anew.

'Therefore if any man can shew any just cause, why they may not lawfully be joined together, let him now speak, or else hereafter forever hold his peace.'

Smosh waited a respectful moment and, when no one spoke up, continued.

'I require and charge you both, as ye will answer at the dreadful day of judgement when the secrets of all hearts shall be disclosed, that if either of you know any impediment, why ye may not lawfully be joined together in Matrimony, ye now confess it.'

There was, Hayden thought, the matter of her age, and perhaps her religion . . . But neither of them 'confessed', and Smosh went quickly on.

'Captain Charles Saunders Hayden, wilt thou have this

woman to thy wedded wife, to live together after God's ordinance in the holy estate of Matrimony? Wilt thou love her, comfort her, honour and keep her in sickness and in health; and, forsaking all other, keep thee only unto her, so long as thou both shall live?

'I will,' Hayden answered clearly, his words echoing strangely along the open gundeck.

Smosh turned to Hayden's betrothed. 'Doña Angelita Campillo, wilt thou have this man to thy wedded husband, to live together after God's ordinance in the holy estate of Matrimony? Wilt thou obey him and serve him, love, honour and keep him in sickness and in health; and, forsaking all other, keep thee only unto him, so long as thou both shall live?'

'I will,' Angelita answered, her voice somehow filled with wonder.

Smosh then spoke to the congregation. 'Who giveth this woman to be married to this man?'

As agreed, Mr Barthe, who was the father of daughters and the eldest present, performed this office.

Hayden and Angelita then turned to face one another, and he took her right hand in his.

Smosh then said to Hayden, 'I, Charles Saunders Hayden . . .'

'I, Charles Saunders Hayden,' the captain of the ship repeated.

Quickly, it was Angelita's turn, though, Hayden thought, she had hardly the breath to manage.

The ring was passed from Mr Hawthorne to Hayden, who placed it on the open book in Smosh's hand. It was then returned to Hayden, who slipped it on to the wedding finger of his bride's left hand.

'With this ring,' Smosh said softly, and Hayden repeated.

'With this ring I thee wed, with my body I thee worship, and with my worldly goods I thee endow. In the name of the father and the son and the holy ghost. Amen.'

Hayden and his bride knelt.

'Let us pray.' Smosh spoke to all the men congregated there. 'O eternal God, creator and preserver of all mankind . . .' When he had finished, he joined Hayden and Angelita's right hands together. 'Those whom God hath joined together, let no man put asunder.'

He then, in the common way, pronounced them man and wife and blessed them.

Hayden and Angelita rose to their feet and the entire gathered crew and guests sang Psalm 128, their voices no doubt echoing around the entire anchorage. Given that it was not the Lord's day, this would surely give them something of a reputation as a pious ship.

'Three cheers for Captain and Mrs Hayden!'

And the men cheered as though they had just defeated all the French that ever were.

Hayden and his bride held hands, suddenly wondering what they were to do now.

Another song was sung, this one more sailorly, but no less heartfelt. The hands went down to the lower deck then, to continue their celebration, and Hayden's cabin was quickly reassembled and the table laid for a light supper, as a traditional wedding breakfast would not answer at that hour.

It seemed passing strange to Hayden to sit at a table with his bride – *his bride*!

And yet he felt a warmth of happiness and amity come

over him so that he thought he must be aglow with it, as surely his bride appeared to be.

The supper lasted barely an hour and his guests went happily and quietly out. Hayden's servant and steward assisted the carpenter, who made a low platform of two grates. Upon this they made as sumptuous a bed as they could manage, and then they too disappeared.

Hayden waved a hand at the arrangement. 'It is a modest marriage bed, I fear.'

Angelita came near, and he put his arms around her.

'It is the bride who is supposed to fear the marriage bed . . .' she whispered, 'or at least feel some small anxiety.'

'And are you anxious, my dear?'

For a moment she did not speak but then said very softly, 'We have taken a great leap of faith together; we shall see where we land. Softly, I hope.'

'As softly as we can.'

Fifteen

Hayden awoke to light filtering into his cabin, his limbs entangled with the limbs of another.

'You wake, my darling.' Angelita spoke softly in his ear. 'I have been lying here admiring my wedding band. It is so simple and perfect. No one could have choosed better.'

She held her hand up in the light so that the newly forged ring glittered.

How delicate her hand is, Hayden thought.

She turned and kissed him on the lips, and then upon the eyelids and his cheeks. 'I am so happy,' she whispered.

'I cannot think you are as happy as your husband.'

'Oh, I am quite more happy, I am certain.' She thought a moment. 'What shall we do with this first day of our marriage?'

'We shall find a house ashore that we might let, for you cannot come to sea with me once I am given orders.'

'Why can I not?'

'It is against the regulations, and it is too dangerous, as well.'

'So we will find a house then. What kind of house?'

'A modest house . . . to go with our modest bed.'

'If I am as happy in our house as I am in our bed, I shall be in ecstasy.'

There came, at that moment, voices from beyond the door. And then one of the voices grew louder.

'Why am I not allowed in?' Miguel said testily. 'I share this cabin.'

'The captain and his bride have not yet risen, sir.'

'His bride!'

Angelita looked at Hayden in alarm.

'Before we find a house,' Hayden said, 'there is another matter . . .'

They rose and dressed quickly, Angelita in her wedding dress, and then Hayden allowed the door to be opened and Miguel pushed his way in, looking much the worse for the previous evening's wear.

'What is this about a bride?' he demanded.

'Before witnesses, and before God,' Hayden informed him, 'your sister and I were married this evening past, by licence and by the rites of the church of this land. It is legal and binding.'

Miguel put a hand up to a beam to steady himself. 'You were married outside of our church?' he demanded of his sister.

'Outside of your church, Miguel. I am a member of the Church of England, now.'

'I do not recognize it. You are not of age. Our church will not recognize this marriage.'

'The Church of Rome does not hold sway here,' Hayden informed him firmly.

'It is done, Miguel,' Angelita said softly, 'and it cannot be undone while we both live.' She took hold of Hayden's arm. 'This is my husband and, if we are so blessed, soon to be the father of my children. Do you wish my children to be born outside of wedlock? That would be a far greater scandal than my marriage to an English officer and gentleman.'

Miguel swayed a moment as though he might fall, then turned his bleary eyes on Hayden. 'I should have shot you when first we landed.'

'I will not allow it,' Angelita said, with utter conviction. 'My husband and my brother . . . ? I would stand between you. I have joined my future to that of Captain Hayden, Miguel. You had best make your peace with it.'

Miguel stood a moment more and then spat out, 'Look what you have become! The wife of a common sea captain!' He turned and stomped noisily out.

Neither Hayden nor his bride moved for a moment, then he turned to her.

A silent tear streaked her cheek. 'He is very stubborn, my brother. Very proud. Will it matter that I was not one and twenty?'

'If he could take us before a judge . . . perhaps, but not likely. And, besides, even if the marriage could be annulled, would you find a husband in Spain once your marriage to me was known?'

'Not of the sort my family intended . . . No, I think they will have to accept us. We are man and wife. And now, we must break our fast and go to find this modest house of which you spoke. Will it have a garden?'

'If you desire a garden I shall move heaven and earth to find you a house so endowed.'

A house, it turned out, was not a difficult thing to come by on the island of Barbados. There were Englishmen in some numbers who spent time overseeing their interests on the island and then returned home to England for extended periods, leaving their homes vacant. With some aid from

Admiral Caldwell, Hayden and his bride found and let a pleasant house set on a street of equally pleasant dwellings on a small rise, which encouraged the breeze to cool the high-ceilinged rooms.

Hayden's letter of credit, secured before departing England, was turned into currency, and the few things needed for the fully furnished house were purchased. A dressmaker was located, measurements taken and a wedding trousseau ordered. Hayden was pleased to see that the new Mrs Hayden showed an admirable restraint in her expenditures, given that she came from circumstances where *restraint* was likely a concept to cause amusement.

A few days of this pleasant flurry passed while the *Themis* was watered and prepared for whatever part the admiral would find for her. Hayden divided his time between his ship and his new home and bride, spending nights ashore while the weather appeared settled, trusting Lieutenant Archer and his officers to keep the ship safe and the crew in order.

One morning, however, as Hayden went down to join his ship, he found three more frigates at anchor, newly returned from their cruise, no doubt. His boat awaited him in the appointed place and at the appointed time. It took only a few moments for the cutter to deliver him to his ship and, when he climbed up to the deck, where the bosun awaited to pipe him aboard, he found four apprehensive Africans standing upon the quarterdeck, being gaped at by one and all.

Hearing the bosun's pipe, Wickham broke away from the group and came immediately to his captain.

Hayden nodded toward the visitors. 'Our rescued slaves, I presume?'

'Exactly, sir. Mr Barthe, myself and Mr Ransome purchased them at auction yesterday. Mr Barthe and Mr Ransome remained for the entire auction, sir, and recorded all the sales so that we might avoid being cheated, which we believe the master of the slaver might have intended, had we not been vigilant.' Wickham turned to look at the family, who were gathered in a tight knot, man and woman clutching each other and their two children.

'And what becomes of them now?'

'Well, sir, we are now engaged in securing their freedom and trying to make them understand that they are free. We do not have a language in common, sir, so it is very difficult.'

'And once the idea of freedom has been grasped? What will you do with them then?'

'We do not yet know, sir.'

'You do realize that we cannot keep them aboard ship?'

'Indeed, sir. We are attempting to find lodgings or a position for them ashore. We fear they will be taken advantage of or worse, Captain, given their inexperience in our world.'

The African family were likely enough looking, Hayden thought. Certainly Barthe had chosen some family in good health, given that they would probably have to endure another sea voyage. They stared back at the men gawking at them with almost as much curiosity as wariness. What were they thinking? Hayden wondered. Did they understand they had escaped slavery? Had they realized it was to that horrifying life that they had been destined? If they could make themselves understood, what would their desire be? To return to the home from which they had been torn?

Archer came forward then, touched his hat and presented

Hayden with a sealed letter. 'From Captain Jones, sir. And there is a Spanish gentleman in your cabin, with Miguel.'

'That will be the merchant to whom Caldwell wrote. I shall go down immediately.'

Hayden took the precaution of knocking on the door to his own cabin.

Within, he found Miguel and another sitting at his table. Both came to their feet and the visitor made a leg.

'I am Don Jenero de Otero, Captain Hayden. Admiral Caldwell asked me to visit your castaways and to aid them if it was within my power.' He shook his head. 'I have just been hearing the story. A terrible tragedy, but out of it a marriage. May I congratulate you, sir.'

'Thank you. Are you able to offer Don Miguel aid?'

'Oh, yes. We have just been discussing it. He will be my guest for a few days until we find him lodgings or a ship that will carry him on to either Vera Cruz, or perhaps Port Royal, from where he would certainly find a ship to carry him the rest of the way.'

'That is good news. Mrs Hayden will be most happy to hear it, though she will miss her dear brother, I am certain. I will leave you gentlemen to your discussion, if you will excuse me.'

Hayden went quickly out of the door and, at the foot of the ladder to the upper deck, he stopped to read his letter – an invitation to dine with the other frigate captains that day at noon. He tucked the letter away in a pocket and, just as he had a foot on the bottom rung, the Spanish merchant emerged from his cabin.

'Ah, Don Jenero, are you bound for shore? Have you a boat?'

'I am and I do not, but a boat can easily be found here. I know all the masters and all the boatmen, too, for that matter.'

'I would gladly have my own coxswain take you ashore.'

'Thank you, Captain, you are very kind.' He stopped a pace distant. 'May I have a moment of your time, Captain Hayden?'

'Of course.'

'You do realize that Don Miguel opposes your marriage to his sister?'

'I do.'

'He assures me she is too young to marry without her parents' consent – even by British law.'

'Mrs Hayden assures me she is of age. I have no reason not to believe her.'

'The Church of Rome would not recognize this marriage, Captain.'

'The Church of Rome holds no sway here, Don Jenero. We were married within the Church of England, in observation of the laws of Britain, while at anchor in an English port. Has her brother considered what would become of Mrs Hayden were he somehow to manage to have our marriage annulled? He should give that serious consideration.'

'I would agree, Captain, and let me say that I personally am unconcerned by this matter. Admiral Caldwell has assured me that you are an honourable gentleman – that your family is known to him.' He made a sweeping gesture in the direction of the island. 'I dwell, here, Captain, and I obey the laws of your country. I will attempt to help Don Miguel to see this more clearly.' He smiled at Hayden, and shrugged. 'It is, as the French say, a fait accompli. There is nothing to be done for it now but to wish you a happy marriage and the blessing of children.'

'Mrs Hayden and I thank you, Don Jenero.'

A boat was manned and Miguel and de Otero were carried ashore. Hayden finally had his cabin back. He consulted with his officers to discover the progress of readying for sea and was more than satisfied with everything that had been done. Archer, to his surprise, was becoming a competent and efficient first lieutenant. When they had first met, Archer had seemed less than interested in his chosen career but, over the past year, that had changed. Hayden now held hopes that the lieutenant would have his own command one day – and Hayden would be sorry to lose him.

His dinner with the recently returned frigate captains was held aboard Sir William Jones's 38-gun frigate, *Inconstant*. In attendance were Captain Peter Oxford of the 36-gun *Thetis* and Captain Albert Crawley, who commanded the 36-gun *Phaeton*. It would be difficult, Hayden thought, to find two more self-satisfied officers than Crawley and Oxford. The source of this apparent contentment was not something they felt a need to keep secret – at least not from Hayden. They informed him that they were making such sums from prize money that, upon their return to England, they could purchase estates.

All three officers were brown from the southern sun, and the handsome Jones, with his sea-blue eyes and yellow hair, appeared even darker for the contrast. Oxford wore a well-groomed wig, and Hayden knew from scuttlebutt that the man had lost much of his hair, though only three and thirty years. Crawley, Hayden had met on several occasions, and had invariably found him amiable, even jolly, and the sun had brought out the lines around his eyes that creased whenever he laughed or smiled. All three men were well made, though none tall. Jones had the kind of bearing people generally associated with the military, and his uniform would have been the envy of a lord.

Sir William, whose knighthood had been granted him by the Swedish King, looked decidedly uncomfortable with all this talk of prize money, though he did agree that harming the enemy's commerce was a valuable contribution to Britain's war.

He changed the subject as soon as it was polite to do so and turned instead to the story of Hayden's crossing and the Spanish castaways – a story that had swept around the island like a cool wind.

'And there she was,' Crawley said, a bemused half-smile upon his face, 'in a ship's boat – your bride to be – dressed as a man?'

Hayden conceded that this was true.

'It seems a very seamanlike way to find a bride, does it not?' Oxford ventured.

'I could not agree more,' replied Crawley. 'Why, I believe every sea officer worthy of his post should find his bride in the middle of an ocean.'

'This acquiring a wife ashore . . .' Sir William added, making a sour face, 'one is all but certain to get a *landswoman*. A very poor mate for a sea officer.'

They drank a toast to Hayden's sea-bride.

The conversation turned to the trials of the British forces in these waters, and the sea officers had little good to say about the efforts of the army – though Hayden knew this might be nothing more than the usual prejudice.

'Are you familiar with the Comte de Latendresse?' Hayden

asked, to which all answered in the affirmative but no one offered more.

'The admiral asked me to sit with him while he spoke with the comte, on account of my felicity with the French language. The comte had just returned from Guadeloupe with news. Perhaps I am wrong, but this nobleman told me his family hailed from Burgundy, yet his accent would seem to indicate he came from the south. My wife's brother was of the opinion that the comte's manners were . . . how shall I say? – somewhat coarse for a Frenchman of that rank.'

Crawley glanced at Oxford. 'Are you suggesting that he is not what he claims, Hayden?'

'I am merely curious as to your opinions?'

Crawley nodded to their host. 'Sir William knows him best.'

Jones, as Hayden and everyone else in the Navy knew, cultivated people of high rank. As well as the King of Sweden, he boasted a friendship with the Prince of Wales and various peers of the highest order. He had dined with the King, or so he claimed, and, at different times, his name had been linked with the daughters of lords, though marriages never ensued.

Sir William appeared decidedly troubled by this question. 'I have always found the comte a most amiable companion. His manners are invariably perfect, in the French way, and I have known many a French nobleman. No, nothing seems the least out of place to me.' He glanced up at Hayden. 'Could you be mistaken about his accent? Perhaps it would be difficult for an Englishman to distinguish?'

'I spent much of my childhood in France, Sir William, and speak the language as a native. Perhaps there is a perfectly reasonable explanation, but his accent is not Burgundian, I am quite certain.'

This seemed to disconcert Jones even more, and he shifted uncomfortably in his chair.

Crawley picked up his wine glass, then hesitated. 'You would appear to be suggesting, Hayden, that it is possible the comte is not spying for the admiral.'

Hayden considered a moment. 'I would not go quite so far, but I do think he bears watching. I have been debating whether I should broach this subject with the admiral . . . You know Caldwell better than I; should I speak to him of this?' he asked the others.

'Unquestionably,' Crawley replied, without hesitation. 'Admiral Caldwell has come to rely very heavily on the comte for intelligence. If this Frenchman is giving the admiral false information, and spying for the French instead, it would put us at a great disadvantage.' He took a sip of his wine then turned the glass slowly, staring into the contents. 'I wonder if there is not some way we could discover if the man is on our side or not?'

'We might put one of our own people in his household,' Oxford offered. 'Though it would have to be someone French.'

'In England,' Hayden offered, 'we could find a Royalist nobleman, who would tell us if he is an imposter. But here . . .'

The others shook their heads.

Hayden considered a moment. 'I have a Frenchman aboard my ship – a Royalist and an excellent cook – I could ask him if he might agree to be placed in the comte's household.'

'That might answer – if he would do it – though he must realize there would be some risk.'

Jones remained unsettled, but finally said, 'I for one do not doubt the man, but if all of you mistrust him, then, by all means, let us endeavour to discover where his loyalties lie. We cannot have a spy giving us false information. Any number of lives might be lost as a result.'

The dinner ended on this note, Jones appearing rather unhappy, and Hayden suspected it was with Charles Saunders Hayden.

As they climbed down the ship's side into their waiting boats, Jones turned to the newest member of his squadron.

'Hayden?' he said quietly. 'Stay back with me a moment, if you please.'

Hayden nodded, and Jones led him aft to the transom, where they might have a private conversation. Expecting to be informed that he did not understand the local situation, having only just arrived, Hayden was prepared humbly to agree, while still asserting that he thought the comte might not be quite all he claimed.

'I know you by reputation, Hayden,' Jones began. 'I have heard what you did in Corsica, and along the French coast. Crawley and Oxford are excellent sea officers, and I do not mean to suggest for a moment that they are shy. They are not. But they are far more interested in lining their pockets than prosecuting Britain's war in these waters. In this, I regret to say, they have the admiral's support. He feels he has been wronged – and, I suspect, in truth, he was – and he knows he will not keep the position he holds now for much longer. For this reason, he has decided to enrich himself to the greatest degree possible while he may. His admiral's share of all prize money is not insignificant. To this end, he has sent us on repeated cruises, ignoring the French possessions and the gains the enemy have made. I believe you understand what is at risk in this war?'

Hayden assured him that he did.

'Then we will carry the war to the enemy. Prizes we may take, but to cripple the enemy, that is our purpose. To control the seas between the islands. Make it dangerous for the French to shift troops from one island to another, which they do now with impunity whenever our armies attack an island we believe is vulnerable.'

'But will we not have orders from the admiral? If he sets us to cruise in one part of the sea . . . ?'

Jones met Hayden's eye and lowered his voice. 'The Admiralty has always expected – even encouraged – me to take more initiative than most post captains would be granted. It is well known that the Prince of Wales and the King admire both my resolution and my independence. Caldwell comprehends this. Once we are at sea, and beyond communication with the admiral, it is incumbent upon me to weigh any newly acquired intelligence and make the best decisions I can, bearing always in mind the interests of King and country. Having dined with His Majesty, I feel I can claim to know his mind as well as any.'

It was as everyone who knew Jones claimed – his character was a combination of patriotism, vanity, boastfulness, gallantry and extravagant imprudence. His gallantry and bravery, combined with a simple, unquestioning patriotism, earned him much admiration and loyalty, especially among the common seaman, but his imprudence and foolish vanity made him an object of much satirical wit among officers. It was said of him that most men who combined so many contradictory qualities would be torn asunder, but Jones was saved by an astonishing naivety – he was utterly unaware that the different parts of his character were at odds. Like a royalist and a revolutionary living under the same roof, oblivious to the fact that their ideals placed them in opposition to each other, and therefore believing the other a most capital fellow.

'I am here, Sir William, to do my duty to King and country, but I will tell you I do not squander the lives of my men. I weigh the benefits of any action against the lives it will cost. I have always attempted to gain the greatest advantage for the least cost, in that regard.'

'I am pleased to see we are of one mind in this,' Sir William assured him.

Hayden found it difficult to hide his reaction. Jones was notorious for undertaking extremely risky actions of very dubious value. The only thing one could say in his defence was that he did not send his men into these dangers while he watched from a distance. Sir William invariably led the charge and risked all the dangers to which he subjected his crews. For this, the men forgave him much they would not otherwise.

'I dine with the admiral this very night, Hayden, and will surely receive my orders then. How soon can you put to sea?'

'Tomorrow, if need be.'

'Excellent. We shall have our ships readied with all speed. Four or five days, we shall require, for the crews shall have leave to go ashore, which will slow preparations to some small degree.' Jones paused. 'You will note that we have painted our ships black – any little thing that will draw our prey nearer . . .'

'I shall have our stripe painted black immediately, Sir William.'

Hayden went down into his boat and Childers steered back to their own frigate. Time would certainly show him what he had fallen into, but he was of the impression that he had fallen in with a brave, perhaps even gallant fool and two prize hunters. The war against France was not the primary concern of any of these men, he suspected. Jones was chasing reputation, while Crawley and Oxford sought wealth. Hayden did not want to tip the balance in either of these directions. It was his desire to prosecute the war against their enemies in a prudent but forceful manner.

As his boat passed astern of *Phaeton*, Crawley appeared at the rail and waved Hayden near. 'Might you have a moment, Hayden?' he enquired as the boat drew near.

'Certainly,' Hayden replied.

'Please, Captain, come aboard.'

Childers brought their boat smartly alongside – a difficult thing to manage when a boat had lost all way and was so near. Hayden went up the side and was invited down into Crawley's cabin, which was fitted out almost as splendidly as a house ashore.

'Do you take tea?' Crawley asked.

'With delight,' Hayden lied. He much preferred coffee but tea seemed to be growing in popularity with some segments of society, though Hayden did not imagine it would ever become universal – the cost was simply prohibitive. From what Crawley had been saying over dinner, he could, no doubt, afford it.

'What did you think of the Swedish King's good knight?'

'He comes much as described, I should say,' Hayden offered, tactfully.

'I do not mean to traduce the character of Sir William, for God knows I esteem, even love him, but he will lead you into the most harrowing dangers for little or no gain. Oxford and I have often been able to balance Sir William's desire to fly into peril at every opportunity, but if you will support him, Hayden – well, I know you are a man of good judgement, which poor Sir William lacks, if I may say it. You will quickly see what he is about, I have no doubt.'

'Does Admiral Caldwell not give him specific orders?'

'Mmm. You must realize that Sir William has a . . . how shall I put this? An inflated idea of his intimacy with the King and of the Admiralty's opinion of him as well. As a result, he feels orders are for lesser men and are not binding upon him.'

'Lacking judgement in all things,' Hayden said.

'I fear so. To be perfectly candid, if left to his own devices, he would kill us all in a few short weeks. Jones, of course, would remain unharmed, as his person is apparently proof against cannonballs. As you are new to the Barbados station, I thought it incumbent upon me to warn you – the man would take on a first rate with a pistol. He has neither judgement nor fear, nor even the common animal trait of self-preservation. Oxford and I attempt to dissuade him of his most absurd plans, and support those that might yield some benefit without the massacre of our crews. You are a very steady officer, Hayden, and I do hope we can count on your support in this endeavour. Jones requires very little encouragement to pursue the most ruinous exploits.'

'I shall attempt to use whatever small influence I might have to pursue those ends which might see this war made shorter, if notably less glorious.'

'And in this Oxford and I are your brothers. Jones, God love him, is rather like a great gun. He requires others to aim him at the enemy, otherwise he would be spending shot to subdue the ocean.'

Tea, which Hayden thought of as particularly thin, bitter coffee, arrived and the conversation turned to other matters. Crawley was a good seaman and knew the local waters intimately. He promised to send his sailing master over to speak with Mr Barthe to be certain his charts displayed all the most recently discovered reefs and rocks – a very great kindness, in Hayden's opinion.

As Hayden rose to leave, Crawley addressed him again. 'Please, Hayden, do not misunderstand me. I esteem Sir William greatly. I have never met a braver man, and I have known many a courageous soul. With but a little aid from those around him, he is a great weapon against our enemies. Let us wield him wisely.'

As Hayden returned to his boat and the short row to his ship, he felt more than a little bemused. Jones had warned him about Oxford and Crawley's predilection to choose profit over duty, then Crawley had warned him to be wary of Sir William's desire for glory while disregarding common sense. He now had only to have Oxford come to his ship and warn him about the shortcomings of both Crawley and Jones and the circle would be complete. He was not, however, expecting that to happen. Hayden guessed that Crawley and Oxford were much of one mind with regards to both the matter of Sir William and how best to prosecute the war against the French.

Hayden returned to the *Themis*, spoke at some length with his officers about the progress in refitting their ship for sea, and then retired to his cabin, sending his writer in search of Rosseau – Hayden's cook.

The Frenchman appeared a few moments later, wiping his hands on a square of cotton. 'Is the *capitaine* displeased with his food?' he asked in French

'The captain is delighted with his food, Rosseau,' Hayden replied in the same language. 'I commend you for it.'

'You are very gracious, Capitaine.'

'Have you been ashore, Rosseau?'

'I have. Your steward and I have been procuring stores at your request and instruction.'

'And I am most pleased to hear it. Did you encounter any of the French refugees while you were on land?'

'A few servants, Capitaine, in the market. I did not speak with them.'

'Have you ever heard of the Comte de Latendresse?'

Rosseau considered this a moment and then shook his head. 'I have not, but there were so many noblemen ... before the revolution.'

'Indeed there were. This particular comte is here, on Barbados, claiming to be a refugee from the revolution. I harbour some small suspicion that he is neither a comte nor a refugee.'

'The Jacobins, Capitaine, they are very cunning. They place men – and women too – into the midst of their enemies. In France, you never know whom to trust. I have seen brother betray brother.'

'Perhaps that is true of Barbados as well. I am in need of a French native to ... mingle with the French refugees. I would like to discover if this comte is a royalist, as he claims, or no comte at all and a Jacobin.'

'You wish to make someone a spy?' Rosseau's mouth turned down. 'It could be very dangerous, Capitaine.'

'That is why I would only accept a volunteer. I would never put a man into such a situation by order.'

A protracted silence ensued, becoming increasingly awkward.

'I have been seen,' Rosseau explained, 'coming and going from the ship. It is no secret who and what I am. To convince anyone I am a Jacobin – even a Jacobin spy . . . But let me go ashore and find out what I may about this man. I do not think there is any way a British captain's chef would win his trust, but he must have servants . . .'

'Do not put yourself in danger,' Hayden said firmly.

'I am already in danger. The moment I agreed to speak to this comte's servants I crossed a border into a lawless land. I will not pursue this matter at foolish risk to myself – assuming I can recognize the dangers in time. I am not like you, Capitaine – a warrior. I am merely a chef. And I am frightened.'

Sixteen

It had been with some difficulty that Hayden had parted from his new bride the previous evening to be aboard ship so that the anchor might be weighed at first light. It was the first time Hayden had gone off to sea – to war – since he had wed, less than a fortnight previous, and he was not certain how his new bride would bear up to this turn of events.

To his surprise, or perhaps disappointment, she had been surprisingly stoic, saying only that she believed God would protect him. Hayden, himself, was not so certain that God approved this, or any, war but then the Old Testament was rife with battles and the perceived intervention of the deity, so perhaps he was wrong on that score.

Their orders were very simple – to cruise the French islands, as far north as twenty degrees, and to disrupt the enemy's commerce wherever this could be managed. It was, to the disgust of Jones, yet another prize-hunting cruise with the single intention of enriching the officers involved – including the admiral. The crews would never complain, because they shared in all prize moneys, and the officers seemed to consider it no more than their due for braving the Yellow Jack. Crawley and Oxford were entirely pleased and prepared to execute these orders with the highest possible degree of diligence.

Both Hayden and Jones were of the opinion that their

squadron's efforts could have been much better directed in aid of the war effort, but Caldwell was yet the commander-in-chief of the Barbados station, so they had little say in the matter.

The four crack frigates had shaped their course to the north-north-west and had hauled their bowlines the moment the trade had found them. This course would allow them to cruise out of sight of the French islands while watching for ships approaching from the west or north.

The frigates stretched out in a line abreast, the distance between being about five English miles. The two most distant ships were then five leagues apart and out of sight to one another. Signals, however, passed quickly between the frigates and this formation allowed them to sweep the greatest area of ocean.

Hayden had been surprised to learn that the frigate captains had not entered into an arrangement to share prize money equally, which was very common on such stations. Jones, of course, did not care much for prize money but had claimed Oxford and Crawley were far too concerned with lucre. It occurred to Hayden that Jones might not approve of such arrangements, as he was only there to carry war to the French, not to enrich himself. The more Hayden considered it, the more likely this explanation seemed.

'Not a sail in sight that does not belong to a fisherman, sir,' came a voice from behind, interrupting his thoughts.

Hayden stood at the windward rail on the quarterdeck – the captain's exclusive few feet of deck. Archer, who had spoken, was by the skylight to Hayden's cabin.

'It is a sadly empty sea, Mr Archer. Let us hope it does not long remain so.'

'It is said to be a rich cruising ground, Captain. I am certain it will not prove a disappointment.'

Hayden beckoned the lieutenant near. 'I have been meaning to enquire, Mr Archer: where have our Africans gone?'

The young officer's eyes went a little wider. 'You do not know, sir?'

'I should not have asked if I had.'

Archer looked decidedly uncomfortable of a sudden. 'Why, Mrs Hayden took them under her wing, sir. They are to learn English and enter service until we work out what is to be done with them.'

Hayden took hold of the rail. 'They have entered service . . . in my home?'

'So I have been informed, sir.' Archer had taken a step back and was not meeting his captain's eye. 'I suppose Mrs Hayden believed that servants were a matter for the lady of the house . . .'

'Indeed. I should agree, especially so as I shall be at sea much of the time but . . . we have saved these poor people from slavery . . . so that they might act as my servants?!'

'Only very temporarily, sir.'

'And who was it approached Mrs Hayden on this matter . . . without first speaking to me?'

Archer looked positively alarmed at this question. 'I – I do not know, sir.'

'Perhaps someone else does. Pass the word for Mr Wickham.'

'Aye, sir.'

The midshipman arrived a moment later, stuffing an arm into his coat as he did so, his colour high.

'I do apologize, Captain,' Wickham began, before Hayden could open his mouth to speak. 'I did not for a moment think Mrs Hayden would fail to mention the matter to you.'

'And how is it, Mr Wickham, that you spoke with my wife without me knowing?'

'Mr Gould and myself encountered Mrs Hayden and a maid returning from the dressmaker. She very kindly asked what had brought us ashore, and we explained our predicament, sir – finding positions for our poor Africans, sir. Not for a moment did I expect her to offer to take them on, sir, or I would never have said a word. I should always have spoken to you first, sir.'

'I believe you would, Mr Wickham. I do wish that someone had seen fit to inform me.'

'I apologize again, Captain.'

'*On deck!*' came the call from above. 'Sail! Point off the larboard bow.'

'Your apology is duly accepted. Lay aloft and see if you can descry this sail, if you please.'

'Aye, sir.'

Hayden watched the boy scramble aloft, his injured hand slowing him only a little.

The Africans were serving in his house! *The Africans they had rescued from slavery!* He could only imagine trying to explain that to a member of the anti-slavery league. He should look a fool in more ways than he cared to count. How he hoped this strange sail belonged to an enemy frigate so his mind would be forced to matters other than feeling utterly foolish.

Hayden called for his glass and made his way forward. The lookout was not wrong: it was a sail and certainly no fisherman. Hayden stood at the rail, gazing through his glass while several of his officers lined the bulwark beside him, their own glasses fixed on the distant point.

'Mr Archer,' Hayden said after a moment.

'Sir?'

'Shape our course to intercept that ship. We shall beat to quarters and signal Captain Jones that we have a strange sail in sight – north by west.'

'Aye, sir.'

The ship fell off on to her new heading, with only minor shifting of yards and trimming of sails. The hands went quietly to their stations, barely controlled excitement apparent on every face. Signals were spread upon the deck and then hauled aloft, where they curled and fluttered in the enduring trade.

They were not half of the hour upon their new course when Wickham called down from aloft.

'*On deck!* They have smoked us, Captain. She is running, sir.'

Hayden ordered the course altered to intercept their quarry then paced the deck while the distant sail grew marginally larger by the hour. By early afternoon it was apparent that they would catch the strange ship up before darkness descended. It was also clear she was a transport.

'*On deck!*' the lookout cried. 'American flag at the mizzen, sir.'

'Mr Archer!' Hayden called out to his first lieutenant. 'If she does not heave-to we will fire a shot across her bow. Have a boat ready to launch. I will send Mr Ransome to see if they have any English hands we might press.'

'Aye, sir. I shall have the boat made ready.'

Hayden alerted the other members of his squadron that the strange ship was an American transport and then watched them return to their previous courses, leaving him to catch them up later.

Realizing that the British frigate would overtake them before darkness, the transport hove-to, resigned to the inevitable. The master of the transport came to the rail and called out to Hayden as the *Themis* lost way a pistol-shot to windward. 'I am an American vessel engaged in legal trade, Captain!' he called out. 'I protest, sir. Protest most bitterly at being searched on the open sea.'

'I am under orders, sir,' Hayden replied. 'Stand by to receive a boarding party. The more quickly you comply with my lieutenant's requests, the more quickly you shall be on your way.'

The British cutter went into the water and a party of marines, midshipmen and hands, under the command of Lieutenant Ransome, was quickly alongside the American ship. The examination of papers, cargo and crew took the better part of two hours, and it was all but dark when the British cutter was manned again. The two ships had drifted a little apart, but Hayden could see Ransome had pressed a few men out of the transport, for they were gathered in a resentful knot in the cutter's bow.

'It would appear we have some new members of our crew, sir,' Archer noted.

'I do hope Ransome has found us some prime seamen, and not troublemakers.'

The coxswain brought the boat alongside, and Hayden went forward through the gloom to see what Ransome had uncovered. The lieutenant came over the side and touched his hat to Hayden.

'General cargo, sir.' He offered Hayden a sheet of paper. 'Cotton and cotton goods, sir. Some lumber.'

'You found us some *recruits*, I think?'

Ransome smiled. 'Yes, sir. And most peculiar, Captain . . . Fowler swears he recognizes one of them. He says the man was an able seaman aboard this ship but was believed drowned, sir.'

'That is more than peculiar. Does this man have a name?'

'Aldrich, sir. Peter Aldrich.'

If Ransome had taken a pistol from his pocket and shot at him, Hayden could not have been more surprised . . . or horrified! He made every effort to hide his reaction to this news, but Wickham, who stood but a yard distant, actually twitched, he was so alarmed.

'Do you recognize the name, sir?' Ransome asked.

'Mmm. Let me see this man.' Hayden turned to Archer. 'Have the American hold her station until I have had a look at these men.'

The newly pressed seamen came over the rail, looking very downcast, if not truculent, and, to Hayden's distress, there among them was Peter Aldrich, a man once falsely accused of mutiny and aided in his escape by Hayden and some of his officers.

A few men began to gather about the pressed men. 'Be about your business,' Hayden ordered them, rather peevishly, and they hastened off to their stations. 'Which one is said to be Aldrich?'

A man was pushed forward, his head down so that his face was barely visible in the failing light. Even so, Hayden had no doubt of the man's identity. It was Peter Aldrich, a man Hayden had warned never to go to sea again.

'What is your name, sir?' Hayden asked.

'Watson, sir. Archy Watson, second mate aboard the *Mystic*.'

'And from where do you hail, Watson?'

'Boston, sir. I was born there.'

Hayden beckoned Wickham nearer, hoping to God that the boy's wit had not deserted him. 'Mr Wickham, you were familiar with the late Peter Aldrich, were you not?'

'Very familiar, sir.'

'Do you recognize this man?'

Wickham, to Hayden's relief, did not hesitate. 'No, sir,' he replied, 'I do not. He does bear a strong resemblance to Aldrich, sir, but it is no more than that.'

'I would concur ... if I were allowed to give my opinion.' This was Hawthorne, appearing out of the gloom. 'He does look a good deal like the late Peter Aldrich – could be his brother – but I have seen such things before. I once met a man who I mistook to be my cousin and was utterly astonished when he was not. There was not a hair difference between them.'

'Mr Wickham, take charge of the cutter, if you please, and return this man to his ship.' Hayden turned to Ransome. 'See these new men settled on the lower deck. I will speak with them in the morning. The rest of you, about your business. We shall make sail the moment the cutter has been taken aboard.'

As the boat crew climbed down the side, Hayden beckoned Aldrich near. 'I do apologize for the misunderstanding, Mr Watson, but you do resemble our late shipmate to a remarkable degree.' Hayden looked quickly around to be certain they were alone then whispered, 'Did I not warn you never to go to sea again?'

'You did, sir,' Aldrich replied, his voice shaking, 'but I have no other trade, Captain.'

'British ships search American ships all the time, as you well know. If this happens again and you are recognized, you will be returned to England, where it is very likely you will be hanged, sir. I should think the life of a common labourer preferable to that.'

'Yes, sir.' Aldrich hung his head like a truant schoolboy.

'Climb down, sir. And do not ignore my warning twice.'

Aldrich went quickly down the ship's side and into the boat, which was immediately away over the dark, restive sea. Hawthorne appeared at Hayden's side. 'That was unlooked for,' he said quietly.

'I shall invite Wickham and the doctor to dine with me this night, Mr Hawthorne. Might you join us?'

'I should be delighted to, sir.'

'Until then,' Hayden replied, and walked aft. He braced himself on the transom rail and for a moment closed his eyes, as though in pain. There had never been any doubt in his mind that Peter Aldrich was naive, but he had never thought him to lack wit. Yet here he was, returned to his former trade, where not only was he taking the great risk of being recognized as one of the *Themis*'s accused mutineers, he was putting Hayden and the others who had arranged his escape in almost equal danger. It could be more than their careers brought to an abrupt conclusion.

The cutter returned quickly from its errand and was lifted directly aboard. A course was set that would see the frigate catch the other ships up in a few hours. Hayden took a turn about the deck then repaired below, where he measured the small distance across his cabin again and again, like a caged beast.

As they had but left port that day, supper was a rather grand affair – though grand in the English way, as Rosseau had remained behind. The meal, however, was not jolly and the conversation was, at best, strained with unusual and slightly awkward silences. It was not until the servants had cleared away and port had been brought out that the diners were left alone.

'It *was* Aldrich, then?' Griffiths asked quietly, with an anxious glance at the open gallery windows.

'You may speak freely – though softly – Doctor,' Hawthorne informed him. 'I have a trusted marine on the quarterdeck ensuring our privacy.'

'Yes, Dr Griffiths,' Hayden said, 'it was Aldrich.'

'Does he not realize he could sink us all?' Griffiths almost hissed. 'Surely, he must.'

'I had only the briefest moment alone with him,' Hayden explained, 'and he excused his foolishness with the claim that he had no other trade.'

'Be that as it may,' Griffiths said, still distressed, 'he has spent much of his life in the Navy and served aboard who knows how many ships . . . He has very likely been aboard British vessels that stopped and searched neutrals, so he comprehends how commonly this occurs. There must be hundreds of British seamen who would know him by sight. This is a very great risk he is taking.'

'And not just to himself,' Hawthorne added.

'Where was he bound?' Griffiths asked.

'Barbados, Doctor,' Wickham replied.

'Barbados!' Griffiths all but reared back in horror. 'Will he go ashore?'

'He will if the ship's master sends him there.'

Griffiths pressed the heels of his hands against his fore-head. 'We take substantial risk to preserve his life, and this is how he repays us? By placing us all in even greater danger! I wish I had him here; I would skin him, I swear!'

'I understand your passion, Doctor,' Hayden answered, 'but I do not think there is much we can do about it, other than to hope he does not give us up in the event that he is recognized and taken back to England.'

'Would he not face a court martial here, in Barbados?' Wickham asked, thoughtfully.

'It is an excellent question, Mr Wickham,' Hawthorne replied pushing his mouth into a sour, thoughtful rose. 'What think you, Captain?'

'I am no barrister . . . but I suppose Caldwell might very well decide, since many of the principal witnesses to the events are present, that we could try the matter here.'

'And this could be to our very great advantage,' Griffiths said. 'Without Landry or Hart to spread their slander and defame him, there would only be the opinion of the officers, and we all believed he had no part in the mutiny.'

'He did run,' Hawthorne observed, 'which does make him look less innocent, I think.'

'He did not so much run as he was pushed – by us,' Hayden answered him, 'but even certain captains of the panel thought it very likely he would be found guilty – and falsely so. We acted to preserve his life.'

'Desertion is a far less serious offence, especially as he was facing persecution and possible execution.'

There was a moment of very contemplative silence and then Wickham said softly, 'My concern is this. Mr Aldrich has always had a most trusting nature. It is entirely possible that, under close questioning by a panel of captains, he might – without ever meaning to – reveal who helped him escape. Even if it were only a single name . . . that would be enough to condemn one of us. And I do not know what the punishment would be for aiding the escape of a man who faced court martial.'

The four looked one to the other, then Hawthorne surmised, with surprising calm, 'Such a thing might be without precedent in the history of courts martial. Officers would not commonly take such a risk for an able seaman.'

'Aldrich was unusual in almost every way,' Hayden remembered. 'I have never known a hand to be addressed as "Mister", even occasionally by officers, but somehow Aldrich garnered such respect. And he was falsely accused by Hart, who never cared for him because the men respected him so while Captain Hart had the respect of no one.'

'Old Faint Hart – I do so miss him,' Hawthorne declared.

'What is to be done about Fowler?' Griffiths wondered. 'He claimed, and rightly so, that he found the late Peter Aldrich alive and hale aboard an American transport. He is not likely to change his mind, and even less likely to keep his peace.'

'I will deal with Fowler,' Hawthorne assured the others.

'Fowler is not the wisest man aboard our ship,' the surgeon pointed out, 'or certainly he would have comprehended that revealing Aldrich's identity could send him to the gallows.'

'There are men on the lower deck, Doctor, with much greater understanding than Fowler,' Hawthorne explained to the surgeon. 'I will have one of them explain to Fowler that he was very much mistaken in believing he had recognized Peter Aldrich, who is most regrettably, but certainly, dead. Do not concern yourself with Fowler a moment more. He shall realize the error of his ways this very night, I am quite certain.'

Seventeen

Upon the sun rising, Hayden found that only a single frigate remained in view – that of Sir William Jones. As the moon had been all but full the previous night, this seemed near to impossible.

'Do you think, Mr Barthe,' Hayden asked the sailing master, 'that they could have lost sight of us when the night had grown so clear?'

'I do not, Captain.'

'Perhaps they went in pursuit of a strange sail in the night and we did not take note of their signals?'

Mr Barthe made a growling sound in his throat. 'I think the explanation will be that they did not believe Sir William quite interested enough in prize money.'

'Perhaps they will return before the day grows much older.'

'And perhaps I will begin to grow again and finally attain the stature that my circumstances merit.'

'You loom large in the opinion of all who know you, Mr Barthe,' Hayden said.

'You refer to his girth, I assume?' It was Hawthorne, making his usual entrance.

Hayden smiled. 'Not at all, Mr Hawthorne. You slept well, I trust?'

'After my mind was put at ease over a certain matter, I slept like a child.' Hawthorne lowered his voice so that the sailing master, who had wandered a few paces off to stare up into the rigging, could not hear. 'Fowler has admitted that he made an asinine mistake yesterday – claiming poor Aldrich had risen from the dead – and feels rather the fool for it.'

'Who among us has not made a mistake?' Hayden observed.

'*On deck!*' the lookout called down. 'Land ho! Land three points off the larboard bow!'

'Martinico,' Barthe announced, his attention drawn away from the rig. 'The current has set us more to the west than I had allowed for, though not by a great deal.'

Hawthorne turned to the sailing master, his look quizzical. 'Was I not informed that the tides in this part of the world were all but imperceptible?'

'So they are, Mr Hawthorne,' the master told him, 'barely a foot or two, but there are powerful ocean currents here not caused by tides. A very strong current flows in through these very islands, but there are counter-currents along the coasts and narrow passes where the current flows north, while not so far off it flows south. Most islands have eddies behind them where the current is strong.'

'But you have been in these waters before, Mr Barthe,' Hawthorne almost insisted. 'You must know these currents well.'

'Only the local men know them, Mr Hawthorne, and then commonly only in their own localities. Ships run aground in these waters with greater frequency than any place on earth, I think.'

'I shall not sleep well again, I am sure,' the marine said, and he did look distressed to a small degree.

Hayden called for his glass and went to the larboard rail. There, upon the horizon, appeared a jagged, green island beneath a bonnet of pure white cloud. In reality, Hayden knew this was the top of a tall volcano – 4,600 feet, if he remembered correctly – the great mass of the island was below the horizon yet. He had a sudden desire to explore this place, for he dearly loved to go ashore in new lands.

'Captain?'

Hayden turned to find the surgeon emerging from the companionway in some haste.

'Doctor,' Hayden replied, 'we have raised the isle of Martinico.' He offered the doctor his glass, which the doctor hardly seemed to notice.

'Might I have a word, Captain?'

'Yes, of course.' Hayden beckoned, and they crossed to the windward side and all the way aft to the transom. The two had been shipmates long enough that Hayden had learned to read the small signs of distress in the doctor's face – signs that most others did not see.

'What is it, Doctor?' he enquired quietly.

'I believe we have fever aboard, sir.'

Hayden shut his eyes for a second, as though he had felt a quick stab of pain.

'Who is it?'

'Drury and James, sir.'

'Two men!'

'I fear so.'

'How ill are they?'

'Not so bad at the moment, but Yellow Fever commonly progresses with great rapidity.'

Neither man spoke for a moment. Hayden could hardly have imagined less welcome news. Yellow Jack was almost invariably fatal.

'Let us hope it spreads no further. We have physic for this, I trust?'

'There is much that is recommended, but I have little faith that any of it will effect a cure. Bark, I believe, helps with the fever.'

'You are too honest, Doctor. Others of your profession are more prone to overstating what they can accomplish.'

'I should never say as much to the crew, sir, but I thought you would prefer the truth.'

'I do, and I thank you for revealing it. Let us hope that these men heal apace.'

Griffiths nodded, but said nothing. He touched his hat and returned to the companionway, where he disappeared down to the secret decks below.

Hayden crossed to the leeward rail, where he stood for a long time, observing the distant green hill, made dramatic by sunlight and shadows. How this drew him, as though it were some promised, mystical isle where man lived at peace with both nature and himself. An isle free of war and disease, and even death itself.

He shook his head. The rest of that long day he found himself glancing often toward the companionway, wondering if the surgeon would emerge again with news. The crew were unsettled to learn that the Yellow Jack had crept aboard, but the older hands kept assuring the others that after a week at sea the fever would be gone – it came out to the ship from the land and clung to it for only so long. Several times over the course of the day Hayden wondered if he was sweating unnaturally. Each time he decided it was only the heat and nothing more, but even so, he was as unsettled as his crew, even if he was at pains to hide it. The invisible terror, that chose its victims by some process men could not fathom, was as frightening to an educated officer as it was to an illiterate seaman.

Perhaps two hours before darkness fell there was a sudden call from aloft.

'*On deck!* Sail! Sail, dead ahead!'

Hayden took up his glass and hurried forward, where he found several officers gathered around Midshipman Wickham, who was standing at the barricade, a glass to his eye.

'A little two-sticker, I think, Mr Ransome,' he said, not realizing Hayden was there.

Ransome looked rather uncomfortable. 'Mr Wickham believes it to be a small brig, Captain.'

Wickham quickly lowered his glass and touched his hat. 'My apologies, Captain, I did not know you were there.'

'It is quite all right, Wickham. I am certain you meant no disrespect. Is she an armed brig or a transport?' Hayden asked.

'I cannot say, sir. She is too distant, yet.'

Hayden raised his own glass just to be certain they were not looking at one of the missing British frigates. 'Make the signal for strange sail to the north, if you please,' Hayden ordered.

'Mr Ransome, I believe she will take more sail.'

'I agree, sir. There is not as much weight in this trade as we have often seen.' Ransome turned and began calling out orders.

'Could you make out her point of sail, Mr Wickham?'

The midshipman shook his head. 'I could not, sir, but perhaps from the foretop I might see more . . .'

'Then lay aloft, Mr Wickham, with all speed.'

Wickham clambered up the ratlines with two of the newer middies at his heels. They were soon all in the foretop, where only Wickham showed the sense to sit and clap on while he used his glass, the other two bouncing about like excited children.

'*On deck!*' Wickham called down. 'I should think she is making for Guadeloupe, Captain, and crowding on sail.'

'How distant is she, Mr Wickham?'

Wickham raised his glass again then looked down to Hayden. 'Two leagues, or a little less.'

'Mr Ransome!' Hayden called out, setting off toward the quarterdeck. 'We will shape our course to intercept.'

A gun was fired and signals run aloft. Almost immediately, *Inconstant* altered her course to converge with Hayden's at some not too distant point. There was a great deal of murmuring around the deck and the watch below came streaming up to see this strange sail. Nothing excited the crew more than the promise of prize money with little or no danger involved, for even an armed brig was no match for a 32-gun frigate and would almost certainly strike if she could not escape.

This was the distraction that all aboard needed. Thoughts of the Yellow Jack were pushed to the rear, and all hands looked forward to the promise of excitement.

When the *Themis* had up all the canvas that she would bear – courses, topsails, topgallants and royals – Ransome came hurrying aft.

'Shall we beat to quarters, sir?'

'Let us wait a little yet, Mr Ransome. We will know how many guns she boasts in an hour or two. With two frigates upon her, her master would be very foolish not to strike.'

During the course of two hours, the three ships drew

nearer the point where they would all converge. The brig, it became clear, was armed and, as she was running toward Guadeloupe, almost certainly French. To the crew of the *Themis*, this meant only one thing – prize money. They fixed their eyes and hopes upon the distant vessel, constantly gauging their speed against that of the chase.

'She'll pass before us,' one man would claim.

'Never will she,' another would declare with equal certainty.

'She has more wind than we.'

'No, it makes here and takes off there.'

And so they argued as the sun slipped toward the west.

The officers were little better, speculating upon whether the brig carried any cargo, how swiftly she sailed, how experienced was her crew. When Hayden could bear it no more, he climbed to the foremast top himself. He found Mr Wickham there, dining on bread and cheese.

'Have I interrupted your meal, Mr Wickham?'

Wickham looked positively alarmed. 'No, sir. I am sorry, sir. I had no supper, Captain, as I was up the mast.'

'Do not rise, Mr Wickham,' Hayden told the boy. 'You are as much deserving of food as any other man. Let me keep the watch for a short while.'

Wickham began to bolt down his meal so quickly Hayden was certain it would result in dyspepsia. Hooking an arm around a shroud, Hayden fixed his gaze on the brig. He then stepped back and lined it up with a shroud. Very slowly, the brig inched to the left of it.

'She is going to pass before us!' Hayden declared.

'She must have caught a gust, sir,' Wickham suggested. 'That was not the case a quarter of an hour past.'

'Let us hope it is only that,' Hayden agreed. But his own observation belied this and after half an hour he leaned over and called down to the deck. 'Pass the word for Mr Barthe, if you please.'

The sailing master soon appeared below, gazing up at Hayden, from that angle looking more than a little like a dumpling in a hat and coat.

'I believe she is going to pass ahead of us, Mr Barthe,' Hayden called down.

'Never will she, Captain,' the sailing master assured him, but in not fifteen minutes Barthe's own observation concurred with his captain's.

Hayden went hand over hand down a stay and found Barthe and Archer awaiting him on the deck.

'I wouldn't advise more sail, sir,' Barthe said, and Archer nodded in agreement.

'We will alter our course to larboard, Mr Barthe, but I think our chase might make Guadeloupe before we can fire a gun to bring her to.'

The master scratched absent-mindedly at a spot on his cheek. 'Our bottom must be somewhat foul, sir,' he offered. 'We might be forced to careen, Captain.'

'Let us hope not.'

The ship's helm was put up a little, and the yards braced and sails trimmed to draw every tenth of a knot from the frigate. Sir William's ship was yet some distance off and would soon be in the *Themis*'s wake, Hayden thought. When Barthe was done trimming sails, he and Hayden repaired below to quiz the chart.

Guadeloupe was actually two islands separated by a narrow channel. At either end of this channel lay a good-sized bay, both well guarded by batteries. Off-lying islands lay to port but Hayden did not think the brig was headed there. Barthe put a finger on the chart.

'She is making for Gosier, Captain, or somewhere in the bay, I would wager.' Barthe made a rough measurement using his thumb and forefinger. 'She will make the bay on the last light, but it will be dark when we arrive.'

'Do we dare follow?'

Barthe pressed his lips together, and a deep crease appeared between his brows. 'There are shoals and coral near the entrance and throughout the bay, Captain, not to speak of the batteries that command much of the bay. I should think it a great risk, sir.' Barthe looked up at his commander. 'Do you think Sir William will attempt it?'

'He might have more local knowledge than we . . . and he is known to be audacious.'

Barthe lowered his voice. 'Some would say "imprudent", sir. If he goes in after the brig, will we follow?'

'I cannot very well let him go in alone, now, can I, Mr Barthe?'

'No, sir. It would be impolitic.'

'Let us hope even Sir William would judge it too great a risk.'

Hayden took a last look at the chart, committing all the major features to memory, and then he and the sailing master mounted the ladder to the quarterdeck, where dusk was quickly turning to night, the sunset fading behind the nearby island.

Archer was standing behind the binnacle, sighting over the compass to the now not so distant brig.

'What think you, Mr Archer?' Hayden asked. 'Will she be ours, or no?'

'She will not, Captain. I have readied the forward chase

pieces in case we might bring her to.' He pointed at the distant vessel. 'We believe they heaved their guns over the side, sir, and pumped their water, too.'

The deck-gun crews all looked very downcast as Archer's conclusion went whispering along the deck. Their prize was slipping away.

'Go forward and take command of the chase guns, Mr Archer. The brig might lose her wind as she comes near the island.'

The first lieutenant hurried forward, where he ordered a gaggle of loiterers off the forecastle. It was the problem of not beating to quarters – the watch below all wanted to see the action.

The trade would take off a little near sunset and, between wind and darkness, night would be bearable, for Hayden often felt he was being baked under the tropical sun.

The brig was clear to the naked eye now – and though still deep in the water she would make it into the bay before the *Themis* could bring her to. Hayden turned to find *Inconstant*. She was almost two miles distant, he believed. Would Jones expect him to sail in after this brig?

'Well, I am damned if I will,' he muttered.

He remained on the quarterdeck and watched the little brig disappear into the darkness and shadows created by the island, the men around all downcast and silent. 'Mr Barthe?' Hayden summoned the sailing master, who stood at the leeward rail.

'Captain?'

'Let us reduce sail. I wish to tack, stand out from the land, and then heave-to.'

'Aye, sir.'

Royals and topgallants were quickly taken in, the ship tacked to give them a little offing, and then hove-to. Very shortly thereafter, *Inconstant* hove-to a pistol shot distant. Hayden admired how smartly she was handled.

'I did not deem it prudent to chase her into waters I do not know well,' Hayden called out to Sir William, who was standing at the rail.

'Come over, Hayden,' the man called back. 'I am sending a boat for you.'

A cutter was quickly in the water and her crew crossing the small distance between ships. Hayden climbed down and was aboard the other frigate in but a moment.

'I am sorry, Sir William, she was too distant for us to bring her to with our guns.'

'Yes, I could see. But come below.'

Hayden followed the man down into his cabin, where a chart was spread upon a table. Wine was offered, which Hayden accepted, and then Sir William leaned his small hands upon the table and gazed at the chart.

'I think we might cut her out by darkness,' he declared after a moment.

'It is a large bay. Will she not be difficult to find by night?'

'I believe her master will take her as deep into the bay as he can and anchor under the guns.' He looked up at Hayden. 'Would you not do the same?'

'If I knew that Sir William Jones had chased me in here, I would. The French know your reputation . . . which makes me wonder if they would not expect you to come into the bay this night.'

'I do not believe the brig could make out my ship at that distance – not given the light when we closed. And your ship is thirty-two guns, so they will know the *Themis* was not *Inconstant*.' He turned his attention back to the chart. 'We will slip in very late – two boats from each ship – board and sail her out. What do you say?'

'It might be done. Certainly, they will rig boarding nets and ferry out more men from the shore, but we might carry her all the same. Let us hope the night is dark.'

Sir William nodded. 'What I propose is I lead the boats in and you will follow—'

'You will lead the boats . . . ?' Hayden interrupted.

Jones turned to him and smiled. 'Why should our lieutenants have all the sport? I will lead two boats and you the others.' He turned again to the chart, putting his finger on the shoreline. 'We will row in toward this little point, Hayden. We will then hug the shore where it will be darkest, all along the north side of the bay.'

'Will we not be at risk of being discovered – so close to shore?'

'We will have to muffle the oars and go along very softly. If we are out in the middle of the bay we will almost certainly be seen . . . and fired upon. The bay has been heavily invested with cannon since we landed our troops there last year. The French are on the watch for us.'

It was a very daring plan, as Hayden should have expected. He stared at the chart and tried to imagine how this plan would unfold in real life.

'The master of the brig put all his guns over the side,' he observed, 'but the crew will have muskets and pistols, no doubt.'

'Yes, I doubt she can be taken without a fight. It is a war, after all. I propose that we make sail and shape our course east, as close to the wind as we can manage – let them at least imagine we have given up. Once it is truly dark, we will slip back and heave-to just outside the bay.' He tapped a finger on the chart, 'Launch boats and slip in as quietly as can be managed.'

'I shall man a barge and a cutter with my strongest men.'

Sir William almost glowed with excitement and pleasure. He raised a wine glass. 'To our success, Hayden.'

'Hear.'

Hayden was climbing back aboard his own ship in but a few minutes.

'Mr Archer,' he called out. 'We will wear ship and shape our course east.'

Archer passed this order along to Barthe, and soon the bosun and his mates had the men running to their stations. No one wanted to bring any shame upon their ship, so yards were braced and sheets hauled with a will, the *Themis*es performing their evolution every bit as smartly as had the crew of *Inconstant*. The order 'luff and touch it' was given to the helmsman and the two frigates were put hard on the wind.

Hayden gathered his officers on the quarterdeck.

'It is Sir William's desire that we sail east for two hours, at which point we shall turn back. Just outside the bay, each ship will heave-to and launch a pair of boats. We will slip in under cover of darkness and cut out the brig that escaped us this day.'

There was great approval of this plan by all concerned.

'Who will command the boats, sir?' Wickham asked.

'Mr Ransome shall have the cutter and I shall take command of the barge.'

Archer looked as though he had been punched.

'Am I not to go, sir?'

'No, Mr Archer. I will need you to command the ship. It is Sir William's desire that he and I shall lead the cutting-out parties, so that is how it will be done.'

This dampened the officers' mood.

'I, for one, think it a damned foolish thing to do,' Barthe stated flatly, 'and I don't care who hears me say it. Two captains leading a cutting-out expedition – putting their lives at risk for a little *brig*!'

No one else said a word but, apparently, Barthe had spoken for them all, as the others, to a man, nodded agreement.

'*Mr Barthe* . . .' Hayden cautioned the sailing master, who made a little bow of concession. He turned back to the others. 'Mr Archer, you will choose the crews. Mr Hawthorne's marines will make up a part of each complement and, Mr Hawthorne, you will sail with Mr Ransome, if you please.'

Hawthorne touched his hat, happy to learn that he at least was not going to be shut out of the fun.

'Have the armourer see to the muskets and pistols. Cutlasses should be sharpened, and we will carry axes as well. I expect they will have rigged boarding nets.'

The two frigates hauled their wind forward and, under reduced sail, shaped their course to leave Pointe la Chaise to larboard. Neither captain wanted to go too far lest the wind took off to the point where it would not bear them back before daylight – not that Hayden was expecting the trade to die away that night. The weather glass was steady and the sky cloudless. The moon would be far into the west by the time they entered the bay – they did not want the moon behind them, that was certain.

There was a buzz about the ship that night, the hands chosen to man the boats the object of much attention and some good-natured ballyragging. The hours seemed to creep by but, finally, the appointed hour arrived and the boat crews set about darkening their faces with burnt cork. Hayden had ordered the boats painted black some months before, when they had cut out a frigate in Corsica, and he had not changed the colour since, quite convinced that black boats were a great advantage for night work.

The ship eventually made her way back to the point Jones had indicated on the chart, and hove-to not far from the *Inconstant*. Boats were lifted on tackles and swung out over the side as silently as the crews could manage. This was a familiar bit of work to any ship's crew and Hayden was quite certain his men could do it without a single order from an officer. The crews went down into the boats, taking their places – marines in the bows, officers in the stern sheets. The coxswains ordered the boats away, and the four boats quickly formed two lines, Jones and Hayden's boats in the fore. Hayden had stepped off the distance into the anchorage at eight and a half miles, so it would likely be two and a half to three hours before they would have the brig in sight. There would no doubt be many other boats in the anchorage, but Jones was strangely determined to take the brig that had eluded them that day – as though this was an affront he could not tolerate.

The muffled oars dipped and lifted, dripping water from the blades. Hayden could hear the men breathing, smell the sweat of their effort and fear. They were heavy, dark shadows in the night, moving in a ponderous, constant rhythm. Hayden knew all the men by now but could hardly recognize any in the darkness.

The coxswain steered toward the land, using the stars as

an aid. Not fifteen yards distant, Hayden could see Jones's barge, his men bending to their work. Despite his reputation for recklessness, the hands followed Jones without the least reserve. To say one had gone on a cutting-out expedition with Sir William Jones was like bragging one had crossed the Styx and returned alive. Assuming one did, of course.

It occurred to Hayden to wonder again what the cargo of this little brig might be. He hoped it was worth risking their lives for. There was no guarantee, however. He knew damned well that, had the choice been his, he would not have risked the lives of his men for this little ship with her unknown cargo. If she had been an armed brig in the French Navy, or a privateer . . . Well, that would be a different matter. But this . . . this was exactly the kind of dangerous expedition with little thought to its outcome or advantage for which Jones had become notorious. Was it any wonder that the other two frigates of their squadron had mysteriously 'disappeared' at the first opportunity?

Hayden hunched his back against the relentless wind. It was a little less than three nautical miles – a league – to the first landmark – the little nameless point at the entrance to the large, open bay. The island called Grande Terre was a black and featureless mass stretching off to the west. Barthe had given the commanders of the boats and their coxswains a bright star to steer toward. A compass was carried, of course, but they did not dare to light a lamp by which to see it.

An hour passed, the boats crabbing against the north-east wind, which never eased its efforts to carry them to the distant side of the bay. Hayden could hear the men breathing hard and bracing themselves to pull.

Childers raised a hand and gestured, and Hayden nodded in return – their point loomed out of the darkness and seemed to separate itself from the mass of Guadeloupe. Many times, Hayden had seen points of land, often joined to the larger landmass by a narrow neck, mistaken for an island. Too often, ships would go aground trying to sail to the wrong side of such points and he had served aboard one little brig that had nearly been lost doing just that. There was no doubt that night, however – this was their point and landmark.

The trade was affected by land and curled around the island so that it blew far more from the west, and a small chop rocked them and slapped against the topsides now and then, throwing a little spray aboard. Hayden strained to hear any sound that might indicate people ashore or out on the bay in boats. The wind hissed and whispered across the land, masking any voices or small human sounds. They must carry on, uncertain the entire way if they had been detected and the alarm raised.

As they penetrated further into the bay, toward the Islet du Gosier, Grande Terre put up its shoulder to the wind, providing the English sailors with calmer waters. The scent of the land carried to them, and the wind felt warmer, as though it passed over hot coals.

'Does Sir William intend to go inside the island?' Childers whispered.

Shoals extended both to the north-west and south-east of Islet du Gosier, and though it was possible they might pass over these, Hayden would not have taken the chance, given his limited knowledge of the bay. Sir William and his two boats lay to starboard, so it was impossible to alter course in that direction without the oarsmen of the different boats running afoul of one another.

'Perhaps Sir William knows the depths better than we,' Hayden whispered.

They carried on for another five minutes, but Hayden could sense Childers' anxiety, as the coxswain stared into the darkness, looking around constantly in an attempt to be more certain of their position.

When he could bear it no more, Childers whispered again: 'Mr Barthe cautioned me to give the shoals around this island a wide berth, sir.'

Hayden nodded. The sailing master had issued him the same warning. He considered for only the briefest moment.

'Alter our course to starboard a little, Childers. I will attempt to speak to their boat.'

Childers edged them marginally nearer, a difficult thing to manage in the dark, where distances were always deceiving. When the two boats were almost oar tip to oar tip, Sir William began to motion Hayden to keep off.

'There is a shoal, sir,' Hayden hissed, hoping his voice would carry.

He could see Sir William consult with his coxswain – perhaps over what Hayden had said – and then Jones cupped hands to his mouth and whispered, 'Follow me.'

'What are we to do, sir?' Childers whispered.

'Assume Jones knows what he is about. Avast rowing, and we will take up a position aft of their cutter.'

Hayden began waving his own cutter back so it did not lumber into their transom, and the oarsmen in the following boat left off rowing. For a moment the two boats drifted, the men lying on their oars, and then they took them up again, Childers bringing them into line with Sir William's two boats.

Hayden thought the tip of the shoal that lay to the north of the little island was less than a mile distant. Half of the hour would see them over it – assuming Barthe was wrong and they *could* pass over it.

The rowers kept up their relentless pace. Hayden would have chosen to proceed more slowly, allowing his men to preserve much of their strength for the coming fight. They would have to speed the last half-mile or so and he did not want his men all in when they arrived at the brig. But they were following Jones's lead, and the *Themis*es would not be left behind and accused of being shy for all the world. Like all men, they needed some things in which they could take pride and they would protect these with their very lives.

A quarter of the hour had passed, when there was a dull thump and grinding sound from ahead and the cutter they followed was backing oars and the men all muttering. Hayden ordered his men to back oars, as well.

'What has happened?' Ransome whispered as his cutter ranged up near Hayden's barge.

'Sir William, I believe, has gone aground. Back the oars, Childers, let us give them room.'

This was done. Through the darkness, Hayden could just make out the shape of the boat, the shadows of men slipping over the side to heave it up and off. Shore was only a quarter of a mile distant and anyone there would certainly have heard this.

Looking about, Hayden estimated that he could make out a boat at sixty or seventy yards, and a group of four boats would likely be visible further off. Given that, he wondered if they would not have been better to come down the very centre of the large bay, as distant from the shores as could be – but he had not been the one making the decisions. He had deferred to Jones, whose experience in those waters was much greater than his.

It took a few moments for Jones to get his barge afloat again, and the other boats to give him room to manoeuvre. Once all was sorted, they set off again, this time giving the shoal room. They bore on in this manner for a short while and then Jones altered course again, almost due west.

'Do you know, Childers, I am beginning to have my doubts about coming so near the entrance to the careenage.'

'I agree, sir. There are batteries there, and men on watch, I have no doubt.'

Hayden did not want to alter his course and lose sight of Sir William but he was also losing his faith in the man's plan to skirt the shore. He gazed out into the bay. The dark mass of a vessel seemed to materialize out of the smoky darkness, riding lights aglow.

'That does not look like a fishing vessel,' Hayden whispered to his coxswain.

'I agree, sir. It would appear to be a transport.'

Then, to the right of this, another vessel came into view, and then another not so very distant from that. And then, as though a little mist had hung over the water and been swept away, a bay filled with ships opened up to them.

'Is it a fleet, Captain?' Gould whispered.

'A convoy, perhaps. I wonder how long it has been in port?' His mind went immediately back to the meeting between the comte and Caldwell at which he had acted as translator. '*The French have no plans for further attacks this season,*' the Frenchman had told the admiral. '*They have not got the ships for such adventures.*'

'*Will they not be reinforced from France?*' Caldwell had asked him. '*Not this season, Admiral.*'

Either the comte did not have the correct information . . . or he had lied.

'Catch us up with Jones,' Hayden said softly.

The oarsmen increased their pace and Hayden's barge quickly overtook that of Sir William, who stood in the stern sheets of his boat, gazing about, his white breeches appearing almost to glow palely.

As Hayden drew alongside he ordered his men to avast rowing and Jones did the same, the two boats drifting on.

'Where is our little brig?' Jones muttered, as he stared into the darkness.

'Sir William,' Hayden almost hissed, 'there is a convoy here . . . and at least one frigate that I can make out. This is almost certainly a military convoy . . . bearing troops.'

'Yes,' Jones said distractedly. 'We shall inform the admiral.' He pointed into the night. 'She must be up in the very head of the bay, where it is too shallow for the larger ships.' He sat down and ordered his boats on.

Hayden sat, dumbfounded.

'Sir,' Childers said softly, 'he is not going after this brig yet . . . There must be five thousand French sailors aboard these ships.'

'Yes . . . Follow Sir William. I shall try to dissuade him from this folly.'

It took a moment for Hayden's boat to overhaul Jones's and, when it did, Sir William pointed up the bay.

'That must be her, there,' he informed Hayden.

'Sir William,' Hayden replied, 'there must be thirty ships in this convoy – at the very least. Two of them appear to be frigates—'

'That is the beauty of it, Hayden,' Jones whispered. 'They will never for a moment be expecting us. We can slip aboard, take the ship by stealth and sail it out without the French being any the wiser.' He pointed again. 'Do you see those lights? I would wager our ship is there.'

'But, Sir William. Why this little brig? There is a harbour full of ships.'

'Come along, Hayden,' Jones replied testily, 'I will lead the way.'

He set his men to the oars again, leaving Hayden, again shaking his head, and all but speechless.

'What shall I do, sir?' Childers asked.

'We have no choice. I cannot leave him to cut out this brig on his own.'

Hayden put his boats in train aft of Jones's. He could sense the mood of the men, though they made not a sound. Like him, they thought this the height of folly.

Hayden looked up at the clear sky and the expanse of bright stars sweeping across the vault. Cloud would have been preferable – cloud and a little rain to mask both the sight and sounds of their approach.

Hayden kept his eyes on Sir William's boats, wondering at what distance they were still visible. He was distressed to find it to be much greater than he had hoped. If there were alert watchmen aboard any of these ships, the British would be spotted at a distance. He could only hope they would be mistaken for Frenchmen.

The stretch to the back of the bay was short – a mile and a half, Hayden thought. He could feel his excitement and anxiety growing; his traitorous stomach gave an audible growl, much to his chagrin. The tension among the men was palpable now, especially among the marines in the bow, who sat stock still, staring into the darkness ahead as though the gates of Hades lay there. Jones was taking them near the little island that lay to the west of the narrow channel that divided the two large islands that made up Guadeloupe. Hayden was certain it was invested with cannon to guard the entry to the channel beyond. He could only hope the gunners stationed there were in their cups or sleeping.

The head of the island drew abreast. Hayden could make out the dark forms of vessels in the anchorage. And then the sounds of voices reached him over the water. He turned his head this way and then that, trying to discern from what direction the sounds came.

Gould pointed at the nearby island, and Childers nodded agreement. The oarsmen slowed their pace without being told, dipping their oars as silently as they were able. It was when the oars returned to the surface, dripping, that they inevitably made noise – a small patter of drops on the surface.

'Listen!' a voice said in French, and Hayden held up his hand; the oarsmen stopped in midstroke – oars in the water. Behind him, Wickham, fluent in their enemy's language, had his men do the same. To his great relief, so did Jones – who often bragged that he had sailed up to the mouth of Brest harbour and spoken to a French Navy cutter there in such impeccable French that they had never for a moment suspected him of being English.

For some minutes they lay there in the dark, trying to control the sound of their breathing, no one moving in the slightest. And then another voice drifted out to them.

'Have some more wine, Mathias,' it said, 'to calm your excited nerves.'

They waited until the conversation resumed, and then a man began a song in French and others joined in. Hayden ordered the oarsmen on. 'Easy. Silent as you can, lads.'

The singing went on without interruption, and every man aboard began again to breathe. At the head of the bay lay another, smaller bight, too shallow for larger vessels and almost enclosed by shoals and reefs and islands. Their brig would certainly draught too much to have got in so far, so Hayden expected her to be lying just short of it, if she was not out among the larger ships.

Jones stood up in his boat, which was now twenty yards ahead and to starboard. He fixed his gaze forward and then turned and began waving Hayden up. Seating himself, his oarsmen suddenly picked up their pace.

'It seems Captain Jones has found his quarry,' Gould intoned.

'Yes, and right up in the back of the bay, where we must sail her out through a French convoy. At least he is right about one thing – they will not be expecting us to come this night – such a thing would be beyond foolish.' Hayden leaned forward a little. 'Put your backs into it,' he whispered, 'let us not have Sir William take the ship before we arrive.'

After a very lengthy ten minutes, Hayden descried a smaller dark mass ahead and ordered Childers to steer for that. He drew his cutlass, felt down into the shadowy bottom of the boat to be certain he could lay his hand on an axe, and prepared to stand.

'Bring us up on her starboard side, head to wind, Mr Childers.'

'Aye, sir.'

Hayden glanced toward the shore – all still seemed quiet, the soft notes of the French song drifting slowly out to them, quieter by the moment.

The smooth cadence of the oarsmen increased to Childers' urging, and the boat surged over the calm bay. Hayden glanced aft, where he found Ransome's cutter keeping pace. The distant brig did not seem to grow larger but instead appeared to be receding, the distance to it mysteriously growing.

Without warning, the brig materialized out of the murk, appearing larger than it should. Childers brought the barge, almost silently, alongside, the oarsmen unshipping sweeps and sliding them silently down on to the thwarts. Fore and aft, men climbed quickly up and made ropes fast to the brig – to their surprise, they found boarding nets! In a bay full of ships! But all remained quiet aboard; if there were watchmen awake, they remained unaware of the English.

Hayden stepped up on to the barge's gunwale and began cutting through the boarding net. Upon the cutter, which had come alongside immediately aft of them, men were doing the same, when a heavy *thump* sounded. Someone in the cutter had dropped an axe. Immediately, Hayden ducked his head.

'*They are upon us!*' came a cry in French.

Hayden rose and went back to cutting through the net, with renewed energy. He could hear the thudding of feet upon ladders, and then there was a flash, hardly ten paces distant.

Musket balls buried themselves in the bulwark planks. A man on the cutter dropped into the bottom of the boat like a sack of meal tossed down. Hayden braced himself, drew a pistol, rose up and fired into the mass of men who were now crossing the deck toward him. The marines in both British boats began firing, the air bright with flashes.

Hayden dropped down, shouldered a man aside and came up with an axe. He took this to boarding nets, hewing through the ropes. A Frenchman came at him with a cutlass, which Hayden managed to evade on first thrust. Gould, who was climbing up beside him, shot the man in the gut and, pressing back the boarding net, tumbled on to the deck, where he immediately became the target for the Frenchmen surging toward them.

Gould scrambled up, drew his other pistol, fired, and then, realizing the odds, turned to lunge back into the barge, but came up against the netting. Hayden drew his own pistol and shot one of Gould's attackers.

'Turn and fight! Turn and fight!' he screamed at the midshipman, who was the lone Englishman on the French side of the netting.

The boy began madly thrusting and twisting, trying to keep from being run through.

Just then, the boarding net was thrust upward and the hands surged over the rail as a single mass. Hayden was pushed upward and over the bulwark, whether he wished to go or not. And then he was alongside Gould, wielding a cutlass and screaming what he did not know.

The battle was fierce and brutal, neither side giving a foot of deck without a man falling. The planks were quickly wet and slick with blood and the footing treacherous.

There were too many Frenchmen aboard to be accounted for by the little brig's crew, so Hayden had been right – they had been reinforced: which meant they had expected – or feared – the English were coming.

A man threw himself upon Hayden, stabbing at him with a dagger and managing, despite all Hayden did, to cut him twice, how seriously could not be gauged. And then this man was torn free and thrown down upon the deck by some of Hayden's crew, and stabbed again and again until he lay still.

Hayden was standing on bodies now. The British had not managed to push the French back but only to hold their little beach-head of deck, and Hayden thought they might not even keep that much longer. The tide turned as Hayden was thinking this, and the British began to step back, even as they fought furiously against the dark mass of shadowy men who tried to murder them with almost invisible iron. A step, and then another, the British sailors were forced into a little crescent of deck so that the men in the centre of the half-moon were hemmed in by their own kind and unable to fight. All forward momentum had been lost and now it was only a question of jumping down into the boats and getting clear before the French followed them over the side and forced them either to swim or to surrender.

'Men in the rear into the boats!' Hayden shouted. 'Men in the fore, hold your ground.'

There was a shout at that instant, and gunfire from behind the French. A moment of confusion, and then the fight was not being pressed; the wall of hostile, dark bodies jostled and lost confidence.

'Press forward! Press on!' Hayden shouted. 'Sir William has come! Sir William is upon them!'

The men around him all shouted and suddenly they were thrusting cutlasses and swinging their tomahawks with deadly energy and purpose. And now it was the French giving ground, frightened and confused, beset from both sides. Men were falling to the deck before them and the British balanced upon the bodies as they fought their way forward. And then the French were casting down their weapons and calling for quarter.

Jones came striding through the surrendering French and, even in the dark, Hayden could see the smile upon his face, the triumph in his step.

'Hayden! Well done! The ship is ours.' He waved a hand at the vessel, unaware that half the still bodies lying upon the deck were British. 'They have a boat streaming aft. I will put all the wounded French and any other prisoners we can into it and set it adrift. Then we will cut the cable and slip out of here before the dawn finds us.'

Jones did not seem to notice that Hayden made no reply. He only turned away and began shouting orders.

The soldiers on the nearby batteries must have decided that the brig had been taken, and they opened fire. Cannonballs screamed through the air and plunged heavily into the waters to either side.

'They will find the range soon enough,' Hayden said aloud. 'Mr Wickham?'

'Here, sir.'

'We will offer aid where we can. Gather some men to go aloft to loose sail, and two men with axes to cut the cable – but not before they are so ordered.' Hayden turned and found another midshipman nearby. 'Mr Gould – see to our wounded, if you please.'

The marines had taken charge of the prisoners, a great number of whom were wounded and, like their British counterparts, crumpled on the deck, many praying and moaning.

An iron ball struck the transom aft, sending up a shower of slivers.

'Captain Jones!' Hayden called out. 'Shall I get this vessel underway?'

'If you please, Hayden.'

Hayden went to the wheel himself. 'Lay out aloft, there!' he called to the men climbing on to the top.

Galvanized by the situation, hands were on the foot-ropes and the yards manned in a trice.

'*Loose mainsail!*' The sail came shivering down and immediately backed against mast and rigging. 'Mr Wickham? Cut the bower cable, if you please.'

There was a dull chopping forward and then Hayden felt the vessel begin to make sternway. He put the helm to starboard and, though it seemed to take forever, very slowly the stern began to swing to larboard.

The men had scrambled in off the mainsail yard and Hayden ordered it braced and then the stay sails set. The latter shot up their stays with the buzz of rings on tarred rope. The mizzen sail was released from its brails and run out.

The ship's movement aft began to ease, she appeared to hover a moment, and then very slowly began to make way, but not toward the harbour entrance; they would never lay that narrow channel on this wind. They would have to slip out to the south, skirting around all the anchored ships – a task difficult enough by daylight when the shallows could be clearly seen from aloft.

'I need a leadsman forward,' Hayden called.

'I'll find the sounding lead, sir,' an unknown hand called back, and hurried off. In a moment Hayden heard the splash of the lead being cast, and then, '*Six fathoms, sand and shell!*'

'Mr Hawthorne, is that you?' Hayden called to the tall figure standing, musket in hand, by the prisoners.

'It is, sir, and very happy I am to see you among the standing.'

'And you, Mr Hawthorne. I need the binnacle lamp lit.'

'I shall have it done in a trice.'

More prisoners were being sent into the boat alongside where the wounded were passed down, with more haste and less care than Hayden would have approved. He set his course by what he could see of islands and headlands, but he was only guessing. Jones came out of the dark.

'Shall I con us out, Hayden?' he enquired. 'I have been in here before.'

Hayden relinquished the wheel with the greatest relief – almost gratitude. He had made a careful study of Barthe's chart but that would be no substitute for local knowledge – there were shoals and reefs and shallows all around.

A man appeared with a ship's lamp and quickly transferred fire from it to the binnacle lamp. Hayden hoped the compass did not require a large correction.

Wickham hove out of the darkness then. 'I have a lookout forward, sir,' he reported, then stood, saying nothing, his face concealed by the darkness. 'We have a great many wounded, sir.' He took a deep breath. 'And dead, too, I fear.'

Hayden nodded. 'We were struck astern, Mr Wickham. Take some of the hands below, if you please, and see if we are making water?'

'Aye, sir.'

Hayden feared that Wickham was absolutely right – there would be a butcher's bill that could never be justified by this little two sticker and her cargo. The French boat was filled to its gunwales with wounded and prisoners and then cut loose. There were not a dozen prisoners left, sitting on the deck.

'Carry the compass up from the barge,' Hayden ordered Childers, 'then stream the boats, if you please.'

More iron balls plunged into the water nearby, and one tore open a staysail, which then hung, wafting, in rags.

The coxswain appeared, with the barge's compass in hand. He consulted the brig's compass and compared the heading with his own.

'Their compass is half a point off, sir,' Childers informed him. 'Our true heading is south-south-east. The brig's compass reads east by south, half a point south, sir.'

'You have an excellent, steady crew, Hayden,' Jones said. 'They do you credit.'

Despite himself, Hayden thanked the man.

'So what do you think of our little brig, Hayden?' Jones asked. 'She is light on her helm and appears properly built. Seventy-five feet, I should think. Small, but handy.'

Hayden could not help himself. 'I should like her a great deal better had her cost not been so great.'

Jones nodded. 'Yes. I should like war better if it could be fought with wooden swords and broken off each day at supper. But it is not so.'

A ball crashed into the midst of the prisoners, smashing the deck and throwing shards of oak in all directions. Both Hayden and Jones fell back themselves, but were quickly on their feet, grabbing hold of the spokes as the little ship tried to round up.

There was then a mewling and calling out in French, as half the prisoners, it seemed, were down and wounded – those who had not been killed outright. There was a moment of stunned helplessness from the English, and then some of the older hands waded into the devastation and began staunching wounds and endeavouring to find who among the very still remained among the living.

'Bloody lucky shot . . .' Jones cursed, half under his breath.

'Not so for the prisoners.'

'No, Hayden. Killed by their own gunners . . .' Jones shook his head.

'I will look to the ship forward,' Hayden said, unable to bear the man's company a second more.

There was calling out from many of the nearby anchored ships now, and lights were appearing. Hayden blessed the dark night. Maybe they could slip out before the French realized what went on. It would be Jones's luck – and would add to his ever-growing myth. Hayden made his way forward to the forecastle.

Wickham reappeared then.

'We are not making water, sir,' he told Hayden. 'But I have the butcher's bill from Mr Gould, Captain.'

Hayden held his breath.

'Seven dead, sir. And four more wounded – two very gravely.'

'Not seven dead just among our own people, surely?'

'I am afraid that is the tally, sir. Sir William has his own losses, which I am informed are not small either.'

Hayden closed his eyes a moment.

'Do you wish to know the cargo, Captain?'

'I am afraid to know it.'

'Bar iron, paper and sundry other goods. Mr Ransome believes it would be valued at four thousand pounds.'

Hayden said nothing.

'Not an insubstantial sum, sir . . .'

'Two thousand pounds less the admiral's share. Is a man's life worth two hundred pounds, do you think?'

'That is not for me to say. I should like to think my own worth somewhat more, though.'

'Mmm. I want you all about the ship, Mr Wickham, keeping lookout. If we run aground, we shall likely be forced to leave this brig behind, which I am now loathe to do.'

'I am on watch, sir. And I shall see to the leadsman. It must be a man who knows what he is about.' A quick touch of hand to hat, and the midshipman hurried off.

The cannonballs were sending up heavy plumes of water astern now, as the brig sailed beyond their range. Hayden felt the muscles in his shoulders and neck release to the smallest degree. If the wind held, they would be free of the harbour in an hour, and out to sea.

'*Eight fathoms!*' came the leadsman's call.

In this darkness, distances to the low-lying shores around the bay were difficult to gauge. There was, Hayden knew, a long shoal that reached out into the bay almost directly south of them. On this wind, they might just weather it, if their leeway was not great. He was tempted to enquire after a pilot among the prisoners but suspected any Frenchman who was not a fool might run the brig aground. They were going to have to find their way out of this bay by their own seamanship – and luck.

'*Seven fathoms!*'

Hayden knew it was something like a mile and one half to the point of the shoal. Their speed could only be estimated at that moment, but he did not think it more than five knots, so a little more than a quarter of an hour. Jones would alter course then.

'*Six fathoms and one half!*'

Taking out his nightglass, Hayden quizzed the bay to all points of the compass. They were going to sail rather near some of the anchored ships when they passed the tip of the shoal.

'*Six fathoms!*'

The guns from the shore fell silent. Either the French gunners realized the brig was out of range, or they had lost sight of her in the murk. Hayden made his way aft along the deck, among the wounded being tended by their shipmates.

'*Five fathoms!*' the leadsman called from the chains.

As he made the quarterdeck, Hayden saw Jones consult a pocket watch. No doubt he was using it to estimate when he had passed the end of the shoal. The man's seamanship was just shy of legendary, and he appeared almost shockingly calm, as though unaware of the gravity of their situation. They would, however, come very near the shoal on this tack, and could not afford the smallest error.

'*Four fathoms!*'

Jones stared out into the darkness ahead, then back to Hayden. 'We will alter our course to starboard once we have weathered the point of this little shoal,' he said. 'Will you arrange the crew to shift our yards and handle sail, Hayden?'

Hayden made a small bow. In a moment he found Ransome, who said quietly, 'I have sail handlers at their stations, Captain.'

'Then we will await Sir William's order.'

'I hope he knows where the end of this shoal lies, sir . . .' Ransome all but whispered.

'No one has ever faulted the man on his bravery or seamanship.'

'*Three fathoms and one half!*'

The men on the deck had fallen silent, half watching Jones, the rest staring out into the dark at the invisible dangers that lay there.

'*Three fathoms!*'

The ship continued to slip over the calm bay, heeling but a little to the warm trade.

'I believe we may safely bear off,' Jones said, as though commenting upon some rather fine weather.

'Mr Ransome,' Hayden said quietly, 'I do not think we shall need to slack the main sheet.'

'Aye, sir.'

Orders were given and, just as Jones began to turn his wheel, there was sudden shouting to larboard and then a flash so bright Hayden could see the face of every man aboard, then he heard a terrible report and all about them the horrifying sound of iron balls tearing apart the night. The deck shook beneath Hayden's feet as at least two balls struck the topsides. A few more passed through the sails, but most, he realized, must have missed the mark.

'Bearing off, Hayden,' Jones informed him.

Ransome and Hayden went about the deck, sending men to their stations. The yards were braced around and sails quickly trimmed. Jones had altered course about six points, and their wind hauled aft accordingly.

The guns on the ship were reloaded, but not with the speed of British gunners, and another broadside was fired, most of the shot penetrating the night, but missing its mark.

'I thought they would rake us, sir,' Ransome whispered.

'They traversed their guns as though we had held our course.'

Ransome peered into the darkness. 'I can barely make

them out, sir. They must have lost us against the land. Thank God.'

Jones leaned forward to consult his watch by the binnacle light. 'Are we making five knots, Hayden?'

'Barely so.'

'The wind will freshen and haul back into the north-west as we go. It is only the land that has caused it to blow from this unnatural direction.' He turned the wheel a spoke. 'In seven minutes I will bring us back, almost to our original course. That should take us out through a narrow pass.'

A British gun crew would fire two broadsides in that time, Hayden thought, and looked up at the sky. Tattered cloud continued to sail over, bands of stars sprayed across the heavens between. Across the anchorage, the vague forms of ships could barely be seen, but in the areas of cloud-shadow, all remained dark. Tails of smoke drifted to them, down the wind, stinging eyes and nostrils.

Not a hundred yards distant, the night opened in a blossom of orange flame and roiling smoke. Hayden froze in place, holding his breath as the report reached them, sails suddenly thrashing about in their gear and balls passing to either side, only to skip off the surface a hundred yards beyond.

'They have found us, Captain,' Wickham whispered. He had loomed up out of the darkness to stand beside Hayden.

'Yes, but they do not have our range. Much of their shot was too high.'

'Let us hope they do not know it.'

Before the next broadside could be fired, Jones ordered the men to their stations again, and then spun his wheel, altering their course five points to larboard. Hayden expected another broadside, but none came.

'They have lost us . . . at last,' Jones announced. 'Half of the hour and we will be in open waters.'

Ten minutes slipped by and Hayden began to hear the men around him breathing more easily; they worked their shoulders to loosen the muscles. In but a few moments they would be beyond the shoals and shallows and into deep water again. The cost in lives had been great but at least these lives had not been lost to no end.

Hayden himself began to feel a lessening of the fear and anxiety that had beset him all that night. He heard a low chuckle somewhere forward, followed of an instant by an officer warning the man to silence.

The wind felt to be making a little, Hayden thought, though it still showed no sign of swinging back into the north-west, where it properly belonged. The slap of wavelets against the sides as they pressed forward, the little sighing breeze and the tiller ropes running through their blocks below were the only sounds. And then without warning Hayden was thrown forward, staggered three or four steps but somehow kept his feet beneath him. The rending sound of timbers running up on rock or coral came to him, and immediately the stern of the brig swung to leeward and was instantly grinding up upon coral. All forward motion stopped and, as the ship swung, the sails luffed and beat the air like broken wings.

'She's hard aground,' came the call from forward, as though every man aboard did not know it.

Men who had been thrown down on the deck got quickly to their feet. Wickham had the presence of mind to grab the lead and begin sounding all along the starboard side.

'Hard bottom all along, Captain,' he informed Hayden. 'I can feel it.'

He made his way quickly aft. 'Three fathoms here, sir. Soft bottom. Sand, I should think.'

Jones looked around the vessel once and then turned to Hayden, his mind clearly made up. 'I will row out the small bower, and my boats will haul as well. I leave the ship in your charge, Hayden.'

He began calling out orders, and his men jumped to with a will. Jones's boats, which had been streamed astern, were brought alongside. Cables were passed up from below and quickly coiled down in the boats. The small bower was lowered with much care, so that it hung under and astern of the barge and could be released of an instant.

Hayden sent men aloft to hand the sails, for the canvas was doing nothing but heeling the ship and pushing it further on to the reef. The capstan was manned. In the dark silence Hayden heard Jones order the anchor let go and Hayden ordered the men at the capstan to be ready for the cable to be returned to the ship. He took his place on the end of one capstan bar, for there were so few men aboard.

The *crack* of musket fire sounded, then, and Hayden jumped back from the capstan to see muzzle flashes coming from out in the dark bay. Upon the instant, Jones's crew began to return fire.

'Mr Hawthorne!' Hayden shouted. 'All your marines to the larboard quarter. Do not fire on Sir William's boats!'

The marines, many of whom were at the capstan bars, took up their guns and hurried aft.

'Mr Ransome! Bring our boats alongside to starboard. An armed boatman in each.'

'Aye, sir.'

Hayden hurried aft, where he found Hawthorne, a musket

to his shoulder, peering into the gloom, where musket fire came from several places.

'How many boats are there?' Hayden asked the marine.

'I cannot be sure . . . Four . . . at the very least. And nearer than I had hoped.'

Hayden heard himself curse. A man was dropping the lead to starboard. 'Are we drawing off?' Hayden asked him.

'Not that I can tell, sir,' was the answer.

Without warning, fire blossomed from several points in the darkness, all very near, and shouting was heard in both French and English. Jones's men returned fire, and splashed oars into the bay without concern for discovery.

'He must come back to the ship!' Hawthorne said in exasperation. 'I do not know who to fire upon.'

Hayden could now make out what the French were shouting and, clearly, they had found the brig.

'Mr Ransome!' Hayden called out. 'Every able-bodied man to repel boarders!'

Hayden could hear boats rowing directly at the brig, and then they appeared.

'Captain Jones!' Hayden shouted at the top of his lungs. 'Call out, or we will fire.'

There was no response.

'Those are your Frenchmen, Mr Hawthorne. Fire as you will.'

Hayden took out his own pistols, which he had failed to load after they had taken the brig, and began madly loading. Ransome ordered the men to the larboard rail, aft, and they lined it, brandishing pikes and tomahawks and shouting defiance at the French.

Hawthorne's marines all fired at once, but there were

suddenly many boats appearing. Six, Hayden, counted, and then more behind those.

'Where is Sir William?' Wickham asked. He stood beside Hayden with a pistol in one hand and a cutlass in the other.

'Driven off, I fear,' Hayden replied, as he finished loading his pistols.

'Fix bayonets!' Hawthorne ordered.

When the first boat was but two boat-lengths distant, Hayden stepped up to the rail, levelled a pistol and shot the man in the bow. Along the rail other guns went off and there was much carnage in the first French boat. But behind came many more.

British sailors were desperately loading their firearms when Hayden realized that the French boats were in such numbers that they were impeding each other in their rush to the brig. He did not need to think a moment more but called out, 'Mr Ransome! All our wounded into the boats . . . upon this instant!'

'Marines, stand in your places!' Hawthorne shouted over the chaos. He looked over at Hayden. 'We will hold them until the men are in the boats.'

'I admire your resolve, Mr Hawthorne, but the French have numbers.'

The first French boat thumped alongside, and another immediately astern of that. For the second time that night a brutal battle began upon the deck of the little brig. The first wave of Frenchmen were held at the rail, murdered, and fell back into their boats, but soon more boats came alongside the first, and more after them, so that the hostile mass became too great. The English were pressed back across the decks, foot by foot. Hayden fought shoulder to shoulder with Hawthorne and another marine but soon they were hemmed in so tight that only a half-circle of deck was left to them.

'Mr Ransome!' Hayden called out. 'Begin getting the men into the boats.'

He did not look back but trusted his men not to break and run. They must cling to their bit of deck until most of the crew was in the boats. The British sailors managed to hold their line so that the fighting did not break up into isolated engagements, which would have been of great advantage to the more numerous French. Pikes thrust out of the dark and Hayden struck them aside with his cutlass, thrusting at the mass of men before him. He held a discharged pistol in his left hand and used it as a small but effective club. The marine to his right was pulled back out of the line and Hayden and the next man closed ranks. A musket fired from among the French, and the man to his right tumbled back. The English were being driven back to the rail. Hayden could not look away to see how many of his men still stood but, finally, when the rail was but two feet behind him, he called out, 'Englishmen! Into the boats!'

Eighteen

'Two post captains going to cut out a little brig,' Archer heard Barthe grumbling to the doctor. 'Why do we have lieutenants, I ask you?'

'We all knew Jones's reputation,' Griffiths replied quietly. 'I have little doubt that our captain will come out of it unharmed. His judgement is very sound.'

Archer only heard Barthe growl in response. The young lieutenant walked aft, out of hearing, along the gangway. All around, the sea was inky black. To Archer, it seemed as if the boats had set off hours before, though it had not been nearly so long.

He went to the rail and examined the dark mass of Guadeloupe, the large open bay. From where his ship lay, hove-to, a few lights could be seen – likely on the shore, though it was difficult to be certain.

Archer realized that he felt both slighted and embarrassed. If anything were to happen to his captain while he remained safe aboard ship . . . well, he would look shy, even if he had been following orders.

'Did I hear a musket, Mr Archer?' the helmsman asked. Even hove-to, a man stood by the wheel ready to cast free the ropes that held it in place.

Archer strained to hear over the sound of wind and sea. For a long moment he thought the helmsman had imagined it but, then, faintly, came the *crack* of musket fire, dulled by distance. The fire was staccato, or perhaps it could be only intermittently heard, and then fell to silence. Aboard the *Themis* the hands and officers went utterly still, listening.

The silence, as much as the gunfire, created apprehensions in the mind. Had the brig been taken or did the gunfire mark the discovery of the cutting-out parties? What did this terrible quiet signify?

And then a flash of distant light and the deep boom of a gun. A regular, if slow, fire began.

'Shore batteries,' Archer heard someone mutter.

Barthe came waddling along the gangway and on to the quarterdeck, the doctor striding purposefully behind. This fire was kept up for some minutes, everyone aboard listening as though, somehow, the reports of the great guns would eventually sum to a comprehensible account of the action in the bay – the meaning of it would be revealed. But then the guns, too, went silent.

'I will wager they have sailed the brig out of range of the shore batteries,' Barthe announced.

That was the meaning of it.

'Or the brig has been dismasted or disabled in some way,' Griffiths suggested softly.

'Perhaps the gunners lost sight of the brig in the darkness,' Archer said, 'or they were not firing at the brig at all.'

Some time, unknown and unmeasurable, passed, the night about them soft and silent, and then guns began to fire again, the flashes lighting up some small part of the bay. Archer called for his nightglass and fixed it on the point where the flashes originated.

'Mr Barthe . . .'

'Mr Archer?'

'There would appear to be some goodly number of ships at anchor; I can make out their silhouettes when the guns flash.'

'Are they ships, Mr Archer, or fishing boats and coasters?'

'I believe they are ships, though I should not wager great sums upon it.' He handed the glass to the sailing master.

Another broadside was fired, the flashes appearing in the dark.

Barthe stared into the night for a long moment more and then returned the glass to Archer. 'I cannot say if you are right or wrong. There is smoke lying upon the water, and a small cloud of smoke can appear to be a vessel at this distance on such a night.'

The gunfire fell silent again.

'I wonder if they could be firing at the ships' boats?' Griffiths asked.

'It would not be impossible, Doctor, though boats are very hard to hit at any distance, as you well know, especially by darkness.' Archer did not believe the surgeon did know, which is why he had taken the trouble to inform him.

'Have we not fired at boats at any time?' Griffiths asked testily. 'I believe we have.'

'And you are quite correct,' Barthe told him soothingly, 'and particularly so if there are several boats close together. In such cases there is a very real chance of striking them. I have seen it done on more than one occasion.'

Again the guns fell silent, and the crew of the *Themis* drew breath and did not seem to let it out. A protracted silence, and then guns fired again.

'That was a broadside, or I have never doubled a cape,' Barthe pronounced.

They strained to hear a moment more, and then another ragged broadside – muffled, distant, the flashes half buried in lingering smoke. A long silence before the guns spoke, yet again. And then musket fire, carried to them over the breathing waters.

It was sparse to begin with, and then concentrated. Archer was quite certain he heard the clash of steel on steel, and men shouting and calling out, but the wind carried so much of this away. It went on sporadically for the next forty minutes and then died away.

Archer began to pace back and forth the length of the quarterdeck, stopping now and then to listen or to call up to the lookouts, who then reported nothing. He was about to conclude that he would never know what had happened inshore, when there was a hail, in English, out of the darkness.

Boats appeared and Sir William Jones drew near.

'I fear the crews of your boats have been taken prisoner, Archer,' he called across the few yards of dark water.

Archer could not quite credit what he had heard.

'But what of our captain?' he called, leaning his hands upon the rail.

'And Captain Hayden, as well. We shall tarry half an hour but then we must make sail. There are frigates and at least two seventy-fours anchored in the bay. They will be upon us at first light if we linger.'

Jones did not tarry but ordered his boats on, leaving Archer at the rail with Barthe and the doctor, the sailing master muttering a stream of curses.

'I, for one, should like to know what occurred,' Griffiths told them.

'Jones said he *feared* "the crews of the boats had been taken". Did that mean he was not certain?' Archer asked. 'If he is not certain, should we not linger as long as we dare on the chance that our captain will return?'

'Several frigates and two 74-gun ships . . .' Barthe waved a hand at the darkened bay. 'The French have reinforced the islands, then. That is what I would conclude.'

'Why, then, did they attempt to cut out a ship?' Archer asked. 'Does that not seem the height of folly?'

'Only if one fails,' the doctor observed softly. 'If one succeeds . . . then it is the stuff of legend.'

Nineteen

As one, they all turned and leapt down into the boats below. Some French came over the rail after them, but the boats were quickly pushed clear and the French either thrown over the side or beaten into the bottom of the boats by the English. Oars went into the water and drew quickly off into the murk, followed by a volley of pistol and musket shot.

To Hayden's relief, he found Childers at the helm.

'What is our course, sir?' he asked.

Before Hayden could answer, a boat of shouting Frenchmen appeared out of the darkness and made straight at them. Hayden grabbed a musket and fired it out to the open waters.

He pointed and shouted in French, 'The English have set off out to sea!'

Taking his cue, Hawthorne fired a musket out to sea and another marine did the same. Wickham began calling out in French from the cutter, 'After them! After them!'

Immediately, the French boats set off in the direction Hayden had pointed. He ordered Childers to follow but in a few strokes had the oarsmen slacken their pace. The instant the French boats were absorbed into the darkness, he ordered Childers to turn south, and watched to be certain Ransome and Wickham did the same.

Seeing how few men were left, and how few could man an oar, Hayden took up a sweep himself.

'I will have that oar, sir,' Childers protested.

'Stay at the helm, Childers,' Hayden ordered softly. 'I will row for a while. Mr Hawthorne? How do we stand for powder and shot?'

'But poorly, sir. Though it hardly matters, we have so few muskets.'

A quick tally was taken: four muskets and six pistols among them. One of the pistols belonged to Hayden.

'Load them all, if you please,' he ordered, passing his pistol, powder and shot forward. 'We may have to fight our way free of this island.'

'How long do you think this ruse will hold?' Childers asked.

'I do not know. Row as quietly as you can,' Hayden whispered to the hands. 'We will slip along the shore until we are well clear, and then out to sea.'

Shots were fired to seaward of them – the flashes seen first then the sharp reports coming to them over the waters. Distant shouting in French followed.

The two British boats slipped along, side by side, as silently as they were able. Every man strained to hear the sound of other boats, to see any danger lurking in the dark. Hayden had studied Barthe's chart before he set off to cut out the brig, but the areas beyond the harbour had received less of his attention than the harbour itself . . . something he should have known would come back to injure him in the end.

A voice called out in French, some distance off, and was answered by others, apparently astern of Hayden.

'I believe they have smoked us, sir,' Gould whispered. He, too, had taken his place among the oarsmen and handled his sweep like a seasoned hand, Hayden was gratified to see.

'Bear a point to starboard, Childers,' Hayden said.

'Are there not shoals here, sir?' Childers asked nervously.

'There are. I hope to skirt them . . . and remain as distant from the French boats as possible.'

Hayden looked up at the sky. Broken cloud streamed overhead, jagged bands of sky appearing in between. Here and there about the bay, the thin, wintry light of stars made a faint glimmer on the water. Hayden prayed that none of these frail patches of light would find them. The boats' black hulls and the men in their dark-blue jackets made the *Themis*es hard to see on such a night, but silhouettes could be made out, and that was both Hayden's fear and the reason he wanted to stay near the land, where boats further out to sea would not discern them against the dark background. It was also not where the French would expect them to be – or so he hoped.

The splash of oars and the hard sound of sweeps working against thole-pins came over the bay. Sound travelled easily over water, so even whispers could be heard at a distance.

Every man aboard strained to hear – and then voices, speaking French, Hayden was certain. Gould made a motion with his hand, toward the boat's larboard quarter – behind and out to sea. And then the sounds of oars astern.

'More to starboard,' Hayden whispered, and Childers drew his tiller a little toward him.

'Who is that?' someone called out in French.

'Laval of the *Saint Amond*,' came the reply from out of the darkness.

'Where are the *Anglais*?' the first voice called out.

'Two boats escaped out to sea, but we believe the others came this way. Be silent, now; we must listen.'

Hayden glanced shoreward, trying to gauge how distant the island was. Half a mile? A mile? He could not say. He knew there was a point south of them, perhaps half a mile distant now. A river emptied into the sea there. Further south again lay a shoal, with somewhat deeper water inshore, where the French would careen their smaller ships. South of that stretched a section of coast – two or three miles – of which, no matter how he tried, Hayden could recall little or nothing . . . until Pointe de la Capesterre, where there was a small marsh at the mouth of yet another river.

A *tunk* of wood on wood sounded almost abeam to larboard. Without meaning to or being ordered, the oarsmen increased their pace as one, fear seeping in among them. A whispering was heard, though the words were lost in the breeze. How close were they?

Hayden wished Wickham were aboard his boat. Strain as he might, he could see nothing but darkness. He made a motion for Childers to steer even more to starboard. How he wished he could cast a lead, but he dared not even speak an order let alone have a lead splashing into the bay. They could let the boats glide to a stop and slip a lead into the waters without a sound, but Hayden was afraid any boats behind would overtake them. It was a danger. The point was somewhere ahead – not far, Hayden thought. If they ran their boat up on a reef of coral it would be all up for them. The sound would not be mistaken by the French. Were Hayden and his men to be forced ashore they would be caught within a few hours, unless they could make it to the hills. But what then would they do?

Now and then there was a small splash like the sound of an oar entering the water – though it was difficult to know its point of origin. Small waves broke upon the shore and were easily confused with any splashes nearby. The tide was high, Hayden knew, which gave them as much water over hidden shoals as they could have.

Without any warning, there was musket fire out to sea and a little ahead – not so distant. The oarsmen lost their rhythm for a moment and some oars collided.

'*Steady*,' Hayden whispered.

The first fire was returned, and then there was shouting. Hayden wondered if it might be Jones, but then he made out a few words – the French were firing on the French. Hayden almost breathed a sigh of relief. It would make any Frenchmen who discovered them less likely to fire without being sure, and Hayden hoped his mastery of the language might pull them through. It had, however, failed conspicuously quite recently.

There was a splash to larboard, even nearer than before. Childers tilted his head toward the island, and Hayden nodded. Their course was altered in that direction.

A shout came from seaward – so close Hayden could hear an intake of breath afterwards. It was a challenge. Every man aboard held his breath, he was certain.

'Does he mean us?' Gould whispered.

Hayden did not know, but then some other called back out of the dark – a name and the name of a ship.

They continued on, oars dipping in a slow, steady rhythm. A patch of moonlight appeared across the bay to the northeast. Almost, Hayden thought he could make out the stricken brig. In a moment he had the terrible realization that this patch of moonlit water moved in their direction.

He removed his oar from the thole-pins, stood and thrust it down into the water until he felt it strike solid bottom.

'*Coral,*' he hissed. '*Half a fathom.*'

An almost imperceptible whisper passed down the boat from the bow. 'Mr Hawthorne believes there is land, dead ahead, Captain.'

Hayden softly ordered the men to ease their cadence. He did not want to run hard on to a coral head.

'*Have Thoms sound with an oar,*' he said as quietly as he was able. Thoms was farthest forward of the rowers and could sound without interfering with the others.

'*Half a fathom yet,*' came the whisper aft.

Land was clearly ahead of them now, and Hayden motioned to Childers to put his helm a little to starboard. He wanted to creep along the shore, not run up on to it.

Whispering reached them – very near, Hayden was certain. Now he was in a bind: they had shore and shallows to starboard and Frenchmen to larboard.

'*Two feet one half, sir. Mud or silt.*'

'Who is there?' someone called out in French. 'Name yourself . . .'

Hayden could see no boat, but the voice was not fifty yards to larboard. He waited, hopefully, for some other Frenchman to answer, as had occurred before, but there was only silence.

The man behind Hayden spoke close to his ear. '*No bottom at one fathom,*' he said.

'*I swear . . . I feel a current on my rudder, sir,*' Childers whispered, leaning near. '*From starboard.*'

The tide was about to turn, Hayden knew, but the ebb would be so small . . . He moved his oar out of place and scooped up a handful of water and brought it to his lips. *Fresh . . .*

'Name yourself, or we will fire . . .' came the French voice again.

Hayden grabbed the tiller, and turned the boat hard to starboard.

'*Row*,' he hissed.

In the darkness, Hayden could not be certain if Childers really looked as alarmed as he thought. Ransome's boat fell into line on their starboard quarter. Hayden could just make out the movement of the oarsmen as they bent to – rowing as quickly as they dared while staying as quiet as they could.

Suddenly there was an explosion in the dark as half a dozen muskets were fired, the balls whizzing about their ears, but none finding either flesh or plank. Trees loomed up to either side. He could almost feel the small current slowing them, for he was quite certain they were at the mouth of a river.

The oarsmen dug their oars deep and surged forward with each stroke. The French boat was so near that Hayden could hear the clatter of lead balls as men loaded their muskets. An instant later they fired again, but the shot all went to larboard, cutting up the leaves of overhanging trees.

'*River bends to starboard, Captain*,' one of the men behind him whispered.

Childers altered his course without being told.

Voices came to them – men calling out in French.

'Have you found them? – *les Anglais*?'

'So we thought . . . but now. We are not certain.'

'Did they pass up the river?'

'Perhaps . . . but it is all in shadow there.'

Hayden could hear the men speaking, as though they were only a few yards distant. If the French came up the river after them, they would be in trouble. He looked about desperately. It was almost black under the trees to starboard – perhaps dark enough to hide their boats. He motioned to Childers, who pushed his helm to larboard, swinging them toward the shadowed tree line.

The shadow, however, was deeper than Hayden had realized. It took a moment for him to comprehend that they were slipping into a small indentation in the bank. He wondered if it might be a separate arm and the land to one side an island, when they slid to a stop on a soft bottom.

Hayden passed his oar to the man next to him and slipped over the side as silently as he was able. The bottom was soft, and his feet sank nearly to the ankles in the silt. He walked forward to the bow, a hand on the gunwale. The little arm of the river appeared to go further yet. There was no current that he could feel, but that might not mean anything. The water was about the same depth for three boat lengths and then began to shallow. To either side were thick, overhanging trees. He returned to the boat quickly.

'Over the side,' he ordered under his breath. 'Silent as you can.'

Ransome's cutter lay not far off. Hayden waded over to it.

'Mr Ransome,' he whispered. 'We will pull our boats further in.'

Lightened of their crews, the boats bobbed up and were easily guided up the waterway, which bent around to the west. When they were as far up the little waterway as they could go, Hayden ordered everyone to hold in place. Under the trees, almost nothing could be seen, but he could hear all the men breathing.

The splash of an oar came from somewhere out on the

main river. The French had muffled their oars – likely wrapping jackets or shirts around the sweeps where they rested between thole-pins.

The sound of swirling water. A few feet off he heard someone cock a musket – Hawthorne, Hayden guessed. He drew his own pistol from his belt. A little breeze stirred the trees, which hissed all around. Hayden expected muskets to fire from a few feet off, carrying them all away . . . but the sighing wind died away and he could hear nothing.

One's imagination, Hayden knew, prayed upon one at such times. It was easy to believe the French lay only a few yards off, having detected the British. One imagined the sounds of men in among the trees. Even in utter darkness – he could not see the man standing before him – the tension of his crew was palpable. And so they remained for an hour, afraid to move, not knowing if the French had come and gone, or if they had ventured into the river at all.

He could not read his watch in such darkness but Hayden knew they were now trapped, for morning would soon be upon them and they did not dare show themselves by daylight. Low-hanging branches touched Hayden now and then, as the breeze stirred among them. He reached up and found a thicker branch, of what variety of tree he did not know, and gently pulled it down, hoping it would not snap and give them away. It did not.

He whispered orders to the men nearest him and in a moment a few were standing upon the thwarts and pulling down branches, which were then tied to the boat by ropes of various lengths. In the dark it was impossible to assess the success of this enterprise, but they did the best they could, and then Hayden ordered the men into the boats. Watches were assigned and the others allowed to lie down in the bottom of the boat and rest.

Grey began to creep out of the east so that the trees were silhouetted against the brightening sky. Hayden waded down toward the main river a distance to gauge the effectiveness of their disguise. A few branches were then adjusted aft to hide the boats as completely as possible and to make the scene appear more natural. He then climbed into the stern sheets, where he found Childers and Gould curled up in the bottom, fast asleep.

Hawthorne sat forward and, when Hayden caught his eye, he shrugged. The marine lieutenant had exchanged his red coat for a blue one and was on watch, musket laid across the gunwales and pistols to hand.

The island's birds began to sing at the first sign of light, and the trees around were alive with them, flitting from branch to branch, some fluttering out to catch insects over the water, where the mosquitoes had found the British sailors. Hayden prayed the heat of the day would drive them to ground.

As morning brightened, Hayden heard, some distance off, the sound of oars working against wood, and then muted conversation. Not five minutes later two boats went by, manned by French sailors with officers in the stern and armed men in the bow. They laid on their oars and drifted by the opening to Hayden's little arm of the river, muskets trained toward the British. Hayden and Hawthorne had both ducked low before the boat appeared, and now Hayden peeked over the gunwale, staying perfectly still. But the boats went on, the officers returning to their conversation. In a moment the sounds of their oars diminished and then was lost altogether.

Beyond the trees the eastern sky caught fire and then the light came angling in among the trees in low shafts, the birds weaving between. Hayden took his pistol and slipped up on to the bank. He went, very slowly, from tree to tree, until he had surveyed all around for some distance. He could not be certain how far the wood extended, but some little way, it appeared. They would go unnoticed there unless someone came right upon them, for the boats were invisible from ten yards off.

'With a little good fortune on our side,' Hayden informed Ransome and Hawthorne, who were both awake and on watch, 'we can sit here the entire day without anyone taking note of us. We will slip out at nightfall. If the *Themis* is not holding position off the bay we will have to sail to Dominica on the trade.' He paused. 'We have fresh water at hand here, but no way to carry any with us to sea.'

Hawthorne reached down, pulled the folded sail aside a little and revealed a small wine cask. 'Liberated from the brig by persons unknown,' he whispered.

Hayden shook his head. Sailors would risk any number of floggings for a good drunk. 'We will drink what we can of it while remaining sober, then tip the rest over the side and fill it with water. The same persons unknown did not liberate any victuals, I would hazard?'

Hawthorne shook his head.

They would be a hungry lot if they were forced to sail back to Dominica, but as long as they had water they would survive – it was not ten leagues to the northern tip of that island. They could easily sail it overnight on the usual trade.

The river, it turned out, was used to transport goods to the plantations upriver and produce back down to the bay. A constant traffic of overloaded boats passed to and fro, the boatmen chattering or singing. None noticed anything unnatural in the cluster of lowhanging branches fifty yards up the side channel.

The tide went out so that the boats sank into the soft bottom, with only a few inches of water lapping their planking. The morning wore on, growing more hot and muggy by the moment. Hayden had almost finished his watch when he heard the sound of laughter – a young woman's laughter.

The voice of a man speaking some patois reached them, coming nearer and nearer. Hayden cocked his pistol and stayed ready. But the voices stopped just short and a soft cooing reached them, unmistakable even if one did not comprehend the language. Very soon this was followed by the sounds of love: sighs and moans and sweet endearments.

One by one the sleeping sailors woke and were signalled to silence by the others. It seemed to go on for an impossibly long time and Hayden could sense the arousal and frustration of the men around him. Finally, the affair was brought to a satisfactory, and rather high-pitched, conclusion. It was then followed by prolonged teasing and giggling. Just when Hayden thought the amorous couple might set in for a second go came the sounds of them rising to their feet, brushing off and pulling on discarded clothing. They set off then, back through the trees, and the sailors all appeared to break into grins at once. Hayden motioned the men to silence or there would no doubt have been many volleys of bawdy jests passing back and forth. As it was, there was some stifled laughter.

One of the men stirred Bamfield, who had been wounded in the taking of the brig, but the man could not be woken. Gould crawled over the hands lying in the bottom of the boat and felt for a pulse or for signs of Bamfield breathing. The midshipman turned to Hayden and shook his head, looking suddenly pale.

They covered the dead man's face with his own jacket, and the others inched away from him, especially the wounded. Hayden feared the man would begin to smell horribly, and wondered if they should not weight his body with stones and sink him there in the backwater. The sun ascended into the blue and, despite their situation, Hayden found himself nodding and fighting to stay awake. When his watch ended, he curled up in the hard bottom of the boat and was asleep instantly.

It was, for Hayden, the usual jumble of dreams: Angelita coming to his swaying cot by night; a storm sweeping across Barbados, lightning revealing the palms bent worshipfully low; Henrietta reading a letter in a garden, face pale and drawn; and Hayden running . . . running through a forest, looking back, pursued by something terrifying.

Twenty

The two ships hove-to not fifty yards apart, and Archer and Barthe were carried across the small divide by cutter. The day had dawned clear and bright, the translucent blue sea rolling by. To the south-west lay the island of Guadeloupe, so vibrantly green it appeared almost to glow.

Archer and Barthe clambered up the side of the ship and were ushered quickly down to the captain, Sir William Jones, who sat at his table without a jacket, poring over some papers. He did not look the least distressed by the events of the previous night.

'Ah. Mr Archer. Mr Barthe, I believe? Would you take a glass of wine with me?'

Neither was the least inclined to, but they could hardly refuse. Wine was duly poured.

'Captain Jones,' Archer said then, 'what in the world happened last night that we lost our captain and shipmates?'

'It was the damndest thing, Archer,' Jones told him, as they all took seats. 'We made our way into the bay, silent as snakes, and there at anchor we discovered a large convoy and their escorts – several ships of war. As you can imagine, it made finding our brig a bit of a problem, but we did find her, finally, anchored at the very head of the bay. We boarded and took her but as we were sailing her out we had the most beastly luck and ran aground. I took my boats to row out a kedge when a dozen boats of screaming Frenchmen came upon us. It was a miracle that we managed to slip off into the darkness. Hayden and his men were yet aboard the brig and attempted to fight them off, but they were terribly outnumbered.' He shrugged.

'You do not know, then, how many survived?'

'We were rowing for our lives, Archer. All we heard was the French attacking the ship and your captain and crew valiantly trying to beat them off. Unfortunately, their numbers had already been reduced by the fight to take the brig, so they did not have much of a chance against a hundred and fifty Frenchmen.'

'I should say not.' Archer felt as though a bucket of the cold North Atlantic had been dashed in his face.

'You are the acting-captain now, Mr Archer, and I have complete faith that you will perform your duties to my greatest satisfaction. Hayden spoke highly of you.' He smiled at the acting-captain in an avuncular sort of way.

'But what of Captain Hayden? What of our shipmates?'

'They will be exchanged. Perhaps not here, but they will be carried back to France and exchanged there. It will all turn out well in the end, I have no doubt.'

Twenty-one

Hayden awoke to a shot, not certain if it was a dream or real. Gould was crouched down, staring into the wood, pistol held ready. Along the boat, others were awakened as well, shaking off their dreams.

'Did I hear a shot?' Hayden whispered.

'Musket, sir,' Gould replied softly.

All the men stirred now, as silently as they were able. They crouched down, peering over the gunnels, apprehensive and struggling to breathe quietly. A little gust pushed through the wood, stirring the leaves and setting branches asway. Above this, nothing could be heard.

Then, nearer, a report muffled by the trees. Hayden guessed, by the sound, that the musket had not been aimed in their direction, so he hoped that meant whoever fired it was not walking toward them. An hour passed without another shot or any sounds of men. The sun had progressed into the west now and darkness was but two hours off, he thought. If they could lie there, hidden, for that short time, they would slip out and pray the *Themis* was hove-to off the bay.

His stomach had begun to complain of hunger, and the others were suffering the same. The confiscated wine had been portioned out, carefully, to the men in both boats, and drunk with officers watching, so none could sell their portion to another. Drunken hands were not what Hayden needed now. Wine – even good French wine – was no substitute for food.

Morris, who was one of the several wounded, awoke at that moment, and cried out in pain. The men nearest entreated him to remain silent, but he was clearly fevered, unaware of what went on, and in terrible agony. In vain, they whispered, cajoled and even threatened the man to keep silent, but to no avail.

Hayden could not help but remember the accidental smothering of a man in a similar situation not so long ago. Finally, Gould gave the man several folds of leather belt to bite down on, and this quieted him at last.

Every man now stared into the shadowy wood beyond and listened apprehensively. For a long time they heard nothing: no sound, no voices. Hayden was beginning to think that whoever was shooting – hunters, he hoped – had passed by. And then a stick snapped.

Immediately, Hayden turned to the right, from where the noise had come, and there, crouched down, musket in hand, was a boy of perhaps fifteen, looking at them curiously.

Gould twisted around and levelled a pistol at the lad, who leapt up and fled.

'*Les Anglais! Les Anglais!*' he cried.

Hayden, Gould and Hawthorne vaulted out of the boat and waded ashore. By the time they had climbed the low bank and gone a few yards into the bush the boy was already lost to sight.

Hawthorne tore apart the air with an array of curses that would have done Mr Barthe proud.

'What are we now to do?' the marine asked.

'We have no choice,' Hayden answered without hesitation. 'We set out this instant and hope darkness finds us before the French do.'

There was no discussion, but only nods from both Gould and Hawthorne. Ransome had climbed up the bank by then and hung back a few paces.

'We are discovered, Mr Ransome,' Hayden informed him as he returned to the boats. 'We must put to sea this instant.'

They clambered down the embankment, into the water and then into the boats . . . but then he stopped. 'We'll leave Bamfield here, under the branches, where he is not likely to be discovered immediately.'

None of the men met his eye, but a few nodded.

The dead man was handed out of the boat, stripped of his British sailor's garb and laid to rest on the shore. No one felt good about treating a shipmate so, but they were in narrow straits now and had no choice.

'Don't leave me here,' Morris whispered, his eyes unfocussed and face flushed and slick with sweat.

'We will not leave you,' Gould whispered. 'Now stay silent, or you will have us all in gaol.'

The midshipman glanced back at Hayden, his look very grave. He did not expect Morris to live, Hayden realized, and wondered if poor Morris comprehended this as well.

The knots that bent the branches low were undone and the able hands all slid over the side and ran the boats over the silt and into deeper water.

'Is our cask full of water?' Hayden asked as the oars were shipped.

'It is, sir,' one of the marines reported.

'As soon as we are in the main river we will rig for sail.'

In a moment they were turning downstream toward the sea. They surprised the occupants of a small fishing boat returning upriver, who stared at them with a mixture of fear and disbelief.

Masts were quickly stepped, gear rigged, and as soon as they emerged from the river's mouth, sails were set. The boat heeled to the trade. Without being ordered, the men all shifted to windward. A scattering of sails could be made out across the pale evening blue – fishing boats and schooners – but no mass of sail large enough to be a frigate.

'What is our course, sir?' Childers asked.

Hayden pointed. 'We will work our way out to sea and then return after nightfall and hope to find the *Themis* there.'

He did not really expect Archer to return until late in the night, but it was always difficult to predict the actions of others. The usual brisk trade was blowing – twelve or fifteen knots – but altered in direction by the islands.

Hayden had only a nightglass, which was of little use by day, so he called out to the other boat just off their larboard quarter.

'Mr Wickham? Can you see our ship?'

The midshipman stood up in the stern sheets and scanned the sea to the west and south. He turned back to Hayden after a moment. 'I cannot, sir, but this schooner seems to be taking an interest in us.' He pointed at a little schooner about half a league to windward.

Hayden could just make out the men on deck, but not why Wickham thought they were interested in their boats, but then the schooner began to wear. She was not large for her type – sixty feet, Hayden thought. Were she a Navy ship, she would have a crew of sixty or sixty-five men, but if she were a trading vessel, that might act as privateer if opportunity arose, then her numbers could be either substantially smaller or – if she were dedicated to prize hunting – greater.

As the starboard side of the distant ship came into the light Wickham turned to Hayden and called out, 'She does have guns, Captain!'

'Privateer!' Childers muttered.

'Not necessarily,' Hayden cautioned. 'I cannot make out more than two dozen men on her deck.'

The little ship crossed two yards on her forward mast but had her square sails neatly furled.

'Mr Ransome!' Hayden called out. 'We shall have to keep to the shallows, and hope to lose her come darkness. Stay near. We may yet need to fight.'

Ransome repeated Hayden's order and the two boats altered course to the south. The shoal that protected the careenage was perhaps one mile distant. They would have to stay off that. Once beyond, they could keep to the shallows. Schooners were employed by navies for inshore work because of their shallow draught, but the ship's boats drew barely more than a foot, even heavily laden.

A gust caught the boats then, heeling them down and dashing spray over the crew. The water, however, was blood warm, or so it seemed, unlike their home waters, where a good dousing would leave a boat's crew shivering and stiff with cold.

Childers glanced apprehensively to windward. 'Will we pass by this shoal, sir, before the schooner reaches us?'

'It will depend, Childers, on how fast this schooner might prove to be.' Hayden considered the privateer that was now most certainly shaping her course to intercept them. 'How much water do you think this schooner draws, Childers?'

'I don't know, sir. That would depend on what work she was intended for and where she was built. If she came from the Chesapeake she might draw very little. If she came from somewhere up north, she might draw ten or twelve feet, Captain. If she's local . . . well, I cannot say, sir.' Childers turned his attention south. 'We will be on a lee shore, sir, and I think the seas will build as we go.'

'Yes. We shall have to sail along the surf line and hope the master of this schooner will not dare come so near.'

'Is it not likely, Captain,' Gould began, 'that he knows these waters better than do we?'

'I am afraid that is very likely true, Mr Gould, and that confers upon him a clear advantage.'

'If I were him, sir, I would pick a place where I might sail in near and drive us up on a shoal, Captain.'

'They might be thinking the same, but any waters that shallow could be clearly seen. He might consider launching boats and coming after us, which he would have to do before it grows dark. Once night has fallen, our boats are not easily seen.'

Hayden looked into the western sky. The sun was now sinking below Basse-Terre and casting an ever-lengthening shadow east. There was very little twilight at this latitude – when the sun set, darkness descended swiftly after. The sun, however, could not be hurried in its course.

Childers was an excellent helmsman and the other boat had Dryden and Wickham aboard, both of whom Hayden would trust at the helm in any situation. Gould was not so experienced but Hayden could take his tricks at the helm if need be.

Hayden turned back to quizzing the privateer, and began to suspect she was both nearer and faster than he had hoped, though very likely on her most advantageous point of sail. She very quickly loomed up, shaping her course to cut

Hayden off at the southern tip of the shoal that protected the careenage. Every man aboard twisted about every few minutes, attempting, with a dreadful fascination, to gauge the speed of the schooner.

A quarter of an hour later, smoke blossomed from its side and, a few seconds after, an iron ball tore into the back of a wave some hundred yards aft.

'They cannot bring their guns to bear yet,' Hayden noted, trying to keep his voice calm.

'Is that a 9-pounder, sir?' Gould enquired.

'Six, I should think, though quite large enough to sink us if we are struck.' Hayden waved a hand at the boat. 'But we are a small target, Mr Gould, on a moving sea. We will soon see how good their gunnery is.'

'I would put money on some of our crews to hit a boat at this distance,' Gould told him.

'But a frigate's decks would not be moving so much in this sea,' Childers pointed out.

The schooner was, however, drawing distressingly near. There was little more than a fathom over the shoal, and the waves mounted up there and became steep. Breaking crests could only be seen over the southern tip, where it became very shallow.

With wind abeam and the sea from the same direction, Hayden did not want to get into the steeper waves and risk being knocked down by a gust. Skirting the edge of shallow water was the best they might do here. It was not necessary to heave the lead; the bottom could be seen down to forty feet, and it was but two fathoms presently.

The schooner fired its 'broadside' of three 6-pounders but the shot all fell astern.

Shading his eyes, Hayden stood and gazed toward the careenage, where he could see another schooner hove down and several smaller vessels swinging to anchors. He then turned his attention to the privateer, trying again to gauge her speed.

'Will we make it, sir?' Gould asked.

'I am not certain where this shoal ends, but it will likely be a close-run thing.'

The privateer held her fire for the next five minutes, realizing, Hayden assumed, that there was no point wasting shot. She was sailing hard toward the end of the shoal, hoping to beat the British boats there and either force them on to the shallow end of the reef or bring them to with her guns. Hayden had no chart for this area but, with the tide near low, he could make out areas of the shoal that were dry.

Again Hayden gazed at the enemy ship for a moment, then he stood and called out to the boat aft. 'Mr Ransome! If that privateer makes the end of this shoal before us we shall wear and sail north . . . upon my order.'

'Aye, sir!' Ransome called back.

'All hands to wear ship,' Hayden said, gaining smiles from all the hands, for she was hardly a ship and did not require even all the men aboard to bring the wind across her stern.

'Will we not be heading back toward the bay, sir?' Gould asked softly.

'Indeed, Mr Gould, but it will be dark before we reach that place and, with a little fortune on our side, the *Themis* will appear off the bay sometime after midnight.' Hayden took another look at the schooner. 'I wonder if we can bring her in so close that she will not risk wearing to come after us but will have to pass some distance south and tack in clear waters.'

It was always Hayden's way to plan for as many different eventualities as he could imagine. Given the vagaries of wind and weather, plans must often be abandoned, and on short notice too. Officers committed to one plan, and one plan only did not last long in the King's Navy. Wind and sea were forces too great to master – men must ever and always adapt to them.

The present matter, Hayden thought, had come down to a three-way race between the ship's boats, the privateer and the descending darkness. The white crests of small breaking waves could be seen, marking the areas where the falling tide had exposed the shoal.

'Helm half a point to larboard, Childers. Let us get as near this reef as we dare.'

'Half a point to larboard, sir.'

Hayden peered over the side, but it was now too dark to make out the bottom, which was one advantage lost. The schooner was yet some distance to windward, sailing fast. She had given up firing, perhaps realizing that seasoned British sailors were not merchantmen who would strike at the first shot. They were clearly hoping to reach the end of the reef before the *Themis*es and Hayden was now beginning to think that she would do just that.

Reaching under the plank-thwart, he took out the folded tracing of Mr Barthe's chart. It covered only the harbour and immediate surroundings; it did not extend to the end of the careenage, as Hayden had never thought for a moment that he would be sailing the brig in these shallow waters. He cursed his foolishness. The brig was on a shoal in the bay and he was without the proper chart.

No one aboard had eaten, now, for a day entire, and Hayden was beginning to feel weak and lethargic, although he was uncertain how much of this might be in his mind and not his body. The schooner passed them now, still too distant to bother wasting more shot.

'Is there deep water off the end of this reef, Captain?' Childers enquired quietly.

'I cannot recall,' Hayden told him. It embarrassed him to do what he did next, but he stood and called out to the other boat. 'Mr Ransome! Is there deep water to the south of this shoal?'

Ransome consulted with Wickham hurriedly, then stood so he could see Hayden. 'Mr Wickham believes there may be, Captain.'

'He is not certain?' Hayden called back.

'No, sir, he is not.'

'Mr Wickham? Can you make out the end of the dried shoal?'

Ransome sat and Wickham rose in his place, leaning out and low to look under the boom. His hand shot up.

'There, sir,' the midshipman called out. 'Not half a mile, I should think.'

Hayden waved and sat back down. The schooner altered her course at that moment, angling in toward the shore. The sun must have set, for the brief dusk was upon them. Hayden could just make out the men aboard the schooner, gathered at the rail.

Three simultaneous blossoms of flame and a shroud of roiling smoke almost hid the hull for a moment. The report reached them, and then shot landed nearby, one ball skipping across the wave tops and passing between the two British boats.

'Imagine missing us at that distance,' Hawthorne observed from the bow. 'Shall I stand and afford them a larger target?'

'In truth, Mr Hawthorne,' Hayden replied, 'their gunnery appears to be up to the task.'

Hayden looked quickly around. If Wickham was right and there was deep water off the end of the reef, then the schooner would cut them off. For a moment he hesitated and then Hayden called out, 'Mr Ransome! We are going into the careenage.'

'The careenage?' the lieutenant shouted back.

'That is correct.' Hayden nodded to Childers. 'As close to the breaking waves as we dare.'

'Aye, sir.'

Orders were given and sheets started as Childers brought the wind around on to the boat's starboard quarter. They were angling in toward the shore. The schooner unleashed another small broadside, but the balls all fell short this time.

'Captain!' came the call from Ransome. 'Mr Wickham believes they are preparing to launch boats, sir.'

'Will they heave-to, Captain?' Gould asked.

'I believe they will anchor. There is not enough surf to matter, and with such a handy little ship they can readily sail off.'

Darkness deepened by the moment, and in fifteen minutes the schooner was lost to sight completely. They were sailing inside the reef now, into a dark anchorage with a narrow pass and spotted with irregular reefs to either side.

'Are you ... content with our course, sir?' Childers enquired.

'I am not the least content, Childers,' Hayden told the coxswain. 'But we shall hold it for a short time, tuck in near the shore where it is darkest, let the privateers pass us by in their boats and slip back out again. Or so I hope.'

The boats went gliding along now across glassy waters. Overhead, the sky was thinly clouded – starless and moonless. The trade began to take off a little but, on such calm waters, their speed remained the same. Hayden strained to hear the splash of oars, but over the small waves breaking on the windward side of the reef no such sounds could be discerned.

Perhaps a little more than half a mile into the careenage, Hayden's boat suddenly ground to a halt, the wind immediately pushing the stern to leeward.

'Let run the sheets!' Hayden ordered.

Before he could call out a warning, Ransome's boat ran up on the same reef to windward of them, the stern lurching to larboard and the sails beginning to flog.

The men went quickly over the side.

'Do not push her off!' Hayden hissed at the crew. 'We must get the sails off her.'

The sails were down of an instant. Hayden ordered the men to crouch behind the boats and distributed arms to the most experienced hands.

'Do not fire until I order it,' he whispered, and the order was passed down the line of men to the crew of the second boat. He waded to the bow of his own boat, where he would be in the centre of the line and his orders most likely to be heard. He had one knee in shallow water and steadied his pistol on the gunwale. If he was correct, the pass was so narrow at this end of the anchorage that a pistol could be fired across it with the very real expectation of inflicting damage.

He could hear no sound of oars over the breaking seas – at least no sound of which he could be certain. And then the privateers' boat seemed to take shape out of the darkness . . . not twenty yards distant.

All breathing stopped.

Hayden prayed that none of his men would lose their nerve. The master of the schooner, if he knew his business, would not have sent only a single boat, even if he did hope to raise the alarm in the careenage.

The French boat, painted some light colour, was going to pass to the right of them, down what was very likely the passage Hayden's boats had missed. The privateers bent to their oars, which had been muffled. Hayden could feel them looking every which way more than he could see them, but no French voice raised the alarm.

Just when Hayden thought he must either order the men to fire or let the boat pass by, a second boat materialized before them.

Hayden leaned near to Ransome. 'If we must fire, the second boat is yours.'

Ransome nodded.

Under the sound of waves, the order passed from man to man. The crew of Hayden's boat tracked the first privateer with their muskets and pistols.

'There!' one of the French sailors cried out, and he leapt up to point, rocking the boat. 'There!'

'Fire!' Hayden ordered.

It was a small volley – four muskets and six pistols, one of which misfired. Ransome's broadside was no larger. Even so, at such close range, every shot likely found its mark. Immediately, French voices cried out in anguish and pain.

'Reload!' Hayden ordered.

A ragged fire was returned, but Hayden's men had ducked behind their boat. When pistols were loaded Hayden ordered a second volley. The privateers who could still man an oar were pulling for all they were worth, but the range was still very short and Hayden guessed that the harm done among the enemy was very great.

'Into the boats!'

Sails were set and quickly sheeted, and the boats set off south, out of the mouth of the careenage. In the dark, and over calm waters, the boat seemed almost to be in flight, soaring low over the sea.

'Mr Gould,' Hayden said quietly to the midshipman, 'ask if any were wounded and have Mr Hawthorne load all the muskets and pistols.' He handed Gould his own pistol and his shot and powder as well.

'No one hurt, sir,' came Gould's report a moment later. 'Captain? Morris has departed this life. Shall we slip him into the sea, sir?'

'Yes, may God have mercy on his soul.'

With barely a splash, the able seaman known as Morris was put over the side and slid past Hayden, his face barely visible in the dark waters. Hayden closed his eyes a second. Nine men, he counted.

'Captain?' came Gould's voice. As he returned Hayden's loaded pistol, he said, 'Mr Hawthorne asked me to inform you that we have not enough shot to load all the muskets, sir.'

'How many can we load?'

'Two, sir. But he has loaded all the pistols and can load half that number once more.'

It was clear to every man who had heard Hawthorne's

report that they had not enough shot to fight off a sustained attack by men in boats. They were on the run and relying far too much on luck.

Within five minutes the boats emerged from behind the cover of the reef and began to bob over the short seas. Ransome's cutter was very slightly ahead and to leeward of Hayden so when someone aboard quietly hailed him, Hayden could not hear. Word, however, was passed back to him in whispers.

'Schooner, sir . . . at anchor, directly ahead.'

Hayden was about to order a course change when he asked, 'How big a crew on that privateer, Childers?'

'Perhaps twenty, sir. Not more than two dozen.'

'And how many men would you have left aboard to man the ship?'

'Six, Captain. Certainly not eight.'

'My thoughts exactly. Mr Gould . . . ? Pass the word to Mr Hawthorne. We will board the schooner and attempt to take her. Have him inform Mr Ransome.'

'Take the schooner, sir?' Gould repeated. 'With two muskets and six pistols?'

'Did you not hear Childers say they would leave six men aboard?'

'It was only a guess, sir,' Childers said quickly, 'not a certainty.'

'An educated guess. We should have the crew outnumbered, and it will be cutlasses and bayonets, at any rate.'

'Aye, sir.'

Twenty-two

Archer could not bring himself to move into the captain's cabin, even though it appeared that he would be in command of the *Themis* at least until they returned to Barbados. Admiral Caldwell would then have the power to confirm him in his temporary position, or replace him. If there were some lieutenant aboard one of the other frigates who was pressed forward by his captain or to whose family Caldwell owed a favour, then Archer could be replaced. It would not be in any way unusual or in the least surprising. Admirals far from England's shores promoted the officers they patronized. That was the way of the Navy.

Even if Archer was not yet prepared to hang his cot in the captain's cabin, he immediately began doing paperwork and conducting ship's business there. The business at hand was placating an indignant sailing master and a quietly seething surgeon.

'The entire enterprise was imprudent from the start,' Barthe complained. 'And then, upon discovering that the bay was full of French ships, he displayed the judgement of an idiot child! Our captain and our shipmates are in a French gaol because Jones is a vainglorious ass! There was a very good reason that Oxford and Crawley decamped at first opportunity. They knew what lay ahead.'

'Mr Barthe, I do caution you to lower your voice,' Archer

said softly. 'I do not think it is wise to let your opinions on this matter circulate throughout the ship.'

'Mr Archer, the entire ship's company is speaking of Jones in far less generous terms than I am, you may be sure.'

Archer suspected that Barthe was right.

'I am much in favour of venting our spleen in regards to Sir William Jones,' Griffiths said, with just the tiniest tremor in his voice, 'but the question remains: what shall we do? If we remain in company with Jones we shall be recruited to his lunatic enterprises, and you, Mr Archer, are not even a junior post captain; you shall be obliged to do as he commands.'

Archer felt as though the planks beneath him grew somehow soft and he was sinking through them – down toward the sea beneath.

The sailing master tapped his index finger upon the table. 'I for one believe we should – entirely without intent – become separated from Jones this very night . . . before he leads us to our utter destruction!'

'It is one thing for post captains such as Crawley and Oxford to lose sight of Sir William's ship,' Archer protested. 'They will both claim it was due to poor weather, or fog, or whatever excuse they agree upon. Caldwell would never accuse them of doing so by intent. But I am only an acting-captain, whom he can replace upon a whim. He might have some other whose career he would like to advance and he will use my separation from Jones as his excuse to replace me. And then you might well have a new acting-captain who will follow Jones through the gates of Hades. I am not certain that is preferable.'

'Without question, Mr Archer,' Griffiths quickly spoke, 'having you as our commander is preferable, but remaining with Sir William is to place our ship and crew in danger to no purpose. I do not know why his own crew has not mutinied.'

'The hands idolize him!' Barthe replied. 'A coward, like Faint Hart, they might come to despise, but a brave man . . . even if he wastes their lives, they will follow him. I still believe we should separate ourselves from Jones at first opportunity. If we make the admiral enough prize money, I doubt he will replace Mr Archer.'

'I will not do it on a clear night,' Archer informed them. 'I need at least a little weather so that I might reasonably claim to have lost sight of *Inconstant*. To lose sight of him on a fine night is to risk losing command, which I will not do.'

Barthe looked at him oddly. 'Mr Archer, if Caldwell has some other he wishes to put in command of our ship he will not require an excuse. He will do so because he can.'

Twenty-three

'Round up on the schooner's larboard side, Childers,' Hayden informed the coxswain quietly, 'and we will let sheets fly as we come alongside.'

'We will have quite a little way on, sir,' Childers said.

'I am afraid you are right. I will attempt to get the stern rope around something and stop us. Mr Gould, I shall trust you to shoot anyone who endeavours to kill me as I am doing this.'

He thought Gould nodded in the dark.

The schooner was an indistinct mass of shadow, then it began to take on definition. Thirty yards off, someone aboard called out, 'Boats!'

Hayden stood up and shouted in French, 'What ship are you? Identify yourself!'

'*La Poulette*,' the man shouted in return. 'Who are you?'

'Lieutenant Mercier of the *La Vengeance*. I will speak with your captain.'

'The captain is away in the boats,' one of the men replied.

They were not ten paces off now, and Hayden could just make out the shapes of men lining the rail.

'Prepare to fire,' he said softly in English. He waited, not wanting to waste any shot. The men at the rail became more distinct, if remaining dark silhouettes. If he came too close, they risked being unmasked.

'Fire,' Hayden ordered. He levelled his own pistol and shot at the small mass of men along the rail.

Judging wind and sea, Childers rounded up sharply and brought the barge alongside, backing the mizzen as he did so. Hayden clambered up with one foot on the boat's gunnel, ran the rope around a stanchion and leaned back against it. Two of the crew jumped up to aid him and they quickly brought the boat to.

The men went over the rail with cutlasses and tomahawks, but there were only two privateers standing and these threw down their weapons immediately upon seeing the British, apparently in numbers. Ransome's boat came alongside, aft of Hayden's, and the men were all quickly aboard.

'We will set sail, Mr Ransome, back a jib to larboard, cut the cable and set off on the starboard tack. Take the men you need; all others, prepare to repel boarders. The privateers might return at any moment. Mr Hawthorne! Secure the prisoners then search the ship for hiding Frenchmen. Mr Gould – a loaded weapon for every man . . . and load this swivel gun as well.'

Despite lack of food, the British sailors ran to their appointed tasks.

The mainsail and gaff, though small by frigate standards, were heavy for such a small crew. It seemed to take an inordinate amount of time to raise and peak the gaff. While this sail luffed and shivered in the wind, the foresail was raised. Before the men could get to the headsail halyards, Wickham shouted and pointed toward the careenage.

'Boat off our larboard quarter, Captain!'

Every man aboard snatched up the weapon they had been given and rushed to the rail. At that instant a cry went up from the French, who realized their schooner had been taken. A musket fired to Hayden's right and Hawthorne loudly commanded men to hold their fire until ordered otherwise by the captain.

Twenty yards off, the privateers opened fire with muskets and pistols, and balls began to strike planking and at least one British sailor, who tumbled back and lay moaning on the deck.

'Fire the swivel gun,' Hayden ordered.

The swivel gun was ignited by match, so took a few seconds to fire. By the sounds of men crying out, Hayden thought they had struck home.

'Fire muskets,' he said, raising his voice just enough to be heard.

A dozen muskets broke the silence. Hayden closed his eyes so the muzzle flash would not destroy his night vision.

'Reload muskets,' Hayden instructed. 'Pistols at the ready.'

The boats of the privateers continued on, rowed by desperate men who realized their vessel was about to be lost if they could not take her back.

Before the muskets could be brought into play again, the first boat rounded up alongside the British cutter.

'Fire pistols,' Hayden said, aiming at the man opposite him.

At that range, the British fire was ruinous. Perhaps half a dozen men clambered out of the boat and into the British cutter as the second boat came up and its crew followed. There was a brief, fierce battle at the rail, and then the outnumbered privateers were falling back and leaping for their boats. Oars went clumsily into the water and, as the single boat containing the survivors pulled away, the British loaded guns and fired two volleys to unknown effect.

Turning his attention back to the schooner, Hayden discovered that the French prisoners who were able had leapt over the side and swum for shore, leaving only the most severely wounded behind. The schooner was quickly got underway, and set off into the darkness, free at last of the island of Guadeloupe.

Hayden stood by the helmsman, Childers.

'Will Mr Archer return for us this night, sir?' Childers asked.

'Left to his own devices, I am quite certain he would, but he will be obliged to take orders from Sir William, and I rather doubt Captain Jones believes us still at liberty.'

'Then what should we do, sir?'

'That is what I must decide, but first the crew and her officers must be fed so that decisions are not made with our wit enfeebled by hunger.'

Hawthorne approached then.

'Sir,' the marine lieutenant began, 'we discovered two men manacled below. One appears to be English and the other claims he is a royalist who was caught while attempting to escape Guadeloupe by boat.'

'An Englishman?' Hayden could hardly credit what he had heard.

'A soldier, sir . . . or so he claims.'

'Well, have them carried up, Mr Hawthorne. I shall speak with them upon this instant.'

The men in question were led up, still manacled, by two of Hawthorne's marines. They were something of a contrast – an ill-kempt man of perhaps thirty-five, small in stature; and a dark young man of rather noble bearing.

'Which of you is English?' Hayden asked.

'Me, sir,' the older man offered, raising his hands slightly. 'Jimmy Ruston. And very happy I am to see you, Captain.'

'Mr Hawthorne tells me you were a soldier?'

'I believe I still am, sir, though the army likely believe me dead. I was a corporal with the 43rd, sir. We were overrun at night while in retreat from Fort Fleur-d'Epée and I was struck on the head and left for dead. I awoke, sir, when I was being rummaged by an old slave woman. When I realized my predicament, I tried to rejoin my company, sir, but I was cut off. I went to ground, Captain, and made my way up into the mountains of Basse-Terre. I'd been living off the land, as it were, for . . . well, I can't say how long, sir, because I lost track. Two Frenchies tracked me down and caught me, sir, and were taking me in when –' he made a gesture toward the other captive – 'Louis, here, stepped out of the bush and shot one with a musket and t'other with a pistol. I didn't know it then, but he'd been watching me for some time. You see, Louis had escaped the Jacobins and was hiding out, too, when he first saw me. He'd jumped out a window and escaped when the Jacobins came for his family. He's a good lad, sir. Only nineteen, but he's got bottom, sir, and steady as they come.'

'Do you speak English?' Hayden asked the young man in French.

'Some small English. Better than Ruston speaks French.'

'Is what he said true? You escaped the Jacobins when they came for your family?'

'Yes. They came at night. They always come at night. I jumped from an upstairs window. Papa feared always that we would be discovered – my family, we were royalists. He hided guns and clothing and some food in case we ever had to make escape to the mountains . . . but I am the only one to escape. They chased me, but I am faster. Then, sometime, I see Ruston. He was very secret, quiet, never having fire by day. Stealing . . . food sometimes but not too much. Hunting but only far away from people. I think he must be like me – a royalist, maybe. But then some Jacobins came and catched him. I shoot them and then find he is an English soldier. He showed me his uniform.' He tilted his head toward his fellow captive. 'These are stolen clothes he is wearing.' He held up his manacled hands. 'Please, can you take them off?'

'Do we have keys, Mr Hawthorne?'

'We do not, sir, but I will set men to searching.'

Hayden turned back to the captives and opened his hands – a small gesture of helplessness. 'The instant we have a key . . .'

'Thank you, sir,' Ruston said. 'We were for the guillotine, without a doubt. They called me a spy. I thought it was all up for Jimmy Ruston, sir.'

Hayden thought the man might break down and weep, his voice was so laden with emotion, but he turned his face away and mastered himself.

Ransome and Wickham arranged watches and stations, the stove was lit and food quickly prepared. It was Hayden's intention to sail away from Guadeloupe toward the island of Marie-Galante, and then return to lie off the bay and hope Archer returned in the *Themis*. Beyond that, he had no plan. Certainly, he could return to Barbados with his prize – which would allow him to see his bride much sooner than he had hoped. He could make the short sail to Portsmouth, on the north end of Dominica – a mere ten or eleven leagues on a fair wind. He hoped, however, that he would rendezvous with the *Themis* that night. He was anxious regarding Archer sailing with Jones. It was very clear to Hayden, now, why Crawley and

Oxford had slipped away at the first opportunity. Hayden had believed it was because they were interested in prize money, but now he was quite certain they did not want to let Jones lead them into disaster. Taking the brig in the midst of a crowded harbour might have been audacious, but it was even more foolish. Hayden had lost nine men in that misadventure. Nine! He had fought engagements with a French frigate and lost fewer men than that. And all for nothing. But then Hayden caught himself. At least they now had this schooner to show for all their losses. Too small a prize for so great a price.

If Archer were to arrive off the bay it would be sometime after midnight – one or two, Hayden thought. The trade commonly eased after dark; Hayden did not want to be left creeping back toward the harbour and arriving too late, but he also wanted to be certain he had left the privateers in their boats behind.

'Sir?' It was one of the hands, with a bowl in one hand and a glass of wine in the other. 'French wine, Mr Wickham said to tell you.'

Dinner was salt cod, boiled pease, hard bread, butter and cheese. A strange sense of relief spread through Hayden's being as he devoured his food, using the binnacle for a table. Hawthorne appeared.

'Will you join me at table, Mr Hawthorne?'

'I would be honoured, sir.' Hawthorne raised his glass. 'To the good men we lost.'

Hayden raised his own. The two ate in silence a moment and then the marine asked, 'Do you think Mr Archer will return this night?'

'To do so, I suspect he will have to defy Jones. A difficult thing for a first lieutenant to do.'

'But we will go there, all the same?'

'That is my intention. If the *Themis* is not there, we will return with our prize to Barbados.'

'What will the admiral think of that, I wonder?'

'He will calculate his share of the prize money and make his judgement accordingly. If he is pleased with his share he will excuse me for appointing myself prize captain and returning to my bride while leaving my first lieutenant in command of my frigate.'

'It is not as if you had any choice in the matter. Jones abandoned us. It is a miracle we were not taken prisoner.'

'Very true, but I wonder how the admiral's particular friend, Jones, will describe what happened? Sir William might suggest that we were foolish not to follow him when he abandoned the brig. If we had done that, we would not have been left behind.'

'Do you think Jones will try to cast some blame on us for what happened?'

'What is the alternative? To admit that it was a vain and risky plan that ended badly and that he ran at first opportunity, leaving us to fight off the French and escape as best we could? I doubt his report to Caldwell will be so honest.' Hayden took a sip of his wine. 'Have you found a key to release our captives?'

'Yes. The master of the ship kept one in a trunk.' Hawthorne leaned nearer to Hayden and said quietly, 'Do you think Ruston ran?'

'It would be a very unlikely place to decide to desert. And if their story is true, they were attempting to sail to Dominica and had the ill fortune to be discovered by privateers. I am inclined to believe them.'

'I agree, Captain. They had even greater good fortune to have us take their ship. Ruston would have been bound for the guillotine as a spy and Louis for being a royalist.'

As Hayden and Hawthorne finished their meal, and one of the hands cleared away their bowls and glasses, Louis approached. He was rubbing his wrists and grimacing as he did so.

'May I speak with you, Captain Hayden?' he asked.

'Certainly.' He glanced at Hawthorne, who touched his hat and backed into the darkness.

For a moment the young man appeared to search for words.

'You may speak French,' Hayden said to him. 'I comprehend it perfectly.'

'On Basse-Terre there are many like me – hiding from the Jacobins. The authorities have offered money to capture them so they are every day being hunted – men, women and children, too. You could save many of these people, Captain.'

'But they are hiding in the mountains, Louis. How would I find them?'

'I would find them, Captain Hayden. There are fifty I know of. I would go ashore in a place I know where it is secret and your ship would not be seen. I would gather together some – not too many, for it would be dangerous to bring so many. Sixteen or seventeen each night. Three nights. Otherwise, they will all be hunted and only the youngest children will be spared. Everyone else . . .' He made a slicing motion with his hand at this throat.

'Where is this secret place you speak of?'

'On the western shore. Near a small island – the Islets à Goayaves. It is very near the mountains.'

'Does anyone live nearby?'

Louis hesitated and then, without looking at Hayden, he said, 'No one to concern us.'

'Ah.' Hayden knew better than to enquire further. 'What you ask, Louis . . . it is very dangerous. I must make four visits to the shore. The chances of being seen and reported will increase each time. A great risk for my crew.'

'But the men and women hiding in the mountains – their chances of being captured are extreme. It is just a matter of when this will happen. You will be taking a risk – I cannot deny this – but compared to them . . . well, it is smaller, somewhat.' He lowered his voice. 'I am told, Captain Hayden, that your mother is French . . .'

Hayden shook his head. 'It is so difficult to keep a secret.'

'There are many women hiding in the mountains who will go to the guillotine if we cannot help them. That is why I sailed to Dominica – to ask the English for help.'

'I will consider your request, Louis. I can promise you no more than that. If we rendezvous this night with my senior captain I will no longer be free to act independently. Do you understand?'

The young man nodded. He left Hayden standing near the transom rail, a small battle raging between wit and heart. His orders were to harass the enemy's shipping – to 'take, burn or destroy' French vessels wherever he met them. Caldwell had made no mention of rescuing royalists.

A memory of Madame Adair came to mind, frightened into distraction as the Jacobins came to her gate . . . and then passed by. Hayden also remembered their desperate coupling and her precious daughter. Was Madame Adair yet alive or had she been drawn into the maelstrom of the guillotine? He did not know, nor did he know what had become of Charlotte, her daughter. The thought of these two – women and girl – being hunted in the wilderness caused such a wave of anguish it was like being wracked with pain.

He wondered how dangerous it would be to slip up to the coast in the depths of the night. Were there royalists or sympathizers living in the place Louis had named? Certainly, that was what he had intimated.

Hawthorne returned at that moment and Hayden waved him near.

'Shall I allow half my men to sleep?' the marine asked.

Hayden nodded. 'Until we return to lie off the harbour. Then I will have every able-bodied man awake and at his station. I do not want to be caught unawares and unprepared.'

Hawthorne touched his hat.

'Mr Hawthorne . . . ?'

'Sir?'

'I have just had a conversation with our young royalist. He tells me there are many people hiding in the mountains and slowly being tracked down by the Jacobins, who then put them upon the guillotine. He has implored me to mount a rescue.'

Hawthorne considered this. 'I am not overly fond of royalists myself, but I prefer them to Jacobins, and at least they are nominally our allies. What would we be required to do, Captain, if I may ask?'

'That is the problem. We would slip in near to the coast and row Louis ashore. He would go searching for the hidden royalists. The difficulty is that he does not think it safe to move large numbers of them at once – no more than sixteen or seventeen at a time – and he believes he can locate fifty.'

'Then what is he proposing?' Hawthorne asked, confused.

'That we bring aboard royalists on three consecutive nights.'

'Four nights in total?'

'That is correct.'

'Well, this cove where we are going to pick up royalists had better be very secluded, otherwise we will be discovered.'

'It is a beach on the western coast of Basse-Terre.'

'A beach can be a very exposed place, Captain . . . even by darkness. And to go four nights to the *same* beach . . .'

'It is a very great danger. And I fear, Mr Hawthorne, that my parentage might influence me in this matter.'

'I do not think, sir, that feeling compassion for people caught up in a war they did not want indicates an improper conflict on your part. If the admiral had given us orders to take these people off, there would be no question, but I doubt his orders covered such an eventuality . . . ?'

'No, they did not.'

'But it would seem, given the numbers of royalists living on Barbados, that the admiral is not unsympathetic to their cause. In which case, it is only a question of the possible risk to your crew and our prize, Captain.'

'And would the crew willingly risk their lives – and their prize money – for a passel of Frenchmen?'

'Fortunately, a ship is not a republic, and they do not have a vote.'

'No, they do not but, in this case, I shall consult with my officers.' Hayden waved one of the hands near. 'Pass the word for Mr Ransome and Mr Wickham, if you please.'

Wickham and Ransome hurried aft and Hayden related Louis's request and asked their opinion. Neither was used to being included in such deliberations, and Hayden could feel them hesitating.

Not wanting to speak before a lieutenant, Wickham turned to his shipmate. 'What think you, Mr Ransome?'

'I think it is a very dangerous endeavour, but if we do not attempt it . . . well, it sounds as if we shall be condemning these people to the guillotine.'

'And you, Mr Wickham?' Hayden asked, noting that Ransome had not committed himself one way or another.

'I think we must try it, Captain, but I for one would be more comfortable with it if we were not returning to the same beach four nights together. Is there not some other place that would serve the same purpose?'

'It is a fair question, Mr Wickham. Find Louis for me, and we shall put the question to him.'

A moment later Wickham returned with the Frenchman, and Hayden asked him if there was not some other beach they could use.

'There are other beaches, but none that will suit our purposes so well. I can bring people there by ways that are safe and where we are unlikely to be seen. Also, the people who are hiding . . . some are very young and others are quite elderly. This beach is not so far for them to travel. As I say, we could use another beach, but I think the risks would be greater.'

'It sounds as though we are taking more risk so that your royalists may take fewer,' Ransome observed.

'No, no. For everyone there will be less risk to go to this beach four times than to go to another. If I cannot reach some other place, because the Jacobins are near and we must stay hidden, then you will come and come again to that place. No, this way is better, *monsieur*, I am certain.'

The four Englishmen were silent a moment.

'I know you would only do this out of goodness,' Louis offered. 'You have no orders from your commander to save people loyal to the King of France, nor is there prize money to be had. All you will have is the gratitude of people who have nothing with which to repay you, for most have lost everything. The gratitude of the dispossessed –' he shrugged – 'it is a worthless currency.'

'Thank you, Louis,' Hayden said. 'I will inform you of our decision.'

They watched Louis retreat.

'If I may, sir?' Hawthorne asked. 'We must both take him on trust and also we must believe he can do what he claims – find and deliver the royalists to the beach without the Jacobins getting wind of it. A lot to ask, given that we have not known him more than an hour.'

'Ruston thinks very highly of him,' Hayden said, 'though we have not known that gentleman any longer. I will tell him I will make my decision after we have attempted to rendezvous with Sir William. I do not want to make any promises to Louis only to have Jones set against them. In the interval, you might all take the time to have some conversation with our Frenchman so you can take his measure and tell me then what you think.'

Hayden had the little schooner stand out toward the island of Marie-Galante until he judged it time, and then he shaped their course to the point off the bay where they had originally launched boats the previous night – which already seemed like many days ago. Under cover of darkness and in deteriorating weather, they stood in toward the bay, Ransome and Wickham taking over the duties of Mr Barthe and piloting them in using the privateer's charts.

The little ship was hove-to off the bay sometime after midnight. The sky had been clouding since the sun had set, and a series of squalls appeared to sweep down from the mountains, laying the little schooner over on her beam end and drenching the crew with rain. It was the kind of night, Hayden knew, on which boats could be launched from inside the bay and would be upon the schooner before they were seen. Watches were set and men armed, though keeping locks dry in such weather was not easy.

Hayden paced about the unlit deck, damp through and surly. The schooner carried but a single lamp, its light shielded from the shore, so that the *Themis* did not run them down if she did return. Of course, the squalls would hide that light altogether, so Hayden had lookouts on the seaward side, searching desperately for the sight of a ship.

The winds shifted about the compass rose, forcing Hayden to put down an anchor, which would make any escape that much more difficult.

An hour passed, and Hawthorne appeared beside Hayden, matching his pace.

'Mr Archer would choose this night to play coy!' the marine observed.

'Perhaps he did not receive our invitation . . .'

'The Royal Mail is going to hell, Captain, there is no question.' The two continued to pace along the starboard deck. 'How long will we wait?'

'Another hour – no more. I want to be distant from this shore when light comes.' A gust struck them suddenly from the south, and the ship seemed to stagger to starboard. 'I do wish this weather would pass. It is all but impossible to see another vessel, and we are at some risk of dragging ashore.'

Hawthorne considered this a moment. 'It is also difficult to know what to wish for, Captain. If Mr Archer
returns, we will once more be subject to the whims of the
vainglorious Sir William Jones. If Archer does not return,
then *he* will be under Jones's command, which could turn
out very badly. On the plus side of that ledger, if Archer
does not return, you, Captain Hayden, will be free to rescue or not rescue royalists – whichever you see fit – without
either consulting with, or interference from, the redoubt-
able Captain Jones.'

'I, for one, am hoping that the *Themis* appears this night.
My ship and crew are in danger of harm or loss while under
the command of Jones. And Archer is at risk to do irrepara-
ble harm to his career, for it seems Jones never suffers the
consequences for his poor decisions. Either he is actually as
dear to the royal family as he would have everyone believe, or
he is charmed.'

'In my experience of men like Jones – and Sydney Smith
– their luck runs out eventually.'

'Those two gentlemen appear to have been granted a
boundless supply of good fortune. While other men I know
have only the opposite – and, often as not, undeservedly so.'

The hour crept, haltingly, by. When Hayden could wait no
longer he ordered sails set and anchor weighed. A froward
gust caught the schooner as she weighed, pressing her toward
the shore but, small and handy as she was, the crew quickly
had sails drawing and way on. In an instant she was racing
through the dark, throwing spray across the deck, a runaway,
carrying her riders with her. The squall did not last, but the
wind continued to change its direction without rhyme or
warning, so that for a time the little ship would be laying her

course and then, not a moment later, she would be hard on the wind going some other way.

Out of the darkness, a sodden Louis appeared – hatless, hair plastered to his forehead.

'I do not wish to be a bother, Captain . . .' he began, and then appeared to run out of words.

Hayden and the young Frenchman contemplated one another and then Hayden said, 'I have taken my ship and crew into danger on more occasions than I care to name, but I never like to undertake enterprises that both my heart and my head tell me are doomed to failure. Rescuing your people is just such an enterprise, Louis.'

The young man nodded. 'These people, Captain, they have no other hope—'

Hayden raised a hand to stop him. 'I have not said I would not do it . . . I have only told you how I perceive the dangers and the likelihood of success. Here is how it will be managed. We will arrange signals to be made by lamps. Once I have received a single from you that you deem it safe, I will send a small boat to the beach with but a single man, or perhaps a pair. You will meet them and, if all is well, you will greet them with a certain phrase I will give you. If you deem it unsafe you will offer a different greeting or, if you can, you will warn them away before they land. I will not commit boats and crews until I have been twice reassured that my people are not in danger. Do you understand?'

'I do, Captain, completely.'

'We will shape our course away from Guadeloupe this night, but in such a way as to allow us to return to your beach after midnight. We will take you ashore as silently as we can and then return the following night if you think you can

290

gather together some of your people and have them there at that time.'

'I will bring them there, Captain. You have my word.'

Hayden contemplated the Frenchman a moment in the dark and then said, 'I should not be so quick to give my word in an enterprise as uncertain as this.'

Twenty-four

The north-east trade swept up and over and funnelled between the island's mountains, producing inconstant winds that swirled and sometimes died altogether. After sunset the trade took off a little and left, along the coast, a narrow band of calms and small, sudden gusts. Laying-to in such conditions was difficult, but Hayden felt they had no choice — the noise of both dropping and raising anchor would easily travel to the shore and to the small islands to their south. They had set Louis ashore the night previous and now returned, hoping he would bring his promised fugitives from injustice . . . and that he would not bring a company of French soldiers.

The two boats from the *Themis*, and a smaller boat belonging to the schooner, had been lowered into the water further from shore to reduce the chances of anyone hearing. They were brought alongside now, and manned. Wickham, a marine and the strongest oarsman aboard went down into the smaller boat. The other boats were lightly manned in anticipation of bearing back refugees.

The schooner lay a little more than half a mile from the shore, in twenty-five fathoms. To the south the Islets à Goayaves were darker masses, distinguished from the black waters because they reflected no glimmer of starlight. To the east lay a small, open bay and a narrow beach, toward which Hayden stared, waiting for three quick flashes from a lantern.

The eyes tended to play tricks, Hayden knew, if one stared intently enough into the darkness. Shapes appeared where there were none, and sometimes little flickers that were manufactured in the brain, or so he had come to believe. He also strained to hear the sound of oars, or of a musket's lock being cocked. There were no sounds but the breathing of the men, and the breeze rolling down off the nearby mountains, hissing and whispering through the trees, then rippling the waters so that the occasional hollow *plunk* sounded against the sides of a boat.

'Sir,' one of the crew whispered, and raised a hand in the dark, indicating a place somewhat north of where Hayden had been looking.

Three flashes, a count of twenty, then three again. Hayden ordered the man standing by with a lantern, hidden from the shore, to return the signal. He then leaned over the side.

'Mr Ransome, keep a good offing until Mr Wickham rows back out and assures you it is clear. Mr Wickham, if you have the slightest suspicion that things are not as they should be, do not press on. We are under no orders to rescue these people, and I will leave them on the beach before I see my crew put at risk.'

'Aye, sir,' Wickham responded, very softly, and then the boats were away.

Immediately, Hayden began to pace the length of the ship, fearing the flash of sudden musket fire or even guns aimed at the schooner. It was a foolish and dangerous enterprise – the kind of thing Sir William might arrange, had he any interest in rescuing French royalists. Hayden paused a moment to watch the boats dissolve into the darkness and realized what he felt was a growing sense of apprehension.

Wickham sat in the stern, manning a small tiller, Bentley rowed, and a marine named Cooper crouched in the bow holding a musket, another ready to hand and a brace of loaded pistols in his belt. They rowed toward a dark shore where they did not know what might await them – a gathering of frightened and grateful French, or a line of marksmen with muskets pressed to their shoulders. Bentley worked his oars for stealth rather than speed, keeping the blades low to the water on the return and slipping them through the surface like sharpened knives. The little boat made hardly a sound as it went, barely a little ripple of wake trailing behind.

Wickham gazed past Bentley at the shadowed shore beyond, thinking as he did so that, if there were anything out of the ordinary awaiting them, he would never know. He also strained to hear any warning sounds, though he hardly knew what they might be. A muffled cough reached them, causing him to flinch, but then he told himself that soldiers hiding in ambush would not cough for their lives. This was some innocent – one of Louis's royalists, he hoped.

A long quarter of an hour, bracing for musket fire the entire time, brought the familiar sound of waves lapping the shore. The boat slid to a gentle stop and Wickham was out and pulling them back, then turning them around so that a quick retreat could be made. He was about to scramble back aboard when he heard a near-whisper in the dark.

'*C'est moi.* Louis.'

Wickham let out a long breath and took another in to a relaxed chest.

'Is that you, Wickham?'

'Yes. How many?'

'Only ten, but I will have more tomorrow – twenty, perhaps. They have brought what little food they can.'

'I will send the boats immediately. Gather them on the beach. Tell them to say nothing.' Wickham pushed the boat for two steps and then swung himself over the side and took hold of the tiller.

'Slowly,' Wickham whispered to the hand at the oars. 'Better to take five minutes more but preserve silence.'

Bentley slacked his pace. In a few moments they found the cutter and the barge, under the command of Gould and Ransome respectively.

'It appears safe,' Wickham whispered. 'God speed.'

He did not hesitate but set Mr Bentley back to his oars. He did not want to linger near the shore any longer than he must. Although Captain Hayden made great effort to hide it, Wickham sensed that he had strong misgivings about this entire enterprise, and if his captain felt this way Wickham was more than a little concerned. He would not draw a full breath until they were under sail and a mile from shore.

Wickham's boat appeared out of the darkness and was quickly alongside.

'All well, Mr Wickham?' Hayden whispered down into the boat.

'All appears well, sir,' came the reply.

The occupants of the boat came silently up and over the rail. Two of the crew took charge of the boat, streaming it with care so that it did not strike the topsides. A very long half of the hour dragged past, and finally the boats took form out of the darkness and a moment later were alongside. Children were handed up, and then women and men. A few precious belongings followed, and last, the boats' crews.

'So few,' Hayden whispered to Ransome.

'Yes, sir. Louis said he would bring twenty tomorrow.'

The ship was got underway and shaped her course immediately to the west to gain as much offing by full light as they could manage. They would then sail north to give them a good slant for returning on the trade.

When they were an hour out from shore, Hayden addressed the gathered French, who had been instructed to sit down on the deck.

'You may speak now, but quietly,' he told them in French.

One man stood. 'I am speaking for us all when I thank you, Captain . . .' Words failed him, or perhaps his English was not up to the task. 'You and your crew. We would all of us have died if you had not escaped us. We cannot thank you enough.'

There was a moment of silence, and then Hayden realized that a woman was weeping.

The tropical sun burned down upon the little schooner, turning the deck into a surface similar to a stove top. Although the sailors ran over it barefoot, Hayden could not hold his hand to the planks for more than a few seconds. An awning had been rigged amidships between the two masts and the French refugees huddled in its meagre shade. A few slept upon the unforgiving planks, some spoke softly, a few children played at cards, for finding themselves upon a ship was nothing but a great adventure to them. All ate and drank parsimoniously, the parents putting aside some of their own food for their children.

On the south-east horizon the tops of Basse-Terre's mountains – impossibly green and crowned with cloud – appeared to hang suspended. Sails could be seen here and there upon the blue, but none seemed to offer any threat, so the schooner sailed on, trying to appear to be hurrying north on some urgent errand of commerce. The officers, young gentlemen and marines had removed their coats to maintain this appearance of innocence, and they were all grateful for it.

Forward, Wickham moved among the refugees, employing his excellent French and seeing to their needs as best he could. Two of the men stood and engaged the young nobleman in serious conversation, and immediately Hayden wondered if there was someone among them ill with fever. Fever aboard this small ship would be catastrophic.

Hayden could see Wickham nodding, and then he gestured toward the stern – toward the captain, Hayden feared. Wickham stepped gingerly among the sprawled bodies and made his way quickly aft.

'You have a most thoughtful look upon your face, Mr Wickham,' Hayden said.

'I have just been given rather unsettling information, Captain, if it proves true.' Wickham turned and nodded toward the two men to whom he had been speaking, both of whom stood watching him expectantly. 'Would you hear these gentlemen, Captain?'

'If you think it important, yes. Send them aft.'

Wickham waved to the men and Hayden retreated to the taffrail, where they might speak in something like privacy.

The men were both dressed in expensive clothing that was now dirty, worn and, in some places, patched. Their very fine riding boots were in ruin and both men looked gaunt and fatigued to their very limits. They introduced themselves – life in the mountains had not eroded their manners – and thanked Hayden again for his kindness.

'How might I be of service?' Hayden enquired of them in French.

'To begin, Capitaine, we must beg that you be most circumspect with the information we are about to impart. Many lives will depend upon your discretion.'

'I am under some obligations to my service and King, but if I can keep your secret without compromising my duty, I will do so.'

The Frenchmen exchanged a look, then one nodded. The younger-looking of the two was spokesman.

'We have a friend, Capitaine, who has hidden his true beliefs so successfully that the Jacobins have recruited his services. He has secretly warned many a family to flee and saved them from capture. This man, at great risk, got word to us that a man we have all trusted and believed in has been playing us falsely. He is neither who he claims to be, nor does he hold the beliefs he so passionately espouses. In fact, he has been betraying us so cunningly that we did not suspect him.'

'I am sorry to hear it, but I am not certain what I might do about it.'

'Our friend believes that this man is in the pay of the English, Capitaine, and is a false informant. His name is de Latendresse and he styles himself a comte.'

Perhaps Hayden did not hide his response to this news well.

'Do you know this man, Capitaine Hayden?'

'We have met. Do you have any proof of his treachery, other than the word of your friend?'

The two men looked at each other again. 'Nothing that a magistrate might hold in his hands. But once we were warned about him, suddenly there were a hundred small coincidences and things that we had explained in some other way that fit more easily into our changed view of him. Our friend . . . he had no doubt. He had been in the room when de Latendresse betrayed a royalist family. These people were taken unawares and . . .' He did not need to tell Hayden what had become of them.

'My commander –' Hayden searched for a tactful way of describing Caldwell's attitude – 'he has a great deal of faith in de Latendresse, I am sorry to say.'

'Do not mention our friend to your superior! Our friend would be in very grave danger.'

'You need not worry. I will not betray your confidence. There is a convoy anchored in the bay off Gosier . . . do you know how long it has been there?'

Between them, they did a hasty calculation. 'Nine days, Capitaine. We are quite certain.'

'De Latendresse was reputedly on Guadeloupe in the last week. Could he have been on the island and not known the convoy had arrived?'

The men tried not to smile. 'The islands are very small, Capitaine. Everyone would know. We knew, and we were isolated deep in the mountains.'

'De Latendresse did not reveal the arrival of this convoy to my people.'

'That is because he is entirely false. He does not want the

English to know that ships came from France bearing troops and guns.'

'What do they intend for these fresh troops, I wonder?'

The two men shared a look. 'They will invade Dominica, Capitaine. Everyone says it is so.'

Twenty-five

The waning moon drifted through a long archipelago of clouds, casting its light down the sounds and channels between. It slipped, now and then, behind the pale islands, illuminating them in a soft glow. In the distance, the lights of *Inconstant* could be seen and, when the moonlight that flowed over the sea found her, Archer could make out the shape of the sails in his nightglass.

He glanced up at the sky, gauging the course of the moon, establishing the positions of the islands of cloud, measuring the time it would take for the moon to transit each mass.

'How distant is Sir William?' Griffiths asked.

'Two leagues,' Barthe replied.

Archer would have said five English miles, but two leagues was near enough.

The three men had gathered at the rail and were gazing at *Inconstant* to windward. Jones always claimed no ship could sail nearer the wind than his, so Archer and Barthe had decided to let him climb to windward of them, which would no doubt feed his substantial vanity and pride. The truth was, the *Themis* was every bit as weatherly.

Archer glanced up at the sky. 'That is great acreage of cloud in the west, Mr Barthe. Do you think it might douse the moon as we require?'

'It might provide an hour of meagre light, Mr Archer. Might I suggest we douse our own lanterns, one by one?'

Archer gave the order, and the larboard stern lantern was snuffed. An area of shadow crept west, slipping over *Inconstant* so that only the pinpoints of light that were her lanterns could be seen, and those but barely.

'Let us douse another lantern,' Archer ordered, and this was quickly done.

The massive shadow that flowed over the sea approached, silent and slowly roiling, down and up, like a languid sea serpent. It reached them, and passed over, more insubstantial than a dream.

'The last lantern,' Archer ordered. 'We will shift our yards and wear ship. I should like to see as many sea-miles as can be managed between ourselves and Sir William, come dawn.'

Archer went and stood at the taffrail, from where he could still see the lights of *Inconstant* as they winked up and down on the trade-driven sea. He could almost imagine it was his first command – even if an acting-command – disappearing over the horizon. Jones might find them on the morrow and install some other in his place. It was the greatest good fortune that Sir William had informed him, in great detail, of his plans for the cruise. If Jones stayed with those plans – to any degree – Archer could avoid him. The only difficulty this threw up was that Jones had chosen the best cruising grounds and, as Archer would not be able to go there, the *Themis* would not likely have as profitable a cruise as her officers might hope, and bringing prizes to Caldwell would likely assure Archer of remaining in command. One choice made seemed to mean another was lost.

The passage north of Guadeloupe would be their cruising

grounds for the next few days, and Archer dearly hoped he would find good fortune and never wake to see the sails of *Inconstant* bearing down upon him.

Twenty-six

In the dark, the schooner crossed an invisible wind-line, and the crew found themselves slipping ever so slowly across an ever calmer sea. With his small crew, Hayden could not man all the guns and sail the ship, so men were assigned to stations to which they could be called of an instant, as circumstances dictated. All the pistols aboard were distributed to the men and muskets were laid ready to hand. Everyone knew their station and duty, assuming they could hear orders being called. A few of the Frenchmen aboard were armed, and a couple of the younger men were stationed to aid the sail handlers. Women and children were sent below.

The little ship slid over the surface with barely a ripple in her wake. There was not a whisper aboard unless it was an order, and everyone who could stared out into the darkness hoping to find any threat before they themselves were discovered.

Hayden had walked forward to gaze a moment through his nightglass. Nothing but a shoreline lost in shadow and the dark mass of the small islands. He passed the glass to Wickham and whispered, 'I will be aft. Keep a careful watch.'

Hayden walked quietly aft, where he found Ransome standing by Childers at the wheel. This was the third night they had crept in to this same beach, and no one aboard felt the least pleased about it. Smugglers who worked along the English coast never came to the same place two nights running but had many landing places which they used in as random an order as they could manage. A smuggler would think what Hayden was doing the height of folly, and Hayden realized that he could hardly disagree.

A small gust swept down off the mountains and would have held them in irons if Childers had not been alert and spun his wheel, putting his helm up and keeping his ship hard on the wind. It was not so good a slant as they had been on, but Hayden expected the wind to come back around when the gust took off. The ship picked up speed on the gust, and a soft, babbling wake was heard behind – not something that could be detected at any distance, Hayden hoped.

Hawthorne loomed out of the darkness, his height and gait unmistakable, even by starlight. 'No one aboard has drawn breath in half of an hour,' the marine whispered.

'When this gust dies we will lay-to, man the boats and await Louis's signal. I shall not risk sailing any nearer.' Hayden waved a hand forward. 'Les Islets à Goayaves lie just there in the dark.'

Hawthorne stared into the dark a moment. 'If you tell me it is so, Captain, I will believe you.' The marine lieutenant was silent for a few seconds, and then whispered, 'I do wish this were the last night we were coming to this place.' He touched his hat and hastened forward, no doubt to see that his men were in position, though Hayden did not doubt that they were. Hawthorne was both liked and respected – not something every officer could manage. His men would be where he positioned them and would not falter if ordered to stand and not give way.

The gust finally withered away, allowing Childers to put the schooner back on her course. Hayden ordered the ship laid-to on the starboard tack with her bow pointed more or less north. A leadsman was set to work in the chains forward, keeping Hayden informed of the depths. There was a shoal outboard of them at fourteen fathoms, and Hayden planned to use it to keep position, though in such a little breeze and small tide he did not expect his ship to move very far.

The boats were brought alongside, and Hayden ordered the crews sent down into them. As the men went one by one over the rail, there was a sudden clatter and a pistol fired in the boat. Hayden went immediately to the bulwark.

'Is anyone hurt?' he whispered.

'No, sir,' came the reply from Midshipman Gould. 'Blew a hole in the planking just below the gunwale, sir.'

'Who was the man who had his pistol cocked?'

'Me, sir,' one of the hands admitted in a small voice.

'Give your pistol to Mr Gould,' Hayden hissed at him. 'You shall not have one again.'

Bloody fool! he thought.

If Louis was watching, and he must be, what would he make of that? A single pistol shot at sea. No shouting. No sounds of a fight. Would he guess it to be an unlucky accident? Or would he pull his people back and retreat to the mountains?

Hawthorne stood at the rail a few paces away, no doubt reassuring himself that this was not the doing of one of his people – which it was not.

'Mr Hawthorne,' Hayden said, trying to calm his voice. 'Let us have another marine in each of the larger boats.'

'Aye, sir.'

Two marines were quickly chosen and sent down into the bow of each boat. Wickham's – the third boat – was small enough that another armed man would simply be in the way. Hayden called for his nightglass and went forward.

Time immediately died away to a little zephyr of drifting minutes. The cosmic wind that pressed it on drew breath, and the night was held in suspension. Hayden began to think that morning would never come.

When he could bear it no more Hayden went quickly below, where there was a lamp lit, and pulled out his watch. It was past the time when they should have seen a signal. His mind made up, he went back up to the deck and quickly forward.

'We will make the countersignal,' he ordered quietly.

The order was acknowledged with a quick knuckle. The lamp was lit and the signal made. For a long moment Hayden did not think that any answer would break through the darkness, but then, dim and distant, the signal flashed.

Hayden leaned over the side. 'Mr Wickham? We have a signal. Keep your wits about you.'

The three boats pulled away and were quickly lost in the darkness. Without meaning to, Hayden began to pace across the width of the deck.

Another oarsman would have been useful, Wickham thought, despite the size of the boat – smaller than a British jolly boat, so narrow that one man could handle two oars. One good oarsman, though, would always be quieter, and that was the captain's main concern. If a rapid escape became a necessity, Wickham planned to take up oars himself.

The beach, which lay half a mile distant, appeared to retreat before them. A low swell broke upon the sand – a ponderous, unrelenting rhythm. Pale crests were visible before the beach, and then the dim expanse of it, running north and south, took form. The boat slid up on the sand and the swell pushed the stern off to one side. All three were in the water immediately, the marine with his rifle shouldered and aimed into the dark forest, Wickham and the oarsman pushing the boat around to allow them to set off, bow first.

A now-familiar voice whispered from a few yards distant.

'*C'est moi*. Louis.'

'How many tonight?'

'Twenty-four, Mr Wickham.'

'So many? I will send the boats at once.'

Louis and another waded into the small surf to push them off.

In but a moment, Wickham found the boats.

'They have two dozen this night,' he told them.

'I hope they have not brought their belongings,' Ransome replied. 'We shall be hard pressed to carry so many.'

'I will return with you,' Wickham told him. 'We might take three or four.'

The boats set off all at once, oars softly swirling water, and were soon gliding to a stop on the sand.

Despite finding Louis there and hearing the phrase that meant all was safe, Wickham was anxious to load his passengers and get shut of that beach as quickly as it could be managed. The French remained back in the shadows until the boats had landed, and then the men came out to help turn them around. The women and children appeared at a word and the men began handing them into the boats.

'Three must come with us,' Wickham whispered in French.

This caused a hushed consultation, and then a woman and

two children hurried over and clambered hastily aboard. The refugees were not yet all aboard when an almost simultaneous flash and report came from just south of them. A musket ball whistled overhead.

Before an officer could shout an order, a volley of musket fire came from down the beach and, in the boat furthest south, there were screams and panicked shouting.

'Push them out! Push them out!' Ransome called over the musket fire, and the sailors and a few Frenchman began shoving the boats out into the small swell. Wickham was doing the same to their boat before he even thought. When the water reached mid-thigh he tumbled over the gunwale and began searching about for oars. They were pulling out into the darkness then. Shouting was heard and then another ragged volley. On the shore he could hear cries and calls to retreat into the trees.

'Pull to starboard,' Wickham grunted, dragging his oar through the water. 'To starboard.'

The sounds of fighting came from the shore, and Wickham feared refugees were being bayoneted. Gunfire came from the trees then, and it was the turn of the Jacobins to take fire. This likely saved his life, Wickham realized, for the Jacobins were on the beach dead aft of them and would likely have killed many in the boats, if they had not been fired upon. He was near to pulling his arms out, keeping up with Watts, and air was tearing at his throat as he gasped.

An orange flash of light dimly illuminated the boats and a deep boom echoed from somewhere out at sea. Wickham turned his head to see the flashes from several guns fading. Almost immediately there was an answer.

'My God, sir! Are they taking our ship?' Watts managed.

'Not if our captain is still standing.'

Everyone's eyes were fixed upon the shore, where musket fire had erupted without warning. Hawthorne came running along the deck.

'Is the shore within range of our guns, sir?' he asked.

'Who would we be aiming them at, Mr Hawthorne? I cannot even see the beach, let alone separate friend from foe.'

It was at that instant that guns fired from behind, slamming into the hull with a rending of timber. Both Hawthorne and Hayden staggered and spun around at the same instant, grabbing the rail. In the muzzle flash of the other ship's guns Hayden could see the shocked faces of every man aboard.

'Man the starboard guns!' he called out.

There was the briefest second of shock, and then the men were running to the guns.

'Traverse that gun aft, Swale,' Hayden ordered. 'Further yet. That will answer. Fire!'

The British guns spoke and the crews went to work, swabbing and loading. All his officers were in the boats, so Hayden was master, lieutenant, bosun, midshipman and captain. He went quickly to the wheel and relieved the helmsman, sending him, and any men to be spared, to raise a headsail.

Even in his instant of surprise, Hayden had realized that the enemy ship had more – and likely larger – guns. With so few men aboard he could not chance being boarded and would not let the other ship alongside, if at all possible. Just as his crew was about to run out their guns, the French ship fired another broadside. Balls beat into the hull and tore through the foresail.

This time Hayden counted them – five small guns – likely 6-pounders. He could make out the masts of the other ship and decided it was a brig – perhaps the very ship they had attempted to cut out but a few nights past. The headsail was sheeted home and the sail handlers ran to raise the main. The ship gathered way and heeled a little to the breeze flowing down from the mountain. The British guns were fired, each as they were loaded – a stuttering fire, but no less effective for it. Hawthorne and two of his marines had manned the aft swivel and were proving quick and able, despite never having fired one before.

Hayden cast an anxious look toward the island, wondering if his boats had escaped the beach or if his men had been cut down. An image of them lying, bleeding on the sand, came to him unbidden. Wickham, Ransome and Gould were among those men, as was his coxswain and other good men. He had sent them to that beach to rescue his mother's people, though he had no orders to do so. If he lost his men and officers in this endeavour he knew the remorse would never be outlived.

The brig was pacing his own ship and angling nearer. 'Hardy?' Hayden called out, hoping his most experienced able seaman was still standing.

'At the gun, sir,' came the call.

'You are now my sailing master, bosun and first lieutenant. If this brig comes any nearer, we will tack. Find sail handlers, and do not hesitate to use Frenchmen. They can haul a rope without understanding English.'

Hardy, who appeared to be a large brute of a man, was a

gentle soul – the guardian of all the ship's boys. He could have been a bosun's mate, but he would not beat a fellow sailor for all the world. The hands would lay down their lives for such a man and do his bidding without question.

'Mr Hardy!' Hayden called out. 'Set a man to swinging the lead, if you please.' He did not want to run his ship aground in the dark, where distances were difficult to measure.

Tacking would have to be timed correctly or the other ship would have an opportunity to rake them from astern. He wanted to put his helm up as the other ship was abreast so it would pass on before it could fire into their stern. No doubt they would tack after, but Hayden assumed they had not enough men to man the guns, stand by to board and handle sail, so it would take a moment for them to get men to their stations.

He sent a marine to bring his nightglass up from the cabin below, and to enquire of the refugees if any he had ordered below had been hurt. The brig was taking on form in the dark, the masts and yards silhouetted against the low stars.

'The French are huddled in the hold, sir, and not a one injured,' the marine reported, handing Hayden his glass. Bracing himself against the wheel so it could not turn, Hayden fixed his glass on the nearing ship. He thought he could make out men lining the rail between the guns, and wondered if extra hands had been signed on for this particular enterprise; there would be no shortage of men, not with a convoy lying at anchor on the other side of Basse-Terre. On the other hand, the master of the ship likely did not want to spread his prize money any further than he must. Hayden hoped he was dealing with a parsimonious privateer.

*

Wickham's oars were not muffled, and knocked and rapped against the thole-pins, drowning out small, distant sounds. The flutter of luffing sails that would indicate their ship was getting underway could not be heard. The report of guns, however, could not be masked, nor could the shouting and calls of men. Those carried to them across the water and filled Wickham's heart with dismay.

He was soon gasping. His arms burned and his muscles and tendons stretched and strained. He did not know how much longer he could keep it up. The Frenchmen on the shore, however, appeared to have lost them in the dark and left off firing.

'Mr Wickham?' called the marine in the bow. 'The ships appear to be retreating out to sea, sir. We are not gaining.'

Wickham heard himself curse.

'Avast rowing!' Ransome called in the dark, and Wickham and Watts laid upon their oars, heaving and gasping.

A boat came gliding out of the murk, accompanied by the sound of muffled weeping – a child.

'Mr Wickham?' came Ransome's voice. 'Have you any wounded?'

'I do not know.' He twisted around. 'Is anyone hurt?'

The Frenchwoman and her children were not and Watts declared the same.

'Just a scratch, sir,' the marine in the bow whispered, as though embarrassed even to be admitting it.

'Just a scratch? And how did you come by this scratch?'

'Musket ball, sir. Nary a drop of blood.'

Wickham whispered across to Ransome. 'As you have no doubt heard, I have one man wounded, and I suspect worse than he will admit.'

The French passengers began whispering back and forth,

enquiring who was in the boats and who left on the beach. Wickham ordered them to be still lest the Jacobins begin firing upon them again. Even so, he could not help but ask, 'Is Louis in your boat, Mr Ransome?'

'No. Mr Gould . . . ?'

'No, sir.'

There was the briefest second of silence.

Then Ransome whispered, 'Mr Gould? How have you fared?'

'One man dead, sir. A Frenchman. Caught a musket ball in the eye, sir.'

'I am very sorry to hear it.'

'May I slip him over the side, sir?'

'Does he have family aboard?'

'No, sir, though some appear to know him.'

'Mr Wickham?' Ransome said softly. 'Will you explain to these people that we must put the man over the side? My French is not up to something so delicate.'

Wickham spoke quietly to the people, explaining that sailors were made terribly uncomfortable by having the dead aboard. The people listened in silence and then one man replied at some length.

'I did not quite understand everything he said,' Ransome whispered.

'They are afraid the body will wash ashore, Mr Ransome, and be recognized, which might put the man's friends or family at risk, especially if they believe any of them were aiding him.'

'Their point is well taken. I will have the dead man in my boat, Gould, if you would prefer it?'

'We will keep him, Mr Ransome. If we can find somewhat

to weigh him down with, I shall slip him over the side once we are beyond soundings.'

'If your Frenchmen are in agreement.'

Guns continued to fire from the two ships, illuminating the sea with dark lightning, and it was true that each flash seemed a little more distant.

'But what shall we do now, Mr Ransome?' Wickham heard Gould ask.

'I do not know, Mr Gould. If the captain is outgunned and in fear of being boarded, then he will have to fly from the enemy ship – in which case we will be thrown upon our own resources. It is thirteen leagues to Dominica – but across a very boisterous channel. I am not confident we will manage it. Our boats are crowded with people who are unaccustomed to the sea. I am reticent to make such a passage under sail in an open boat with a cargo of landsmen.'

'Is there some river nearby where we might hide ourselves through the day?' Gould asked. 'We might then return here tomorrow night in hope of meeting the captain.'

'I am not aware of any such place. Are you, Mr Wickham?'

'I am not. And even if such a place could be found, I greatly fear we would be discovered, and though we would face the uncertain prospect of prison, these people would face the guillotine. I think our best chance is to make for Dominica. We might complete a good part of the crossing by dark, so there would be no fear of discovery before daylight; by that hour we would be halfway there, at the very least.'

Wickham could just make out Ransome in the faint starlight but could not read the look upon his face. The lieutenant was, no doubt, contemplating all the possibilities and, Wickham assumed, did not much like any of them. The passages between the islands were open to the great fetch of the Atlantic and the winds funnelled between the islands and were stronger than the normal trade. They would have a quartering wind and sea, which meant broaching would be ever a danger. If a boat overturned it would be difficult in the extreme to right and bail it in such conditions, and especially so with frightened people in the sea, most of whom would not swim. If they did not make for Dominica they were in great danger of being discovered by the Jacobins, who would certainly be on the lookout for them.

'I believe you are correct, Mr Wickham, we have but one course,' Ransome declared. 'We must sail for Dominica.'

'The privateer's boat has no sail,' Wickham observed, 'and might be a bit small for such a crossing.'

'I will empty your boat of its people and take it in tow, Mr Wickham. I shall cut it free if it proves a danger.' He turned and spoke to the other boat. 'I do not mean to slight your abilities in any way, Mr Gould, but Mr Wickham has had much more experience in open boats in rough conditions, so I shall put him in command of your boat. You shall be his second. We shall rig for sail but must be prepared to reef if we feel broaching is a danger. We will make every effort to keep the boats together, for we may need to come to the other's aid.' He turned back to Wickham. 'I shall take your passengers in my boat, Mr Wickham; Watts and Cooper shall join you in the cutter, Mr Gould. And Mr Cooper? Show your scratch to Mr Gould, if you please.'

Passengers were transferred, masts stepped, sail set and the schooner's boat taken in tow on a doubled painter. It was a good little boat, if a little battered from hard use, and they did not want to lose it.

The instant sails were sheeted, the boats gathered way, leaving the small islands to larboard. Wickham left Childers at the helm, as there was no better man for the job on their ship, unless it was their captain or Mr Barthe. He would take his own trick, as it was forty miles to Dominica and would very likely take eight or ten hours – perhaps longer, loaded as they were.

They had left too many refugees on the beach – only fifteen had made it into the boats – and of these one had since been killed and three were wounded – all in Ransome's boat, which had been nearest the Jacobins on the beach and had shielded the other boats somewhat.

The winds coming over the island would gust suddenly, sweeping down upon them with no warning so that the men handling the sheets were ever on the alert to let them run. The wind would then die away or push their head off for a few moments so that they could not sail within two points of their course but it would come around again, die away, gust, then disappear yet again.

The southern tip of Basse-Terre was a little more than three leagues distant. They must then give a small group of islands called the Saints a reasonable offing. Dawn was yet some four hours off and sunrise, at this latitude, not long after. The compass was shipped. They bore a lamp, which carried their fire, but this was kept shuttered until needed. Gould used it briefly to examine and bind Cooper's wound, which he pronounced innocent enough, though any wound could go septic and, this far south, many did. Wickham counted himself lucky that he was unhurt.

A mile to the north and out to sea a single gun fired and then fell silent. Wickham did not know where the schooner had gone, but the running battle he had expected had been cut quickly short. As there were no sounds of victorious celebration he assumed that his captain had given the enemy the slip. Where Captain Hayden might be heading in their prize, he could not say.

The stars were bright and sharp, hanging in the depths of the sky and illuminating the boat and its occupants with a faint, chill light. The passengers were arranged to weather and the British sailors made up the moveable ballast, which might have to shift from one side to the other of an instant in these fickle winds. One or two of the refugees slept, exhausted from walking who knew how far. Others lay still, eyes open, perhaps frightened; Wickham could not say. One woman whispered a story in the ear of her son; Wickham caught a few words now and then. A story of a brave boy sent to sea who saved his ship and was made an *aspirant* – a midshipman. Wickham hoped only to see his cutter and all aboard safely across the Guadeloupe Passage – hardly more than thirty miles. That would be difficult enough for him. He glanced over at the other boat, which was keeping pace to starboard. The idea that his boat might go over while Ransome's did not filled Wickham with anxiety. And then he chastised himself. He was thinking of his own pride and not the safety of the people who were in his charge. Vanity.

The sea was somewhat confused, as far as could be told in the dark: a low, ponderous swell overridden by smaller seas; though largely striking the port bow, some appeared to come from the west and still others from the east, despite the shore being distant less than half a mile. Once they were out of the lee of the two islands, Wickham expected the seas to originate from a single direction, though grow greatly in size.

He wondered how many people had been left dead or wounded on the beach and if Louis had been among them. Certainly some of the royalists had run back into the trees, but whether they could escape through the bush he did not know. Under the trees the darkness would be complete and one could make one's way only by feel. The captain had been correct when he said that they were returning too often to the same place, not that he would take any pleasure in being right. He had, as everyone knew, great feeling for his mother's people.

With all sails drawing, the schooner was outpacing the brig by a small but noticeable margin, Hayden was certain. The prize was also, to a degree, more weatherly than the square-rigged brig, which was unable to close with them on this slant for that very reason. For the brig to bring her guns to fire on the schooner they would have to bear off to the west, which would allow the schooner to get that much further ahead – and it appeared the master of the privateer was not choosing to do that. Hayden was beginning to think that he might lose the brig while it was still dark and return to find his boats. As this thought was forming in his mind, the wind died completely away.

The prize drifted on, sheer mass carrying her through the dark waters. Hayden fixed his glass upon the brig, which appeared to have some small wind yet.

Hawthorne left the aft swivel gun, which he had manned with two of his marines, and crossed over to Hayden, who stood staring through his nightglass at the inverted image of the brig sailing upon a dark, liquid sky.

'Will the wind carry her up to us, Captain?' he asked softly.

'It might. We should prepare to repel boarders, in that event.'

'I think we are well prepared, Captain.'

The entire crew fixed their attention upon the distant ship, which every moment appeared to take on form. She was a shadowy apparition, then a black mass moving through the dark air, and then a cloud of sails, and finally a ship bearing down on them.

'How is it that she has wind and we do not?' Hawthorne asked no one in particular.

'The devil aids them,' Hardy cursed.

'I thought them Papists, not Satanists,' the marine replied.

Hayden chuckled in spite of himself.

'I believe we have lost steerage, sir,' the helmsman said.

'Let us hope the French sail into this same calm or their wind precedes them.'

A gun fired on the brig, and a ball went tearing through the air some few yards to larboard.

Hayden sent a man below with his nightglass and removed a pistol from his belt. The helmsman was right: the ship had lost steerage and was turning slowly to larboard, which would allow the British to bring guns to bear if it would but continue in that fashion.

A little breeze pressed against the sails, which had begun to thrash slowly from side to side with the rolling of the ship. Everyone glanced up toward the mountains as though they might see a wind. Immediately, it died away, causing sails and spirits to slump. A second ball fired from the chase piece, and it appeared to pass between the masts, miraculously damaging nothing.

A gust of wind struck them, pressing the ship so far over that Hayden thought masts might carry away or sails part. One instant, the ship lay motionless, and then she was heeled over and tearing through the darkness.

'Let the main sheet run!' Hayden hollered above the wind now moaning through the rigging. He jammed the pistol back into his belt and took hold of the rail with both hands, wondering if the ship might be thrown upon her beam ends. He glanced to the brig, which had a moment ago come so near, and was almost certain she had been caught aback.

Off the schooner went, the wind still pressing her down so that water gushed in the scuppers and the shrouds stretched and creaked like rusted hinges.

'Sir!' Hayden heard the helmsman cry, and turned to find the young man braced against the wheel as the ship tried to round up.

Hayden pushed off the rail and struggled up the sloping deck to aid him, and the men eased the main sheet at that same moment, the schooner righting herself to some degree and the helm suddenly manageable. Under normal circumstances, there would always be two men at the helm – and an officer standing by to give them orders – but with such a small crew and a privateer bearing down upon them, they had needed every man possible for the ship's defence.

With the ship back on her feet, Hayden had a moment to take stock. He called another of the hands to the wheel and made his way aft. The brig appeared to have recovered from being caught aback, if that was indeed what had happened, and was also on a westerly course. The gust that had laid them over reached a crescendo, howling for a moment through the rigging and forcing him to brace himself against the force of it, and then it began to take off.

'Keep your wits about you,' he instructed the helmsmen. 'This wind might haul aft, and quickly too.' He glanced forward along the deck. 'Pass the word for Hardy, if you please . . .'

A moment later Hardy came hurrying out of the gloom.

'If this wind takes off – and hauls aft – the brig will certainly return to her pursuit. We will fire all our larboard guns to give us a screen of smoke, then wear ship. If we have a little luck on our side in this darkness we will cut across her bow before she knows what we are about. We will rake her – twice if we can manage it – turn to larboard and give her another broadside as we pass.'

Hardy hesitated a moment and then said very softly, 'It is a great deal to ask of a small crew, sir.'

'Yes, but they are steady men and can run between guns and sail handling. I will explain what is to be done to the Frenchmen, and they can give us their aid. I do not believe this privateer will expect us to turn on him, and that is much to our advantage.'

The crew were quickly assigned stations and duties and stood ready to execute the complex evolution Hayden required – *and* fire the guns – but the wind took off only a little, pressing both ships on. A quarter of an hour passed and Hayden feared the wind would not alter or take off that night, when it fell suddenly away and the ship came slowly upright and slowed, as though she had run up on the softest mud.

Although the brig was out of range, Hayden ordered the guns fired and then, as quickly as it could be managed without carrying away any gear, they wore ship and brought the wind on to the larboard beam. They were now bearing down upon the brig, which lay off their starboard bow.

The master of the brig, perceiving what Hayden did, turned north, so that Hayden could not rake him from astern. But that was never Hayden's plan.

The two ships converged and appeared about to pass broadside to broadside. Hayden leaned out over the starboard rail to get the clearest view possible. Aboard his ship the gun crews reloaded madly and then all stood ready to fire again.

The helmsman was also watching the approaching privateer.

'Shall I port my helm, sir?' he asked, unable to contain himself a moment more.

'Upon my order . . .' Hayden said.

He could see the murky shape of the privateer, but distances were so difficult to judge in the dark. If he turned too soon their small guns would not have the effect he hoped for. If they turned too late the ships might collide. There was no margin for error, and it would be difficult enough to measure the speed and distance in broad daylight.

'Fire the starboard guns,' Hayden ordered, and flame and smoke erupted from the muzzles, creating a dense, black cloud that obscured any view of the privateer.

He ordered the main sheet eased, counted very slowly to twenty . . .

'Port your helm,' he said, loud enough to be heard, but no more.

The little schooner was very handy and turned into the heart of the smoke cloud. He did not know if this small ruse would work, and he was counting on the smoke being carried away by the wind so they could see the enemy to fire.

Hayden had crossed to the larboard rail and stood staring into the night and the drifting, acrid smoke, which caused his eyes to water to such a degree that he could hardly see and was forced to wipe them constantly. He had ordered the guns traversed so that they might fire, reload, traverse aft and fire a second time, but wondered now if this was a mistake. Certainly, the brig should be almost abeam . . . unless she, too, had turned to bring a broadside to bear.

A little, irregular thinning of smoke, like a jagged window.

'Fire!' Hayden called.

The little 6-pounders jumped back, and the men went immediately to reloading.

The brig was lost in the smoke again.

Hayden touched one of the men nearby on the shoulder. 'Jump up the larboard shrouds and see if you can discover our brig.'

The man was up on the rail, swinging around the shrouds and climbing as fast as hands and legs could propel him. When he was almost at the maintop he turned and gazed south a moment, and then called out.

'Almost abeam, sir. Half a point aft.'

'Traverse guns aft,' Hayden called.

Immediately bars were employed, the guns scraping over the deck a few inches at a time. Each was fired as it came to bear, and Hayden was not certain all had found their mark, but the effect on the brig was audible as the cries of the wounded penetrated smoke and darkness.

'Helm to starboard,' Hayden ordered the men at the wheel.

Gun crews went efficiently about reloading and running out guns.

The ship turned – too slowly, it seemed to Hayden. As she turned, however, the smoke that clung to her swept away to leeward. The brig emerged from this cloud, not twenty yards distant, sails shaking, a yard angling down and foretopmast hanging in its gear. At such close range, the small guns had done much damage.

'Fire as she bears,' Hayden ordered, and the guns spoke one by one, the French running out guns but managing to fire only the two aftmost.

And then they were past.

'We are away, Captain!' Hawthorne almost crowed as he came aft. When Hayden did not answer, he enquired, 'Are you not pleased, Captain? You look out of sorts.'

'I am just wondering – if we press our French passengers temporarily – would we have enough men to sail both the brig and schooner to Dominica?'

Hawthorne appeared dumbfounded for an instant. 'You are suggesting we can take the brig . . . ?'

'Her rig, for the moment, is in ruins and I believe we shot away her wheel. We could tack back up to her, lay our ship across her stern, and rake her until she strikes.'

Hawthorne almost laughed, partly from disbelief. 'And I thought they were chasing us!'

'And so did they, I expect.'

Hardy came hurrying aft at that instant. 'Captain!' he called out. 'I believe there is a fire, sir!'

Keeping the boats moving and making the best of the inconstant winds required an alert man at the helm and the constant trimming of sails. There was almost always too much wind or hardly any at all. Everyone aboard understood the importance of putting sea room between themselves and Guadeloupe, so no man shirked in the performance of his duties.

It had come as something of a surprise to Wickham, when he had first come into the Navy, that a boat so small as a cutter was organized with as much structure and discipline as a 110-gun ship. Everyone had their station and, on longer passages such as this, their watch. Orders were just as precise, and their execution even more rapid. The off-duty men were given a place to rest and did not shift from it without permission or orders to do so. An expedition on a small boat was not a holiday from ship's discipline, and officers made certain that the hands were never for a moment in doubt of it.

Two hours after the decision to make for Dominica had been made, one of the crew pointed aft into the darkness.

'Is that fire, Mr Wickham?' he asked.

The midshipman twisted around and, indeed, there was – fire, some miles distant.

'Is it on the water or on the land?' Wickham wondered aloud. 'Mr Ransome!' he called at the top of his voice. 'Fire, sir. To the north.'

Ransome's barge was some fifty yards to leeward – just visible in the darkness. A moment of silence followed and then Ransome's voice carried to them. 'Is that a ship, Mr Wickham?'

'I cannot say, sir. Perhaps it is on the land . . .'

No one spoke what was in everyone's mind: was it Captain Hayden's prize or an enemy vessel that was afire?

For a few moments everyone but the helmsmen stared aft

326

in horrified fascination and then the ball of orange flame swelled of an instant, blazed hotter and within three minutes disappeared altogether, leaving a dark stain upon the stars.

'Let us hope that was the enemy,' Ransome called out. 'May God have mercy on their Papist souls.'

Whispering began among the royalists and Wickham was forced to remind them – sharply – that they were in enemy waters and that silence was required so that orders could always be heard. Muttered apologies in French followed – and then a deep, troubled silence.

If the captain's prize had caught fire and sunk so rapidly there would almost certainly be loss of life. The enemy ship would no doubt search for survivors, but then they would begin looking for the escaped royalists. It would be a race for Dominica, the boats having a head-start but the ship being swifter.

The four and a half leagues to the southern tip of Basse-Terre used up much of the night's remaining store of darkness, so capricious were the winds. Dawn found the boats hardly beyond Pointe à l'Aunay, though a league and a half to the west. Wickham knew they must pass by the islands called the Saints next. He would much rather have done so in darkness, but there was nothing for it now.

The trade winds finally reached them and the boats began to race across the blue, sails full and drawing. A quartering sea would pick them up and almost toss them forward, the boat attempting to yaw and the helmsman fighting it with all his strength. The heat of the day was not far off and there would be no shade from the sails all through the forenoon.

The Saints were half drowned in an early-morning mist which Wickham knew the sun would burn away before it had risen too high. Already, the sails of fishing boats could be seen, running out to their fishing grounds. Some of these boats they might pass quite closely, but Wickham was not overly concerned. The English sailors were well armed and certainly more than a match for any fishermen they met.

Water from the cask was rationed out carefully to the French and to the hands. They had learned a hard lesson in the recent cutting-out expedition and the captain had made certain the boats set off with small stores of both water and food on the chance that they could not return to the ship when planned. All would be thirsty by the time the boats reached Dominica, but not dangerously so.

Once daylight was upon them, Wickham twisted around often to survey the horizon to the north and then to quiz the ocean in all quarters. Fishing boats could be seen at almost all points, and several larger vessels – these all at a distance – but no sail that should be feared. The greatest danger was the sea itself, which was steep and swift running. The wind blew a gale in this narrow passage, and that day had more northing in it, bringing the quartering sea aft somewhat and making the threat of broaching more likely. The helmsman was constantly at work, never for a moment allowing his mind to wander and always steering to anticipate the seas rather than reacting to them, which would many a time have been too late.

The buffeting and constant howling of the wind, Wickham found, deadened the senses somehow, and men turned their backs to it and fell into a kind of lassitude. The sun rose relentlessly and the heat grew by the hour until it baked them, even as the warm wind dried their skin and mouths. Water was rationed with absolute care and Wickham would not allow parents to preserve their portion for their children lest he have these men and women become ill from thirst.

Seasickness beset refugees cruelly and they were often helped to leeward to disgorge their rebellious stomachs of their rations. One or two marines, who were not so used to the motion of small boats, also suffered, but not so badly. The hands, however, took no notice of it but fulfilled their duties silently and even slept when not on watch.

The small boat that Wickham had commanded was towed for some time by Ransome, though it made the barge difficult to manage, for it would fall behind and drag it back or suddenly forge ahead on the face of a wave and release its pull on the barge, catching the helmsman unaware. More than once a broach was the near-result. Sometime in the forenoon, it slewed sideways just as the painters pulled taut and, helped by a breaking crest, the boat overturned. Immediately, the painters parted and snapped like whips into the transom of the barge.

'We will leave it!' Ransome called out to Wickham, who acknowledged this with a wave and nod.

The little boat was abandoned, overturned, its bottom barely awash in the fair blue, where it was carried slowly off by the seas and currents.

The sun attained its apogee and Wickham ordered his small rations distributed among the many, though they would have needed a miracle of loaves and fishes to satisfy everyone.

Often the helmsman was relieved, for it was taxing of both strength and wit to keep the boat from broaching and, many a time, when the gusts came, sheets were let run. The day wore on and Wickham, though he was supposed to have his mind on his duty, wondered constantly if the ship that had burned was the schooner with his captain and shipmates aboard.

Flames climbed up the tarred rigging and into the sails, which set the sea afire all around. In the terrible light Hayden could see dark figures running about the deck, and boats swinging out. There were shouts and calls – some orders and others clearly panic. Hayden, Hawthorne and Hardy all stood transfixed, watching the fires spread over the enemy ship beyond all hope of control.

'What do we do, sir?' Hardy asked, his voice filled with awe and dread.

This question seemed to shake Hayden out of his dream. 'Buckets,' he answered. 'Wet down the sails and sluice the deck!'

Quickly, the crew was organized and buckets were passed up the ratlines to be splashed on to the sails. The decks, too, were sluiced and water dripped down from above.

When less than half a mile distant from the brig, there was a sudden eruption of flame through the side of the enemy's hull. Not a great, horrifying explosion, but still the heat from it carried to the British and the report could be felt through one's body. Everyone, including the officers, ducked and threw up their hands, but whatever debris was blown out did not reach them. The burning ship began to go down. Her mainmast toppled forward and the ship listed heavily to larboard. Hayden could see men leaping into the sea and others into the only boat that appeared to have been launched.

'Hardy!' Hayden called. 'Immediately this gust takes off we shall wear ship and search for survivors!'

The gust, which was not so great as many they had experienced that night, did not die away for some minutes, and then the British wore ship and came back as quickly as the wind would allow, reaching the brig on one tack.

Here and there, pieces of the ship floated, some still burning, and men who were in the water or clinging to bits of wreckage called out. The single boat that had been launched was filled to overflowing, but still made its way through the wreckage, pulling men from the water.

Hayden had no boats to aid in the rescue – Wickham had taken ashore the only one the privateers had left when they had gone chasing the British. Quickly, though, he called out in French and assured the men in the boat that he would take them aboard and they would not be harmed. The boat was swiftly emptied alongside the schooner, and then set out again. A few men swam to the British prize, which lay-to in the fickle wind. Many more called out and waved, just visible in the light of burning debris.

Of the men who came aboard, many had small blisters, but a few had been burned horribly and lay on the deck moaning and praying in French. Hayden had no doctor aboard, likely little physic, and the only man with any understanding of medicine – Gould – had gone off with the boats. There would be little they could do for these poor men, and Hayden feared that most would die in agony.

One of the royalists came up on the deck at that moment, took one look at what was going on and crossed straight to Hayden.

'Capitaine,' he began in French, 'I am a physician, and, though these men would hunt me and put me upon the guillotine, I cannot leave them to suffer. If you will allow it, I will do what little I can . . .'

'By all means, yes. I will send men to search below for any physic that might be found.'

A few other men and one woman came up the ladder and went among their enemies. From the captain's cabin, a box was carried up that contained a few instruments and even less physic – bottles with names even Hayden did not recognize. The physician, though, was in no doubt and was quite certain none would offer any aid. Burns were commonly treated by oil of olive, of which there was none.

The night turned dusky and then greyed to a pale dawn. Beyond Basse-Terre the sun coloured the horizon then floated up, searing the sky. The last of the survivors were found and brought aboard. Hayden and Hawthorne stood watching the brig's boat being lifted aboard.

'What shall we do now, sir?' the marine lieutenant asked.

'We shall search for our shipmates, Mr Hawthorne.'

'Do you think they made it off the beach, Captain?'

Hayden shook his head. 'I do not know. We shall head back to the bay where we saw them last and see if the boats are on the beach. If not, we will sail south along the coast and hope to find them.'

'If they did escape the beach, sir, what would they do?'

Hayden had been contemplating this very question. 'They cannot know what happened to us. We were caught unawares by a more powerful ship. They must have seen the fire and cannot know which ship it was.' He considered only a few seconds. 'I believe they would set out for Portsmouth on the northern end of Dominica; getting out of French waters would be imperative. It is not so far, though the winds in the channel can be strong and seas short and steep. Even so, I think they would be up to it. We shall see.'

The boats were overburdened. Wickham was taking his trick at the helm and felt how ponderously the cutter responded to the tiller. Each wave would pick the small boat up and carry it forward, then slide by, leaving it to settle a moment in the trough. It was that moment when the wave lifted the stern that the boat would begin to yaw and the helmsman would pull with all his strength to keep the boat from broaching.

The boats sat deep in the water, so the waves, as they raced beneath, rose up within inches of the gunwale. Only once, when they had transported 18-pounder guns at the island of Corsica, could he remember the boats sitting so deep, and that had been on calm waters. The men all sat farthest to windward, the women were in the centre and the children perched to leeward. It was the best arrangement Wickham could make, as there was not room for everyone on the windward side. Heavily ballasted boats were inherently more stable, as any fisherman could attest, but this assumed the ballast was both deep in the hull and fixed in position. Human ballast fulfilled these conditions but poorly.

Sometime around midday, one of the men exclaimed something incoherent and pointed to leeward. Wickham turned just in time to see Ransome's barge broach to and then slowly go over, throwing all her occupants first to leeward and then into the sea. Of an instant, this boat was left behind.

'Childers,' he said as calmly as he was able, 'we shall have the sails off her and oars shipped. Oarsmen, take your places.'

'Can we not sail back to the barge, Mr Wickham?' Childers

stood and fixed his eye upon the overturned vessel so it would not be lost among the seas.

'I will not risk wearing ship with so many inexperienced people aboard, for all the men must shift from one side to the other at the right instant, or we will be swimming. When I give the order we will back the starboard oars at the same instant as we go forward with the larboard.'

He then explained in French exactly what must be done. As soon as he had nods of understanding from the passengers and the oarsmen had taken their places, Wickham began watching the seas coming up behind, looking for a suitable moment to turn, for a miscalculation would see them rolled as well.

When a smaller sea approached the order was given and the boat turned in place. The crew were aided by French passengers, who rowed with a will, for their people were in the water, too, and Wickham could only guess how few were swimmers.

It took almost a quarter of an hour for the cutter to reach the overturned boat where men and women could be seen struggling to find some purchase on the hull. A few children lay over the bottom like dolls.

As they drew near, Wickham stood and tried to count the heads, which was difficult in the high-running sea. Fewer than he hoped – perhaps many fewer.

As they ranged up, they found the barge, beam on to wind and seas, bottom awash, and a few frightened souls clinging to whatever purchase they could find. Hair was plastered flat and, even in the hot sun, all seemed pale with fear.

Childers threw a rope to one of the hands in the water so that the boats might be linked together. Ransome and several others were clinging to the rudder, and the lieutenant waved a hand at Wickham.

'Have you places for those who cannot swim, Mr Wickham? I shall send you children and women first.'

'We have, but we are overburdened as it is, Mr Ransome.'

'There is nothing for it,' Ransome called back. 'They are not strong enough to hold on much longer.'

'Then send them one at a time; we do not want our own boat overturned.'

The English sailors maintained order among the passengers, passing the children over first and then aiding those who could not swim. Swimming was such a simple art Wickham was always surprised how few had mastered it.

'We will get a rope across the hull and to the masthead, and pull the barge over, Mr Wickham,' Ransome informed him.

Ransome himself was not a strong swimmer, Wickham knew.

'Have you someone to swim down, Mr Ransome?' the midshipman asked. 'I will do it if you wish.'

'Very kind of you, Mr Wickham, but Gould assures me he can manage.'

Gould stripped off his blue coat and threw the sodden mass to one of the hands in the cutter. Catching the rope as it was thrown across the overturned barge, he dived under the boat. All waited, holding their breath in sympathy.

'Should he not be up by now?' Childers whispered after a moment.

'A moment more . . .'

Wickham began to count the passing seconds and, when he could bear it no more, he stood and pulled off his shoes, but, before he could go over the side, Gould broke the surface, gasping and coughing. An oar was thrust out from the cutter for him to cling to and in a moment he recovered and passed the end of the rope to Childers. The men remaining in the water were rearranged so their weight might be employed to right the boat, the rope to the masthead was fastened to the stern of the cutter and, at a word from Ransome, the cutter began to pull and the men stood up on the gunwales of the overturned boat and, with aid from a wave, the boat rolled slowly over, where it floated with only an inch or so of the gunwales above the water.

The cutter was manoeuvred back alongside and made fast. Buckets were employed from the cutter, though with each passing wave the barge appeared to fill again, but then slowly the gunwales began to rise and, as they did so, less water flowed back in with each wave. After an hour, the boat was floating high enough that men were able to stand in the boat and bucket water out, which they did for only a short while before their places were taken by others.

'Mr Wickham,' said one of the hands bailing, 'shall I cut loose the water cask and put it over the side? It is weighing the boat down, sir.'

'Nash,' Wickham replied peevishly, 'do you not know that a cask filled with seawater weighs more than the same cask filled with fresh? The drinking water is providing buoyancy at this time, not weight. Bail on.'

'Aye, sir.'

The men continued to bail, though it was heavy work in a boat rising and falling and rolling as well.

'Mr Wickham,' Cooper said, standing in the crowded boat. 'Might I draw your attention to these boats downwind of us? They appear to have called a parliament, sir.'

Wickham twisted around and, there, a mile off, a group of

fishing boats had congregated, but there was no sign of active fishing.

'What do you think they are about?' Ransome asked. The lieutenant had pulled himself over the transom and was seated on a thwart, water washing about his buttocks.

'I doubt they have gathered to plan our rescue,' Wickham stated.

Cooper trained Wickham's glass on the distant boats. 'More like crows, perched on branches, trying to decide if they can eat us or not. Half an hour ago a boat set off for the Saints with all haste – it did not appear to be loaded down with fish.'

'If they begin to draw near, Mr Cooper,' Ransome ordered, 'fire a warning shot.'

Wickham asked for his glass and fixed it on the distant islands. The Saints were an odd little outpost of France. There was no sugar production, nor any wealth to speak of, so slaves were rare. The French occupants were employed in fishing and market gardening, but there was a small fortress, Wickham thought, and certainly a French garrison.

'Mr Ransome,' he said, lowering his glass. 'I think we should get underway as soon as humanly possible. I believe we shall have French soldiers coming our way as swiftly as it can be arranged.'

'Damn Sir William and this entire enterprise,' Ransome muttered, clearly exhausted and out of patience. 'We shall find ourselves in a French gaol yet.'

This spurred on the efforts of the men bailing, and buckets of water splashed over the side with a speed Wickham would not have thought possible in the heat. An old sailing adage ran: 'There is no pump so efficient as a frightened man with a bucket.'

Even so, a boat the size of a frigate's barge held several tons of water and it had to be emptied out one bucket at a time, which, no matter how frightened the bailers, could not be managed quickly.

Ransome shifted on his seat and beckoned Wickham near.

'We lost eight when the boat capsized,' he said quietly, 'two of them woman and three children.'

'I am very sorry to hear it,' Wickham whispered.

'I believe the stern was thrown up on a steep sea and the rudder left the water. There was naught we could do.'

'It was bad luck, not poor seamanship, I am quite certain,' Wickham replied. 'No one is to blame for it. This is a dangerous crossing for overloaded, open boats. We have been lucky not to do the same ourselves.' Wickham waved a hand at the distant fishermen. 'Even they turn over occasionally, who sail here almost every day of the year.'

'It is kind of you to say, Wickham, but it was the boat under my command that capsized and people under my care who were lost. There is no one else to blame . . .' The young officer looked entirely miserable, sitting drenched to the skin, his hat lost, hair plastered tight to his skull.

'We all knew this crossing would be dangerous, but we had no choice. To try to hide on Guadeloupe would have resulted in capture – and the guillotine for the royalists. Every one of them would have made the choice to attempt the crossing. Do not doubt it.'

Ransome nodded, but Wickham did not believe his words provided much comfort.

The bailing continued for some time, the sea occasionally

breaking over the boat and replacing water that had so recently, and at great cost, been thrown out. Handling the bucket required two hands, so the men in the boat were constantly being thrown off balance as the boats rose and fell, which slowed the process terribly. Finally, Wickham sent other men into the barge, who knelt and steadied the men bailing, and the water level in the boats dropped much more quickly.

The French passengers were ill and frightened, the children exhausted and crying. Everyone was overly hot and not a few peevish. Dominica, which had been in view since the sun had risen, seemed never to grow nearer.

'Sail to the north, Mr Wickham,' Childers reported, and pointed off toward the western edge of Guadeloupe.

Wickham retrieved his glass and gazed at this distant vessel – not an easy task aboard a small boat on such seas.

'Is it our captain?' Ransome asked.

'I can make out course and topsail. Whether it is a schooner or a brig I cannot say. It is, at the moment, shaping its course toward us, so we shall know soon enough.'

By mid-afternoon the barge was finally declared sea-ready, and the crew and occupants returned to their boat. The two vessels made sail, and were again sliding over the steep seas, the helmsmen both more vigilant and more anxious. The crew of the barge continued to bail for some time after, and Wickham could see the pails being emptied regularly over the side.

The capsize had taken several hours to remedy, and Wickham glanced up at the sun now, wondering if they would make Dominica by sunset.

*

The boats were not on the beach, where Hayden had sent them into an ambush. There was no way of knowing what had happened – if the British sailors had been taken prisoner, or, if they had escaped, how many might have been wounded or even killed. If the French ambush had succeeded and the boats were captured, the French might well have sailed them south, it being the quickest way back to Gosier.

Hayden shaped his course down the coast, staying inshore as far as was safe. Unfortunately, near the shore the winds were even more fickle and often absent altogether. Ship's boats could be rowed through the calms, but the schooner, though a small ship, was far too large for that.

The coastline was empty of the *Themis*'s boats and their crews – just long stretches of sand backed by palms and dense forest with hardly a living soul to be seen. Pointe à l'Aunay came abreast late in the afternoon and the wind finally found them not long after. It came like a great sigh, after so many hours of drifting and frustration.

Hawthorne found Hayden doing a circuit of the ship, and the two stopped on the forecastle for a moment to speak. Hayden had found a glass aboard and employed it to quiz the horizon at all points.

'I do hope you are not finding French warships in the offing?' the marine said.

'Not at this precise moment.'

'Excellent, I do need a day's holiday from the war occasionally. A terrible admission of weakness upon my part.'

'We all need such days, Mr Hawthorne, and, fortunately, the war provides many of them.'

'Not so many under your command, Captain, if I may say

so. You appear to follow the fighting so that we have far more than our share of it.'

'Poor luck, is all I can say. Speaking of war, how do we stand for powder?'

'More than enough for this war, I should think.'

'That much?'

'Well, perhaps I exaggerate to some small degree. Enough to see us home.'

'And I thought we were about to go into the business of selling powder. Well, we shall have to make our fortunes some other way. Piracy, perhaps?'

Hawthorne laughed. 'When I was a boy it was my only dream.'

'If every boy who ever dreamed of becoming a pirate grew up to do so, Mr Hawthorne, it would be a frighteningly lawless world.'

'Indeed, sir. I understand they have all retired to Jonathan's Coffee House, in recent years.'

'They have called it the "Stock Exchange" for some time now.'

'Ahh . . . piracy by another name.'

'Not a good place for the unwary to take their morning coffee, that is certain.' Hayden raised his glass to search the sea again. 'Have you heard? The brig that had the misfortune to burn last night was the very brig Sir William ran aground and almost saw us all killed.'

'Even war has its ironies, I suppose, Captain.'

'More than its share.'

'No sign of our boats, sir?'

'There are many small boats to the south, but the Saints has a fishing fleet and I cannot, at this distance, distinguish one boat from another.'

Hayden handed the glass to Hawthorne, who began to

search the blue. 'You still believe they will have sailed for Dominica?'

'If they survived the ambush on the beach? Yes. Where else is there for them to go?'

'England does seem a bit distant . . .'

One of the two marines hunkered down in the bow pointed off to the north-west of a sudden. 'Mr Wickham! Boat, sir.'

The midshipman, who was standing his trick at the helm, twisted around to see.

'I'll have it, sir, if you like?' It was Childers, reaching immediately for the tiller, not so much helpful as wanting the helmsman concentrating on one thing only.

Wickham allowed the coxswain to relieve him at the helm, and found his glass. A small vessel, perhaps a cutter, was emerging from the narrow Passe des Dames at the eastern tip of Grand Islet, the nearest of the Saints.

Wickham lowered his glass, stood, and called over to Ransome, whose boat they were now making an effort to keep near, in case of further calamities.

'A French Navy cutter, Mr Ransome!' he called out. 'I cannot tell if there are soldiers from the garrison aboard, but nor can I say there are none.'

'Are you certain, Mr Wickham?' Ransome called back. 'I have lost my glass.'

Wickham lifted his and examined the little ship again. It was a single-masted vessel, crossing yards, a bit wall-sided, straight-stemmed. 'Fifty or sixty feet, flying the French flag, and uniformed men aboard, Mr Ransome. From this angle I cannot tell you what guns she carries.'

'Let us hope it is not us they are looking for. No matter, there is little we can do but carry on as swiftly as we dare.'

The lassitude of the royalists dissolved in that instant and the hands were suddenly more alert as well. Neither boat dared carry more sail, but more human ballast was shifted to windward and the helmsmen became determined to squeeze every last quarter-knot out of their vessels.

Ransome reported that aboard his boat there remained no dry powder and that they had lost most of their weapons when they were thrown into the sea. A glance at the sun told Wickham that sunset was perhaps three hours off – and the northern tip of Dominica about the same. To the north, the strange sail was clearly closing, the ship heeled to the trade and rocking over the cresting seas.

'It appears we might have two Frenchmen bearing down on us, though we might hope the one to the north is nothing more than a transport,' Wickham said quietly to Gould and Childers.

The coxswain did not look convinced by this. 'Will darkness reach us before either of these ships?'

Wickham tried to gauge the speed of the closing cutter – the nearer of the two vessels. 'It will be a close-run thing,' he concluded.

The sun appeared to hover on the wind, hanging in the sky and barely moving westward at all. The royalists in Wickham's boat whispered among themselves, cast glances over their shoulders at the French cutter ranging up, and then fell to whispering again.

Childers made a small gesture with his hand toward the French, clearly wondering what was being said, but Wickham could not hear the whispers, which were carried away on the wind. One did not need to speak French, however, to see the fear in their faces.

Every quarter of an hour or so Wickham would quiz the French cutter in their wake, more certain on each occasion that it pursued them.

'Do we dare to carry more sail?' Wickham quietly asked Childers and Gould.

'We have already had one broach,' Gould answered quickly.

Childers considered a moment and then nodded. 'I agree with Mr Gould, Mr Wickham. Another broach and they will have us, without a doubt. Do you think they will overhaul us before we reach the island?'

'It is always difficult to be certain of distances over the ocean, especially from so near the surface.'

'Mr Hawthorne would offer to go up the mast,' Gould said and they all laughed in spite of themselves.

Mr Hawthorne climbed on to the foretop, where Hayden sat with an arm looped around a shroud and a glass up to his eye.

'What do you make of it, sir?'

'I think it is a Navy cutter, though it is yet too distant to be certain.' He passed the glass to Hawthorne, who took his place opposite Hayden.

The marine lieutenant stared at the sea a moment and then lowered the glass, a look of concern spreading over his handsome face. 'The small sails that I see before the cutter . . . are they fishing boats?'

'Some might be, but I fear two of them, at least, might be boats bearing our shipmates and perhaps some French royalists as well.'

Hawthorne raised the glass again, perhaps hoping to see more upon a second look. 'If our boats are out there, will this cutter overhaul them before they reach Dominica?'

'I cannot even be certain our boats are there, Mr Hawthorne, but if the cutter does overhaul them, I hope their people have the wit to surrender rather than fight.'

'Surely they would not take on a ship – even such a small ship – with a handful of muskets and pistols? Even Ransome has more common sense than that!'

'I agree, but if the French royalists are captured, their deaths are certain. They might prefer to die fighting . . . The other royalists who came aboard all bore muskets, and not a few pistols as well. Under such circumstances they might not be willing to surrender.'

'In which case our own people would have no choice but to fight . . . even were the situation hopeless.'

'Exactly so.'

'Certainly they must be able to see us?' Hawthorne said, thinking aloud.

'I am quite certain they can – but can they make out what ship we are on this point of sail? I rather doubt it.'

'And the French cutter will reach them before we can?'

'Yes. I am afraid they will.'

The French cutter did not have a proper chase piece and was forced to round up somewhat to bring a forward gun to bear. This was a dangerous operation which could easily lead to a broach, and the 3-pound balls fired never threatened the British boats.

'They are merely trying to see if we will lose our nerve,' Wickham observed as a ball from the French ship splashed into the back of a wave some thirty yards to larboard and dismally short.

He twisted around in time to see the upper limb of the sun sink into the sea; in half of an hour it would be dark – unlike in northern latitudes, where the summer light could linger almost an hour. Dominica floated upon the sea some few miles distant, just out of reach, Wickham feared.

The royalists aboard were silent and utterly apprehensive, the gunfire from the French cutter causing them all to start. Children hugged their parents, and husbands tried to re-assure their wives, but they appeared as people being carried to the guillotine.

Originally, their destination had been Portsmouth in Prince Rupert Bay, but now the boats were shaping their course for the most northerly point of the island, which was also the point nearest to them. If they could, they would try to land in the protection of a small point. If not, they would have to go through the surf to land, which was not to Wick-ham's liking with so many landsmen aboard. Turning over in the surf was common enough with lightly loaded boats.

Wickham took up his glass and fixed it on the distant ship, struggling to keep it in the circle of his lens, especially with his damaged hand, which now clung to things but poorly.

'I am beginning to believe that is our prize, in the offing,' he observed.

'Our captain?' Childers responded.

'So I hope – pray, even.'

'Then it was the French ship that went up in flames, God have mercy on their Papist souls.' The coxswain cast an embarrassed glance at the French passengers, but none had noticed, or perhaps they pretended not to.

Wickham raised his glass and watched the chasing cutter a moment more, then lowered it and cursed under his breath. 'They are mounting a half-pounder swivel on the bow.'

Even without his glass, and in the failing light, the midshipman could make out men on the bow of the cutter. He glanced again at the island – too distant, he thought.

'Does the bottom shoal up near the shore?' Childers asked him, tilting his head toward Dominica.

'Not enough to matter to us. They will be able to sail in as close as they dare to a lee shore, and launch boats, if they so desire. If we can get ashore before them, however, they will have a difficult time finding us in the forest.'

The newly mounted swivel gun fired and, though the ball missed its target, it came a great deal nearer than any previous shot.

'Pass loaded muskets aft for Mr Gould and myself,' Wickham ordered, and then he arranged to have men load for the two midshipmen.

Gould and Wickham sat with their muskets aimed at the sky, waiting until the French cutter was within range – which would be too damned close, by Wickham's estimate. He glanced again at the island, which had grown large in the growing dusk.

'I think we shall have to chance the surf, Mr Wickham,' Childers said.

'Yes, I believe we have no choice. Keep the seas dead astern, Mr Childers. It is our only hope.'

The red and bloody sunset overspread the western horizon and then began to slowly fade. The swivel gun was fired again, and the ball splashed into a wave not two yards distant from Wickham's cutter, then shot back out at an almost oblique angle, passing just over the heads of his crew.

Everyone aboard shifted position at once, and there were exclamations and oaths in two languages.

'Stay in your places!' Wickham ordered. '*Restez-là!*'

Wickham felt his heart pounding and forced himself to breathe slowly. It was something Hawthorne drilled home to every man trained to fire a musket – a pounding heart will shake your hands. He began to say it over and over, silently: 'A pounding heart will shake your hands. A pounding heart . . .'

There was a flash and a puff of smoke at the French cutter's bow, but the boat fell behind a wave at that instant. Wickham raised his own musket, trained it on the ship and pulled back the cock.

'Aim for the men at the swivel gun,' he said evenly to Gould. 'Wait until the bow reaches the bottom of the trough, Mr Gould, then fire above the men's heads. Or, when she has reached the crest, fire just below the rail.'

When the ship next sank into the trough, the instant before she began to heave up again Wickham fired above the heads of the men and, without looking, passed his musket back to the loader behind. A loaded gun was placed in his hand at almost the same instant and he could hear the sounds of the first musket being reloaded.

Gould's gun went off and Wickham raised his own to fire. The French cutter was a larger target which rose and fell more slowly, but Wickham and Gould were firing from a less stable platform. Wickham did not know who had the advantage. Behind him, parents shifted to shield their children. Small blossoms of smoke appeared at the bow as muskets were fired. The balls whistled by or plugged into the sea, but none struck home.

The swivel gun fried and the ball sank into the back of the very wave that raised the British cutter. Childers glanced at Wickham – the shots were getting nearer.

Gould and Wickham kept up a steady fire and were making the men on the forecastle of the enemy vessel pay. A man started up the rigging of the French ship, a musket over his back, and Gould shot him before he'd gone a dozen feet. He slid down the ratlines and shrouds and was caught by another before he could tumble into the sea.

Ransome's boat had ranged ahead a little and was not the target Wickham's boat remained. It was an unfortunate arrangement, Wickham thought, for most of the royalists were aboard his vessel, which was the object of the French gunners.

Dusk was rapidly turning to darkness, and it was harder to see the individual men on the bow of the enemy ship, but the flash of their muskets gave them away. Gould was just raising his musket to fire when Wickham reached out and put a hand on his arm. 'Belay firing. Let us see how easily they can find us in the dark without our powder flash to alert them.'

'They are overhauling us, Mr Wickham; surely, they will see us.'

'Work us a little to larboard, if you can,' Wickham said quietly. He turned to gaze forward a moment. Dominica was large now and he thought he could make out the sound of surf some distance off.

'Manson? Have you room to heave a lead?'

'Aye, sir. I will manage,' came the reply.

The lead was broken out and the splash of it plunging into the sea heard: a moment of someone letting the rope run and then hauling, hand over hand.

'Nine fathoms, Mr Wickham, sand bottom.'

Wickham looked back once at the enemy vessel, which had ranged up even nearer.

'Mr Childers? No matter what occurs now, do not surrender. If Gould and I are shot, keep on for the island; the surf is nearer than it appears.' Wickham glanced over at the other midshipman. 'Mr Gould, if they make us out or draw alongside, we will keep up fire until we are felled. Everyone who has a musket or pistol, make ready. We will attempt to fight them off. The shore is very near.'

A shout was heard on the enemy vessel and volley of musket and swivel-gun fire was unleashed, but it was somewhere to starboard.

'I think they have discovered the barge, sir,' Childers observed quietly.

'Yes. Poor Mr Ransome,' Wickham replied softly. 'He cannot even return fire.'

The skilled hand of Childers worked the boat to larboard, little by little, until the enemy ship, which had been dead astern, was on their starboard quarter – the sails dark and angular against the low-hanging stars.

'They must give this up soon, mustn't they?' Gould asked, leaning toward Wickham and whispering. 'It is a lee shore and no small wind.'

'Perhaps they know these waters better than we,' Childers offered.

'Or do not know them at all . . .'

A shout was heard aboard the enemy ship, and then muskets

began to fire, striking one of the young royalist women and hitting the topside strakes with sharp reports.

'Return fire,' Wickham ordered.

Every man aboard who held a gun began firing at once. Childers was thrown down, suddenly, and lay staring up at the sky, stunned.

Dropping his musket, Wickham grabbed the helm in time to prevent a broach. Seas were suddenly steeper.

'Surf ahead, Mr Wickham!' one of the hands forward called out.

There was shouting aboard the enemy vessel and, immediately her helm was put over, slowly she turned, her mainsail resisting the helm, and then she jibed, all standing with a great crash of breaking gear.

All musket fire aboard the French cutter ceased in that moment and, from Wickham's boat, only a few more shots were managed.

'Clap on, everyone. Clap on!' Wickham called out.

The seas became precipitous and pressed together, crests toppling to either side. The cutter was picked up on the face of a wave, the stern tossed high, and then there was the sound of rushing water as she raced along the face. The wave passed beneath and the boat settled, stern first, into the trough. Again she was lifted, carried forward and settled, Gould and Wickham together struggling to keep her on course.

'Childers?' Wickham said, genuinely frightened. 'Are you shot, sir?'

To his surprise, the coxswain sat up, putting a hand to the side of his head and taking the fingers away, stained dark. 'I think I was, but grazed, though it seemed I had been shot through the brain for a moment.' Without another word, he moved up on to the thwart and took Gould's place on the helm, the midshipman giving it up gladly.

Gould then probed the coxswain's wound. 'You will have a hell of a lump, but I believe it was not a ball but a splinter from the gunwale that struck you. Or a ball that deflected off the rail, perhaps. God was looking out for you, I think.'

Wickham did not know how many waves passed beneath them, and he had lost sight of Ransome's barge altogether when they were picked up by the steepest sea yet. A crest broke heavily over the transom and, of an instant, the stern was thrown to starboard, the boat turned beam on to the sea, and she rolled over so quickly that Wickham was thrown into the warm water before he could cry a warning to others. He surfaced to the night, feeling himself rising up the face of a wave. Arms flailed the waters nearby and instinctively he reached out and took hold of a thin wrist. Immediately, a hand clapped on to him so tightly it almost caused him pain. And then a panicked woman had an arm around his neck and he was being forced under. For a moment they wrestled, and then he broke the lock around his neck, ducked under her arm, took hold of her beneath her arms and began to kick to the surface. A sharp crack on his skull told him he'd surfaced into an oar. He took hold of this and slid it in front of the frightened woman.

'Take hold of the oar,' he ordered in French, and was relieved when she did as he instructed.

For a moment he was treading water, attempting to part the darkness and determine their situation. He could hear voices calling out, some not so near. A dozen feet away, the dim whaleback of the capsized boat lay half awash, heads bobbing around and men thrashing the waters to reach it.

'Mr Wickham . . . ?' someone called.

'Is that you, Childers?'

'It is, sir.'

Before Wickham could reply, a wave lifted him, but as he settled again into the trough, his feet touched soft bottom.

'There is bottom here, Childers. I felt it just now. We must make an effort to get everyone ashore. I should not be surprised to find an undertow in such a place.'

'Aye, sir.'

Orders were given that were lost on the wind, and then Wickham realized that the men holding the boat were kicking and paddling, pushing the overturned boat toward the shore. He twisted his neck around, took a bearing on the beach and began to paddle toward the island, the sodden skirts of his royalist wafting about his legs as he swam.

On his back, as he was, Wickham could not see the island, nor could he judge their progress, but he could look out to sea, and little pinpoints of light could be descried some distance off. Calls and voices were carried down the wind.

'Can you make out what they are saying?' he asked the woman, who he could almost feel fighting her panic and fear.

'They are launching boats,' she whispered, hardly able to speak, she was breathing so rapidly.

Wickham let his legs sink again and this time there was sand beneath his feet. He began to stand, but a sea knocked him down, the woman landing atop him. and then they were both struggling up, water to their chests. They stumbled ashore, her dress like a sea anchor, resisting her progress so that Wickham had all but to drag her through the water.

Once she was in the shallows, he turned back into the

waters, took a moment to find the overturned boat and then waded out into the breaking surf. A wave lifted him and he struck out toward the cutter. In a moment he found the painter and began swimming for shore with it wrapped about his shoulder and held firmly in one hand. For a time it seemed he made no progress at all, but then the beach seemed to appear before him, nearer than he had dared hope, and he was wading into the shallows, then putting his weight on to the rope, digging in his heels and pulling with all he had. A sailor came in along the painter, stood, and did as Wickham did. Finally, the boat was picked up and tossed ashore, where it rolled upright, three-quarters full.

Childers staggered up on to the beach and dropped down, gasping. He held something up in the dark.

'I have your glass, Mr Wickham,' he announced.

'My glass! How in this world did you manage that?'

'Just as the boat went over, it rolled almost into my hand and I kept hold of it the whole time, sir.' He passed it to the midshipman rather proudly.

'I cannot begin to express my gratitude. I thought it lost without a doubt, and knew I should never get another like it in Barbados.'

'I knew it was a gift from the marquis, Mr Wickham, and you placed great value upon it.'

'Childers, I shall give you a suitable reward for this kindness, I swear I shall.' Wickham rose and walked among the castaways, counting heads. 'Where is Cooper?' he asked suddenly.

'We could not find him, sir,' Childers replied. 'I fear he might have received a blow to the head as the boat went over, for he never broke the surface nor was seen by anyone. He is our only loss, Mr Wickham, though a great loss it is, for he was as good a marine and shipmate as any.'

'Mr Wickham . . . ?' a voice called from the darkness.

'Here!' the midshipman answered, like a schoolboy.

The man appeared out of the dark, a sodden sailor, clothes clinging and hair plastered flat to his pate. 'Mr Ransome sent me to find you, sir. Have you many lost or hurt?'

'We lost Cooper, sadly. I am not certain of our hurt.' Wickham turned around on the sand. 'Mr Gould? Have we many hurt?'

He could just make out the other midshipman, crouched beside a dark form on the beach. 'Many a bruise, I suspect, and one Frenchman with a broken arm – or so I believe. The doctor would know better.'

'No one bleeding dangerously?'

'Not a one, Mr Wickham. Except for Cooper, we have fared remarkably well.'

The hand dispatched from Ransome's boat bent over, hands on knees. 'Were you overturned in the surf as well?' he asked.

'We were, and there was little we could do about it. A crest broke over our transom and our stern was swung sideways against anything the rudder could do.'

'It was the same with us, sir. We were overtaken by a sea and then all pitched into the water of an instant. We lost no one, though our boat was not so overburdened as yours . . . We had lost so many before.'

There was a call from out in the surf, Wickham thought, almost certainly in French.

'We have almost no weapons and not a grain of dry powder,' the hand from Ransome's boat declared, staring out into the dark sea.

'We are no better off.' Wickham turned to the crew and passengers of his boat. 'Everyone up; we must make our way into the forest or we will be captured.'

'They may have no better luck landing than we,' Gould observed.

'Unless they know what to expect here . . . And they will not be racing along under sail, as were we, though there was bloody little we could do about that.'

The hands and the French were helping each other to their feet. Ransome and his people came along the beach at that moment, and they all made their way toward a gap in the trees. Just as they were about to proceed into the impenetrable darkness of the forest, without a single light to aid them, guns fired out at sea, and everyone brought up and turned to look.

The entire day they had been chasing this distant cutter, and had closed to within a few miles at sunset.

'Ten 3-pounders, and as many half-pound swivels,' Hayden guessed. He was answering Hawthorne's question about the guns likely carried by the cutter.

'Then she has a greater weight of metal than we?' the marine lieutenant asked. Despite his time at sea, he would always be something of a landsman, Hayden thought.

'I could carry our entire broadside in my pockets,' Hayden told him, 'and I do not exaggerate when I say this.' Hayden looked up at the shadowy sails, full and drawing. 'I even wonder if they believe this is the privateers' schooner yet – news might not have reached them.'

The two men stood upon the forecastle of the schooner, gazing out over the briefly twilit sea, the mountains of

Dominica rising up out of the waters, solid and unmoving in the ever-changing seascape.

Hayden called up to the lookout on the foremast. 'Bradley? Can you make her out yet?'

'I can, sir. Dead before us. Not half a league distant, Captain.'

There had been time, through the long afternoon, to train the royalists in the firing of guns and to take some basic orders. Hayden had paired most of the Frenchmen with an experienced sailor and given the French instructions to aid them in every way. The islanders were intelligent, practical people used to doing a variety of tasks and would quickly comprehend what was required, even without anyone telling them. It did not take much native wit to realize that they could jump to and aid men hauling ropes, and they did just that whenever needed. Some of the women had clapped on to ropes during the day and aided the men hauling, much to the amusement of the British sailors.

'I don't think you'd see my missus turning her delicate hands to such work,' Hayden had heard one of the hands observe.

'I've seen your missus, Huxley, and I don't think "delicate" is the proper term for her claws.'

Of course, traducing the honour of one's wife was not acceptable at any station, so threats were made, apologies offered, Mrs Huxley's hands rated as delicate as a duchess's, and they all laughed for they were a kindly and good-natured crew and Hayden held them in great affection for this as much as anything.

The firing aboard the French cutter ceased, and the musket fire from the British boats went silent as well. Hayden guessed the French had lost sight of the *Themis*'s boats, painted black as they were, and Ransome and Gould or Wickham had the good sense not to fire and alert the French to their position – or they had run out of powder, he could not say which.

A few moments passed and then the swivel and muskets were fired at once. Then silence again. Hayden had no desire to fight this French vessel, which was almost certainly better armed than his privateer and would have trained men aboard – not a crew that spoke two languages, half of whom were landsmen. He could not, however, stand by and allow the British boats to be taken. All the afternoon he had endeavoured to overhaul the Frenchman and force him into a running battle which would allow the British boats to make Dominica. Hayden's hope had been that the schooner would prove swifter and he would keep enough distance between the two vessels that the French would not be able to batter his prize into submission. Once the boats were safely clear, Hayden would then crack on and race the French for the town of Portsmouth and the bay, which certainly would have British vessels at anchor and where the French would not venture.

But the French were so near his boats, and the north end of Dominica so close by, that this plan was no longer to be contemplated. Darkness might let the boats escape, he thought, and then he would do the same, keeping distance between himself and the French cutter, which would likely not wish to be discovered so near the British island at dawn.

Hayden did not like his position overly. The north shore of Dominica was a lee shore, and the winds, which commonly took off somewhat after the sunset, had been making for the last few hours and showed no signs of easing.

For a short time the schooner bore on, rising and falling with the quartering sea, the wind moaning softly in the rigging. And then there was an unholy crash and distant shouting.

'*On deck!* Somewhat has happened aboard the Frenchman, sir! Perhaps she's lost her topmast, Captain.'

'Has she run aground?' Hayden called up into the dark.

'I don't know, sir. She seems to have sheered to starboard, sir. Mayhap she jibed all standing.'

'Mr Hardy! Sail handlers to their stations.' Hayden began hurrying back toward the quarterdeck. 'We shall tack ship!'

The moment the men were at their stations, he ordered the helm put over and the ship was brought around and through the wind. Immediately she was on the other tack, Hayden ran her down toward the position where the French cutter had last been seen, a leadsman calling the depths as they went.

'Bradley?' Hayden called to the lookout. 'Can you see the Frenchman?'

'I have kept my eye on her, sir,' came the lookout's voice from above. 'Point off the larboard bow. Half a mile distant. I believe she's come to anchor, sir.'

'Well, let us thank the imprudence of French captains,' Hayden muttered, and crossed to the larboard rail where he leaned out to see if he could make out the enemy. And there she was, some distance off, bow to wind, or so he thought, and riding up and over the waves.

'*On deck!*' the lookout cried again. 'Captain? I believe she is anchored just outside the line of surf, sir.'

Hayden ordered the helmsman to shape their course to come across her bow. Sheets were eased accordingly.

'We have luck on our side again, it seems,' he told Hawthorne, as the marine appeared on the quarterdeck. 'They must have run in too near, realized they were almost in the surf, jibed all standing and carried away gear. They have anchored to effect repairs and we can rake them as often as we are able.'

Almost broadside to the waves, the schooner rolled terribly, so their fire would have to be timed perfectly. Steady men had been made the gun captains and Hayden had cautioned them to hold their fire. It was his intention to come as near as he dared to the cutter to make the most of their small broadside and reduce the chance of missing. The silhouette of the enemy vessel was almost lost against the darker island, but Hayden could see it, even with the sails off her.

They ranged in at speed, the brisk trade pressing their little ship on, and then as they passed, on the roll, Hayden ordered the guns fired and the 3-pounders kicked back, spewing smoke and fire. There was distress aboard the French ship, he could hear, but then, as Hayden was about to call for sailhandlers, the French cutter swung to larboard, turned broadside to the seas and carried toward the surf line.

'My God!' Hayden said to no one, not quite able to believe what he saw. 'We have shot away her anchor cable . . .'

Aboard the French cutter, all thought of defence was given up, even though their broadside came to bear upon the schooner. Men scrambled to make sail, though he could see numbers yet aloft undertaking repairs.

'Can she make sail, Captain?' the helmsman asked. 'Had

she not too much damage to her rig? They would never have anchored in such a place otherwise.'

'I do not know . . .' Hayden watched as the ship was carried into the surf. The mainsail crept slowly up, luffing and snapping, the gaff only half under control.

Hawthorne had stepped away from his swivel gun and came to the rail beside Hayden. 'Can they sail out of such a place?' he asked quietly.

'Only if God has taken notice.'

But all deities appeared to have their attention elsewhere that evening, for the French ship was carried into the surf and in a moment had found bottom, her mainsail not yet raised. Her decks tilted wildly toward the beach as she was driven higher with each wave. Hayden had been aboard a ship wrecked some distance from the shore, though in harsher conditions than these – a late-spring gale – and he knew the horror of it. There might be fifty men aboard the cutter and, if lucky, half might survive. Boats could be taken through the surf and perhaps back out again, though much would depend upon the nature of the shore. Was there a landing place?

Where, for that matter, were his own ship's boats and their crews? How many of them had been lost?

'We have no boats to send to their aid . . .' Hawthorne said.

'No,' Hayden replied, 'but we shall stand by until daylight. Let us hope this cutter is driven ashore. If she comes to rest some distance out . . . well, God have mercy on their souls.'

The castaways stopped at the shadowy edge of the bush and turned to look seaward where the flashes and reports of guns had originated.

'Is it Captain Hayden?' someone asked.

No one knew the answer. The chasing ship – the vessel they had seen closing all the long afternoon – had no doubt found the cutter, and she was not a French privateer, that was clear. She was British or perhaps Spanish, for the Spaniards plied these seas in numbers.

'What shall we do?' someone asked. 'We cannot stand here. The French have launched boats.'

'Tarry but a moment,' Ransome ordered. 'Let us see what will happen now. I believe the boats will return to their ship if they can. They will not risk being left ashore should their ship make sail.'

In the darkness it was difficult to see what went on, even a few hundred yards distant. The rigs of the ships tended to be more visible than the hulls, which were lost against the dark sea. Starlight glittered dimly off the moving waves and the breaking crests were palely visible. Wickham would have given anything for a nightglass, but they had only his single glass remaining and it was of little use by darkness.

Something changed in the appearance of the French cutter, and voices were carried to them over the sound of breaking seas. For a moment Wickham was confused by what he saw, and then he realized. 'She has swung broadside to the seas! Her cable has parted!'

'Are you certain, Mr Wickham?' Ransome asked.

'I am. Look! She is rolling and thrashing. They attempt to raise the main.'

'Never will they sail out of there,' one of the hands asserted, and Wickham thought he was likely correct. If they could not make sail immediately, they would be in the surf.

'Whatever led them to anchor so near?' someone asked, but no one replied. Clearly, it had not been by choice.

Wickham started down the beach and in a moment was standing with the waves dying about his ankles. There was shouting out among the seas now, distinct from the voices carried from the ship. For a moment he stared, and then, there on the back of a wave, he made out a boat being frantically rowed out, away from the shore.

He turned back toward the people still standing at the margin of the wood. 'Do you see? The boats are attempting to return to their ship. They have given up on us.'

En masse, the castaways hastened across the beach and gathered in a line where the seas died.

'Mr Wickham.' Childers broke the silence. 'That ship is in the surf. There can be no doubt.'

'I believe you are correct,' Wickham replied.

A terrible cry reached them – distress from every soul aboard – and then an odd lurch from the French ship. She seemed suddenly to stop in her progress toward the shore, and Wickham thought her deck was slanted heavily toward the land.

'Hard aground,' one of the hands declared. 'There is no saving her now. The seas will drive her up the beach and there will be no getting her off without a dead calm to allow it. Otherwise, she is a loss there.'

'Mr Ransome?' Wickham said softly to the lieutenant. 'Should we not empty our boats and launch them if we can? We might preserve some lives this night if we act smartly.'

Ransome nodded. 'All able-bodied men to the boats. Mr Wickham, can you ask the French to search along the shore? We will need our oars.'

The boats lay half submerged and were being battered back and forth by the seas. They would soon have been damaged, left to the whims of nature. Water was thrown out by the bucket until each was light enough that all the men together could roll her on her side and pour the remaining water out. Sweeps had been gathered off the beach, and now were shipped. Most of the French were left ashore but helped launch the boats into the surf, wading in waist deep and steadying each one until a sea passed beneath and then the boat was shoved out bodily on the ebbing wave.

Immediately, they met a sea and dug in to crest it, for if the first few seas could not be surmounted the boat would be tossed back ashore.

It took everything the men aboard could muster to pass over those first few waves. Wickham and a young Frenchman had manned the aft sweep and pulled for all they were worth.

After the initial seas, the waves grew less steep, though they were commonly as high. Childers was at the helm and steered them unerringly toward the stricken French vessel, Wickham was certain. He did not need to glance over his shoulder to ascertain their course, though he was constantly curious as to their progress.

'How distant is she, Childers?'

'Some way off, sir. I can make her out quite clearly, even by starlight.'

Over the sound of the surf – a constant low thunder in which no individual breaking wave could be discerned – apparitional voices carried to them, now and then, barely within the range of hearing so leaving Wickham to wonder if he imagined them. He realized, as he rowed, that he grew tired more quickly than he should, and knew this was exhaustion. Desperately, he needed sleep and a few days' rest to recover his strength. All the men were in the same state, he was certain, and yet had forced their way out through the seas breaking on the beach despite barely having the strength to stand.

'Can you make out the French boats?' he asked Childers, who stood to look over the seas.

'One, I believe, Mr Wickham. No . . . there is another. Both making their way back to the ship, the first all but there.' He was silent a second, his knees flexing to keep his balance in the rough conditions, done as easily as a dancer. 'I do hope these men are steadier than those of *Les Droits de l'Homme*, sir.'

A memory of Franks's boat being overwhelmed by panicked French sailors and being swamped and turned over . . . and lost. Their poor bosun, who had volunteered to take the boat through the surf, a victim of the chaos in the French Navy. And here they were again, taking a boat to rescue the same, barely governed sailors – sailors who believed in ideas of liberty and equality, both noble sentiments but with no place upon a stricken vessel where only order would save lives.

'Fifty yards, Mr Wickham,' Childers informed him.

The midshipman left his French rowing partner to handle the sweep and stood to get a better view. The stricken vessel lay with the tips of her yards in the surf, her masts angled low, the deck slanted and half awash. Seas broke over her windward side and the wind howled and moaned, luffing Wickham's coat, which was being rapidly dried by the warm trade. Wickham could see men in the rigging and up the masts, clinging to these last little islands of hope. The two

French boats, which had been dispatched not so long before to hunt down the British sailors and royalists, made their way to the rigging hanging down into the sea to take off the men clinging there.

Wickham made a quick assessment of the situation and ordered Childers to lie off the quarterdeck. 'Five yards off, hold our place a moment and let me speak with the French. Let us hope there is an officer there whom the hands respect.'

Childers nodded and brought the boat near in the tumultuous seas. The oars were backed a moment and Wickham found himself staring at a dozen men clinging to the windward rail, frightened beyond description. He had half a mind to pull away, for these men were past taking orders from their officers.

Wickham pulled the pistol from his belt and held it up where all could see. 'You will come aboard this boat one at a time in an orderly fashion,' he told them in French. 'The first man who jumps into my boat out of order I will shoot through the heart. We will then back our boat away and leave the rest of you here. Do you comprehend what I am saying?' There were nods and words of acceptance. Wickham ordered the boat brought alongside and lines were thrown to the men on the French vessel.

Wickham hoped his bluff would stand; his pistol had been soaked through and the powder drenched when they were thrown into the sea, but the French did not know that.

'Line handlers,' Wickham said loudly. 'Be prepared to cut those lines of an instant upon my order.'

Behind him, where the French boats were taking men from the rigging, Wickham could hear shouting and cursing, but he dared not turn to see what went on. He was determined that his boat would not be swamped by panicked men.

The strongest French sailors formed a chain down the deck and the men slid on their buttocks, passed from man to man and then into the boat, which rose and fell with each sea, slamming now and then into the submerged rail, which threatened to turn them over. Finally, several French sailors stood upon the French cutter's rail, in water that rose as high as their necks at times, and held the English boat off, other men steadying them.

Men were coming aft along the windward rail and being warned to stay in their places by the other Frenchmen, who nodded to the young English officer who stood sternly, holding aloft a pistol.

Behind him he heard what sounded like fighting, the night full of curses and threats.

'Mr Wickham,' came Ransome's voice from out of the night. 'When your boat is full we will take your place.'

'Draw your pistol, Mr Ransome,' Wickham called back, not turning away from the men coming aboard his boat. 'I have told these Frenchmen that the first man to jump aboard my boat out of order will be shot and we would leave the rest of them here to drown. You must tell them the same.'

'My pistols are drawn and ready, Mr Wickham.'

When the midshipman thought he could carry no more in safety, he informed the officer present that he would return as soon as he had carried his cargo ashore. He then ordered his boat away and, loaded to the point of overcrowding, the men took up the oars and sent them toward the beach. Immediately, Mr Ransome's boat manoeuvred to take his place.

The distance to shore was covered in less than half the time it took to reach the wreck, for the seas picked them up and carried them along, like great hands passing them from one to the next with only a brief lull between. As they neared the beach and the waves mounted up, Wickham and Childers had a brief conversation as to how they would get their boat in without the same calamity that had befallen them before. Wickham gave careful orders in both English and French and, at a word from him, the rowers reversed their positions so that they faced forward and took hold of the oar which had previously been manned by the hands at their backs. All the oarsmen now faced forward and could back oars with all their strength.

As the boat was lifted on the face of the wave, the men rowed for all they were worth, keeping the speed of the boat manageable. In this way they approached the beach but slowly. When the last wave before the sand picked them up, and at the very last second, Wickham and Childers unshipped the rudder lest it be broken and the boat was cast up, not too ungently, on the beach. It did slew to starboard to some small degree, but the sailors all clambered out and very quickly slid the boat up the beach, where the waves died around it.

The Frenchmen gave thanks to their saviours and even pounded them on the back, they were so relieved to find themselves on land and not swimming for their lives. A moment of rest, and then Wickham ordered the boat turned around, which was done bodily by all the men who could muster about it.

The British sailors took their places and manned oars again, the rudder was shipped and, at an order from Wickham, they began again to battle their way out through the seas toward their enemy's ship, to rescue the men who had been intent on their murder not two hours before. It was, Wickham thought, the strangest irony that sailors would risk their very lives to kill their enemy and then, when an enemy's ship was discovered sinking, risk their lives to save the men aboard. He rather thought the latter was the finer impulse.

They had not gone fifty yards when Ransome passed them in the barge.

'How many remain?' Wickham called out to him.

'Your boat shall be the last, I think. And, Mr Wickham . . . ? Be prepared to defend your boat from the French both as you return and when you are upon the shore.'

The idea of the French taking their boats and sailing for Guadeloupe, or some other possession, had not occurred to the midshipman and he thought it a sign of his terrible fatigue.

'We shall have our pistols ready,' he called back, largely for the sake of the French aboard Ransome's boat, some of whom likely had a little English.

'God speed, Mr Wickham.'

'And you, sir.'

The wreck lay much as they had left it, the masts perhaps a little nearer the water. The seas continued to break over it and Wickham thought it unlikely that she would ever swim again.

'Mr Gould, do you have a pistol?'

'I do, sir.'

'Do we have any other firearms?'

A musket and another pistol were reported; all the guns had wet powder and would not fire. Wickham ordered these distributed to the steady men.

'Blackwood,' he said to their remaining marine, 'you will take station in the bow, and Ruston, you will stand by him. When we approach the wreck, stand and make your weapons seen. Gould and I shall do the same. Let them see that we are vigilant and that we are prepared to defend our lives and our vessel with blood, if it is required.'

The others took their stations, and an air of seriousness settled over the little vessel. None had thought of fighting the men they attempted to rescue, let alone killing any, but it was clear now that they must be prepared to do so. After all, their captain had done almost that exact thing, taking the schooner of the privateers who hunted them.

As they neared the wreck, Wickham could make out the last of the men gathered at the stern, more grim now than frightened.

Wickham had Childers keep clear and he gave this group the same warning before he would lay his vessel alongside. It was the same exercise again, holding off the boat and loading the men one at a time. As the men came aboard, Wickham ordered them to sit down in the bottom and crowded them all in the middle, so that they would have to overcome the oarsmen before they could reach the men bearing arms.

That being done, he set out for Dominica for what he hoped would be the last time this night. Landing on the beach was managed as before, and they were soon wading ashore as men dashed out from the beach to pull the boat up out of reach of the breakers. Both the French and the British collapsed on the sand but, noting Ransome and several others standing with guns in hand, Wickham touched Gould on the arm and then did the same. The French, it must be made clear, had only very briefly been castaways – they now were prisoners.

'Where have the French boats landed?' Wickham asked, looking around and seeing only their own two boats.

'They did not come ashore, Mr Wickham,' Ransome replied. 'I should think they have sailed for Guadeloupe.'

'Well, they shall have a wet passage. It was difficult enough with a fair wind. I should not like to make it in an open boat hard on the wind. I wish them luck.'

'They have not had much luck this night,' Gould observed softly. 'They would have been wise to come ashore. Better to be a live prisoner . . .' He did not finish his thought, nor did he need to.

At that moment guns fired aboard the ship that yet lay off the shore.

'The private signal,' Gould declared. 'That is our captain.'

'We will send a boat out to him at first light,' Ransome announced quietly. 'And Mr Wickham? Inform the French sailors that a British ship lies off shore. Let them not have any ideas of escape.'

Wickham relayed the message to the prisoners, who outnumbered the British sailors. They appeared to accept their lot, glad, no doubt, to be alive.

Wickham could have lain down on the sand and slept for a day, he was certain, but, as an officer, he was required to stay on his feet and be an example for the hands. He almost trembled with exhaustion.

'What will tomorrow bring?' Gould asked him.

'We will all be taken aboard the prize and the prisoners likely deposited in Portsmouth. After that . . . Barbados, I will wager, and perhaps a few days of shore leave and respite.'

'A little holiday from making war will not go amiss,' Gould replied.

'No, it will not,' Wickham said with feeling. 'I could sleep for a sennight and not be recovered.'

Twenty-seven

After three frustrating days in delicate negotiations with the authorities in Portsmouth, on the island of Dominica, they had finally agreed to accept Hayden's rescued royalists if he would take the prisoners on to Barbados. The crossing to Barbados had required a further two days, due to the trade choosing those particular days to become indecisive. Barbados was raised, finally, and Hayden's excitement could hardly be hidden. How happy Mrs Hayden would be to find him home weeks before expected!

When the anchor was well and firmly down and the schooner holding her position without doubt, Hayden ordered the boats launched and, leaving Ransome in command of the prize, went ashore and hurried through the twilight streets to his island home. His pulse was speeding somewhat, and his colour high when he reached the door, his imagination running ahead of him to the sweet delights of married life and his comely bride, who would be more than surprised to find him returned so soon.

The house, however, was dark, not a candle burning, though the smell of smoke permeated the air. Hayden found himself rushing from room to room, lest there was a fire as yet undiscovered. Very quickly he found the source. A family of Africans were crouched around a fire built on the tile of the covered porch that looked out over the small garden. They were in the process of cooking a fish on a makeshift spit, and the smoke was being carried through an open door and into the house.

'Where is Madame?' Hayden asked. 'Mrs Hayden. Where is she?'

They looked at him as though he were nothing more than a mild curiosity – a strange animal making unintelligible noises. He hurried inside, banging the door closed behind him.

Very quickly, he mounted the stairs, calling out as he went, but there was no reply. Their chamber was empty, the bed unmade. The windows were opened and leaves had blown in and collected in the eddies behind furniture. The other rooms were undisturbed.

Frantic, Hayden pummelled down the stairs and was out of the front door where he collided with Rosseau, who was so red-faced and gasping that he could not speak immediately.

'Where is Mrs Hayden? Where is my wife?' Hayden demanded, as though Rosseau might somehow be responsible for her absence.

'Gone . . .' the little Frenchman gasped. He held up a hand and tried to master his breathing. 'They have taken her . . .' he managed after a moment.

'Who have taken her?'

' 'er brother . . . and the comte.'

'*The comte!*' Hayden realized he had shouted.

Rosseau nodded and then went on in his native tongue. '*Oui. Le comte.* He . . .' Then he shook his head. 'Let me begin in the proper place. You were right, Captain 'ayden. The comte is not a royalist but a Jacobin and a spy. Miguel, he knew something – a secret, that he never told to you. The Spanish frigates . . . they sailed to Vera Cruz for silver. That was their commission. The Spaniard, the merchant whom the admiral sent to Miguel, he never found a ship to carry Miguel to his uncle. He wanted only to lend Miguel money at interest and keep him here as long as possible. Miguel, I think he suspected the comte from the very beginning. He went to him and they made some arrangement – I cannot say precisely what – and then they took Madame in the middle of the night and they were gone.'

'Madame is gone? Where?'

'On a boat for Guadeloupe, I think.'

'How do you know all this?'

'I found a woman, a maid in the comte's house, and I put the suggestion in her mind that her employer was not a royalist but a Jacobin spy. At first she said it was impossible, but then she began to see that there were little things – many little things – that could better be explained by the comte being a spy than by him being a royalist. It was she who told me Miguel had come to meet with the comte. And now she has come to me to tell that the comte and Miguel and Mrs 'ayden all went off in the night, leaving the comtesse and her children behind.'

'When did this happen?'

'Two nights past.'

'Have you gone to Admiral Caldwell?'

'I have only just learned of it myself this evening. You are the first I tell.'

Hayden considered only a moment. 'I will see the admiral this night.'

He closed the door behind him and began down the street.

'Do not tell him it was me,' Rosseau said, trotting along beside him, as he walked as quickly as he was able. 'Do not even whisper my name. The Jacobins must not learn it was me.'

'I will keep your name back,' Hayden told him. 'Do not be concerned. Your part will not be known. I have other evidence that the comte is a traitor to us.'

'Where is it they have taken Madame, do you think?'

'I do not know, Rosseau, but I would wager all I have that Miguel and de Latendresse will have hired or come to an arrangement with French privateers to apprehend this Spanish frigate.'

Caldwell's residence was not distant and Hayden was there, knocking upon the door, in short order. The admiral was at table and came away from it rather offended and surly. He did not invite Hayden to join him.

'What is this matter, Hayden, that could not wait until I had finished my meal?'

'Mrs Hayden has been abducted against her will, by her brother and de Latendresse—'

'Latendresse!'

'Yes, Admiral. I have recently taken a group of royalists from the island of Guadeloupe and they are certain, beyond any doubt, that de Latendresse betrayed a number of them to the Jacobins and that he has been in the employ of the Jacobins all along, only masquerading as a royalist.' Hayden did not add that the man was likely only pretending to be a comte as well.

'Royalists . . .' The admiral took a chair. 'I can see you are distraught, Hayden, but you must begin at the beginning so that I might catch up.'

Hayden was too agitated to sit and paced forth and back across Caldwell's office, relating the events of his recent cruise. Caldwell did not interrupt once the entire telling but sat behind his massive desk, following Hayden's progress as he tacked back and forth across the room. Finally, Hayden brought it all to a conclusion with news of the Spanish treasure frigates and his own 'spy's' observations of the comte.

Caldwell sat in his chair, rather dumbfounded, Hayden thought. He had just been told that his favourite frigate commander was a vainglorious ass and his royalist friend was a spy and had, in fact, been playing him for a fool. It was a great deal to absorb in a short time.

'You do not think these royalists who singled out de Latendresse were engaged in some grudge or other – the French are forever turning in their neighbours and sending people to the guillotine because they mislike them.'

'I am quite certain that these royalists were telling me the truth. De Latendresse has found a way to enrich himself tremendously, and he has gone off with Don Miguel Campillo, abducted Mrs Hayden and left his own family behind. I do not believe you will ever see the man again unless we capture him and bring him to justice.'

Caldwell considered a moment, perhaps searching for another defence he might throw up in the path of Hayden's assertions.

'If I understand you correctly, Hayden, there will be at least one, and perhaps two, Spanish frigates bearing silver?'

'Unless there are more waiting in Vera Cruz but, very typically, it seems there has been but a single frigate or a pair performing this service in recent years.'

'A far cry from the treasure ships of only a few years past,' Caldwell observed, almost wistfully. 'I can send word to the Spanish in Havana, but it would seem this will likely be too late.' The admiral contemplated a moment more. 'I should wonder if there is a privateer powerful enough to match even a single Spanish frigate. There are a few converted merchant vessels operating in these waters, but even they would carry only two dozen 12-pounders at most. They fly from our frigates wherever they are met.' Caldwell looked up at Hayden. 'I do wonder if de Latendresse can muster the ships to take a Spanish frigate.'

'It would seem that he believes he can, Admiral, or he would not have disappeared the day after Miguel approached him with the news of the Spanish silver being shipped.' Hayden knew the privateers often sailed with large crews and relied on boarding rather than guns.

'Mmm . . .' Caldwell still seemed to resist the idea that the comte had been playing him for a fool – as any man would, Hayden realized.

'It would seem to be an act of treason for this Spaniard – Mrs Hayden's brother – to give the French the date the Spanish frigate intends to sail and perhaps the route it will use as well. He is divorcing himself from his country quite decisively if he has done this.'

'Miguel is a desperate man, sir. And perhaps he believes his part in this matter can be kept dark.'

'He is rather naive if he believes that,' Caldwell asserted, and Hayden nodded agreement.

'There is the matter of the French and Spanish abducting my bride . . .' Hayden reminded the admiral, hoping to appeal to his British – not to mention male – pride and sense of honour.

'And how do you propose we get her back?'

It was the very question Hayden had been asking himself.

377

'The Spanish frigate will almost certainly sail to Cádiz through the New Bahama Channel . . .' he said, almost thinking aloud.

Caldwell nodded. 'If it does not first stop in Havana, though that is much less frequent now.'

'If I had my ship I would go searching for the privateers in the channel.'

'You do not expect to find your bride aboard a privateer?' Caldwell smiled.

'In fact, I do. After he has betrayed this information to de Latendresse, Miguel will not return to Spanish soil until he is certain it is safe and that no one knows his part. The comte will take his money and travel to some neutral nation until he is certain France is safe for him. I believe they will sail north to one of the United States . . . and Miguel will not go without his sister.'

'It is a great deal of conjecture, Hayden. Perhaps even wishful thinking. How certain are you that there is a Spanish frigate transporting bullion?'

Hayden thought it the wrong moment to give a realistic assessment. 'Quite certain, sir.'

'But you have no ship.'

'Unless I have the good fortune to run across my first lieutenant in the *Themis*, I have only the privateer's schooner.'

'A very undermanned little ship, Hayden, you must admit.'

'Sir Benjamin, if it were Lady Caldwell abducted, would you not go after her in a jolly boat if that was all you had?'

'When I was your age, Hayden, I would have taken on all of Spain and France with a pistol to have my bride back, but I am older now, if only the smallest amount wiser. I do not think you will accomplish what you hope without your own frigate and likely the aid of the other captains in my little squadron ... and they are at sea and beyond recall. The schooner you have sailed here is a prize and not yours to employ in personal matters. However, having said that, I deem this threat to our Spanish ally's treasure ship to be a serious matter and therefore I am willing to take extraordinary measures to avert it.

'As the only ship we have at our disposal is your prize, I will send you with orders to warn, if at all possible, the captain of the Spanish frigate. If you are not able to do so, you must employ whatever means possible to ensure the safety of that ship and not let the treasure fall into enemy hands. I will give you a letter to Sir William containing the same orders, in the event that you should meet him or any of your fellow captains. I will also send a boat north to attempt to deliver orders to any of the frigate captains to sail to your aid, but I should not hold out hope of that. You will note that the interests of His Majesty's government in this matter are to take priority over your desire to rescue your lady in distress. Do you comprehend what I am saying, Captain? Naturally, I am in great sympathy with you personally, but the British government, you must realize, does not care a fig for your bride.'

What Hayden comprehended was that, if he used a Royal Navy ship to rescue his bride and the Lords of the Admiralty decided to court-martial him for it, the admiral would claim his orders were only to preserve the vessel of their ally from capture. Given that Caldwell did not seem to be in the favour of the Lords Commissioners, it was a very wise course. The written orders would make no mention of Hayden's bride and the admiral would deny any suggestion that he had given Hayden tacit approval to attempt to find and return Mrs Hayden.

'I do understand. And thank you, sir.'

'I cannot imagine why you would thank me. I am sending you into danger in a little schooner with a few 3-pounders. You have nothing for which to thank me.'

The admiral pulled a sheet of paper from a drawer and unstoppered a bottle of ink. 'Now,' he said, taking up a quill and examining the tip in the poor light. 'Tell me what you require to get underway.'

'Powder, shot, victuals, water . . . and men, sir. We are terribly short of hands.'

'Men . . . The entire Navy is short of men, Hayden . . .'

Twenty-eight

The men came in twos and threes, sometimes alone. A number had been in the care of a physician ashore and were from the British frigates stationed in Barbados. They were easily picked out among the other men, for they moved stiffly, as if they had become fragile while in hospital, and they were pale among the sun-darkened hands. Hayden did not think they would be much use in a fight. Two men who came aboard had been serving Admiral Caldwell as servants ashore. That Caldwell had given them up and returned them to sea service astonished Hayden. In the end, the crew numbered thirty-two, with Ransome, Wickham and Gould as officers. He even had his own coxswain aboard. Men had taken to touching Childers for luck, as he had been grazed by a musket ball while running from the French and wore a dressing around his head yet, to prove it. Had he leaned an inch to one side at that instant he would certainly be dead.

It was a day of utter frustration for Hayden. He paced the deck with anxious energy, and implored his men to make haste with every task, with the result that they were then lacking employment while they awaited the victuals or the powder. And so the day dragged on. Ransome had ordered awnings rigged over the quarterdeck and between the two masts, giving a little shade to the vessel, which baked beneath the tropical sun.

Hawthorne and his few marines had laid all the muskets

and pistols out on an open section of deck, where they cleaned and serviced each one to be certain it would perform its duty when required. Ransome and Wickham went over the ship from stem to stern and keel to truck and put everything to rights that they could, in the brief time allowed.

The time, however, did not seem brief to Hayden, who imagined his bride sailing further and further from him into a vast, featureless ocean where the track of a ship disappeared not long after it passed. Her absence and loss was more than just something he comprehended in his mind, he felt it in his body and chest as though a part of him had been cut away. The pain of it never left him, not for an instant.

The sun was setting when everything was stowed and the ship trimmed to the lieutenant's satisfaction. The anchor was weighed and the schooner began to gather way and shape her course north on the vague little zephyrs and gusts that made their way over the island of Barbados. The brief tropical twilight descended upon ship and sea, and then darkness and a clear, starry night. Lamps were lit, watches set and hammocks piped down. The familiar routine of a ship of the British Navy established itself without any need for explanation or extra discipline, the officers and men falling into it like it was the natural order of the world.

Hayden had taken the cabin aft that had been the residence of the former master, and slung a cot there. It was a cramped little space compared to his cabin on the *Themis*, and a closet compared to his cabin aboard *Raisonnable*, but its former occupant had been a fastidious man, he had come to realize, and it was clean and relatively fresh, aired by an overhead skylight and small windows in the transom. The schooner would be swifter to windward than a brig of simi-

lar size, not much different with the wind on the beam, and
not as swift or as easily steered as her square-rigged cousin
with the wind aft or on the quarter. Of course, the topsail
schooner carried square canvas as well – sometimes only the
square topsail by which she was distinguished, but sometimes a course and even a topgallant, if the owner or master
was determined and had the manpower to make use of every
little puff of wind that came his way.

Wickham approached the captain's little patch of deck, a
man of perhaps thirty years trailing in his wake. Hayden
waved them forward.

'Sir, this is Henry Scrivener. Before he took ill, he was
master's mate aboard Sir William's *Inconstant*. He has spent
many years in these waters and has brought both his own
instruments and his charts aboard with him.'

Hayden refrained from making any comment upon the
man's name. 'How long have you been a master's mate,
Scrivener?'

'Six years, Captain. I was rated able before that, sir, but took
a keen interest in navigation and was always pestering Mr Ches-
ter with questions. Finally he said he could bear it no more and
taught me his trade so I would leave him in peace, sir.'

'Are you familiar with the Old Channel of Bahama, Scrivener?'

The man nodded. 'I have traversed it on two occasions,
sir. It is fraught with cays and shoals not on any charts, Captain, and a good lookout is worth more than the best pilot.'

Hayden invited Wickham and Scrivener below and spread
a chart upon the small table in his cabin. The route Hayden
had drawn took them east of both the Windward and Leeward Islands over open ocean.

Scrivener contemplated this a moment, a freckled hand to his mouth. He was a tawny-haired man, and freckled all over his face, hands and arms. He was half a hand shorter than Wickham and appeared thin and a little stooped. 'If I may, sir?' he said after a moment.

'Yes, by all means. Your knowledge in these waters is far greater than mine.'

'It would be shorter by a hundred miles to pass south of St Lucia, then to shape your course to take you through the Mona Passage, which is both wide and deep, sir. Open water the whole way. Then down the New Channel of Bahama, where we should have fair wind, even if it does turn a little north, as I have often seen it do, sir.'

Hayden could see the sense in it immediately. 'Would you be my acting-sailing master, Scrivener?'

'It would be my honour, sir.'

'Then lay out your courses, and we will inform Mr Ransome.'

'I shall do so this moment, sir.'

Hayden returned to the deck, feeling a little lightness in his step. It was a stroke of the greatest luck to find a master's mate who knew the waters! It buoyed his spirits somewhat. To reduce their route by a hundred miles would get them to the New Bahama Channel in nine days rather than ten, and every day counted.

The little schooner made good speed all that night, passing south of St Lucia in the forenoon. Hayden had slept poorly and been on deck before sunrise, spotting St Lucia to the north-west and St Vincent to the south as the sky turned to light.

The exact date that the Spanish frigates would set out

from Vera Cruz was not known to him, but he reasoned that, if de Latendresse decamped from Barbados the day after Miguel had revealed his intelligence regarding the silver, then he must have believed he could reach some point where he might intercept this ship – and the only place narrow enough to make finding the frigate a reasonable possibility was the New Bahama Channel.

The crossing to Mona Passage was about one hundred and fifty leagues. He hoped to be through the passage in four or five days . . . if the trade would hold. If he had followed his original route, passing to the east of the long chain of French and British islands, he might have found Sir William, or Archer, or the other British frigates cruising there, which was part of the reason he had chosen it. This route made finding aid all but impossible. They would be on their own.

Hayden knew, from conversations with the other frigate commanders, that there were several privateers cruising these waters which had been merchant vessels and were well armed – twenty 12-pounders and various small deck guns, Sir William thought. He, Oxford and Crawley had been attempting to find and take them for some months, but they had eluded them on two occasions, flying from them and then slipping away by darkness. The masters of these privateers knew their business and were more familiar with these waters than were the British. It would be one or more of these ships that he believed de Latendresse would need to take the Spanish frigates. How long it would take him to find these ships, come to an arrangement with the masters or owners, outfit them for a month's service and get underway, Hayden did not know. If de Latendresse knew from where they operated presently it might make this task easier and swifter. Whenever the privateers suspected that the British knew what port they used, they would change to another harbour on another island altogether.

How Hayden was going to fight off or take even one of these powerful privateers, he did not know, and it did make his enterprise seem more than a little Quixotic. This brought a sudden memory – had not Henrietta once, in jest, named him 'Don Quixote *del Mar*'? It was likely his penchant for rushing headlong into danger that had inspired her to break off with him and take up with a landsman who would never risk life and limb in some doubtful venture. This thought of Henrietta, for some reason he could not explain, only increased his pain at the loss of his bride and added to his feelings of confusion.

St Lucia dropped astern, dwindling all through the long afternoon, and then they were out of sight of all land and would be until they raised Hispaniola in a few days' time. The trade blew constantly, day and night, driving the long ridges of translucent blue across the empty expanse of the Caribbean Sea.

It was the fourth day before land appeared – just the top of a green mountain under a little wreath of white cloud. And then this mountain appeared to grow out of the sea, rising up until a great island was revealed beneath.

The afternoon saw them draw near the Mona Passage. Winds, interrupted by the land, grew fickle in both strength and direction so that it took them several hours to work up to the entrance of the passage. The passage itself was wide – over fifty miles – with a good-sized island in the middle and a few smaller islands as well. The wind blew directly through the pass out of the north, so Hayden brought the schooner into the gap from the south-east, as near the shoals that extended out from Punta Aguila as he dared. This would give them the best slant to pass through, and Scrivener assured him that the winds would back to the east as they pressed deep into the passage. The sun dropped behind the hills of Hispaniola as the little ship shouldered aside wave after wave, spray slatting down hard on the deck.

It was morning before they were well and truly through the passage and the wind did back to the east, though not so much as Hayden had been promised. Even so, it was a fair wind, and they shaped their course to carry them along the northern shore of the mountainous island of Hispaniola, which would lie off their larboard beam for two and a half days . . . if the wind held.

They were seven, long, frustrating days away from their hunting grounds, and Hayden well knew that the strait the Spanish frigates would pass through was wide enough that they could slip by unseen. It was not, however, the treasure frigate that was on his mind. It was the privateer he hoped was carrying his bride that he was looking for – and if this vessel had aboard neither his bride nor her brother, he did not know what he would then do. It was a thought he tried to press down whenever it arose, which it did often, especially by night.

Hispaniola passed in due course, the Windward Channel opening to the south and offering a glimpse back into the Caribbean Sea, for they were, strictly speaking, now in the Atlantic. The passage itself was fifteen leagues wide and, beyond it, the long, narrow island of Cuba lay in a shimmering sea. Cuba, however, appeared to have broken free of her moorings and was drifting west at the same pace the schooner sailed. Hayden began to think they would never leave it behind.

By midday, however, four days out from the Windward Channel, they reached the area Scrivener thought their best chance to intercept the Spanish frigates, and the area where they were most likely to find the French privateers Hayden prayed would be lying in wait with de Latendresse, Miguel and his bride aboard.

Hayden climbed to the crosstrees of the mainmast and surveyed the straits at every point of the compass. Not a single sail in the great expanse of blue. Dolphins passed in numbers, whales blew and pilot fish swam lazily in the ship's shadow, but men did not appear to venture into that small portion of the watery globe.

Two sail did appear on the second day and proved to be a pair of Spanish transports. Hayden spoke to both ships but neither master had seen signs of either Spanish Navy vessels or French privateers, for which they were thankful. Taking Hayden's warning seriously, they pressed on, doubly vigilant.

It was the third day, at dawn, that Hayden woke to distant thunder. Bare feet came pounding down the ladder and the marine guard knocked immediately on the captain's door, though Hayden had already rolled out of his cot and was pulling on clothes in the dark.

More reports reached them before he mounted the deck, where he found Wickham climbing to the maintop with a glass slung over his back. Hardy was on watch and pointed immediately to the east as Hayden appeared.

'There away, sir.'

There were flashes on the horizon just then, and Hayden counted the seconds evenly.

'Ten or twelve miles,' he pronounced. 'Let us shape our course to the east.'

Ransome appeared at that moment, still straightening his uniform.

'Gunfire, due east, Mr Ransome,' Hayden informed him. 'Call all hands. We will have breakfast and then beat to quarters. We shall be two hours or a little more coming up to them.'

'Aye, sir.' Ransome went off, calling orders, as the schooner was brought on to a new course, yards shifted and sails trimmed to get the greatest possible speed out of their little ship.

The wind shifted from north-east-by-north to east-north-east and every point between, keeping the sail handlers on the hop and the helmsmen ever ready to work the ship a little to windward when the wind allowed, and tight on the wind when it did not.

Hayden forced himself to eat a little breakfast, though afterward he would not have been able to tell anyone what he had eaten. Coffee was welcomed like a dear friend and, though it gave an increased edge to his nerves, it sharpened the mind, which Hayden knew would be utterly necessary – for how he was going to take a more powerful ship with such a small crew was still a question he could not answer.

Flashes and reports continued as the sky brightened and the sunrise spread over the sea. The flashes were then largely obscured by the growing light, but the reports continued for three quarters of the hour and then abruptly and ominously ceased. The quiet was more disturbing than the sounds of battle. Smoke, however, stained the horizon, rising up and spreading, before being swept down the wind. The smell of it reached them just as Wickham, astride the topsail yard, called out that he could see the tops of masts.

Hayden took his glass and climbed the foremast shrouds to perch with Wickham on the yard. The impossible blue of the tropical sea spread out around them, and there, to the east, the masts could be seen in a mass so that the number of ships could not be counted.

Hulls began to float up, backlit by the morning sun.

'I make it six, Captain,' Wickham pronounced with some certainty.

'Six?' Hayden was more than a little surprised. 'Are there frigates?'

Wickham did not answer immediately, but gazed a moment. 'I cannot say, sir. It would appear some ships are alongside others, but some are behind and I cannot make them out clearly. I do see Spanish colours, though . . . of that I am certain.'

The little schooner bore on toward the gathering of more powerful ships, and Hayden could almost feel the trepidation of his crew emanating up from the deck below and growing by the moment. The schooner was, undoubtedly, swifter than any of the vessels lying before them, but winds were never even across the face of the sea and many a slower vessel had been carried up to one more swift by favour of the winds.

As they sailed on, the scene before them began to take on substance and clarity.

'Two frigates, sir,' Wickham announced after a time. 'Four other ships – converted transports, perhaps.'

'Our privateers,' Hayden said.

'Yes, and they are the ships flying Spanish colours, sir.'

'Which I should have guessed. No doubt they were masquerading as a small Spanish convoy. I wonder if they had a private signal to put the frigate captains off their guard and draw their vessels near?' Hayden leaned over so that he might see the deck below.

'Mr Ransome! It would appear we have found our frigates and our privateers. Let us lay-to on the starboard tack and see what they will do next.'

Ransome acknowledged this and began calling out orders to the sail handlers and helmsman. In a moment the ship lay-to under reduced canvas, less than a league distant from the gathering of ships.

Hayden gazed through his glass until his arms grew tired.

'Will they move bullion from one ship to another?' Wickham wondered.

'I cannot imagine they would,' Hayden replied. 'It would be a difficult thing to manage at sea, and would you not rather have your treasure aboard the most powerful ship?' He gazed through his glass a moment more. 'Tell me, Wickham, if you believe they transfer more prisoners off one frigate than they do from the other.'

'Aye, sir.' A brief pause. 'You believe they will not risk Spanish prisoners retaking the frigate carrying the bullion, sir, and will take the crew off?'

'Assuming only one frigate carries silver . . . It might be both.'

An hour the two sat upon the yard, observing the distant ships and the boats passing between them constantly, like bees among flowers.

'Do you see the most southerly frigate, Captain?'

'With her stern to us?'

'Yes, sir, and no mizzen topmast. I believe they remove the most men from her, sir, and carry them to the other frigate and one of the privateer ships.'

Hayden stared into the little lens of his glass a moment more, watching the boats, unable to be certain Wickham was right – but then the midshipman's eyes often proved better than his.

'Sir, at the stern rail of the ship without the topmast . . . do you see, sir? All in white? Is that not a woman, sir, in a dress?'

Hayden brought his glass to the ship Wickham named, and there he could make out several figures, some moving and others stationary. Among them, still as morning air, Hayden imagined he could make out the form of a woman dressed all in white, and he felt, as absurd as it might seem, that she gazed back toward the little schooner that bore her husband – for what other woman might this be? De Latendresse had left his own 'countess' and family on Barbados – abandoned them, Hayden guessed. Could this be anyone but Angelita?

Hayden lowered his glass reluctantly. 'At least she is dressed as a woman this time,' he said.

Wickham lowered his own glass. 'Well, we have found them, sir,' he addressed his captain quietly. 'What now shall we do?'

Hayden glanced down at the deck below and aft. The cutter and barge, employed so recently on the isle of Guadeloupe and in Wickham's escape from that island, sat upon the deck, the cutter resting inside its larger sister.

'Do you remember, Wickham, whose idea it was to paint our boats black?'

'I confess, sir, I do not.'

'I cannot remember, myself, but whoever it was has my eternal admiration.'

The privateers were several hours in transferring prisoners and repairing damage to the ships and their rigs. Hayden expected to see them sway up a mizzen topmast to replace the spar the frigate had lost, but this did not occur; the frigate would almost certainly be faster than the converted transports even without the topmast and the sails that could be set upon it.

About the time the sun reached its zenith, the little convoy got underway and shaped its course toward the Santaren Channel. Hayden kept his schooner some distance in the wake of the privateers and their prizes so that the ships were clearly visible from the masthead. He wondered if de Latendresse and Miguel guessed who followed in their wake. The loss of the schooner would have been news on Guadeloupe – everyone would have known the British had taken her – but exactly which British officer might not have been generally known.

'So, where do you believe they are headed now, Captain?' Hawthorne asked.

The two men stood upon the forecastle, gazing after the ships they followed.

'I thought they might sail directly to an American port, but it would appear I was wrong on that count. A French port, therefore, must be the answer. The privateers must have investors who do not want to see the treasure they have captured divided up out of their sight. Guadeloupe is as good a guess as any.'

'Guadeloupe is some distance off . . .'

'Yes, and once we reach an island populated by Frenchmen, the odds swing drastically in their favour.'

'So they would rise from "merely impossible" to "utterly impossible"?'

'Why, Mr Hawthorne, I have never known you to be such a pessimist. I should think they would not alter any more than from "merely impossible" to only "*somewhat* more impossible".'

'If I may say so, Captain, I believe you are being overly optimistic.'

'Perhaps so, but my heart is more involved in this matter than your own.'

Neither man spoke a moment and then Hayden broke the silence. 'May I ask you a favour, Mr Hawthorne?'

'Of course, sir. What might I do for you?'

'If you believe I am making a particularly foolish decision, clouded by my feelings in this matter, would you be so kind as to bring this to my attention?'

Hawthorne did not immediately answer, and then he replied, 'I must tell you, Captain, I am more of a landsman than many comprehend. I might not possess the knowledge to judge your decisions. I should confess that on more than one occasion I have wondered at the . . . *prudence* of some of the enterprises you have undertaken, and in almost every case I was proven to be wrong and you in the right.'

'But, Mr Hawthorne, you are sensible of the mood of my officers and can judge for yourself when they are wary of some enterprise I am proposing.'

'Perhaps, sir, but your officers have come to trust in your judgement and abilities to a degree that, for reasons of modesty, you might not believe. Many's the time you have weighed the odds to a nicety and succeeded in some enterprise that none of them would ever have dared.'

'You would think that losing my ship to the French, not so long ago, would have shaken their confidence more than a little.'

'Everyone agreed that, if not for fog and a bit of bad luck, we would have slipped away, sir.'

Hayden let this pass without comment; in truth, he wondered if he had not made several errors in judgement which had led to that particular calamity.

Hawthorne nodded, his eye fixed on the sea before them. 'If you wish it, Captain, I will endeavour to speak if I believe your emotions are clouding your judgement.'

'Thank you, Mr Hawthorne.'

'I am honoured, Captain Hayden, that you would ask me.'

The matter, then, was left to silence.

Twenty-nine

Two men had been lost to the Yellow Jack, and the captain and two boat crews were prisoners of the French, but, beyond those not insignificant calamities, Archer was beginning to count their cruise a success. The cruising grounds had proven richer than anyone expected, and though they had not taken a single prize which, on its own, would bring a man wealth, smaller prizes had been numerous enough that officers and hands were well content.

The weather had been excellent, the cold, English winter a broad ocean away. The West Indies, Archer had begun to think, could be something of a paradise but for the Yellow Jack and the war.

The hands worked about the ship, kept busy by the officers, and the watch below gathered here and there in the shade of the sails to discuss how best to squander their prize money upon return to England's shores.

Along the deck, Archer saw Mr Barthe staring aloft and speaking to the bosun, who nodded agreeably. The two had become a society of mutual respect in the last months. Archer missed poor, unlucky Franks, but it was a great comfort to have such a capable bosun. Barthe spotted the acting-captain as he approached and touched his hat.

'Captain Archer,' he said, with barely a trace of irony.

'Mr Barthe. Do we have trouble aloft?'

'Chafe, Captain,' Barthe informed him. 'Nothing a properly positioned thrummed mat will not address.'

'Chafe has become like a troublesome relative, one who constantly requires a little propping up, a little fluffing, to keep her happy.'

'*On deck!*' came a deep-voiced cry from aloft. 'Sail, south-by-east.'

'Can you make her out, Adams?' Archer called to the lookout, chafe and thrummed mats forgotten.

'A two-sticker, sir. Schooner, looks like. Sailing north, Mr . . . Captain Archer.'

'Let us shape our course to intercept her,' Archer said to the sailing master.

'Aye, sir.'

Archer walked aft and called for his glass, which soon revealed the smudge of sail, heeled well over and showing no signs of running.

'They must have seen us by now,' he muttered.

'She looks very swift, sir,' Maxwell observed.

'Indeed she does. Which is why she shows no fear of us. Despite her truncated length, we would never catch her close on the wind, and her master appears to know it.'

'Could she not be British, Captain?'

'It is not impossible, though here . . . unlikely. We shall see. We will show her our colours if it appears she might outrun us.'

The ensign was arranged on deck and made ready to send aloft. It was entirely possible this little ship was Spanish or a neutral – American ships plied these waters in great numbers, and ships from the British colonies further north traded here as well.

The two vessels approached each other and, when the schooner was distant some mile and a quarter, she sent British colours aloft and made the private signal. Archer ordered this answered and hauled their own ensign aloft. Within half an hour the two ships hove-to within hailing distance and the lieutenant in command of the smaller ship swung out a boat and came aboard the *Themis*. Archer recognized him from Barbados, a thin, young officer with an oddly stooped carriage for someone so young.

'I have orders for you from Admiral Caldwell,' he said, after pleasantries had been exchanged.

'For Captain Hayden, you mean,' Archer responded.

'No, sir, for you. Captain Hayden sailed from Barbados several days ago and I have been searching for you or Sir William . . . or any of the frigate captains ever since.'

'Captain Hayden was not captured?' Mr Barthe interjected.

'No. He managed to escape Guadeloupe in a captured French schooner, with most of the men accompanying him, I am told. Caldwell sent him off in this schooner with orders I was not privy to.' He handed a sealed letter to Archer. 'And I was sent to deliver these to Sir William if possible, but if not to any commander of a British frigate.'

'Well, you have managed that,' Archer replied. 'What are you to do now?'

'I shall continue to look for Sir William for a few more days and then return to Bridgetown.' The young man lowered his voice. 'Before I sailed, a rumour had begun to circulate that Mrs Hayden had been abducted by her brother and perhaps a French spy.'

'That sounds very dramatic,' Archer said. 'Was there any truth to it?'

The young officer shrugged. 'I cannot say, sir, but the rumour was believed to have begun with the admiral's servants.'

For a moment the three men stood awkwardly silent.

'Have you any idea where I might find Sir William or the other frigates?'

'Cruising east of the French islands. They planned to watch the passes between.'

The lieutenant nodded. 'I should be about my business, Captain, if you have no further need of me?'

'By all means. And good luck to you.'

A few moments later Barthe and Archer retreated to the captain's cabin and Archer opened the admiral's orders, which were addressed to Sir William Jones, Captains Oxford and Crowley, and himself.

I have discovered, beyond reasonable doubt, that the Comte de Latendresse is not a loyal ally of our King and adherent to the royalist cause, as we believed, but is, in truth, a Jacobin spy who has played us false. De Latendresse, through the agency of Don Miguel Campillo, has come into possession of information regarding a Spanish frigate sailing from Vera Cruz to Spain bearing silver. Captain Hayden and I believe that de Latendresse and Campillo have engaged ships to intercept this frigate belonging to our Spanish allies, very likely in the New Channel of the Bahamas. I have dispatched Captain Hayden in a schooner to find and warn the Spanish of this plot. As there is a very real danger that he will not intercept the Spanish vessels or that he will arrive too late, you are to set out immediately for these waters or toward any place that subsequent intelligence would indicate, to warn our allies or protect these ships from predation by enemy vessels. If you find yourself in company with Captain Hayden you are to place yourself under his command until such time as he sees fit to release you.

Archer passed the letter to Barthe, who stood fidgeting nearby. He took it to the window and angled it to the light, his face growing more serious with each sentence.

His hand, holding the paper, dropped down in apparent anger. 'Then it is Campillo and that Frenchman who abducted Mrs Hayden.'

Archer shrugged. 'So I would assume. I am relieved beyond words to learn that our captain and shipmates are not in a French gaol, but where we might find him in this maze of islands I cannot say.'

Thirty

For several days they followed the privateer convoy, into the Old Channel of Bahama and along the coast of Cuba. The fickleness of the trade, highly uncommon at that time of year, continued to plague them, making an already difficult feat of pilotage even more dangerous.

Whether the privateers would pass through the Windward Channel or continue on became a question hotly debated. For his part, Hayden did not know what they would do. Clearly, they would want to get their prizes as far away from the Spanish islands as quickly as they could manage, but the Windward Channel saw a great deal of Spanish traffic and might be more dangerous even than the course they were on now.

Hayden went aloft often and watched the ships they followed. A privateer went first, then the frigate Hayden believed bore both the bullion and the passengers, Mrs Hayden among them. In the rear came the second Spanish frigate, so a powerful vessel always separated Hayden from the main prize. This arrangement never seemed to vary, no matter how often he went aloft to quiz the convoy.

Two nights before the Windward Channel was reached, the winds fell so light that the schooner lost steerage and Hayden was forced to anchor lest the current sweep his vessel on to a reef. It was a particularly dark night with ragged cloud passing over – high up where the wind had retreated.

Hayden took his nightglass and climbed to the topsail yard. It required a moment but he found the privateers and their prizes – nearer than he expected.

He leaned over and called quietly down to the men below. 'Pass the word for Mr Wickham.'

A moment later the midshipman climbed on to the topmast yard, and Hayden immediately passed the young man his nightglass.

'There away,' he said, pointing. 'Do you see?'

Wickham gazed a moment. 'Yes, sir. I can make them out clearly.'

'Which ship is in the rear?'

Wickham continued to hold the brass tube to his eye. 'I cannot be certain, Captain. It has ever been the frigate with the missing topmast, sir.'

'But you cannot be certain . . . ?'

'I am sorry to say that I am not, sir.'

Hayden considered only a moment. 'Have Mr Ransome call all hands, if you please, silent as can be managed.'

Wickham did not ask a single question but merely touched his hat and began to climb back down to the deck. Hayden took one last look through the glass toward the distant ships, and then followed the midshipman down.

Acreages of moonlight moved slowly over the surface of the flat, calm sea, shifted here and there by passing cloud. Hayden watched them for a moment while the men streamed up from below. There was no pattern to it, he was certain of that.

Ransome, Gould, Hawthorne and Wickham gathered about him on the quarterdeck. Hayden motioned them near and spoke to them quietly.

'We will launch the *Themis*'s boats, and man them for cutting-out. Arm the men, Mr Ransome, and have everyone wear their blue jackets. Let no light colour show. We will all darken our faces with burnt cork. With all haste, Mr Ransome. The moonlight wanders here and there over the sea and we want to manage all of this by darkness.'

Hawthorne remained by his captain as the others hastened off to execute their orders.

'Are you sure of this, sir?' he asked, with some difficulty, Hayden could tell. 'There are half a dozen enemy ships not too distant. I should think these are odds Sir William would relish, but Charles Hayden . . .'

'I hope only to take one of them and in this I believe we shall have aid. I have a special task for you, Mr Hawthorne. You will need half a dozen strong men you can rely upon . . .'

The boats were quickly readied and swung out, the men careful not to let them knock against the topsides or splash into the sea – these vessels might have been made of china, so carefully were they treated.

Ransome chose the steadiest men, leaving most who had come recently from their sick beds to man the schooner, which Gould would command in the captain's absence – much to the young gentleman's chagrin.

Down into the boats the men climbed. The darkly painted sweeps were manned, and the boats set out for the convoy which lay at anchor ahead. The men, with their blackened faces, would almost have appeared comical if their looks and manner had not been so grim.

Ransome had the cutter, with Wickham there to take his place should the lieutenant be wounded. Hayden took command of the barge. He had only two dozen men in the boats, all well armed and seasoned in such endeavours, but, even so, very small numbers. Hayden and Wickham had been observing the aftmost frigate in the convoy for several days and were both convinced the prize did not have forty privateers aboard. All the frigate's evolutions had been executed terribly slowly and there were never enough men aloft to take in or loose sail efficiently. Prize crews were often small, and this one, he hoped, was no exception.

Clearly, the privateers did not believe the schooner sailing in their wake could be a threat to them. Hayden's few 3-pounders did not compare to a gundeck of 18-pounders and an upper deck with carronades and chase guns. Whatever the purpose of the little schooner that dogged them, it was not to take any of the ships but likely only to follow and report where they had made port.

Oars had been carefully muffled between thole-pins and the rowers took up a cadence that allowed them to keep near-silence, oars entering the water cleanly and staying low to the surface on the return.

Hayden kept gazing around at the patches of moonlight that swept across the darkened sea, trying to gauge their speed and direction. As they moved, these patches changed shape and size, some growing, others shrinking and some even disappearing altogether. Areas of light would suddenly appear, as though a lens were uncovered in the heavens, allowing the moonlight through.

'Avast rowing,' Hayden ordered quietly, and a moment later Ransome's boat followed suit.

For a long while they laid upon their oars, as Hayden watched the progress of a small lawn of moonlight that came rippling over the sea. It changed shape and size as it flowed, as though some monstrous, glowing jellyfish slipped along just beneath the surface. All the while, he glanced up at the cloud, attempting in vain to find where the cloud might send this illumination, but to no avail. The cloud would send it where it would.

Just when Hayden thought it should pass over them, revealing two boats of British sailors, it shrank a little and passed a hundred yards to the west, leaving them yet hidden by darkness. Every man aboard breathed a deep sigh and Hayden set the oarsmen to work again, bearing them on toward the anchored ships.

How far apart the privateers had anchored was a concern to Hayden, as he knew the other ships would send boats or even train their guns upon the aftmost frigate if they believed it was attacked or in danger of being taken. With no wind, all the ships streamed to a small current that ran more or less toward the west, lining up the ships, bow to stern. This meant that the privateer lying ahead could train only her stern chase pieces on the Spanish frigate, unless they could clap a spring on to their anchor cable, or row out an anchor.

There had been no sign of wind for some time but Hayden knew full well it could return without the least warning. In such a case, the undermanned frigate would require all hands to make sail. Hayden was counting on there being lookouts awake, a watch sleeping below and the watch on deck largely asleep at their stations. The discipline of the British Navy – or even the French Navy, for that matter – would not be found among privateers . . . or so he hoped.

The only real advantage the English sailors had in this matter was surprise. No sane officer would expect the captain of so small a schooner to attempt to board a powerful frigate with five other ships anchored only a few cable lengths distant. Hayden had taken advantage of this kind of thing before. In Corsica the French had not believed it possible to carry guns to the hilltops, and so had made no defence against this – Hayden had proven them wrong. He hoped he was about to catch his enemy unawares again.

Wickham had been ordered to keep his keen eye fixed upon the aftmost frigate and warn Hayden of any untoward movement of men upon the deck. At this distance Hayden could make out the mass of the ship and lamps upon the transom, but nothing more. The posted lookouts and the guards were invisible to him.

If the British boats were spotted, Hayden hoped the lookout would cry out, thus warning the British. A smart lookout and an astute master might keep it all silent, man guns and blast the boats as they came near. Although he thought the latter unlikely, it was still in Hayden's mind, and he continued to approach the frigate from astern, where only the chase pieces might be brought to bear.

Hayden's thoughts were drawn back to Corsica again, where he and his men had cut out the French frigate *Minerve* by painting their boats black and doing exactly as they did now, slipping up on the ship from astern as silently as they could manage.

The men rowed on and the frigate came more and more into focus. Hayden felt his own stomach and muscles begin to tighten. He checked that he had a pair of pistols in his belt yet and that his cutlass would not hang up as he rose to climb on to the frigate's deck. His mouth was utterly dry and he would have given almost anything for a drink of water – anything that his orders would not sound as though they were formed in a mouth stuck together by fear.

Upon the frigate's deck he saw a man pass through the illumination of a stern-lamp, but he could see nothing more than that. Hayden expected the cry to go up at any moment, but none did, and the rowers continued in their slow, steady cadence.

Ten yards distant, Hayden began to believe they would not be detected until they mounted the deck, when a voice cried out, '*Bateaux! Bateaux! Les Anglais sont ici!*'

At an order from Hayden the oarsmen dug in and shot the boats forward so that they were alongside just as men appeared at the rail with muskets. Hayden had pistol in hand and fired immediately, but did not know if he hit anyone at all. Of an instant he was climbing over the rail, pressed upward by the men behind.

He shot a man at two yards, clubbed another with his pistol before he cast it down and drew his sword. Privateers were rushing up the companionway and spewing out on to the deck, some shirtless and without a weapon.

The British were on the deck in numbers and flew at the French, screaming like madmen. Hayden saw the red coats of Hawthorne and his marines crouching and jumping down to the gundeck.

The combat was now general all across the deck, the British fighting in small knots and attempting never to allow one man to become isolated from the others. It was a melee, in which neither side appeared to be winning. Hayden stepped over fallen British sailors as often as privateers.

There was, in the darkness, no way to be certain which side was winning and which losing. Men fell, with the thud of bones and flesh on wood, but Hayden had no idea if they were British or French. He thrust his sword at a man, struck his sternum direct, and immediately drew back and put the blade into the man's stomach, crumpling him to the deck.

There was shouting at the head of the companionway, and voices crying out in Spanish. Hayden could see Hawthorne at the head of this column and in a moment privateers were casting down their weapons and crying for quarter.

There was a great 'Huzza!' from the British, and Hayden stood a moment, gathering his wits and trying to catch his breath, for he was gasping for air, heart racing. The sound of more distant voices, shouting, came to him, and he realized it came from across the water – the other privateers were launching boats.

'Where is Mr Ransome?' Hayden called out.

In a moment the lieutenant came staggering out of the mass of men, his hat gone, coat torn across the front.

'Are you hurt, Mr Ransome?'

'Man ran into my chest with his head, sir. Knocked the wind from me.'

'Have Mr Hawthorne take charge of these prisoners, if you please. We must clap a spring on to the anchor cable on the starboard side and run it out the aftmost gunport.'

'I do not know the explanation, but she is anchored by her small bower, sir.'

'Then we shall run it out the larboard side, Mr Ransome. Have Wickham make up gun crews for both batteries and make ready to fire. We shall require the aid of the Spaniards, for we have not enough men ourselves.' Hayden did not have to be any more explicit. Ransome would know what he meant and what he planned.

The lieutenant went running off, calling the names of men.

Hawthorne came forward then, a Spanish officer beside him.

'Captain Hayden, this gentleman claims to be the former captain of this frigate.'

The man made a courtly bow. 'Agapito Serrano,' he said in good English. 'At your service, Captain Hayden.'

Hayden made a quick leg; there was no time for courtly formalities. 'I will need your aid, and the aid of your men to sail this ship, Captain Serrano,' he said. 'We are about to be attacked by boarders.'

'I shall resume my command,' Serrano said, 'and dispose my men to defend the ship. When that is done, Captain Hayden, I shall have the time to express my gratitude properly.'

'I believe you have mistaken the situation, Captain Serrano,' Hayden informed the man. 'This ship was taken from French privateers and I consider her a British prize of war. She is no longer yours to command; she is mine.'

Hawthorne took a step away, pulled a pistol from his belt and began immediately to load it.

The Spaniard was so taken aback that he was unable to form words for a moment. 'Captain Hayden, this ship is the property of the Spanish Crown! You have liberated us from the French, for which we are grateful, but I demand this ship be returned to Spanish control . . . this instant.'

Hawthorne pulled back the cock on the now loaded pistol and handed it to Hayden, who held it, finger on the trigger, pointed at the deck. Around him British sailors began picking up discarded pistols and muskets and loading them. The

Spanish had them outnumbered, and Hawthorne had clearly found the arms room and given their 'allies' weapons, so Hayden hoped this Spanish captain would realize that he would not hesitate to shoot him if he attempted to take back the ship.

'When we reach Barbados, sir,' Hayden said evenly, 'you may plead your case to my admiral. Until then, you must give me your entire support or we will all be the prisoners of privateers within the hour.'

'Sir,' the Spaniard replied, 'this will be considered an act of war against Spain. Are you certain you are willing to create a rift between our nations . . . you, a mere post captain?'

'If there were no Spanish prisoners aboard this ship,' Hayden said, 'she would be considered a British prize without question. It would then be up to our two governments to decide what should be done with her. I am only a mere post captain; it is not my place to return this ship to Spain. We have no time to argue the finer points of the laws of the sea. You will either submit to my command or we will lose this ship to the French. I must have your answer this instant.'

The Spaniard looked around, glancing toward the not so distant privateer, where boats were now in the water.

Ransome appeared at that moment. 'Sir, we have rigged the spring.'

Hayden looked at the Spanish officer, who hesitated yet.

'Until we reach Barbados,' the man stated evenly.

'Thank you, Captain Serrano,' Hayden ceded, making a small bow. 'Mr Wickham is forming crews to man the guns. Will you aid him? And we must be prepared to repel boarders.' He glanced up at the rigging. 'There is not a breath of wind upon which we might escape.'

'Where is Mr Wickham?' the Spaniard asked.

'Mr Hawthorne will take you to him.'

Captain Serrano made a small bow and immediately attached himself to Hawthorne, calling out orders in Spanish as the two retreated toward the companionway.

'Veer the bower cable, Mr Ransome. Bring us beam on to the other ships.'

'Aye, sir.' Ransome went off at a run. Hayden had no doubt that he had men standing ready to veer cable. He was becoming a surprisingly competent officer.

The deck guns were manned by Spaniards, and Hayden was surprised to find they were all long guns – there were no carronades.

'Shall we fire grape at the approaching boats, Captain?' one of Serrano's officers enquired of Hayden.

Hayden assented to this suggestion.

The bower cable was veered and the head of the ship payed off so that the ship would have wind on the larboard quarter – assuming the wind, when it returned, would come from the north or north-west. The small current moved the bow of the ship at an almost languid pace, causing Hayden to worry that they would not bring their guns to bear before the first boats reached them.

He raised his nightglass and realized, though boats appeared to be manned and away from the ship, that they were backing oars and hovering in place. Waiting for reinforcements, Hayden realized, knowing that the retaken frigate would now be, with all the prisoners moved aboard her, very well manned indeed.

Hayden estimated that the nearest privateer was just out of range of the Spanish guns, but he went to the waist and called down to the gundeck. He was very happy to find the Spaniards at their guns, silent and purposeful.

'Mr Wickham . . . ?'

'Sir?'

'Elevate a gun to its greatest degree and fire a shot at that ship. I believe she is out of range, but let us be certain.'

'Aye, sir.'

Orders were given to one of the British gun crews, the gun elevated and, at a word from the midshipman, fired.

Hayden had walked away a few paces to be clear of the smoke, raised his glass to his eye and watched with some anticipation. There was a sudden fountain of water, not just short of the ship but shy of the gathering boats as well.

Wickham's head appeared at the top of the companionway ladder. 'We could remove the aft wheels, sir . . . ?'

'Let us keep the wheels in place. Rate of fire might be our advantage yet. Reload with grape, Mr Wickham. Some of these boats might reach us, but we will make them pay for it.'

Hayden returned to the rail and gazed off toward the privateers through his nightglass. A wandering patch of moonlight illuminated them a moment and, though it was difficult to be certain, Hayden thought there were at least eight boats gathered there and perhaps as many as ten. There could be two hundred privateers in those boats. He hoped the Spanish gunners knew their business.

Without any order that carried across the water, the boats all set off at once, their bows aimed directly at the Spanish frigate so recently taken. Hayden was more than a little surprised at this, as he would have divided his force in two, circled round and approached the ship from both bow and stern, where only chase pieces could be brought to bear.

Hawthorne appeared at his side at that moment.

'Do they row directly for us, Captain?' the marine officer asked quietly, as though the privateers might overhear.

'It appears they do, Mr Hawthorne.'

'Is that not the height of folly? Do they not realize we have brought our ship around?'

'I cannot say. A moving boat is a difficult target to hit, especially by night, as you well know. They may simply believe our gunnery is not up to the task . . . but at a hundred yards grape will cause great slaughter.'

'Perhaps they are admirers of Nelson, Captain, and believe you must always "go straight at her".'

'Which will catch up with even Nelson, one day.'

'Luck to you, Captain,' Hawthorne said, touching his hat.

'And you, Mr Hawthorne.'

The marine retreated to take command of his men and whomever else Ransome had assigned him. Men began to climb aloft with muskets at that moment, many of them Spaniards. Hayden raised his glass again, and gazed a moment at the flotilla approaching. Privateers often favoured boarding as a tactic – their ships seldom bore enough guns to offer an advantage – but men could be had at small cost. A privateer usually sailed with a surprisingly large crew. And it appeared the privateers intended to use that advantage here.

A gun fired on the deck below, catching Hayden entirely by surprise. He stormed over to the opening to the gundeck, where he could hear shouting in both English and Spanish.

'Mr Wickham?' Hayden cried over the voices. 'What goes on down there? Where is Captain Serrano?'

Wickham appeared directly below Hayden, his face a shadow surrounded by a halo of pale gold hair. 'It was a Spanish gun crew, sir. Captain Serrano has disrated the gun captain and replaced him with another. I believe the man fired the gun as a protest against the British taking his ship, sir.'

Hayden turned immediately away. 'Pass the word for Mr Hawthorne!' he called. He had no time for this now and felt his anger boil up.

The marine appeared on the run, having no doubt registered the tone of his captain's voice.

'Take your marines to the gundeck, Mr Hawthorne. If there are signs of insubordination or mutiny among the Spaniards, you may deal with it as harshly as you see fit.'

'Aye, Captain,' Hawthorne replied quickly. He began calling for his men and in a moment they were thumping down the companionway.

Hayden returned to the rail, only to find the flotilla of ship's boats dividing into two. He let out a string of frustrated curses. Ransome appeared just then.

'Do you see the boats, Captain?'

'Yes. These privateers are not so foolish as we hoped. Is the spring rigged so we can let it run?'

'Indeed it is, sir, though it would be quicker and easier to cut it.'

'We might have need of it again. Clear everything the cable might foul and be prepared to let it run on my command.'

'Aye, sir!' Ransome touched his hat and went off at a run.

Hayden went immediately part way down the steps to the gundeck. 'Pass the word for Captain Serrano!' he called out, and the Spanish officer appeared a moment later, very grim-faced and appearing to suppress anger.

Wickham stood a few paces distant, a pistol in hand, and Hawthorne and his marines claimed the centre of the gun-deck with their muskets ready.

Hayden had no time to mollify an angry Spaniard. 'We shall have the privateer's boats approaching from bow and stern. Both batteries must be ready. Once the boats are too near to be fired upon, gunports must be closed tight. All men will then be needed to repel boarders.' Hayden turned to Wickham. 'Mr Wickham? Have you heard?'

'Aye, sir.'

'Then let us be about our business. Good luck, Captain,' Hayden offered to the sullen Spaniard.

He mounted the ladder and returned to the rail with his nightglass. The privateer's boats had split into two small flotillas, each of which carried somewhere near a hundred men. Hayden dearly wished he'd had more time to prepare his defence, assign the men to stations and create a plan with his officers. The truth was, though, that every experienced man aboard – both officers and hands – comprehended exactly what must be done. Fire upon the boats with the great guns until they draw too near, then take up arms and prepare to defend the ship. As his former captain Bourne often said, 'War at sea is not a complicated business.'

The two flotillas were giving the frigate a wide berth, but Hayden needed to keep them as distant as possible for as long as possible. 'Mr Gould,' he called out to the midshipman who was commanding the forward deck guns. 'Jump down to Mr Wickham. Have him traverse a pair of guns, one fore and one aft, and fire on the boats. Let them not become too bold.'

Gould touched his hat and disappeared to the gundeck.

When Hayden anchored his schooner he had been pleased to find the current was not strong – now he wished it were running a great deal faster. He was about to employ it in defence of his ship.

A forward gun fired at that moment, and he turned to see if there was any possibility that he might make out where the shot struck water . . . but he could not. A second gun fired aft and that ball landed somewhere in the dark ocean as well. Hayden fixed his glass on the forward flotilla and was quite certain it had altered course to keep out of range of the great guns.

'Mr Gould! We will use the chase pieces fore and aft to keep these boats honest.'

Hayden wanted both flotillas to approach from directly fore and aft, and to be as distant as possible when they began that approach. He turned his head from side to side – the faintest zephyr caressed his cheeks.

Hayden crossed the deck and again called for Mr Wickham.

'Sir?' The midshipman spoke from the darkened deck.

'Inform Captain Serrano that I intend to fire both batteries at once.'

'I will, Captain.'

Even as Hayden gave this order he wondered if it might be a mistake. He would hide his ship in the smoke so that the enemy could not see what he did, but the smoke would also obscure their view of the enemy, making it difficult to aim their guns. He held his hand up again. Was it enough of a breeze to carry the smoke away in time? Once they began firing guns at the enemy boats the smoke would obscure all anyway . . . but the first clear shot is what would allow the gunners to get the enemies' range and to gauge their speed.

Perhaps war at sea was more complicated than Captain Bourne had suggested.

Hayden drew a lungful of air. His course was set and there was no changing it now. It was all a matter of timing. He gazed up at the lookout.

'Aloft there! We shall fire both batteries to hide the ship. Climb as high up as you can to get above the smoke. I will rely on you to tell me what the boats do.'

'Aye, Captain,' came the cry from above and the man, who was among the musketeers on the maintop, went crawling up.

Hayden turned his attention back to the boats, quizzing both flotillas with his nightglass. They were only a few moments distant, but he needed them closer yet. He cursed the privateers who had not replaced the frigate's lost top-mast . . . he could have used the mizzen topsail with this little zephyr appearing.

The boats finally drew almost in line with the frigate and Hayden called for Ransome, who appeared at the ladder head.

'Fire both batteries, Mr Ransome, and then let the spring cable run. Be certain the guns are reloaded with grape. We will hold our fire until the boats are within range.'

Ransome repeated Hayden's orders and disappeared below. There was a mighty blast as all the guns on the gun-deck were fired as one, and a cloud of smoke utterly enveloped the ship and seared Hayden's nostrils and throat.

The spring was let run at the same instant and the ship began a slow turn, her stern swinging with the current, aided to the smallest degree by the faint breeze. The movement of the ship, however, appeared to be so slow that she would never swing to the current in time.

The privateer's boats were obscured by the cloud and the night, and Hayden began to wonder if he'd misjudged the distance in the dark and that they would be upon them before the ship swung around and the guns brought to bear. It would then be a battle against boarders, and Hayden did not have his steady British crew around him. He did not know if the Spanish were more determined fighters than the French. He was, however, about to find out.

He could hear, in the distance, the coxswains crying out the beat in French, exhorting their oarsmen to row faster. The ship continued her turn; Hayden believed he had seen seasons turn more quickly. The smoke swirled around the masts and rigging, caught in eddies and backdraughts. It clung to the ship like a skein of silk entangled in thorns. The faint-hearted breeze could not collect it all and carry it off in one single direction. Hayden had the horrifying feeling that he had made a terrible misjudgement: the French would be upon them before the smoke cleared and guns brought to bear.

Hayden felt himself leaning out over the rail, trying to catch a glimpse of the boats he could hear approaching, but the smoke appeared to mass before him.

'*On deck!*' came the cry of the helmsman, who was himself lost in the smoke. 'Boats to starboard, three hundred to three hundred fifty yards, sir! To larboard . . . a little less, Captain.'

Even if the lookout were correct in his distances, the frigate had not yet turned far enough that guns could be brought to bear. The only good thing Hayden could think of was that it would be very unlikely the privateers could see the frigate was being turned.

'Captain Hayden!' Gould's voice reached him from somewhere forward. 'I can just make them out, sir.'

Hayden all but ran down the deck to the forecastle, where he found Gould standing on the rail, gazing out to larboard.

'Can we traverse guns and bring them to bear, Mr Gould?'

'Not yet, sir. Not quite.'

Hayden climbed up on to a gun carriage and stared in the same direction as the midshipman. Smoke yet whirled languidly about him, but then, off in the dark . . . movement.

'I see them!'

Very quickly, Hayden gauged the position of his ship, how quickly she turned, and then the speed of the enemy's boats.

'Shall we prepare to repel boarders, Captain?' Gould asked softly.

'It will be very close, Mr Gould. Keep the men at the guns a little longer.' Hayden jumped down off the carriage and crossed the deck, climbing on to another carriage there. The vague little breeze did not hold its course for a moment together but came most of the time from the north-west, so the smoke was eddying behind the starboard topsides. Hayden could see nothing here.

'*On deck!* Two hundred and fifty yards, Captain.'

Hayden cursed almost silently. He realized then that, if the smoke cleared, they would only be given a single, clear shot, and then new-made smoke would obscure the sea again. As it was, the boats would soon be too near to be fired upon, as the guns could be lowered only a small degree more before they would come up against the sills.

Slowly, ever so slowly, the smoke began to clear, as though someone drew back a curtain, but an inch at a time. Gould ordered a gun traversed to its furthest degree. The gun captain sighted along it and shook his head.

'Not yet, sir,' he reported, then aimed his gun a little lower.

As the curtain of smoke drew back, the flotilla to either side came into clear focus, the men sending the boats on with long, powerful strokes. A small star of flame appeared on one of the boats and the report reached the frigate a moment later, but the boats were not yet within musket range.

Gould turned from his position at the rail and raised an eyebrow toward the gun captain, who dutifully sighted along his gun again.

'Almost there, sir.'

Hayden suspected the privateers were saying the same.

The captain of the starboard chase gun stood tall suddenly. 'We have a shot, Captain.'

'I wish to keep the ship free of smoke until all the guns can be fired at once. Do not fire until I give you the order.'

The man made a knuckle but was clearly disappointed. Left to their own devices, the hands would ever waste shot and powder.

The small current pushed the ship, little by little, even as the boats drew nearer, a few feet to each thrust of the oars. Hayden envied the men in the boats, who drove toward the frigate under their own power while he was forced to wait upon the whims of a dilatory current.

'Sir?' the captain of the first gun said. 'I believe we can risk a shot . . .'

Hayden walked back to the next gun aft and sighted along it. Quickly, he went and called down to the gundeck. 'Mr Wickham? Can your guns be brought to bear?'

'Very nearly, sir.'

'Inform me the moment they can.'

Hayden could feel the tension on the ship, the men urgently wishing to fire their guns, the captain holding them in check. The silence on both decks was so complete that Hayden thought he could hear the ticking of his watch, even within its pocket. How slowly it measured time!

'Captain Hayden . . .' came the voice of Wickham, out of the darkness. 'We have a shot, sir.'

Hayden raised his voice only the smallest degree. 'On my order . . . fire!'

Both batteries exploded in flame and smoke, the blast assaulting the ears, disturbing the very air. It was not uncommon for gun crews to need more than one shot to find the range – powder was ever varied in its strength – so Hayden wondered if there was any chance they might get their shot near.

The crews set to work immediately, reloading and running out the guns.

He gazed up and called to the lookout, 'Aloft, there! Did we hit a single boat?'

'One to larboard, sir. Most of our shot went fifty yards long.'

Hayden looked down on to the gundeck. 'Did you hear, Mr Wickham? Fifty yards long and the boats draw nearer by the moment. Lower your guns and fire again.' He gave the same order to the captains of the upper deck guns and in a moment the heat of a second volley swept up and over the ship, smoke so dense that Hayden could not see thirty yards.

'*On deck!*' the lookout sang out. 'We struck two boats to starboard, Captain Hayden. One appears to be going down.'

'Do they stop to aid that boat?' Hayden called back.

'They don't 'ppear to be, sir.'

'What is the range?'

'Hundred yards, sir . . . a little less.'

Guns were being run out at that instant.

'A hundred yards, Mr Wickham . . . one last shot and then close gunports – let us fight them on one deck only.'

Guns were lowered one last time, fired and Hayden heard the creak and slam of gunports being shut and sealed. Men came streaming up the companionway, armed with cutlasses, tomahawks and short pikes. Some of the older hands were given pistols, and marines and seamen bore muskets with bayonets fixed. Captain Serrano and Ransome soon had the men organized into larboard and starboard watches and spread along the rail.

'There they are, sir!' one of the hands shouted. He pointed out through the slowly clearing smoke.

And so they were, not fifty yards distant and coming straight at them.

The privateers began firing muskets, and Hayden ordered the musketeers in the rigging to return fire. Lead balls began to hiss by and bury themselves in the bulwarks. Hayden had been blessed with an active and vivid imagination and at such times it was best to keep it well in check. To imagine being struck by one of these invisible balls was enough to give any man pause, and officers were expected and obliged to stand resolutely on the quarterdeck under the most concentrated fire and show not a sign of trepidation.

A man not ten feet distant was struck in the eye by a ball

and fell to the deck like a dropped doll, never to move again. Hayden tried to swallow, but there was no moisture in his mouth.

Pulling back the cock on his pistol, Hayden raised it so that it pointed at the sky. The smoke was wafting away, finally, and the boats, loaded with armed men, could be made out clearly. They shouted and screamed threats as they came, but the Spaniards held their peace, standing in their places with what Hayden hoped was resolution. Their ship had been taken once by privateers, and that was not a comforting thought. His twenty-some steady British sailors would not be enough to fight off such numbers.

Judging the boats near enough that even the worst marksmen could not miss, he ordered muskets fired from the deck, and all around him the *crack* of musket fire was followed by rapid reloading. He intended to wait until the boats were alongside before employing his pistol so that there was almost no chance of wasting a shot. His second pistol he would hold in reserve; it might save his life or the life of one of his crew.

The first boat came neatly alongside amidships and, with a cry, the men began scrambling for the upper deck, where Hayden's mixed crew of Spaniards and British sailors fired upon them and then set to work with pikes and cutlasses, attempting to throw them back.

A boat came alongside the quarterdeck and Hayden chose the largest man he could see and shot him in the chest. He tossed the pistol down and drew his cutlass with one hand and his second pistol with the other. For a moment it seemed that the French would not gain the deck, but then they broke the Spanish line amidships and came pouring over the side.

Instinctively fearing the enemy would get behind them, men turned away from the rail, and the French then broke the line in several places.

Hayden was forced back, and it was parry and thrust and hot work all around. Having been schooled by a marine captain as a midshipman, Hayden never drew back his blade to slash, for whenever a man did, Hayden would put the tip of his blade into his chest. With the blade always pointed before him he could parry as needed and thrust when opportunity presented itself.

Hayden threw himself to the side to avoid a pike, tripped on a body and went down hard on his back. Immediately, a man was upon him with a dagger and would have done for him, but Hayden managed to deflect his first blow and then shoot him through the chest. Pushing the man aside, he found his sword, which he had dropped to fend off the attacker, swept up the man's dagger and staggered up, bleeding from his right arm somewhere.

'Captain! Captain!' a cry came from aloft. 'The privateer . . . she is bearing down on us, sir.'

For a few seconds, Hayden did not comprehend what the man meant, and then he saw it. The ship anchored nearest them had slipped her anchor and was bearing down on them on the current, broadside to the flow with all her gunports open.

Hayden was along the deck and down the companionway in an instant. Here he found a few Spaniards, bearing wounded to their surgeon. 'Leave them!' he ordered in Spanish. 'We must cut our bower cable – this very instant!'

The men hesitated only a second and then gently set the men on the deck and hastened with Hayden. They were hewing the cable with axes in a moment, and then it let go with a sudden snap.

Hayden gathered them all to him. 'When the ship is broadside to the current, cut the spring. Do not take the chance of it fouling. Cut it right at the gunport.'

The men hurried aft.

Hayden went up the ladder to the deck, two steps at a time.

He was allowed only a second to assess the battle, which was yet being contested all along the deck, and then two men were upon him with cutlasses. They had been properly tutored in the weapon's use and neither drew back to slash, which might have given Hayden an opening. Instead, they trapped him against the break to the gundeck, one feinting while the other attempted to make the killing thrust. Twice, Hayden avoided being run through with a quick sidestep.

'Again,' one of them said in Breton. 'But feint and then kill him.'

Hayden had no time to bless his Breton family: the first man feinted again and as Hayden parried he threw the dagger, left-handed, at the man's face, parried the second man's thrust and ran his blade three inches into his chest then drew it out in time to parry a thrust from the first. It was now one on one and Hayden began to force the man back, parrying and retreating. He ran the edge of his blade up the man's forearm, cutting arteries and tendons. The man dropped his sword and went down on one knee, clutching his wounded arm.

Hayden hovered the point of his blade at the man's neck. 'Ask for quarter,' he said in Breton, surprising the man overly, and, without hesitation, the man did.

Snatching up the man's blade, Hayden turned back to the fighting, which, he realized, was over everywhere but on the quarterdeck. Spanish and British sailors corralled the privateers, while all around the still lay upon the deck, and the wounded moaned and cried out. Wickham passed, leading a company of English and Spanish to the quarterdeck. Hayden went to the rail, and leaned out. The spring had been cut and the frigate was drifting with the current. At that instant, guns fired from the nearby privateer, shot hissing through the rigging.

Hayden climbed up on to the rail and turned back to the deck. 'Where is Captain Serrano?' he shouted in the brief silence after the guns fired.

There was muttering and whispering and then Serrano appeared, his coat gone and his right arm bound in a bloody dressing.

Hopping down from the rail, Hayden went to him. 'You are injured, Captain . . .'

'It is nothing,' Serrano insisted. 'Shall we man the larboard guns, Captain Hayden?'

'Immediately, if you please.'

Serrano began calling out orders in Spanish. Men hastened to the guns in an orderly manner, which Hayden approved heartily. Gunports creaked open and the rumble of wooden wheels rolling over the deck planks came to him. Ransome appeared, looking rather done in, but intact, as far as his captain could tell.

'Are you hurt, Mr Ransome?'

'No, sir. I seemed to be in the thick of it, though, and if the French had not surrendered I might have fallen to the deck from exhaustion.'

'It was bravely fought, all around. I want you to take charge of the gundeck. This is our ship and I don't want the Spanish losing sight of that.'

'Aye, sir.' Ransome reached up to touch the hat which he had not, until that moment, realized was gone. He crossed to the ladder, his gait a little wandering, as though he had received a blow to the head and was not quite recovered.

Hayden sent a man below to carry up his nightglass but, before it arrived, the privateer fired a second broadside and this one did considerable damage to their rig and sent four or five men plummeting to the deck.

'Give me a whisper of wind,' Hayden muttered, to no one in particular.

Hawthorne and a Spanish lieutenant had taken charge of rounding up prisoners, and the wounded Spanish and English were being borne down to the surgeon before the wounded privateers had their turn.

The frigate's guns all fired at an order from Ransome, which was repeated by Gould on the upper deck. Whether they did any damage to the privateer, Hayden could not tell through the darkness and smoke. With no wind, the cloud of smoke remained stationary, hanging over the water in a thick mass as the current carried the ship slowly away. The cloud obscured the enemy vessel, which, carried on the same current, was travelling at precisely the same speed, the distance between the two ships neither growing nor becoming less.

Hayden's nightglass arrived and he quizzed the darkness with it, but the mass of smoke hanging over the water hid her quite effectively.

'Aloft there . . .' he called out. 'Did we do any damage to that privateer?'

A second of silence, and then an English voice, 'Sir . . . Much of our shot fell short.'

'By what distance?' Hayden called up.

'A cable length, sir.'

Hayden went to the waist and called down into the darkness of the gundeck.

'Did you hear, Mr Ransome?'

'A cable length shy, sir. We are elevating guns, Captain.'

'Fire when you are ready, Mr Ransome.' Hayden stared up into the rigging. 'Aloft . . . Have you a nightglass?'

'We do not, Captain.'

'I will have mine carried up.'

Gould sent a man scurrying Hayden's way and he swiftly bore the valuable glass up to the lookout. Hayden wished to go aloft himself, so he could assess what the enemy was doing, but did not want to cede the deck to Serrano.

Ransome called out again, and the larboard battery hurled fire and smoke into the night. The smoke hung so thick about the deck that Hayden could hear men coughing from all points. For a moment an unnatural silence overspread the ship and then the lookout called down.

'*On deck!* Our fire struck home, Captain.'

Hayden called down to the gundeck. 'Well done, Mr Ransome. Let us pour in as many broadsides as we can.'

He stood at the rail while the gunners plied their trade. It was soon obvious that the Spanish gun crews were not nearly so efficient as the British, whose rate of fire was almost double that of the Spanish and never less than three for two.

It was a strange battle, the two ships drifting down-current, firing, through dense clouds of smoke that hung in the air, at an enemy who could barely be glimpsed.

With direction from aloft, Hayden was able to concentrate his fire so that much, if not most, of it found its mark, while the fire from the privateer was far less effective, much of it passing overhead, some landing in the water, short.

Using numerous 18-pound balls, Hayden made up two 'anchors' and deployed them, one at the stern and one at the bow. When the frigate exhibited a tendency for either her head or her stern to get a little ahead, the 'anchor' was deployed long enough to slow that part of the ship and keep the frigate square to her enemy. All the while Hayden glanced aloft and watched for the smallest signs of wind.

Scrivener appeared with a Spaniard bearing a rolled chart.

'You appear terribly grave, Mr Scrivener,' Hayden observed, beckoning the two men forward.

'I have been consulting with the frigate's master, sir.' He nodded to the man and introduced him. 'My Spanish is less than perfect and his English is not up to my Spanish, but the charts and a pointing finger are the same in all languages. The sailing master believes we might very well be swept up on to shoals within the hour, sir.'

Hayden had ordered all deck lamps extinguished, so the three repaired below, where they unrolled the chart in the dim light of a lamp.

The Spanish sailing master tapped the chart, 'We anchored here, Captain Hayden. The current in this channel can vary from one to as many as four knots, though at this time of year I would estimate it to be two knots.' He put his finger on a conspicuous reef. 'Therefore, we must not be too distant from the reefs that lie off this island.'

Hayden gazed at the chart only a moment. 'We cannot go

aground. Given a little wind, the enemy would be upon us of an instant.'

He looked quickly along the gundeck, where the crews went about their business. The guns had been traversed a little aft at the directions of the lookouts.

'How certain are you of our position?' Hayden asked.

The two men glanced at each other. 'Quite certain.'

'How near to the reef do you dare to take us?'

The Spaniard blew air through his lips in a small explosion. 'Well, Captain, I should not like to risk going too near. It is dark, the speed of the current not precisely known . . .'

'I understand,' Hayden said. He looked around. 'Find Captain Serrano and bring him to me, if you please.'

Hayden went back up on to the deck, where the gun crews were also hard at work. Again he looked for signs of wind, but found none.

A moment later the sailing master appeared with Captain Serrano, the two deep in conversation. Before Hayden could speak, Serrano began.

'I do not think it wise to risk going near these reefs, Captain Hayden.'

'It is not my intention to go any nearer, Captain Serrano. But here is what I intend to do. I will fire every gun on the ship at once and create an impenetrable cloud of smoke. Immediately thereafter, we will drop anchor and swing head to wind.'

'But they will rake us, Captain, three times, perhaps.'

'Only if they see us. Either they will pass close by to starboard, whereupon we will rake them, or they will tangle in our bow sprit, swing alongside and we will board. How many men do you think this privateer carries?'

'Not so many as we, I should think,' Serrano replied, 'but I am not even certain which ship it might be, nor was I ever aboard her.'

'But do you believe their numbers greater?'

'I very much doubt it.'

'Then we will board if we have the chance. If not, we will weigh and drift down on them. If they strike the shoals we will anchor and fire on them until they strike or we inflict so much damage to their ship it can never float free.'

Serrano shook his head, his face drawn tight as if in pain. 'With all respect, Captain Hayden, it is a very risky plan. So many things could go wrong. We might be raked from bow to stern, they might drop their own anchor and be only a pistol shot distant. They might carry away our bow sprit and jib boom—'

'But there are spars aboard to replace these,' Hayden interrupted the man.

'Yes, in time, that is true, but we could lose our foremast . . .'

'I do not think there is much chance of that – with so little sea running and no wind at all.'

'I simply think it is too great a risk, Captain Hayden. I say this with all respect; I have been at sea twenty years longer than you and I should never attempt such a thing.'

'And I say this with equal respect, Captain Serrano: I think the risks are smaller than you imagine. It is a dark night, we will be hidden by a dense cloud, and if they penetrate our intentions and anchor, then we must have the advantage in weight of broadside; if they tangle in our rig and swing alongside, then we will have the advantage in men. If they pass us by, we will rake them and drift down until they either anchor or are swept on to the reefs. It is not without risks, I realize, but we cannot continue on to the reefs and must anchor sooner or later at any rate.'

This last argument even Serrano could not counter, though he appeared to be desperately searching for a rebuttal. The man might have been at sea twenty years longer, but Hayden wondered how many battles the man had fought, for he seemed to be the type who could envision only the disasters and never the successes.

'Station men to drop anchor, Captain,' he said, no longer able to tolerate the man's indecision, 'and to fire both batteries at once on my order. We will prepare to fight the starboard battery or board, as the situation requires.' He made a small bow – a respectful dismissal, he hoped – and turned back to Scrivener. 'Pass the word for my officers, if you please, Mr Scrivener.'

The Spaniards went off and, within a few yards, were whispering to each other. Hayden watched them retreat, thinking as they went that boldness in battle was ever more preferable than caution, for the enemy almost always expected what they would do themselves. Serrano would never expect what Hayden was about to do and he hoped the privateers were of the same mind.

Hayden lurked about the deck, listening to the orders given to the Spanish sailors. It appeared that Serrano's lieutenants approved the plan more than their captain, for they passed the orders along with barely concealed enthusiasm, which revealed more about Serrano than the man would have liked, Hayden guessed.

Ransome, Gould, Hawthorne and Wickham were quickly informed of Hayden's plan and approved it most heartily.

Guns were run out on both sides and, at an order from Hayden, all fired at once. The cloud this created roiled for a second from the violence of the explosion and then settled into a languid mass. For a long moment it clung to the ship, and then the ship appeared to drift away from it. Hayden attempted to calm his racing heart, and counted to sixty slowly. He then gave the order to let the anchor go, which was managed with only the smallest splash, the cable running out ever so slowly. Immediately upon being snubbed, the ship began to swing.

The deck guns were then reloaded with grape – an order Hayden almost hated to give.

Shot from the privateer continued to land near, but in only a few moments Hayden noticed that most passed overhead and none struck the hull. As the ship turned, she presented a smaller target and even more shot hissed by to either side. The dense storm of black smoke continued to hang over the water, hardly dissipating, only a few tendrils reaching out toward the Spanish frigate, as though reluctant to let it go.

The boats, which lay alongside, were moved aft and streamed with the current.

'Aloft there!' Hayden called to the lookout. 'Can you see our privateer?'

'I cannot make her out, Captain.'

'Inform me the moment you can.'

'Aye, sir.'

'If we cannot see them,' Hawthorne said quietly, 'does it mean they cannot perceive us?'

'So we might hope.' Hayden looked up at the clouds sailing over and the moonlight knifing down through the channels between the clouds. The sea was still illuminated here and there by shafts of moonlight, but none of these drew near.

The men at the deck guns on the quarterdeck were silent and unnaturally still, as though they listened for their pursuers' footsteps. No one knew when the privateer would appear and whether she would come through the cloud dead ahead with raking fire or if she would pass to starboard, as Hayden had predicted.

'Which do you expect, Captain,' Hawthorne whispered, 'that we will rake her as she passes or that she will tangle with us and we will board?'

'I do wish I knew, Mr Hawthorne. Certainly, she appeared to be ever so slightly south of us, nearer the coast, but precisely where the current will bear her ... Anyone's guess would be as accurate as mine.'

'I rather doubt that, Captain. Your "guess" is the one I should take most seriously.'

The two stood at the rail – "friends", as much as their respective ranks and positions allowed, and Hayden found comfort in the marine lieutenant's presence. He wished he felt less like he was proceeding to his own hanging, but thus were the trials of command – the captain was the individual who would be held accountable for decisions such as the one he had just made; the captains of the court martial would be told of Serrano's expressed reservations. Hayden hoped his youth and inexperience would not lead to a disaster here, costing many lives from both his and Serrano's crew – there would almost certainly be a Spanish mutiny at that point.

He could not allow the Spanish to regain control of their ship. Somewhere, beyond the cloud of smoke, he imagined his bride, lying awake, hoping with all her heart that Hayden would not fail her. The marine officer standing beside him had once warned him of this propensity in men – to attempt the rescue of maidens in distress – but they had then been discussing the doctor and the maid of all work whom he had rescued. Hayden, however, seemed as prone to this as any man – as his recent history proved.

'*On deck!* She is coming through the cloud, Captain.'

A shaft of pale moonlight fell upon the cloud at that instant, illuminating it and, if anything, making it more impenetrable. And then the masts and yards of a ship appeared, high up, and then the ship itself, beam on and a little to starboard. Her stern was to them and she fired a broadside, none of which struck Hayden's Spanish frigate.

It was so silent aboard the ship that Hayden could hear the shouting in French as the privateers realized their situation.

He pushed off the rail and called down to the gundeck. 'Mr Ransome, we will rake her as she passes. Fire each gun as she bears.'

Before the lieutenant could answer, Hayden heard the splash of the privateer's anchor being let go in panic. The captain is certainly no fool, Hayden thought, as he must have had his cable faked upon the gundeck and ready to veer. The privateer was not seventy-five yards up-current from them and would certainly pass just beyond pistol shot, stern on if the anchor did not hold immediately.

Hawthorne ordered his men to open fire, and the crack of musket fire sounded from both ships. A ball struck a gun on the quarterdeck, ricocheted and came so near Hayden's ear that he swore he felt the wind of its passing. He touched his ear to be certain it was intact.

The bottom of the channel was, as Hayden knew, uncertain. Much of it was sand, but there were numerous coral heads as well. The Frenchman's anchor might snag one of these and they would be able to snub her up on very little cable. They might also try to snub her to lay her alongside the Spanish frigate, only to find their anchor ploughing ineffectually through soft sand. If the Frenchman's anchor held as it should, the two ships would be less than pistol shot distant and Hayden would not have the usual advantage provided by his British crew — a higher rate of fire. If this was one of the privateers Jones had told him about, she would likely carry only 12-pounders, and Hayden's ship bore the Spanish equivalent of the British 18-pounder.

With one eye on the enemy ship, Hayden ordered guns traversed as far forward as possible. He then positioned himself a few yards behind one of the deck guns so that he might sight along it. There was no shot.

The forward chase piece fired at that moment — but it was a small gun and Hayden could not see if it caused any damage at all.

If he had been the French captain, Hayden knew he would not snub his cable until the last possible instant, which would allow the most cable to be veered, increasing the chances of the anchor holding. Hayden thought he would snub it just where he thought it would bring the ship to before it came under the Spanish frigate's guns. If he had the men, he would attempt to board and carry the frigate by main force.

What the master of the privateer would do, Hayden could not say. The man was formidable and not the least shy, he believed. To have slipped his anchor and ridden the current down to the frigate as it was being attacked by boarders was enterprising in the extreme. Hayden was not certain he would have thought of it himself – nor dared it if he had.

The privateer continued to be carried down-current at the pace of an old man out for a stroll. So close were the ships to one another that Hayden heard the master order the cable snubbed. All eyes were fixed upon the enemy ship as she drifted . . . and then, almost imperceptibly, her bow began to lag behind, and then it was clearly so. Where the ship would fetch up or whether her anchor would hold once the entire mass of the ship came upon it, no one knew.

'Pass the word for my officers, if you please,' Hayden said to a British sailor at one of the guns. 'And Captain Serrano, as well.'

In a moment, Ransome, Wickham, Gould and Hawthorne appeared, followed almost immediately by the Spanish captain.

'Are we to board, her, Captain?' Ransome asked, clearly both excited by the prospect and anxious as well – as any sane man would be.

'It would appear to be the most logical course, Mr Ransome,' Hayden replied. 'Mr Wickham, I will leave you in command of the ship.'

Before Hayden could say more, one of the Spanish lieutenants came on to the quarterdeck; Hayden had seen the man hurrying along the gangway.

'Captain,' the man said, but he addressed Hayden, not Serrano, much to the Spanish captain's surprise, 'the privateers are rigging a spring. We could hear their orders from the forecastle.'

Hayden needed only a second to comprehend what that meant.

'Then we must do the same,' he ordered, 'in all haste.'

The privateer was going to swing his ship to bring his broadside to bear on the frigate, and from the angle his ship would achieve he would be firing diagonally across the deck – not a raking fire, but damned close.

The Spanish lieutenant and Ransome went running off, calling out orders as they went. No doubt the French would hear – just as they had overheard the French – but it did not matter. They must swing their ship to bring their own guns to bear or they would be at the mercy of the privateer's cannon. If one of the frigate's masts could be brought down . . . the ship would be lost.

Hayden found himself standing at the rail with Serrano and Hawthorne. 'Have you ever seen what can be done with a ship in a tideway or a river when a spring is employed, Mr Hawthorne?'

'I do not believe I have, Captain.'

'When a ship is set at an angle to the flow so the current strikes one side of the vessel, she can be shifted to one side or the other – and quite substantially.'

Hawthorne contemplated this but a moment. 'Could they swing their ship down upon us?' he wondered.

'It is a weak current,' Serrano answered, in Hayden's stead, 'but then, the ships are not distant one from the other. I should say it is just possible.'

'This privateer . . .' Hawthorne observed with something like admiration, 'he is a cunning dastard, is he not, Captain?'

'Indeed he is, Mr Hawthorne. I do wonder how large his crew might be.' Although he had asked this question of Serrano once already, he glanced at the Spaniard again. The man shrugged.

'I wish I had an answer for you, Captain Hayden,' he offered softly. 'When they boarded our ships, they did so in overwhelming numbers.'

At that moment, Hayden wished above all things that he had his own crew about him, for they would have a spring rigged in a trice. As it was, Hayden did not know if he should allow the French to come alongside. If they had superior numbers he might lose his frigate – for which he had paid dearly already. Better to use his greater weight of broadside – the very thing this privateer was attempting to nullify – damn his eyes.

Hayden felt himself leaning out over the rail, attempting to part the darkness. He could barely make out the ship, but the tops of her masts could just be distinguished against the star-scattered sky. Her chase piece had ceased firing and Hayden wondered if it could no longer be brought to bear because the ship was turning. He suspected that the French would fire bar or chain into the frigate's rigging. At such close range a great deal of damage could be inflicted – even by 12-pounders.

A flash and simultaneous report left no doubt about the privateer's position. The sound of iron tearing through the rigging could not be mistaken. A foremast yard came swinging down but did not strike the deck. A man tumbled out of the rigging and struck the planks just before the mainmast. He lay utterly still and was quite certainly dead.

Everyone aboard held their breath while the privateers reloaded their guns.

Wickham appeared at the head of the companionway. 'We have a spring rigged, sir.'

'Veer the bower cable, if you please, Mr Wickham.' Hayden spoke the order as clearly and calmly as he was able.

'Aye, sir.' The midshipman thumped down the ladder, leaping the last three steps, Hayden could tell, and went running forward, shouting Hayden's order as he went.

The privateer's guns fired again, tearing through the rigging, doing untold damage. Hayden held his breath, but the masts stood. The head of his ship was paying off quickly to larboard and would move more quickly once the current caught it.

The men stood at the guns, which had been traversed as far forward as was possible. Gun captains positioned themselves to sight along the barrels, but it seemed to take for ever for the guns to be brought to bear.

Hayden thought the privateers would fire a third broadside before his own guns could be fired, and he felt himself bracing for it, as did all the men around him, hunching up their shoulders and stiffening. None, however, shied or tried to hide.

Ransome appeared at the ladder head to the gundeck, his body facing Hayden but his head turned back so that he could hear what was being said on the deck below. His head snapped around suddenly.

'Guns are bearing, Captain,' he called out.

'You may fire the battery, Mr Ransome.'

Ransome's order and the firing of the frigate's broadside occurred simultaneous with the firing of the privateer's guns. Flame erupted from both ships and then a dense pall of smoke hid even the stars. British and Spanish crews went about reloading and Hayden believed the Spaniards were trying not to be outdone by the English, crack gunners whose rate of fire had never yet been equalled by the enemy.

Hayden's greatest worry was that the privateers would

sever his spring line, but their guns were aimed into the frigate's rigging, attempting to disable her, and nowhere near
low enough to find the spring.

For a quarter of an hour, the two ships fired broadside
after broadside at one another but, with each explosion of
guns, the French rebuttal was reduced, as her gun crews were
decimated and guns dismounted.

'*On deck!*' the lookout cried. 'The privateer is moving,
Captain . . . down-current.'

Hayden hastened to the ladder head. 'Veer the spring, Mr
Ransome! With all haste!'

Out of the smoke, the privateer drifted. Between the darkness and the smoke lying on the water, Hayden was not
certain of the ship's attitude, but it appeared she had slipped
her anchor again and was drifting free, attempting to get
clear of the frigate's guns.

As Hayden's spring was veered and the ship turned slowly
head to wind, she shifted to starboard, nearer the enemy vessel. Guns were hurriedly traversed and, after the briefest
interruption, began again to fire. At such close range the
18-pounders were devastating.

The privateer was borne along the current until the two
ships were almost abreast.

'She is very near, Captain, is she not?' the gun captain
beside Hayden asked quietly.

'Distances are ever deceiving by darkness,' Hayden replied.
But then he began to wonder if the man was not correct, if
the French ship was not swinging nearer. For a moment he
stood, trying to measure the water between the ships.

'Prepare to repel boarders!' he cried suddenly. He ran to
the ladder head and called down to the gundeck. 'Fire a last

broadside, Mr Ransome, and then close and secure gunports. All men to the upper deck. They are swinging their ship alongside!'

Hayden pulled a pistol from his belt, thumbed back the cock and then drew his sword. As guns were fired aboard his ship – at less than pistol shot – he went to the rail. A curtain of grey wafted before him, the enemy ship ghostly, glimpsed and then lost. Men came crowding up from behind, bearing arms and swearing oaths. A few jumped up on the guns or on to the rail, waving cutlasses and shouting threats and defiance. Musket and pistol fire began in earnest, and this first group of the foolishly brave paid the price for it, being taken down from their perches and tumbling into the mass of men behind.

The cloud thinned and out of it the rail of a ship appeared. Hayden lowered his pistol and shot a man not ten feet distant. The two ships were moving so slowly that they came almost gently together, even as violence spread over their decks. For a long moment the two crews fought at the rail, neither able to press forward on to the other ship's deck. One of the Spanish lieutenants then led a charge, up on to a quarterdeck gun and over the rail, leaping down into the mass of Frenchmen and breaking the line. Hayden followed immediately after, jumping from rail to rail and then down on to the deck and into the melee.

Two British topmen and Lord Arthur Wickham came to his side, and the four of them pressed forward, a deadly little squadron of fighters, taking a foot of deck and then another. Hayden felt a point penetrate his left arm above the elbow and realized it had been a thrust aimed at Wickham which the midshipman had parried. There was no time to stop and assess damage; they were beset on all sides.

It was a long battle and, when finally it appeared that his side had carried the day, Hayden had to use his cutlass as a cane to hold himself up. All his reserves were spent and he heaved and gasped like a man who had been too long beneath the water.

Although he could still hear the sounds of battle forward, the Frenchmen around him were surrounded in little knots and began throwing down their arms and suing for quarter. Wickham went off into the dark as though on some urgent errand and returned a moment later with midshipman Gould in tow.

Immediately, Gould approached his captain and Hayden realized that he and Wickham were removing his jacket and that his forearm and hand dripped with blood. He felt suddenly a little light-headed.

'It was my doing,' Wickham explained to Gould. 'I parried a thrust and it went off my blade and caught the captain unaware . . . and I am heartily sorry for it.'

Hayden wanted to tell Wickham that it was not his fault in any way at all, but could not, somehow. The two midshipmen sat him down on a gun carriage while Gould tore away his sleeve and used it for a dressing.

'Have I ever told you, Mr Gould,' Hayden said, carefully forming his words, as though he were a few drinks drunk, 'how pleased I am that your brothers studied medicine?'

Gould managed a smile. 'Never have you, sir.'

'Well, now I have. How have we fared, Mr Wickham?'

'Ransome and Hawthorne are gathering up the prisoners. I do not know how the other *Themis*es have done, but Captain Serrano shall have a butcher's bill such as he has never seen, I suspect.'

'And has our good Spanish captain survived?'

'I saw him but a moment ago,' Gould replied, 'going below . . . looking for prisoners, I should imagine.'

'Let us hope there are some . . . we need to make up a prize crew . . . and Serrano needs a command, I think.'

Gould finished tying Hayden's dressing. 'No major arteries were severed, sir, so I should hope it would stop bleeding soon.' He did not say a word about the possibility of the wound going septic.

'Thank you, Gould.' Hayden's moment of light-headedness had passed and he rose to his feet. He turned back to the rail and called up to the men in the rigging, 'Aloft there! Can you yet see the other ships?'

'I can just make them out, Captain. They haven't moved, sir.'

'And I am more than glad to hear it,' Hayden muttered. 'How much damage is there aloft?' he then called.

'A good deal, sir,' came the reply from the heavens. 'It shall be a job of work to put it aright.'

Ransome came striding out of the dark, cutlass still in hand. 'She swims, Captain,' he declared. 'We managed not to hole her below the waterline.'

'Are there prisoners, Mr Ransome?'

'Not so many as on the frigate. Appeared to be fifty or sixty, sir. Captain Serrano is seeing to them.'

French prisoners were being herded on to the forecastle and made to sit down on the deck. Hayden glanced up at the stars, wondering how distant dawn might be. Wind remained in absence – not enough to stir a lock of a maiden's hair – and even in the darkness the heat was oppressive, the air close.

There was a flurry at the ladder head. Out of the gaggle of men rushing on to the deck appeared Serrano, holding a square of linen over his mouth and nose.

'Fever,' he blurted from behind his hand. 'They have fever aboard this ship.'

Thirty=one

Every man who heard retreated from Serrano and his small entourage. The word passed along the deck like a hissing little breeze. *Fever! They have the fever!*

Hayden fought an impulse to retreat over the rail back on to the frigate.

'How many?' he asked quietly, displaying composure he did not feel.

'I did not count,' Serrano replied. 'The sick-berth is over-flowing.'

'Has it spread among the Spanish prisoners?'

'I – I do not know.'

'Send a man below to find out. I shall not release them if there is fever among them.'

'But I have released them already.'

'They might have to go into quarantine. Have a lieutenant find out if they have the Yellow Jack.'

Serrano nodded. He spoke a moment to one of his offic-ers and then retreated to the rail. Certainly, he would have gone back to the frigate but could not while Hayden and his officers remained aboard the infected ship. His pride was not yet overruled by his terror of the fever, though this was clearly substantial.

Hayden felt for a moment that the decisions he had to make were too complicated for his brain to encompass. He had a Spanish frigate bearing too many French prisoners. A privateer's ship with likely one hundred and fifty more. He had fever among the French on this ship and perhaps among their Spanish prisoners as well. He had hoped to use this ship in his pursuit of the privateers and his bride but now he had other difficulties.

Serrano's lieutenant emerged from below, found his captain by the rail and shook his head. Hayden almost sighed aloud.

He went to the Spanish captain at the rail and waved the others away.

'I shall put you in command of this ship and send you into Havana with all of our French prisoners. You will have to go into quarantine there, but you might send us aid. There must be Spanish Navy ships there.'

Serrano was clearly taken aback by this and did not offer an answer.

'Shall I put one of your lieutenants in command and send him to Havana?' Hayden whispered.

Serrano looked around, as though searching for something that might save him from this command. 'No,' he said quietly. 'I shall take her in. But we might have trouble with the prisoners if they know they are going into a ship with the fever.'

'It is likely known among all their ships, but we will quarantine the sick and keep them separate. I will speak with the French master.' This brought another matter to hand. 'Where is the master of this ship? What has become of him?'

Enquiries were quickly made, and it was revealed that the French master – the formidable captain who had fought his ship so cunningly – had been killed in the hand-to-hand fighting. Hayden was sorry to hear it, for certainly the man had been a brilliant officer . . . even if a privateer.

Hayden put Serrano and Hawthorne in charge of transferring prisoners, and sent Ransome and Wickham aloft with a Spanish bosun and his crew to begin putting the frigate's rig to rights. Serrano mastered himself and began to effect repairs on the privateer.

Hayden went about his ship, seeing to everything being done. As he did so, he encountered an acrid smoke hanging over the ship and on her lower decks. Finding Ransome, he enquired of it.

'Some leaves and twigs, sir,' the lieutenant informed him. 'The Spanish surgeon has ordered it burned to keep back the Yellow Jack from the other ship.'

'I should think it would hold any contagion at bay,' Hayden said. 'It is the most wretched odour!'

Ransome smiled. 'I agree, sir. It seems to keep the insects away, so it is not altogether useless.'

Light found all the ships, becalmed only a few miles from the Cuban coast, men clambering among the rigging, swaying up topmasts, crossing yards and renewing shrouds and stays.

Almost forgotten in the fighting was the schooner. Hayden asked Serrano to make up a small crew of experienced men and sent it off for Nassau to carry word of what had occurred, hoping to find Navy ships there that might be sent to his aid. Commonly, he would have put a lieutenant or midshipman in command but he was so short of officers he could not spare them. Using a Spanish crew was less than ideal, but he could see no way around it, and watched the vessel set sail with some misgivings.

It was noon before the ships were ready for sea, and still the wind did not blow over that part of the ocean. Hayden and all his men were exhausted beyond measure, for none had slept that night and they had fought a hard battle and refitted their ship – much of it by darkness.

Hayden had kept one of Serrano's lieutenants aboard the frigate to translate his orders and station the Spanish crew as necessary. Watches were arranged, messes organized and the ship put into order.

The lieutenant, whose Spanish rank Hayden believed was *Teniente de navío*, was named Reverte, and he seemed rather pleased to find himself in the chase – despite the odds – and not returning to Havana to seek help. The fact that the ship Serrano commanded had the Yellow Jack aboard was likely something of a relief as well.

While the watch below slept, the deck watch were kept busy about the ship, despite their exhaustion. With the enemy so near, Hayden did not feel he could allow these men to rest but kept them constantly employed so that they might be ready to defend the ship of an instant should the privateers again launch boats.

He questioned Reverte closely about the other frigate – the one he believed carried Angelita. She was a sister ship to the frigate he had taken, with identical guns arrayed in the same manner. Reverte did not believe either ship to be swifter or more weatherly, and both, according to him, were fresh from refit and in near-perfect condition. It was obvious he believed them to be superior to both French and British frigates of similar rate.

'The privateers would never have taken either ship, but they employed a ruse no one had before seen,' he explained to Hayden. 'We first saw smoke on the horizon and, upon approaching, the Spanish-flagged ships taking off the crew of a transport that appeared to be afire. Boats were plying back and forth with all haste and some men on the burning ship plunged into the sea and swam. Immediately, we went to their aid but all the boats in the water bore armed men and suddenly we were beset by overwhelming numbers and our ships, which were utterly unprepared, overrun.'

'I have never seen such a ruse before,' Hayden admitted, 'and almost certainly would have fallen victim to it myself.'

'You are being very gracious, Captain. We abandoned all common caution. I believe it was the men leaping into the sea – to avoid burning, it seemed – that convinced us what we saw was real.'

'And you did not note that these ships carried more guns than any transport would?'

Reverte held up a finger, 'Ahh, but here they were clever as well. We could see canvas strips painted with gunports, which transports sometimes wear to appear to be what they are not. But these canvas strips concealed *real* gunports! As though one wore an obviously false beard to hide one's real beard.'

'Do you recall seeing, among the privateers, a young woman?'

'This is Mrs Hayden, Captain?'

It was uncanny, Hayden thought, how easily rumours could penetrate the language barrier. He nodded.

'Yes, there was such a woman. Not the sort one would expect to see aboard a French privateer. She was with a young man I assumed must be her husband. I should have realized they were Spanish by his dress, but my mind . . . We had just lost our ship to a ruse and my career was finished.'

'Perhaps we can resurrect your career, Lieutenant.'

'Perhaps . . .' The young man, who appeared to be about Hayden's age, glanced over at the prize so recently taken and now under command of Captain Serrano. 'My captain will never revive his career. It is a tragedy, for he is an admirable man and an exceptional officer.'

Hayden thought the captain something of a fool for approaching strange ships without first beating to quarters, or at least being utterly certain of their nationality and intentions before drawing near. Panicked men leaping off the burning ship, though . . . Hayden suppressed a smile of admiration – it was a brilliant bit of theatre.

'On deck?' the lookout cried. 'The privateers appear to have wind, sir.'

Hayden and Reverte hurried forward, where they found Ransome gazing through a glass. A glass, however, was not necessary: Hayden could see sails being loosed.

'They will sail their anchors out on that wind,' Ransome declared.

Hayden glanced up at the masthead. There was hardly a breath stirring. The crew was already at quarters, in the event that they must repel boarders.

'Prepare to heave our anchor, Mr Ransome. We shall keep the crews at their guns but have them ready to loose sail at a moment's notice. These privateers might let the wind carry them down to us, and could reach us even as the wind does.'

'Will we cut our anchor cable, then, sir?' Ransome asked.

'If we are forced to. I am loath to give up another anchor.'

'I believe they will run,' Reverte declared.

'But they are four ships and we are but two . . .' Ransome handed the Spaniard his glass.

Reverte raised it to his eye. 'That is true, but Captain Hayden has already taken two of their ships. They will not want to risk losing the prize they have taken. I believe they will run . . . but perhaps I will be proven wrong.'

An anxious half of the hour followed and, just as wind began to stir about the ship, it became clear that Reverte would not be proven wrong. The privateers gathered way and shaped their course to follow the coast away from Hayden and Serrano's vessels. For a frustrating hour Hayden and his crew watched their quarry fly, gathering speed, it appeared, by the minute.

But, finally, the wind reached them, almost on the beam. Setting just enough sail to give them way against the current, they retrieved their anchor, the men at the capstan almost trotting in a circle to keep up.

Perhaps two hours after noon, they were under sail and in pursuit of their enemy, the lookouts calling out when reefs or coral heads could be seen, and the officer of the watch giving orders to the helmsman and sail handlers to shape their course to avoid these obstacles. While they had been refitting, Hayden had ordered the mizzen topmast and yards swayed up so that his ship could carry all possible sail.

Ransome and Wickham had gone over the ship's stores and reported that, as expected, they were victualled and watered for an ocean crossing and had enough powder and shot to take on a good-sized fleet.

The four ships of the privateers sailed in a line, the distance between them short and the frigate second in line. Two of the converted transports, with their twenty 12-pounders, lay between Hayden and Mrs Hayden – and the same two ships lay between the British members of the crew and a cargo of Spanish silver. Avarice, Hayden thought, could be seen shining in their eyes and upon their very faces. Although they did not know the value of this cargo, everyone imagined it large enough to make them wealthy for life. Hayden did not tell them that they were treading into a legal quagmire. The Spanish remained their allies (or so Hayden assumed), they were aboard a liberated Spanish ship which the Spanish captain had claimed to be property of the Spanish Crown. Hayden contended the frigate was a British prize until superior officers deemed it otherwise and, if they were to take the frigate bearing bullion, it would be the same. However, it was possible, given the delicacy of Britain's alliance with Spain, that the Admiralty or the British government might choose to return the ships – and their cargos – to Spain. In which case the Admiralty might compensate Hayden and his crew for this loss, or they might not. More litigation, Hayden felt, with a distinct lowering of his spirits, might lie in his future.

The weather remained unsettled. Great continents of cloud passed over; the flattened, dense landscapes oppressively grey and unvarying. The wind, though constant in its direction, would take off, then make, then fall almost calm so Hayden ordered the anchor cable faked down upon the gundeck so that they might let go the anchor should the ship lose way altogether. The current, though small, could easily sweep a ship up on to a reef and do her considerable damage.

Hayden was forced to slip down to the captain's cabin and sleep for a few hours, as he could hardly stand for fatigue and he knew he would need a clear head and excellent judgement over the next few days. He did not want to be making decisions out of exhaustion and desire. His men deserved better than that. He emerged in the late afternoon, feeling somewhat befuddled, hoping the wind would clear his mind.

The brief tropical day wore swiftly on, and the sun was soon astern where the vast plains of cloud had not yet travelled. A honeyed light illuminated the fleeing ships and their tanned sails against the grey so that they appeared to be revealed in some holy light. All aboard gazed at this sight in solemn silence, as though they could see the very glitter of Papist silver going before them.

Hayden called together his senior officers, and both Scrivener and the Spanish sailing master, and spread a chart upon the table in the captain's cabin.

'The channel grows broader and again broader as we approach the Windward Channel. Even this night its width is much greater than when we weighed. I do not think we should give the enemy the slightest indication of it, but I propose we man all the guns on the gundeck, keep our gunports closed, and in all ways prepare for battle except upon the upper deck, where such preparations might be observed. With this dark sky, we will slip up on the aftermost ship and use our 18-pounders to our very great advantage. We might knock one ship out of the fight this very night.'

The young officers shifted about in excitement, but Hayden looked to Hawthorne, whom he had charged to be his common sense over the next few days – given that Hayden's own might be pushed aside by his feelings.

Hawthorne gave an almost imperceptible nod, which, for some reason, forced Hayden to hide a smile. There was something oddly amusing about a *marine* who was known to become ill in small boats sanctioning his plans.

'Shall we return the anchor cable to the cable tier, sir?' Ransome enquired.

'No, let us wet it down most thoroughly and leave it ready. The wind might die at any moment, as it has several times this day.'

'We will lose the use of two forward guns,' Ransome stated.

'I comprehend that, Mr Ransome, but, even so, our broadside will be greater.'

Ransome nodded. Hayden could almost see him ticking off a list of objections, a process of which his captain approved. He wanted his officers to think every action through most thoroughly and consider all eventualities – especially those that might see events turn against them.

'We will slip up on her larboard side,' Wickham asked, 'and have the weather gage?'

'For whatever small advantage it might provide us in these circumstances – yes.'

'Will they attempt to come alongside and board us, Captain?' Gould wondered.

'They might, especially so if we do not have much room to larboard, given the restrictions of the channel. Yet, I think we can keep distance between us for long enough that we can pour in sufficient broadsides either to disable their ship or force them to sheer off. We shall put them in a difficult position, for if they wear we will rake them.'

'Will no other ships come to their aid?' Reverte asked, contemplating the chart with a rather distant look, as though he could see the battle taking place upon it.

'We will find that out. I do not think they will risk bringing the frigate bearing the silver into the action but, certainly, the privateer next in line might come to her comrade's aid. We have men enough to fight both batteries and handle sail as well. It will be very dark and that will hide most evolutions until they are well underway.'

The idea of fighting two ships sobered the gathered officers somewhat. Broadside to broadside, the privateers were no match for the Spanish frigate, but if one ship could get astern of them and direct a raking fire on to their decks . . . well, even 12-pounders could cause a great deal of damage, not to mention many casualties, in such a situation.

Questions were asked, answers provided, and when everyone was certain of their plan and the sailing masters had agreed upon their exact location, the officers hastened out to ready the ship.

Hawthorne lingered behind, and Hayden fixed his friend with a questioning look.

'You approve this course of action, Mr Hawthorne?'

'I should approve it more had we our own ship and British crew but otherwise it seems a typically audacious Charles Hayden-like action.'

'You make me sound like Sir William, whose Jones-like endeavours are notorious.'

'There is a world of difference between you and Captain Jones. He is brave – almost absurdly so – as are you, Captain, but you are inside the mind of the enemy, or so it always appears to me. You have somehow penetrated their thoughts, or perhaps their way of thinking, and are able to predict what they are most likely to do.'

Hayden tried not to laugh. 'Mr Hawthorne, the truth is I

have no more knowledge of the enemy than you – or anyone else aboard, for that matter. I simply put myself in his place and ask what I would do in any given situation. I then weigh what I believe to be their own motivations in that same situation and then make my best guess as to what they are most likely to do. Not magic.'

'And what would you do in their situation, given you were being chased by a Spanish frigate under the command of a British captain desperate to regain his bride?'

'I would lure that captain into a trap.'

'And will they not do the same?'

'Perhaps, but their common sense is overridden by greed. I do not think they will risk the frigate unless she is brought to and they have no choice. The privateers wish to preserve their prize at all costs.'

'But the other three ships – though I do understand they boast only 12-pounders – could they not overpower us should all three of them attack us at once?'

'If they are properly managed, yes.'

'And why will they not do that?'

'I think it is possible that they will.' Hayden looked back at the chart laid upon the table. The Old Channel of Bahama would grow substantially wider over the next few days. 'They will not attempt to attack us where we might simply avoid battle – our frigate is faster than the converted transports.' He ran his finger along the north shore of Cuba until he came to its very end. 'If I were a privateer desiring to preserve my treasure at all costs, I should find the narrowest point and use my other three ships to set up a blockade, forcing us to battle.' Hayden tapped the chart. 'Here. The Windward Channel is only twelve leagues in breadth at its narrowest. If the two frigates are more or less equal in speed, the other ships would need to hinder us for only half a day and we would likely never catch the other frigate.' The one that bears my bride, Hayden thought.

'Can three ships blockade a pass so wide?'

Hayden considered a moment. 'Three frigates could manage it under most circumstances. They could not resist a strong squadron, perhaps, but they could space themselves so that no ship would pass through by day. These three privateers, nine miles distant one from the other . . . We might pass through under cover of darkness.'

'That sounds like a great risk, then,' Hawthorne said.

Hayden almost smiled, partly for being so obtuse. Hawthorne had inveigled him into reconsidering all his thoughts on this matter – aloud – so that the marine lieutenant and he might examine them together.

'Do you know, I believe the safest course for the privateers is to remain as they are in tight squadron where they might all support one another. We are only one ship, after all. The frigate and her three escorts are far more powerful than we. As long as they have shot and powder they can hold us at bay.'

'What will they do, Captain, if we attack the aftmost ship this night?' It was almost a prompt.

'The other ships will come immediately to her aid.'

'I wonder if there is profit in that?' Hawthorne rubbed his chin as he gazed at the chart.

'Only to put them on their guard.' Hayden paced to the transom windows and stood a moment looking out. A glorious sunset spread across the western sky.

'If they keep to their formation, then, Captain, and do not

allow us to pick off any stragglers, is there any way at all that we might hope to take this frigate bearing both the Spanish treasure and your own?'

'Short of terrible misfortune or divine intervention? None.'

'I do not much like that answer,' Hawthorne informed him.

'I like it a good deal less than you, Mr Hawthorne. When I served as Captain Bourne's first lieutenant, he often said, "Always assume your enemy is as intelligent as you." We cannot assume they will do anything foolish.'

'Then what is the point of attacking the trailing ship?'

'To see how they will respond – though I am not much in doubt of what the other ships will do. But we will see. Let us discover how great their understanding might be.'

Hawthorne nodded. 'It seems like a very long shot, Captain.'

'Indeed. But I can think of no other course at this time.'

Hawthorne nodded. 'I will muster my marines and musket men.'

Left alone in the captain's cabin, Hayden stood at the open window and watched the sunset as it progressed through all its glorious stages until there was but small gilding upon a few low, distant clouds. Hayden was standing there yet when the tropical night slipped silently in from the east. Stars began to appear, and then there was darkness, the heavens lit by uncounted points of light.

Hayden turned away to return to the deck and, even as he did so, there was a change in the motion of the ship. Mounting the ladder, he emerged on to deck to find the ship rolling in the low swell, her sails and gear slatting about.

Wickham was the officer of the watch, and he approached his captain the moment he appeared.

'We have lost our wind, sir,' he offered, rather unnecessarily.

'For how long, I wonder?' Hayden looked up at the pennants and around at the horizon. 'Can you make out our chases, Mr Wickham? Do they have wind?'

Hayden's nightglass was retrieved and carried to the deck. Wickham and Hayden both went forward, where the midshipman focussed the long glass on the privateers' ships.

'I believe they are becalmed, as well, Captain,' he declared after a moment, and handed the glass to Hayden.

It took a moment for Hayden's eye to adjust, but he thought he could make out the sails slatting back and forth as the ships rolled.

'What is our depth?'

'Twelve fathoms on sand, Captain,' Wickham answered promptly, impressing Hayden again with his efficiency. 'We appear to be over a shoaling bank.'

Hayden glanced up at the sky. 'If we do not have wind within the quarter-hour we will have the sails off her and anchor, Mr Wickham.' It was almost a law of the sea that once the sails were properly furled and the hands down from the yards, the wind would fill in again. He had seen it a thousand times, he was certain.

The quarter of the hour passed swiftly and the hands were called to anchor, then sent aloft to take in sail. The ship lay rolling in the swell, uncomfortable, but not terribly so. Hayden paced the deck. His plan to attack the aftmost ship was now impossible. They would be very much on the watch for boarding parties and would no doubt have rigged boarding nets. It was even possible that the privateers might attack him, by drifting down the current as they had before. His men were on the lookout for it.

As matters stood, the privateers were too distant to be fired upon. Hayden found his mind drifting back to the conversation with Hawthorne. If the four remaining privateer ships could not in some way be separated, they were, cumulatively, too great a force for his single frigate. For the life of him, however, Hayden could think of no way to separate them. The privateers were sensible of their situation; they would stay together at all costs.

These were the kind of circumstances that army officers did not comprehend – that one could be so near to the enemy and unable to mount an attack. One could not simply march forward. Batteries could not be established anywhere to attack these fortresses. Sappers could not dig their tunnels and undermine the enemy's walls. No, all that could be accomplished was to watch and wait. Even a seasoned sailor like Hayden found it frustrating.

'I wonder ...' Hayden whispered, a thought so absurd coming into his mind that immediately he rejected it. But then it returned in a slightly altered form. Objections rose up, and were, by more alteration, dealt with. It was risky to the point of foolishness – the kind of thing which William Jones would heartily approve. But, even so, the idea would not go away.

Hayden sent for Hawthorne, who arrived at the stern of the ship a moment later.

'An idea so appallingly dangerous and improbable has taken hold of my mind, Mr Hawthorne, that I am in need of your aid to banish it.'

'I am most anxious to hear it.'

'The privateers are, for the time being, beyond the reach of our guns . . .'

'That is true. I can see it myself.'

'Indeed. I do not believe there is any way we can separate these four ships and, together, they are too great a force for our single frigate.'

'I am awaiting the "appallingly dangerous" part.'

'Have you ever been witness to sappers tunnelling under a wall, causing a massive explosion and collapsing a section of a fortress wall?'

'I have had that particular pleasure. Are we going to tunnel under the seabed? Because I would agree that such a plan was somewhat improbable.'

'Very nearly. I propose taking the boats and towing a large explosive charge to the stern of the frigate, where we will set it off and damage her rudder beyond repair – at least beyond repair at sea.'

'Ah, that is the improbable and appallingly dangerous part.'

'I did warn you.'

Hawthorne contemplated this idea a long moment. 'How would we lay a charge against the ship? In a boat, I expect?'

'I propose lashing barrels together.'

'And have you ever seen, or even heard of this being done before?'

'Never.'

'Well, for that reason alone I am predisposed to approve it. You would carry these barrels in a boat, lash them to the rudder in some way, light a long match and row like the devil pursued you to get clear?'

'I should think we shall have to tow our barrels but, otherwise, that is very nearly what I am thinking.'

'If they see or hear us – and they will certainly be on the lookout – they will kill every man in the boat—'

'Did I mention that it might be appallingly dangerous?'

'It slipped my mind for a moment.' Hawthorne made an odd face and tilted his head slowly side to side, as though physically weighing the arguments for and against. 'We have slipped up on ships on many occasions to cut them out. In some ways, this is no different. It must be said, however, that in many of those cases the enemy did not expect us – as they will now. I suppose it is no more dangerous than a cutting-out expedition into a crowded French port to take a little brig of little value. It is a war and risking lives cannot be avoided . . . but I wonder if there is any reasonable chance of success? That for me is the question that must be answered, even though I am well aware that fortune ever plays too large a part in such endeavours.'

'It will be dependent upon our ability to get our charge near without being seen. Shall we propose this to Ransome and Wickham and have their opinions?'

'You are being rather parliamentary,' Hawthorne observed.

'It is such an unusual idea that I am in need of others to knock it down.'

'I am sorry to have failed you in that office. By all means, let us ask Ransome and Wickham . . . and Reverte as well. I am gaining a hearty respect for the man.'

The named officers were summoned and Hayden's proposal was put to them.

'If the charge is strong enough to damage the rudder beyond repair,' Reverte asked after but a moment's thought, 'might it not sink the ship? The stern is ever a vessel's most vulnerable part.'

Ransome and Wickham both nodded.

'It is a point well made,' Hayden said. 'And I am not certain I have an answer for it. Sinking the frigate would be no bad thing if it were not for the bullion aboard, which I have been charged to preserve by my admiral.' He did not add that his own bride was on that ship.

'It is dangerous because we have already used boats to take this frigate, so they will have watchmen in place and be highly alert.' He looked about. 'It is not such a dark night that we cannot be seen, even after the moon has set.'

'We must have them looking somewhere else,' Wickham pronounced.

'We could feign an attack on another ship,' Ransome suggested, 'though I am not certain how we might manage that without men being wounded or killed.'

No one could think of a way to feign an attack that would be believed by the enemy without actually attacking or at least getting within pistol range.'

'Fire ships!' Wickham blurted out.

'I do not believe we have ships we can put to such purpose, Mr Wickham,' Hawthorne observed, 'unless we have escorts of which the rest of us are unaware.'

'No, but we have boats – our own from the *Themis* and the frigate's boats. I suggest we find some way to put fire aboard them – perhaps in barrels we could line with copper. Take them up-current from the privateers, set them alight and position them to drift down on the enemy ships. They might not cause any real difficulties or even come terribly near the ships, but they will certainly have every eye upon them.'

This idea received much approval. Discussion then began as to which ship to attack and how the barrels might be lashed together in such a way as to keep the powder dry.

It was soon clear that the ship to be attacked would be the aftmost privateer, as any ship further up the line would have men upon the bow staring forward at the fire boats, so any British boats would likely be descried as they came to the stern of the ship ahead.

The French ships had not anchored in a perfect line, bow to stern, but were spread over a small area, the frigate perhaps fifty yards to starboard of the ship ahead, and the next two ships staggered yet again. It might be possible to send the boats drifting in among them, therefore, which would cause great panic, or so it was hoped. Fire was one of the seaman's greatest fears.

Small water barrels were commandeered to contain the fire, as the staves were thoroughly soaked through. Wickham took charge of this, having them lined with thin copper plates used upon the bottom of ships.

The others put their minds to making the craft that would bear their explosion. Four small barrels were weighted with shot until they floated half out of the water with their round ends up. A fifth barrel was set in the centre of these, so that it was above the water for the most part, and then filled with powder. All this was lashed together with a small frame of wood, and then lowered into the sea. It floated much as expected but was too large to be carried aboard a boat and then got over the side. A towing bridle was arranged.

Night wore on, so the work was done as quickly as possible. Not long after midnight, the two fire boats rowed off with a third to take off the crews. They were to skirt the enemy ships beyond their sight and row up-current of them before setting alight the old rope and tar in the barrels and releasing them to drift down on the privateers. Hayden took command of the boat that would lay the explosive charge against the rudder, as he would not send anyone else on such a mad endeavour. It had been, after all, his idea to begin with, and he was not about to ask another to perform it.

It was the task of Hayden's boat to hold position just beyond sight of the aftmost privateer and wait until the fire boats had been released and caused what Hayden hoped would be considerable confusion.

The "mine", as Hawthorne had named it, for so the sappers called their tunnels, was not easily towed, even against so weak a current, but it showed no signs of going over, so at least there was a chance they would get it to the ship with the powder still dry.

Childers steered them faithfully out on to the dark sea and, when it was believed they were just beyond the distance where their darkly painted boats might be seen, the rowers slacked their pace to hold position; and glad they were of it, for towing the mine was difficult work.

They waited for the sight of fire drifting down on the French ships.

From where they lay in the dark, Hayden could easily make out the lanterns on the nearest ship's stern, and through that light marched a sentry every few moments. One of these made a brief stop and a second figure appeared. It took a moment for Hayden to realize that the first man was the stern sentry and he had likely been wakened. Unfortunate timing, he thought. If the man were asleep when they arrived it would make their task much simpler.

A light appeared within the master's cabin, illuminating the transom-gallery windows, which would certainly be open on such a close night. He thought he could see someone moving about in the light, and prayed this man would make his nightly toilet and fall asleep easily. Hayden reminded himself that this hardly mattered – once the fire boats were discovered, everyone should soon be awake . . . with their attention fixed forward.

The rowers worked their sweeps in utter silence, and the depth of that silence told him how frightened they really were.

'Where are Mr Wickham's boats?' Childers muttered, perhaps unable to remain silent a moment longer.

'Be patient,' Hayden whispered. 'If they had been discovered, there would be firing and noise, so they are not yet to their places.'

Hayden glanced back to be certain their strange tow had not turned over and drowned the powder barrel or broken loose to bear down upon their own ship. Hayden himself had coiled down a short length of match cord into the powder hole on top and then pressed in a bung to keep all dry.

There had been a lively debate about how much powder would be required to damage a rudder beyond repair and the side that argued they would only get one chance at this, better make it count, won, so there was powder enough to do the job, Hayden was quite certain.

Childers touched his arm and pointed. Far off, before the anchored ships, a flicker, which then disappeared. But then it appeared again and began to swell. Somehow it then split in two and began to burn in earnest. Hayden was just wondering how long it would take the privateers to discover fire bearing down on them when a cry went up, carried over the open water.

Hayden held his men in check for a moment longer – until he hoped all eyes aboard the ships were focussed on the burning boats – and then he sent them away, as stealthily as they could row.

It would be a matter of timing, he thought. The attention of the privateers would be drawn forward to begin with but, at some point, he was certain, some man who had his wits about him would think to look around to see if their enemy could be found on any other quarter. The English sailors needed to have their mine in place before this occurred.

Fixing his eyes on the transom of their intended target, Hayden tried to gauge the reaction aboard this particular ship. There was both consternation and confusion, of that he was certain. Men were rushing on to the deck and all seemed to hurry forward. There were calls for poles to fend off the fire boats, though he suspected they did not yet quite know the nature of the threat drifting down on them. In the darkness and at distance, they might be actual ships.

Orders were called out aboard the privateer. Men were sent to stand by the anchor cable lest it need be cut or let run. Others were sent out to the tip of the jib boom with poles to prepare to protect that delicate spar from collision or fire. Others soaked down the deck forward and even the topsides. All the while, Hayden's black boat crept nearer, as though he and his men were crawling through the undergrowth to surprise their prey. He even felt at that moment like a heartless predator.

The stern of the ship took on height and then loomed over them. Aft, Hayden could see no sign of sentries and hoped they had been sent off to soak down decks, or to some other task to protect the ships from fire.

Childers could not bring the boat neatly alongside – the tow being dragged back by the current would not allow it – so he nudged the bow up to the ship's transom so that the men there could grasp hold of the rudder. Hayden scrambled forward through the rowers, a rope from the tow in his hand. There was very little purchase on the rudder, and the men attempting to hold on had it slip free of their grip. Without a thought, Hayden shrugged off his coat, pulled free his boots and went over the side as silently as he was able.

In two strokes he had his hands on the rudder. Feeding the rope in around it took a moment, as it was not a small timber, but he managed, and then, bracing his feet against the hull, he pushed with all his might, hauling in a length of rope, and then another. It was almost more than he could do, the current's drag on the tow was that great. Four times he did this, and then had to pause a moment to recover. The boat was unmanaged now, the men pulling the mine along its starboard side, but, with no oars in the water, it was quickly being swept aft.

Again Hayden braced his feet and pushed. And again. The mine was not two yards off now. Another heave and it was all but home. A final push, and it brought up short. Quickly, he made it fast and then clung to a barrel a moment, gasping and shaking from the effort. Childers got the boat under control and brought the bow up to Hayden.

The lamp, closed to let no light out, passed from hand to hand forward, and the man in the bow held it, waiting for Hayden to regain his strength. He forced himself to put a foot on one of the narrow boards that made up the frame, and very, very tentatively put his weight upon it, hoping all the while the mine would not turn over. It heeled to his weight, but all the ballast in the barrels resisted him and it stayed more or less upright.

He was dripping wet and dared not open the bung or handle the match cord for fear of getting it wet. As he perched there, trying to think how he would dry at least one hand, a cry came from directly above his head.

'*Les Anglais! Les Anglais!*'

Immediately, a musket fired and the man in the boat's bow fell back, his lamp falling into the sea with a splash, and disappearing. Fire was returned from the boat, which began to drift aft on the current. More men came running to the transom rail and began firing, and Hayden crouched low and pressed himself up against the transom planks, the overhanging stern hiding him from the men above.

Childers ordered the rowers to take up oars, and the desperate men sent the boat off to larboard, seeking the protection of darkness. Hayden did not know how many had been hurt – and they were being fired on yet.

Footsteps came thumping across planks almost overhead and a man leaned out of the transom-gallery window a few feet above Hayden's head and fired. With all haste, he set to reloading and, when his gun emerged again, Hayden stepped up on one of the barrels, grabbed the startled man's arm, hauled him half out of the window and clubbed him several times over the head with his drowned pistol. When he was utterly still, Hayden reached the sill and pulled himself up and then swiftly in. There was no one else in the cabin and Hayden dried his hands on the abandoned bedclothes in a swinging cot and snatched down the lantern.

For a second, he hovered at the window, listening. Childers had steered the boat to larboard, and most of the men on the deck above had moved to that quarter, where they were still shouting and firing muskets. Even so, Hayden hesitated. He was about to go out of the window, bearing a lantern, which would almost certainly reveal him to the enemy. He would have to carry the lantern in one hand and climb with the other, which he realized would be all but impossible.

Hayden looked around the cabin in desperation, and his eye lit upon a pistol, lying on the floor near the man he'd clubbed to death. It must have fallen from his belt. He seized it, checked that it was loaded, made certain the flint was both new and firmly in place and went to the cot. He tore a piece of sheet free and wrapped the pistol in it before shoving it into his belt, then went again to the window.

He glanced up to see if anyone looked his way, but could not be certain. No one had spotted the English mine, it seemed, and, with a deep breath, he lowered himself out of the window. It was far enough down that he was forced to drop the last foot on to the centre barrel, which held the powder. Half falling from that, he landed on one of the lower barrels and managed not to go into the water altogether. He paused there a moment, still, but when no cry went up he went to pull the bung from the powder barrel, when he realized he had left too much water there.

Carefully, he unwrapped his pistol and used the cloth to dry the barrel head, then pulled the bung. He fished out the match cord, positioned the bung so that it covered most of the hole, and then added the damp cloth to this, covering the hole completely, but for the tiniest hole where the match emerged. Balancing himself, he held the cord in one hand

and the cocked pistol in the other. For the briefest second he hesitated, took a long deep breath, then aimed the pistol at the cord, which dangled a few inches from his hand, and pulled the trigger.

He turned away from the smoke for an instant, and then opened his eyes, which were swimming from the flash. The match burned! Gingerly, he pulled the cloth away, expecting all the while that the powder would light and blow him to his final glory, but it did not.

He slipped into the water, took a few deep breaths and then submerged, swimming as far as he could dead down-current and then surfacing as silently as he was able. He floated on his back, breathing and not letting his feet break the surface as he kicked. He went under again and swam until the need for air drove him up. He then began to swim quietly, desperate to get away. He glanced back once and, though there were men on the quarterdeck firing into the dark, it did not seem to be at him, nor was there any sign that the mine had been discovered.

Hayden had not swum very far when there was a flash and then an unholy explosion. He was propelled forward briefly and felt as though a massive fist of water had landed a blow to his entire body. He spun around in the water, holding up an arm to protect himself, and saw what appeared to be the entire transom of the ship explode in a monstrous moment of fire.

Hayden could not tear his eyes away, and hovered there, treading water, watching the stern of the ship heave up and then settle and immediately start to go down.

'My God!' he muttered. 'We have done for her.'

Fire consumed the transom and burned in the rigging and

furled mizzen sails. Hayden could see men on the deck picking themselves up.

'You must launch boats,' he heard himself say.

But the French did not yet seem to comprehend their situation. And then there was a mad rush to the boats. The ship, however, was going rapidly down by the stern, sinking ever lower as water rushed in. Hayden was certain they would not have a single boat over the side before the ship slipped beneath the surface.

He watched in fascinated horror as a gun, broken loose by the explosion, rolled and then tumbled down the slanting deck, taking with it men who could not get clear in the press. The ship began to roll on to her starboard side, a great wounded animal going to ground, but this one would never rise again.

Men began to slip into the water as half the deck went under. One of the boats was manhandled upright and floated off from the sinking vessel, with men leaping aboard and others clinging to the gunwales. The mizzen rigging burned yet, the flame casting a stained hellish light over the scene.

'I never meant to do this,' Hayden whispered to no one. It was, he realized then, the truth of war – men endeavoured to bring destruction to the enemy, but, once achieved, they then looked in horror upon their own accomplishments. One looked in horror upon one's self.

He trod water, floating high above the earth, watching as a hundred men or more began the slow fall toward the earth's surface. What kind of man could murder a hundred of his own kind?

Only the forecastle of the sinking ship remained, and there was enacted a scene of such chaos as he had never witnessed, men climbing over their fellows to keep from the sea. Others were shoved over the bulwarks, and then those were pushed over behind.

A burning ship's boat came drifting by the stricken ship and he realized it was one of their fire boats, still afloat, carried by the sea. It was a macabre sight, sliding by the sinking ship, as though it had come to cast light on Hayden's own handy work, like a rebuke from some higher power.

Aboard the ill-fated ship there was such keening and howling, as though these were not men at all but some wild beasts trapped and about to give up their lives. And then Hayden saw two small boys, holding hands, leap down into the sea, where they disappeared beneath the surface. For a long moment he watched, but they never surfaced again. Hayden realized that he wept, silently.

'Captain Hayden!' came a cry out of the darkness. 'Captain Hayden . . .'

'Here!' he called back. 'I am here.'

'Where away, sir?'

'South! Row south!'

A moment later, a boat came gliding out of the dark and he was being helped over the side by many hands.

'It worked, Captain,' Childers pronounced, as Hayden tumbled down on to a thwart.

For some few seconds Hayden could not reply. 'I never meant to sink her with so many souls aboard.'

'They are privateers, sir,' Childers replied. 'They have been raiding our commerce and causing all manner of mischief.'

'For which we might send them into our prisons and later exchange them for our own people. but we would not execute them.'

Childers was struck dumb by this. Clearly, he had been elated by their success – which had been far greater than they expected.

'It is a war, sir,' Childers said, almost under his breath, glancing at the men who lay upon their oars.

'Perhaps mankind's most wicked contrivance. Row me back to our ship,' Hayden demanded, and then, more softly, 'How did our crew fare?'

'Four lost, sir. Three wounded.'

'I am mortally sorry to hear it.'

'Look!' One of the rowers pointed toward the stricken ship.

A boat appeared then, and a second. The boats from the other privateers had come. Hayden did not want to see what happened next and turned his head away. The oarsmen set to their sweeps, and Childers put his helm over to take them back to their Spanish prize.

It seemed to Hayden then that, if he managed in the end to have Angelita back, all the joy and goodness of their marriage would be fouled by this one act – to have murdered so many to have her returned. It was unspeakable.

They were soon alongside the ship, and passed up the wounded first, before Hayden climbed over the side, a puddle forming about him where he stood, watching the hands come up on to the deck.

Gould came hurrying up. 'We have done for that privateer! Congratulations, Captain!'

Hayden gave the smallest nod in reply. As he turned to make his way down to his commandeered cabin, he found Hawthorne before him.

'An accident of war,' the marine said, as though he knew

Hayden's thoughts. 'Nothing more. Never was it intended. Just misfortune – almost freakishly so.'

'I do not think the French will believe it so innocent. Our names will be black among those people – my mother's people. Even my own family will turn away from me. It was a monstrous act, Mr Hawthorne, a monstrous act, and it will haunt us until the day death knocks at our doors.'

Sleep did not come to Hayden that night. He wanted nothing more than to remain in his cabin, alone, and speak to no one, but he was afraid the French would desire revenge upon them for this terrible act, and he returned to the deck and paced his private section.

So distraught did he find himself that he was left muttering to no one.

'Never was it my intention to sink them,' he whispered. 'To disable them, yes, but never to murder so many.'

This thought seemed to possess him, and he repeated it over and over as it echoed in his mind. 'An accident of war', Hawthorne had called it, but Hayden wondered now how he could not have realized what would occur. Had not Reverte even suggested as much? To ignite so much powder so near to the ship's weakest point . . . What other result could it have had? Why had he not comprehended that? Was his mind so clouded by emotion that he had not been able to perceive that obvious truth?

Ransome and Reverte prepared the ship for an attack by boats, but the stars blew into the west and no attack came. It left Hayden and perhaps others to a long night of self-recrimination.

Wind and a thin, grey light reached them at the same instant, as though the morning were pressed on by the breeze.

Pennants began to stir, flutter and then stream. Hands were called to make sail and to break out the anchor.

A short distance off, the privateers did the same. Hayden more than half expected the three remaining ships to turn and come after him, for the odds were very much in their favour, but they did not. Instead, they returned to their previous course, along the Old Channel, as though they had not noticed what had occurred the night before. Indeed, Hayden half wondered if it had not been a nightmare.

The wind, almost from the north, remained, throughout the day, froward and moody. For a time it would blow and hurry the ships on, but then it would die away so that they all but lost steerage-way, then, for a few hours, it would be but a breeze, falling away and coming back like a soft breath. And then it would make with a vengeance, howling among the rigging so that the ships heeled and were in danger of carrying away spars. Sails were set and handed, and then set again, until the men were exhausted from the work.

The three enemy ships were kept always within sight, but Hayden could not now imagine how he would take one of them, let alone overcome three to find Angelita. He wondered if she knew what he had done? What would she think of a man who murdered a hundred to have her back? Would she have even the slightest desire to call such a man her husband again?

The Windward Channel was reached at dawn and, though Hayden expected the ships to continue on, passing through the Mona Channel as they had come, they instead turned down the channel.

Ransome and Reverte were standing on the forecastle

when Hayden arrived, having been alerted to the privateers shaping their course to the south.

'They will draw nearer your port of Kingston,' Reverte said.

'Yes, but I doubt this channel is being watched as it was when we were enemies of your nation. It is unlikely we will meet English cruisers here now.' Ransome caught sight of Hayden and he touched his hat. 'Captain. There goes our quarry, slipping off down the Windward Channel, though I cannot think why.'

'They never want to be becalmed again where the ships can anchor,' Reverte said with certainty. 'They have had too many bad experiences with that. Perhaps they also think they will find fairer winds in the Caribbean Sea. Who can say?'

Employing Reverte's glass, Hayden quizzed the ships retreating down the wide channel. It was just over a hundred miles through to the other side, past the long peninsula that grew out of the south-west corner of Hispaniola. If the winds held – and the channel did not have its name for no reason – they would be through in a day.

'We will shape our course to follow their own, Mr Ransome,' Hayden ordered, lowering the glass but gazing yet at the distant ships.

Over the course of the last day, he had felt Angelita slipping away from him, as though she were beyond his grasp now, though, maddingly, he could see the ship that bore her off as it made its way toward the horizon, where it would disappear and she would be lost to him, utterly and irrevocably.

During the afternoon a high, gauzy cloud formed, dulling the day and drawing the colour from the sea so that it appeared a drab blue and, in the distance, grey. By sunset, the cloud had become denser and drowned the stars. A black squall swept down upon them out of the dark, pressing the ship over and throwing the sails about so that they luffed and shook. The helmsman put the ship before the wind and she went racing off toward the south-west, where, fortunately, they had sea room.

Hayden went to his berth sometime after the darkness had settled in, exhausted from his lack of sleep the previous night. Even so, sleep eluded him for some time and then it was fraught with nightmares and he woke often.

As was his usual habit, he rose before dawn, broke his fast and was on the deck before the first signs of light. All the planking was wet from rain, and the sails and rigging dripped.

Hayden stood with a hand on the binnacle, staring off into the south. Gould was officer of the watch and he appeared at that instant.

'Where are our chases, Mr Gould? I cannot make them out.'

'Nor can we, sir,' the midshipman admitted.

'And how long have they been out of sight?'

'Two hours, sir.'

Hayden could hardly believe what he had heard. 'And why did no one wake me?'

Gould stood, embarrassed and hesitant. 'I – I do not know, sir. We expected them to reappear and then we would have woken you for naught, Captain.'

'And what is our position?'

'Perhaps five miles north-north-west of Cap Tiburon.'

'Have they disappeared around the cape?'

'We did not think them so distant from us, sir, but it is possible.'

Hayden considered a moment. 'Have my nightglass carried up, Mr Gould. I shall be on the forecastle.'

Hayden paced the length of the gangway to the forecastle, where he gazed a moment into the dark night. A spattering of rain was heard on the planks around, and on his coat and hat, as the wind drove it down at an angle. Hayden moved to leeward to gain some protection from the sails.

A moment later, his nightglass arrived and he began a careful search of the sea at all quarters. On such a dark night the long peninsula that made up the south-western corner of Hispaniola could not be descried, which Hayden did not like overly. Currents were often unpredictable and his ship might have been set more to the east than either of his sailing masters realized.

Ransome hurried along the gangway, pulling on a coat. 'We have lost our ships, I am informed, sir.'

'Indeed, Mr Ransome. But you are not officer of the watch and had no part in it.'

'I did leave orders to wake me for any reason at all, Captain.'

'I have no doubt of it.' Hayden passed Ransome his nightglass. 'I cannot find even Hispaniola, let alone a ship on this dark night.'

Ransome began to quiz the sea in the same manner his captain had but a moment before.

Hayden turned to one of the forecastle hands. 'Enquire of Mr Gould who the lookout aloft was when the ships disappeared.'

'A Spaniard, sir. He's only just climbed down.'

'Find him for me, if you please.'

'Aye, sir.' The man ran off.

'What see you, Mr Ransome?' asked Hayden,

'A bloody, dark night, sir, but neither ship nor land.'

'Mmm. My eyes have not failed me yet, then.'

The hand returned with the lookout a moment later.

'This is him, sir, though I don't know his name. We call him Georgie, sir, because he looks somewhat like the Prince of Wales.'

Hayden had not realized previously that one could hear a smirk, but he certainly did in this statement – though its intent did not seem malicious.

'You were aloft when the privateers disappeared?' Hayden asked the man in Spanish.

'I was, Captain. We had lost sight of one ship or another throughout the night.' He waved a hand at the sea. 'Squalls and mounting seas, sir. When we lost all three I thought nothing of it, but we have not caught sight of them since.'

'And when did you lose sight of them for the last time?'

'About four bells, Captain.'

'About or exactly four bells?'

The man shifted from one foot to the other. 'I heard the ship's bell, sir, and within a few minutes we lost sight of all the ships' lamps.'

'And how distant were they when you lost sight of them?'

'More than a league, sir, but not two.'

Wickham had arrived on the forecastle as the man spoke, and hovered on the edge of the conversation.

'You may go,' Hayden told the Spaniard. He turned to the lieutenant. 'We shall beat to quarters, Mr Ransome.'

'Aye, sir.'

Ransome hastened off, calling out orders.

Hayden beckoned the midshipman forward. 'Mr Wickham, have a look through my nightglass, if you please, and see if you cannot find our privateers.'

Wickham took the glass and went immediately to the barricade. 'You think they are lying in wait, sir?' he said, as he peered through the glass.

'Their lamps all disappeared at the same instant – at four bells – as though it had been so arranged. If I were them I should darken my ships so that we would come up to them just before dawn. We would not perceive them lying in wait but there would be light for the battle.'

'Should we heave-to, Captain?'

'If we have merely lost sight of them in the dark, heaving-to will let them slip further away, increasing the chance of us losing sight of them altogether.' Hayden found himself looking around as though someone would fall upon him out of the darkness.

'I do not care for either possibility, sir.'

'Nor do I, Mr Wickham.'

The Spanish crew came up the ladders into the rain and darkness, sullen looks upon their faces as though to say, What does this Englishman want of us now? Can he not see it is a dark night and we have need of sleep?'

Reverte hastened on to the forecastle and Hayden informed him of their situation. The Spaniard looked positively alarmed, and he went about the ship exhorting the men to take their stations and stand ready.

After interrogating the darkness for some minutes, Wickham handed the glass back to his captain. 'I can make out nothing, sir. Though perhaps there is an area of more concentrated darkness off our larboard bow, some miles distant. Hispaniola, I should think.'

'I shall feel better once we have weathered the cape,' Hayden growled. He looked around again. 'Damn this black night.'

The men stooped by their guns, backs to the wind, which was surprisingly cool for the latitude.

'I shall keep you on the deck for your sharp eyes, Mr Wickham. Send Gould down with Reverte to command the gundeck.'

Wickham went off, calling the midshipman's name.

Hayden took one last look into the darkness with his glass and then made his way along the gangway, which was both slanted and heaving in the quartering seas.

As he came on to the quarterdeck he met Hawthorne, who was bearing a musket.

'You have heard our small news?' Hayden asked, as the marine fell into step beside him.

'I have. And where have these ships gone?' he asked.

As they reached the binnacle there came a flash of light aft and then the report reverberated over the water. Hayden did not know where the shot went, but he stood all but transfixed a moment.

'Should I thank them for answering that most pressing question?' Hawthorne wondered in the silence.

And then came another shot, from their larboard quarter, which struck the back of a wave not two dozen feet aft of their transom.

And then the night was illuminated for an instant as a broadside was fired to starboard, though too distant to do damage.

Hayden took one look around, comprehension coming over him like cold rain. 'They intend to trap us against the lee shore of the peninsula.'

A moment of silence, and then the gun aft fired again. Then the gun to larboard.

Hayden turned his head, listening carefully.

Guns fired again from somewhere out to the west.

Hayden pointed to this last. 'That is the frigate,' he announced, 'so the others are the privateers. Mr Hawthorne, would you be so good as to find Lieutenant Reverte on the gundeck and send him to me?'

Hawthorne made a quick salute and went for the companionway ladder at a trot. As his head disappeared below, Ransome shot out of the companionway.

'They have come after us, sir!' he blurted.

'Mmm. But their timing is imperfect. We still have a little darkness left to us and we had best exploit it to our greatest advantage. Ah, here is Reverte.'

The Spaniard remained significantly calmer than Ransome, who was clearly in a lather.

'Will our ship tack in this wind?' Hayden asked of the Spaniard.

Reverte looked about, assessing the wind a moment, and then nodded. 'I believe she will, Captain.'

'I would like to turn to larboard, rake the privateer on our larboard quarter if we can, carry on until we are well clear, and then come through the wind on to the starboard tack. The seas are not so great as to prevent us opening gunports.'

Ransome and Reverte acknowledged the orders and hurried off to prepare the men for these evolutions. Hayden sent men to the ship's lamps with orders to snuff them just before the helm was put over.

He then called for Wickham and stationed the young reefer on the larboard side of the quarterdeck, clear of the gunners, and had him fix his glass upon the enemy lurking there in the dark.

'I have her, sir,' Wickham announced.

'Do not take your eyes off her, Mr Wickham. I shall need you to tell me when she is directly abeam.'

The privateer was almost invisible in the darkness, and Hayden was counting on them continuing to fire their chase piece to give his gunners a target. Like all such manoeuvres, this one relied for its success upon timing. The privateer would have a chance to rake Hayden's frigate as it passed by but Hayden hoped to turn through the wind at that instant and prevent this. Whether the ship would prove as handy as the *Themis*, he could not say. There was also a question as to how distant the privateer was . . . If she were nearer than Hayden believed, then he would not have time to turn into the wind, and he might well get raked – and at close range, too. If she were further away, then Hayden's broadside would likely do little damage.

To the east lay a deep, open bay – over a hundred miles to its head – encompassing one large island and several smaller ones. Its southern shore was made up of the long peninsula that grew out of Hispaniola's south-western corner. Its eastern shore curved up somewhat toward the west and terminated at the point that made up the northern entrance to the Windward Channel. Despite the great size of the bay, Hayden believed that, had he a squadron of three ships under his command, he could trap a ship in it by daylight. This was why he felt he must get on to the starboard tack before dawn. He could not let the enemy ships herd him into a corner.

It occurred to him, at that moment, that he might be better *not* to fire his broadside, which would alert the other ships that he had changed course, although they would not know if it was to the east or to the west. He weighed this option for only a few seconds before deciding that opportunity to do damage to one of the three ships – especially at close range – could not be passed up. Who knew what the result might be? The privateer might lose a mast and be out of any subsequent action. It was not particularly likely, but the outcome of a broadside at such range could not be predicted.

When all was in readiness, Hayden gave the order, lamps were doused and the ship began her turn, yards being shifted, and sails sheeted in. He went and stood by Wickham, who braced himself in the aft corner where transom met bulwark, Hayden's nightglass fixed upon the enemy ship.

'Will she pass astern of us?' Hayden asked, still unable to make her out.

'I do not believe so, Captain, but it will be very near. We might traverse guns aft . . . ?'

The order was given and the sound of carriage wheels being forced across the planking ground around the ship. The chase gun fired on the privateer, but she had clearly lost sight of them, for the ball went well aft.

'We have a shot, sir,' the nearest gun captain announced quietly, sighting along his gun to the place where the flash had been seen.

'Mr Wickham . . . ?' Hayden prompted.

'I agree, sir.'

The order was given, and the larboard battery fired, shaking the deck beneath Hayden's feet. All listened for the sound, and a terrible rending and crash of iron on wood came to them over the water, though the extent of the damage could not even be guessed.

Immediately, yards were braced and the helm put over. The frigate forced her way up into the wind. Before she had come into irons, the privateer fired her own broadside, and much of it struck home, some passing through the sails and rigging, and other balls striking the hull. Nothing carried away, and the ship, after hovering a moment in indecision, came through the wind and in a moment settled on to the starboard tack.

Gunports were closed, though guns had been reloaded and were in all ways ready to fire. Every eye was now fixed to the west, trying to find the other ships to see what they did. None bore lamps, for they had come upon the frigate by stealth, and now that they realized Hayden had changed his course, they left off firing, rendering them near to invisible on such a dark night.

'There away!' one of the hands called out. 'A light, sir.'

Hayden stared into the dark and, after a moment, found it, wafting slowly up and down.

'Why would they light a lamp?' Wickham wondered.

'They have lost sight of one another and cannot risk collision – a great boon for us, for we may remain dark for the little night that remains.'

'What shall we do now, sir?' Wickham asked.

'Remain on this course until we see what they intend. Will they chase us yet, or will they continue on for whatever island is their destination?'

'I would certainly choose to go on, sir. We cannot challenge three ships alone, and they would be foolish to let us lure them back up the channel. British ships do come here, even if not often.'

'I agree, Wickham. Let us see if they are cool-headed or still desire revenge for our murdering so many of their fellows.'

Wickham continued to search the darkness with Hayden's glass.

'Have they worn, Wickham?' Ransome asked as he came aft. 'Can you not see?'

'I believe they might have, Mr Ransome, but cannot yet be certain.'

The frigate stood on for a short time, when signal guns were fired on one of the enemy ships and then answered by the others, extinguishing any doubts as to their positions.

'They are wearing now,' Wickham told the others. 'Even the ship we raked seems to be able to wear, so we did not damage her as we had hoped, I should guess.'

'Will they come after us again or will they bear off and pass south of the cape?' Ransome asked.

It was the question in everyone's mind, Hayden was certain, but it would not be answered until daylight found them. Dawn, however, lay concealed behind a thick layer of woolly grey that had overspread the Caribbean sky that night. When it did finally come, slowly, but slowly revealing the heaving sea and the great islands to both east and west, it cast only a dim light over the silvery-grey waters. There was no doubt, however, that the privateers had chosen to stand on and were nearing Cape Tiburon.

Hayden felt a strange hollowness inside at this sight. A

heavy lassitude and something like melancholy came to fill the void. The ships bearing his wife were slipping off.

'*On deck!*' came the cry from aloft. 'Sail! Sail, just rounding the cape!'

Thirty-two

'Aloft there!' Hayden called up to the lookout. 'Does she bear colours?'

'No, Captain. Not that I can see.'

Wickham, who stood by the rail, hatless, the wind ranging his gold curls about his face, handed Hayden his nightglass. 'Shall I fetch my glass and go aloft, sir?'

'If you please, Mr Wickham.'

'Immediately, sir.'

A moment later, Wickham was climbing slowly up the ratlines, his glass slung over his back. He settled himself on the maintop and fixed his glass upon the distant ship.

'She's a three-master, Captain,' he called down. 'Painted like a transport.'

In itself, this did not signify a great deal, as Sir William had ordered all his captains – including Hayden – to paint their ships a single colour so that they were not obviously Navy ships.

'Are there other ships, Mr Wickham, perhaps just behind the cape? Can you see?'

'Just a single sail so far, Captain.'

'A single French cruiser in the Windward Channel, sir,' Ransome observed quietly. 'That seems improbable. Much more likely that she is either the transport her appearance claims or a Spanish ship. She might be British, but our cruisers have tended to sail in squadrons.'

'She is very likely a transport, Mr Ransome, and a most fortunate one as well, for these privateers will not dare harass her with our frigate so near.' Hayden glanced up at the sails, gauging the wind. 'We will stand on for half an hour more and then wear ship, Mr Ransome. Once we have worn, we will send the men to their breakfast.'

'I shall send word to the Spanish cooks,' Ransome replied. 'Though I do miss a good English breakfast,' he confided softly.

Hayden, who had grown up with French cooking, nodded. 'What man, Mr Ransome, could find fault with the English breakfast?'

'My thinking exactly, sir.'

No other ships appeared around the cape, distant now only a few miles, and the strange ship bore off, hard on the wind on the starboard tack, prudently giving the unknown ships sea room.

'*On deck, Captain!*' Wickham called down. 'She is sending colours aloft, sir – British colours.'

Hayden considered this a moment, and then summoned one of the English hands. 'Pass the word for Reverte and Mr Gould.'

Hayden stood at the rail, gazing off toward the four ships. He could make out the British colours without a glass now.

The frigate taken by the privateers sent aloft colours at that moment, and these, Hayden was quite certain, were Spanish.

'Aloft, there! Is that the Spanish flag, Mr Wickham?'

'So it is, sir.'

Reverte and Gould arrived at the same instant.

'Who is your signal officer?' Hayden asked the Spaniard,

uncertain of the proper term in Spanish and using a less than correct translation.

'He went with Captain Serrano on the prize, Captain Hayden,' Reverte answered.

'Do you know if you carry a British ensign?'

Reverte's countenance did not change in the least. 'I shall have the colour-chest carried up, but I believe that it is possible.'

Hayden refrained from commenting on allies bearing British colours. Of course, his own ship had carried Spanish colours – such was the fragile nature of the two nations' alliance.

Hayden turned to the midshipman. 'Mr Gould. Do I recall correctly that you committed much of the signal book to memory?'

'I did make an effort to, sir.'

'We may have need of signals. You might be forced to tear apart the Spanish flags and improvise, but you should stand ready.'

Gould looked a little perplexed. 'What signal will be required, sir?'

'I wish I knew; we shall see what transpires.'

The colour-chest arrived on the deck and, to the slight embarrassment of the Spanish, there was indeed a British ensign therein. Hayden ordered it sent aloft.

Gould went through the Spanish flags, laying out those of different colours.

'*On deck, sir!*' Wickham called down. 'The strange ship, sir – I do not find her so strange, after all. I believe she is ours, sir. I believe she is the *Themis*!'

Hayden called for a glass and quizzed the distant ship.

French and British frigates were much alike and easily mistaken one for the other, but there was something about the proportion of this particular ship's rig that did seem familiar.

As Hayden looked, the rig began to change shape.

'She is clewing up her mainsail, Captain,' Wickham called down.

'No, Mr Archer,' Hayden muttered.

'What are they about, sir?' Mr Gould asked.

'They are heaving-to so that they might speak with one of these ships they believe to be Spanish. Can you make up "Chasing enemy ships", Mr Gould . . . this very instant?'

Gould looked over at the flags he had laid out on the deck. 'It will be very makeshift, sir.'

'It does not matter. Do the best you can, and quickly as you can.'

Gould began tearing up the Spanish signal flags for the colours he would require. Reverte called for the sail maker and his mates, and they began furiously making up flags to Gould's directions. The stitches were so far apart that Hayden wondered if they would hold together in the wind but, in a little more than a quarter of an hour, something that resembled the signal for 'chasing enemy ships' went aloft. Hayden ordered a gun fired at the same time to draw the attention of the *Themis*, and prayed that their lookouts were not so focussed on the nearby "Spanish" vessels that they did not notice.

'Mr Ransome. Lieutenant Reverte. Let us wear ship and run down upon our privateers.'

Hayden looked up into the rigging. 'Aloft there, Wickham. Has Archer seen our signal? Can you see what they do?'

'He has hove-to, sir. That is all I can tell you.'

'Have they gone to quarters, Mr Wickham?'

'I cannot be certain, sir. Gunports are closed.'

'Damn!' Hayden whispered. Archer was about to have three enemy vessels fire broadsides into him, and he seemed utterly innocent of their intent.

It occurred to Hayden, then, to wonder how the *Themis* had arrived at this place, but he decided Caldwell's messenger must have found her. He kept hoping that Jones would round the headland in *Inconstant*, but no other ship appeared. There was only the *Themis*, hove-to some distance off the headland, with the three ships bearing down on her.

'Aloft, Mr Wickham?' Hayden called out. 'How distant are the privateers from the *Themis*?'

'Not a mile, sir, I should think.' Wickham raised his glass again. 'Sir? Mr Archer is getting her underway. Mayhap, he has made out our signal, Captain.'

Getting a frigate underway could not be done instantly, even under the most pressing need, which no doubt Archer felt at that moment. Hayden watched as yards were braced around and sails loosed. Staysails jerked aloft, flailed for a moment and then were sheeted tight.

The instant sails were set and drawing, he saw gunports open, and not, it appeared, an instant too soon. The nearest privateer began a turn to larboard and unleashed her broadside of 12-pounders. Before Hayden could even wonder at the effect on Archer's command, smoke erupted all around the *Themis*, and the privateer, whose deck canted toward the *Themis* on that point of sail, was a scene of carnage, sails torn and flailing and men strewn across the deck.

Immediately, the other privateers bore off, shaping their course to weather the cape.

'Mr Ransome!' Hayden called out. 'We will pass that privateer to weather and give her a broadside.'

'Aye, sir!'

Ransome and Reverte went immediately about the ship, disposing the men to their proper stations.

Hayden stood at the rail, holding a shroud as the ship rolled on the quartering sea. A bit of rain rattled down around him, though Hayden hardly took notice but to note that powder must be kept dry, something of which the Spanish gun crews were cognizant.

Aboard the nearest privateer, men were scrambling about, trying to put their ship to rights. They dared not bear off, lest Hayden rake them, so they stood on, knowing that the Spanish frigate flying a British flag was about to bring ruin to them. Hayden wondered if they would strike, given that a much more powerful ship was about to engage them, but their false ensign continued to stream.

The Spanish frigate was the swifter vessel, but not by a great deal, so overhauling the privateer took half of the hour.

'*On deck, Captain!* The *Themis* is wearing, sir.'

'Climb down, Mr Wickham,' Hayden ordered. 'I shall need you on the deck.'

The frigate finally drew abreast of the privateer, just beyond musket shot, and both ships fired their broadsides at almost the same instant. Smoke obscured all for a moment and then the wind carried the cloud away. The privateer was a ruin of dangling rigging and unmounted guns. Almost reluctantly, Hayden ordered the guns reloaded and fired, and then they passed the privateer by, leaving her bobbing on the waves, her wheel shot away and turning slowly broadside to the seas.

The remaining privateers disappeared behind the cape at that moment, and Hayden ordered their course altered, so that he might sail within hailing distance of the *Themis*. Gunports were conspicuously closed, and he sent Wickham out to the end of the jib boom with a speaking trumpet to hail Archer. There were a few moments of wary hesitation, and then the *Themis*es recognized their shipmate and there was a great cheer aboard the British vessel.

The two ships drew abeam and Hayden found himself standing at the rail, looking over at his ship and officers, gathered at the rail, grinning like men in their cups.

'We were told to look for a schooner, Captain,' Archer called, 'but it has been miraculously transformed into a frigate – a Spanish frigate.'

'I shall tell you the story entire at some time, Mr Archer,' Hayden called back, suspecting that his own grin was not immoderate. 'For now you should know that we chase a privateer like the one you just dished, and a Spanish frigate bearing both bullion and Mrs Hayden – or so I believe.'

'Have you a plan, sir?' Archer asked.

'A very simple one. We overhaul them and disable the privateer first. We then range up to either side of the frigate and hope her master has the sense to strike.'

'Then we should not let them get any further ahead, sir.'

'I agree, Mr Archer. Luck to you, sir.'

'And you, Captain.'

The two ships swiftly made sail and shaped their respective courses to weather the tip of Hispaniola, which lay less than a mile distant. Although the Spanish ship had the longer waterline, Hayden was not displeased to see that the *Themis* kept pace with her. The two crews, Spanish and British, were immediately competing, and the lieutenants and sailing masters of both vessels were all about the deck, bracing yards and trimming sails to get every tenth of a knot from their respective vessels.

Hayden took a glass and went forward to the forecastle, where he might get a better view of their chases. The masters of these ships were not fools and gave the cape a wide berth, not wishing to be becalmed in its lee. The wind, which had been blowing north by east to north-north-east for some hours, chose that moment to shift to north-east by north, and the privateers found themselves in the lee of the hills all the same, where they rolled terribly in the quartering sea.

Reverte and Ransome came forward, and the three considered their best course for a moment, studying the dog-vane and pennants at the masthead and quizzing the sea all around.

Ransome pointed to a flight of white-feathered birds some distance before them. 'Those gulls have wind beneath their sails, sir. Have they not?'

A quick look with a glass confirmed this observation.

'Perhaps this wind will carry us up to them, Captain,' Reverte observed.

'Perhaps, but in this sea a small wind will be rolled out of our sails in an instant, as you both well know.'

It was, perhaps, one of the most frustrating experiences of sailors – and not an uncommon one – to have seas greater than the wind justified. The wind would then be too small to steady the ship and the seas would roll and throw the sails about so that they might flog themselves to ribbons. If the seas, however, were the proper height such a wind should make, this would not occur, and the ship would slip along happily.

It was decided to shape their course more to the south-west, trying to skirt the area of calms beneath the cape and hope the wind did not shift back into the north, sending their chases on their way east, while Hayden's frigate and the *Themis* had gone further west. It was a gamble, and Hayden could not guess how it might pay off.

All through the forenoon they made their way south-west, the lookouts aloft trying to discern the edge of the calm so as to keep their ships in wind, though the area of fickle winds grew and shrank without any apparent cause.

For half of an hour before noon, the privateers found wind and shaped their course south-east, but then the wind left them again and they rolled and slatted about in the seas, gear threatening to carry away, such was the violence of their motion.

By four bells Hayden's two ships were some seven miles south-west of the privateers, which Hayden did not care for, but both Ransome and Reverte, and Mr Barthe aboard the *Themis*, all concurred that they might risk altering their course into the east. Yards were shifted and the helms put over and the two ships, now broadside to seas blown out of the Windward Channel, rolled on toward the west at good speed.

When they had covered perhaps five miles, the two privateers found their wind and shaped their own courses to skirt the southern coast of Hispaniola.

When Hayden's little squadron was due south of Cape Tiburon, the fetch grew so short that the seas went down to a low, long swell and the ships suddenly surged forward, their motion eased so that the worst landlubber aboard could dance a jig upon the deck without fear of falling.

The two ships raced on, carrying every sail they could

safely send aloft. Wickham asked permission to climb to the foremast tops, where his view would not be impeded by sails, and there he watched their chases for half an hour before leaning over and calling down to Hayden on the forecastle.

'Sir, we are gaining on the privateer, but the frigate ranges ahead.'

Hayden turned to Reverte. 'Will the frigate reduce sail to protect her consort or will she abandon her and run?'

Reverte shook his head. 'I cannot say what the master will do. This frigate and the one we chase were built from the same draught. One is as swift as the other.'

'Then it might come down to which has the cleaner bottom,' Hayden replied.

'Or the better seamanship,' Reverte observed.

'This is your ship, Lieutenant,' Hayden said. 'Can she be made to sail faster?'

'Perhaps, if I might suggest a few small things? She is like every ship and has her own little likes and dislikes.'

'By all means, do with her as you will.'

For the next hour it seemed the master of the frigate could not make up his own mind as to what to do, but then he began to crowd on sail and left the other privateer to her fate, a rather cowardly act, all aboard the chasing ships agreed.

Hayden went back and forth between quarterdeck and forecastle, trying not to look as unsettled as he felt. After chasing these ships for so many days it now appeared he might actually overhaul them, which forced him to consider another matter. His bride was aboard one of them . . . and he might be forced into battle with the ship that bore her, endangering her life.

Upon one of his visits to the foredeck he found Reverte standing at the forward barricade.

'I realize I have asked this before, Lieutenant,' Hayden began, taking his place beside the Spaniard, 'but you are quite certain no bullion was transferred off the frigate?'

'I am quite certain.'

'And the lady you saw – the woman I believe was Mrs Hayden – she is aboard the same ship?'

'Certainly she was, at the time our ships were taken.' Reverte paused. 'Even privateers would put such a woman down into the deepest part of the hold so that she would be in no danger in the event of a battle.'

'I have seen ships explode – more than once – catch fire, and even founder. I have witnessed vessels sinking after collisions and I have been aboard a ship wrecked upon the coast with great loss of life. There is no place aboard a ship that is truly safe.'

'There is no place in this life that is truly safe, Captain Hayden. I once saw a man run down by a carriage that had escaped and rolled down a hill. He later died of his injuries. Mrs Hayden will be as safe as is possible. I cannot say, "Do not worry" – you are her husband so that would not be possible – but I am quite certain all of your concern shall be for naught. Mrs Hayden will not be harmed. You might ask yourself how many times you have seen a ship's surgeon wounded in a battle.'

'I have never seen it, unless the ship itself was destroyed.'

'Because he is down in the cockpit, deep in the ship where Mrs Hayden will be.'

Hayden felt himself nod, his anxiety very slightly eased, but not erased.

It became apparent that the course set by the privateers would not take them to Guadeloupe, but to the north of it. It did not take Hayden long to realize that de Latendresse and his allies were likely steering for one of the neutral islands that lay nearer. At the speed they were presently sailing, St Croix was not four days distant, and that island's port would shelter them from the British more than adequately. Hayden could not let the enemy ships reach that island.

The wind gods seemed to have taken the side of the privateers, that day, providing them wind when Hayden's ships were left floundering in near-calms that appeared ever to impede them. Day gave way to darkness and the lookouts were on the alert for any attempts by their chases to slip off in some other direction. Hayden slept as poorly that night as he could remember, and was on deck often, assuring himself that neither frigate nor converted transport had disappeared but remained always before them.

Well before first light, he gave up sleep altogether and found himself on the forecastle when dawn began to brighten in the east, silhouetting the enemy vessels as they dipped their bows into each sea.

Wickham and Reverte came up to the barricade, where Hayden stood with a nightglass tucked beneath his arm. The Spaniard pointed toward their chases.

'The frigate was not so far ahead at sunset,' he observed. 'And look . . . we are drawing up to the privateer.'

Hayden nodded. Even in the thin light he was certain Reverte was correct; they would overhaul the aft ship before midday.

'I do not think that the frigate has any intention of protecting her consort. She is more than a mile ahead, perhaps a mile and a half.' Hayden turned to Wickham and Reverte. 'We will beat to quarters but keep the fire in the galley stove yet. Send the hands down for breakfast a few gun crews at a time. I want a well-fed crew ready to give battle.'

Hayden crossed to the starboard rail, where he found the *Themis*, almost a mile distant on their quarter. Archer was not risking collision by night – he had been witness to that variety of calamity – but now he would almost certainly have to tack to bring his ship up to Hayden's.

Apparently, the privateers came to this same realization, for at that moment the lookout called down, '*On deck, Captain!* The frigate is making ready to tack, sir.'

Ransome came running along the gangway at that moment, coatless and shaking off sleep.

'Ah, Mr Ransome,' Hayden said to his lieutenant. 'Call sail handlers to their stations and coil down. We shall wear ship upon my order.' He turned to his other officers. 'Mr Wickham. Lieutenant Reverte. You have the gundeck.'

The two touched hats and hurried off at the same moment as Hawthorne appeared, bearing a musket.

'What are the French about now?' he asked as he passed Ransome, who was calling orders as he went.

'They were hoping to catch us unawares, Mr Hawthorne,' Hayden informed the marine, 'and pass us to either side, allowing each ship to fire at least one broadside. I suspect they would target our rig, and then hope to do something similar to the *Themis*.'

'But the second ship does not appear to be tacking.' Hawthorne pointed.

'No, Mr Hawthorne, but we shall soon see how deeply he comprehends the situation – the master of the privateer, I mean. He should allow the frigate to pass ahead of him, for if they approach us at the same time we will wear and rake the privateer – unless she also wears, of course. If the frigate is allowed to range ahead, then we will not dare wear ship for fear of being raked ourselves.'

The crew, both Spaniards and Englishmen, came streaming on to the deck and began immediately to coil down ropes in preparation to wear ship. Ransome stationed himself on the gangway, just forward of the quarterdeck so he could relay Hayden's orders to the hands who would brail up the mizzen, allowing the ship to turn downwind.

The distant frigate came through the wind, sails flailing and beating the air a moment, and then calming as they were set to drawing properly. The second ship was doing as Hayden's command was, sail handlers at their stations, ropes removed from their belaying pins and coiled down on the deck so that they might run freely.

'It would appear that this captain comprehends the situation well enough,' Hawthorne said, clearly disappointed.

'I expected no less,' Hayden replied.

'Shall we wear ship, then, sir?' Gould asked anxiously.

'Mr Gould, are you not assigned a station at this time?' Hayden enquired peevishly.

'Most certainly I am, sir. The forecastle, Captain.'

'Then see to your duties, Mr Gould, and I shall see to mine.'

'Aye, sir. My apologies, sir.'

Although it was Hayden's policy to allow his young gentlemen to ask questions of him, on the principle that this would aid them in acquiring their trade, there were, clearly, some questions that served only to vex him, and these he felt should be discouraged . . . sharply, when necessary.

He turned to find that Archer was tacking the *Themis* in an attempt to get to windward so he might bring his ship into the action. The privateer's frigate was now coming toward them, on a slant that would take it to windward of Hayden's ship.

'Mr Ransome,' Hayden called. 'Open the larboard gunports, if you please.'

'Larboard gunports, Captain,' Ransome called back, and relayed the order to Reverte and Wickham.

There was a moment of utter silence on the forecastle. The gun crews had released their guns, removed tompions and run them out, and now they waited.

'At the risk of sounding like a green reefer,' Hawthorne said quietly to his captain, 'do you plan to stand on or wear ship?'

'That depends, Mr Hawthorne, on what our enemies do. I will order whichever seems most advantageous, but it will be determined by the arrangement of the enemy's vessels and when each will reach us. Do have a little patience, Mr Hawthorne. I have not gone to sleep.'

'Aye, sir.'

Hayden assured himself of the *Themis*'s position and then estimated the speed of the approaching captured frigate. It had the wind more or less on the quarter and was closing with them at what appeared to be great speed, for the combined velocity of the converging vessels was easily eleven or twelve knots, he was certain.

The second privateer began to turn into the wind, but her master seemed to have incorrectly estimated the speed of the other vessels and was making his turn too soon.

'There,' Hayden announced. 'Mr Ransome! We will alter our course to pass to leeward of the first privateer.'

Ransome repeated his orders and went immediately to the helmsman.

'Do you see, Mr Hawthorne? We shall attempt to manoeuvre the privateer between ourselves and the captured frigate, which will not be able to turn downwind to rake us, for fear of running afoul of his consort. If he wishes to come after us, he must tack, which I intend to do myself the moment we have passed the privateer.'

Hayden turned and made his way back along the gangway so that he might be upon the quarterdeck before the ships met. The helm was put up a little and the bow of the ship fell off the wind. Hayden could see the privateer tacking.

'Will she not try to force us up by sailing below us, Captain?' Ransome asked quietly.

'I do not think she can tack so quickly.' Hayden exchanged his nightglass for one made for the day and quizzed the nearest ship. 'Does it not appear, Mr Ransome, that she is undermanned?'

Hayden passed his glass to the lieutenant, who gazed into it a moment. 'Could he have manned both batteries, Captain?'

'Perhaps, but I wonder if much of the crew has not been transferred to the other ships?'

Ransome brightened noticeably. 'I do hope you are correct, sir.'

'Let us prepare to fire our larboard battery as we pass, Mr Ransome.'

Ransome moved immediately to the break in the deck so that he might relay his captain's orders to the gundeck.

Marines and other men with muskets were settling themselves on the tops, preparing to fire on the enemy's deck as she passed. Hayden would not, under different circumstances, have left his lower square sails drawing where they might be set afire accidentally from sparks blown back by the wind, but he had need of all the speed he could manage. Ransome had ordered the hands to wet down the sails with buckets, but the trade would dry them in a moment. It was simply an unavoidable risk.

Despite the number of actions Hayden had been through, he still felt both his heart pounding madly in his chest and a shortness of breath. A sea officer might steel himself to stand upon the quarterdeck in the midst of gunfire, but fear could never be eliminated. It was elemental, he believed, more animal than human.

As the sun broke free of the horizon, the enemy vessels appeared to grow larger, the light picking out the details of the ships and casting long, stark shadows. The privateer came through the wind just before her sister ship reached her, and just as Hayden's own vessel passed her to leeward. Had she tacked a moment sooner, she could have turned downwind and raked Hayden's ship but, as it was, she was forced to pass him beam-on, and almost dead in the water after tacking. Her gunports, however, were open.

'Mr Ransome, we will fire our larboard battery all at once,' Hayden said, loud enough for the lieutenant to hear. There was silence all along the deck at that moment.

The two ships came up to one another, and their respective guns fired almost at the same instant, a great, jarring explosion of fire and smoke. All about Hayden there was a rending of timbers and shouting. Shards of wood and deadly slivers spun by in the pall of smoke. Hayden picked himself up and began tugging slivers out of his coat, some with bloody ends.

He wondered that he remained whole and could still stand. The smoke blew off quickly, revealing the damage all around, and men thrown down on the deck, twisted into unnatural positions and some still as stones.

He tore his eyes from this horrible scene and looked aft to the enemy ship, which was in far greater ruin than his own. Hayden had half expected her to turn downwind in an attempt rake him from astern, but she did not.

'We shall tack, Mr Ransome.'

Immediately, the lieutenant began calling out orders.

The privateers' captured frigate stood on, and Hayden wondered if she would tack. But then he realized that the *Themis* was tacking, even as he did, and would be on a course to intercept the frigate in but a moment.

The master of the captured frigate must have come to the conclusion that his ships would be overtaken and so had chosen to turn and fight, likely hoping to inflict damage on Hayden's rig, but the captain of the second ship had not perfectly understood his intentions and came about too soon, allowing Hayden to avoid the heavier broadside of the frigate. Ship handling and tactics would now come to the fore, as the privateers had no hope for escape but to run off downwind, into the great expanse of the Caribbean Sea, where there was no land to impede them for a hundred leagues.

Hayden watched the two ships, fascinated. What would they do now that their plan had failed?

'We appear to have taken no damage below the waterline, Captain,' Ransome called out.

'And how have the men on the gundeck fared?' Hayden enquired, not taking his eyes from the enemy.

'We have lost some men and we have one gun dismounted, sir, but it is no danger to us.'

Hayden's ship came through the wind with a shaking of sails and gear, and then the sudden, percussive *thup!* of sails filling. Yards were shifted and braced, sheets drawn home. The frigate gathered way and set off in the wake of her sister ship – the ship carrying Hayden's bride, or so he prayed.

Hawthorne trotted along the deck to where Hayden stood at the rail, watching his adversaries and trying to divine what they might do.

'I do not know how best to station my musket men, Captain,' he said. 'Will Mr Archer come up into the wind and attempt to rake the frigate?'

'I do not believe he will, Mr Hawthorne – not with two ships bearing down on him. I believe he will stand on and exchange broadsides.'

'Two knights riding along the barrier . . . ?'

'It is very much like that. Rate of fire will count for nothing, as there will be opportunity for only a single broadside. There is, however, a very great change in our situation. In a few moments, our ships will lie between the privateers and any French or neutral islands to which they might reasonably sail. They have, I think, made a very grave error.'

'If you were the master of the French frigate, Captain, what would you do?'

'I would run off downwind and hope to slip away by darkness.'

'That sounds like an act of desperation,' the marine lieutenant stated. 'The Frenchman made an error turning to fight.'

'The master of the converted transport made an error. He tacked at the wrong moment and allowed us to use him as a shield. Now they are in a difficult situation, as our two ships have the greater weight of broadside.'

The gun crews and sail handlers on the upper deck all stood silently at their stations, eyes fixed upon the three ships before them. The frigate and the *Themis* were closing on one another rapidly. Gunports of both ships were open, and on the upper decks the gun captains could be seen elevating or lowering their weapons. The *Themis* was not going to pass as near to the French ship as Hayden had, he could now see but, even so, they would be close enough that much damage could be inflicted.

Hayden's own ship was being put to rights by the Spanish sailing master, the bosun and his crew, who hurried about the decks and climbed aloft, shouting to one another in rapid Spanish.

The two combatant ships came abreast of one another and Hayden was sure every man on deck held their breath an instant. At such short distance the flash of powder and the sound of the explosion were simultaneous. Dense, roiling smoke enveloped both vessels. Immediately, it began to blow off in long tendrils, even as it swirled into the back eddies of the sails.

The ships emerged from this darkness, and Hayden could see that the enemy frigate had much damage to her sails and rig.

Hayden pointed. 'I believe Mr Archer has fired bar and chain, Mr Hawthorne. Do you see the ruin he has made of the Frenchman's rig?'

As the *Themis* emerged from the veil of smoke that

clung to her, the second French ship – the converted transport, sheered off, shifting her yards to run dead before the wind.

'At least that privateer has mastered rudimentary sums,' Hawthorne observed. 'A dozen 12-pounders opposed to a broadside of 18-pounders . . . Clever lad.'

'And his rig has less damage than Mr Archer's, so he will have the advantage for a short while.'

The two British ships converged in but a few moments, and Hayden climbed up upon the rail, holding on to the mizzen shrouds. He pointed off at the retreating privateer. 'That ship is yours, Mr Archer,' he called.

Archer waved back and nodded, turning to call out orders. The two ships passed of an instant, and Hayden's vessel held her course, quickly gaining on the frigate that Archer had partially disabled.

Hayden went striding forward on to the forecastle, where he might see his chase more clearly. Gould was there with a glass screwed into his eye, though the ship was so near Hayden had to wonder why.

One of the hands quietly warned the midshipman that the captain approached and he hastily lowered his glass and touched his hat. 'There is a great deal of damage to her rig, sir,' he reported. 'I think her topmasts might carry away with but a little more encouragement, and they are taking in all sail above the topsails.'

Even without a glass, Hayden could see that this was true. He could also see that they would overhaul this ship in but a few moments.

'Mr Gould, go down to the gundeck, if you please, and inform Ransome that I intend to range up to windward of this frigate and engage her at close range. Pass the word for the Spanish officers.'

'Aye, sir.' The midshipman went off at a run.

A moment later, sailing master and junior lieutenants hurried on to the deck.

'We will overhaul this Frenchman in a moment,' Hayden informed them in Spanish. 'Let us clew up our courses. We will be to windward of her, so she will be in much smoke, but I do not want to give them an opportunity to board, as I believe they have numbers.'

The Spaniards nodded approvingly and immediately began sending men to stations. Hayden took one last look at the frigate before them and strode back to the quarterdeck. Two ships built to the same draught and identically armed were about to engage each other at short range. Around him, Hayden could see a smouldering and determined anger. These were the Spaniards who had fallen victim to and been made fools of by these same French privateers. The opportunity for redemption, if not revenge, was welcomed most heartily.

Hayden's frigate slowed just as they caught up the privateers, the Spanish sailing master estimating the speed of the two vessels precisely, and clewing up sails at the appropriate instant.

Hayden returned to the quarterdeck, where he could stand near the helmsman and where Ransome could both relay his orders to the gundeck and take his place should he fall. As his ship drew near the privateer, Hayden found himself hoping above all things that Angelita would be deep within the ship, as Reverte had suggested, and would remain untouched by the violence.

As the bow of Hayden's ship came abreast of the privateers' aftmost gun, it fired, and then the next. Clearly, the French hoped to do damage and kill members of Hayden's gun crews before his ship could fire a broadside – and it was certainly worth trying, in Hayden's view.

'Mr Ransome,' he called out between shots, 'order Mr Wickham to fire as she bears, if you please.'

Immediately, the forward guns spoke and then each gun aft of that in order. It took a moment for Hayden's ship to come abreast of the Frenchman, as the difference in their speed was so small, but then they were firing guns as quickly as they could be loaded and run out.

Around Hayden, chaos erupted. Splinters from the bulwarks spun past, even as musket fire and iron balls from the deck guns murdered his crew and tore away his rigging. When men of the larboard battery fell, others stationed at the starboard guns took their places, sometimes pulling the dead or wounded clear, and leaving thick smears of blood upon the planks.

The binnacle exploded not a yard from Hayden, and he picked himself up from the deck a second later, dazed and uncertain if he were injured. A moment he stood, searching his side, where he felt pain, but decided he was bruised only.

For a quarter of the hour the two ships battered one another from close range, until it became clear that the guns on the privateer spoke less and less frequently, and then they fell silent altogether. The enemy vessel was half hidden in smoke, but Hayden ordered his own crew to leave off firing and, in a moment, the wind cleared away the great cloud. There lay their sister ship, her rig in ruins, her decks littered with bodies and debris, her guns blasted from their carriages.

Men draped a flag over the ruined bulwark of the quarter-deck, but it was not, as Hayden expected, a British flag to signal their surrender – it was a yellow ensign. The *Yellow Jack*.

Thirty-three

Hayden ordered boats launched and went himself aboard the prize, anxious the entire way and searching among the Frenchmen at the rail for a sign of Angelita. As he came up the side, he found the crew gathered on the quarter-deck – a smoke-stained and beaten group who to a man appeared to bear some small wound or other. Among these downcast sailors he found both de Latendresse and Don Miguel Campillo, the latter with his arm bound in what appeared to be a bloody shirt.

'Who is the master of this vessel?' Hayden asked in French.

De Latendresse replied. 'The captain was killed in the action – may God have mercy on his soul.'

May he have mercy on yours, Hayden thought.

'I am in command,' de Latendresse admitted. 'I am the captain.'

'You are no officer,' Hayden said coldly. 'You, sir, are nothing more than a spy. And you,' he said to Miguel, 'aided this man. In good faith, I offered you my help, and you chose this course instead – to become a traitor to your own nation.'

'Better than accepting handouts from the likes of you,' Miguel replied in Spanish.

The blood drained from his face as he said this, he wavered an instant, and then slumped slowly down on to the deck. Although he looked as though he might pass into unconsciousness, no one seemed to care or even to take notice.

'Mr Wickham? See to their surrender. And Mr Gould?'

'Sir?' The midshipman stepped quickly forward.

'Will you examine Don Miguel's wounds? God help me, he is my brother-in-law yet.' He turned his attention back to de Latendresse. 'Where is Mrs Hayden? What has been done with her?'

'She is below,' de Latendresse said, and ordered a man to lead Hayden to her.

Marines went ahead with muskets at the ready, but there was no resistance, only wounded and dead lying on the ruined gundeck, which was slippery with blood.

Hayden was taken down to the hold, where he found all the ship's sick and hurt, lying upon barrels, but for one cot, suspended and screened off from the others by a bit of sail.

Hayden went there, unable suddenly to breathe. And there he found his bride, shiny with sweat, her beautiful face a sickly yellow hue.

'Do not come near,' she whispered. 'I have the fever.'

Hayden went immediately to her side, all but collapsing down on a short stool that stood on planks by her cot. He took up her small hand, which was inhumanly hot.

'You are always a bit late,' she said, her voice so thin it was not even a whisper. 'But here you are, all the same.'

'I will have Griffiths here of an instant,' Hayden told her. 'He has physic for every hurt. He—'

She put up her hand to quiet him. 'There is no physic that will heal this hurt . . . The true apothecary comes for me.' She closed her eyes and tears pressed between the lids and, though she made no sound, her shoulders shook.

'Is Mr Smosh nearby?' she managed after a moment.

'He is . . .'

She nodded, and then with effort whispered, 'I will be buried in the religion in which we were married.'

'You are not going to die.'

'Charles . . .' she said softly, but very firmly. 'That is my wish.'

Hayden found he could not speak, but nodded.

She put a hand upon his heart. 'You will keep me there – I know. There, safe . . . until we are both called from our long sleep.' Tears flowed freely then. 'So short was our time together in this life but all of eternity awaits us.'

Thirty-four

Hayden had arrayed her in the dress in which she had been wed and then sewn her into a cocoon of sail cloth. He paused then to weep the most bitter tears of his life. She appeared so very small when they bore her up to the deck, as though whatever had made up Angelita in life had already fled.

The officers and crew gathered on the quarterdeck, where Smosh spoke in his deep, sonorous voice. His words, as kind and profound as they might have been, seemed nothing more than bits of air to Hayden. They hardly registered.

The day appeared somehow imbued with solemn beauty, the sea of tropical blue spreading out to the south, a little whisper of wind, and hardly a cloud to sully the sky. Gulls ranged about the ship, mewling sorrowfully.

What occurred seemed somehow impossible to Hayden, and he had difficulty believing that he attended the funeral of his young wife, who but a few weeks before had been vibrant to the point of overflowing with the life she had been given.

The voice of Mr Smosh penetrated Hayden's numbed mind, and the final words registered.

'We therefore commit her body to the deep,' he said, 'to be turned into corruption, looking for the resurrection of the body when the sea shall give up her dead . . .'

They slipped her into the endless depths, and condolences

were again offered, until Hayden found himself alone on the quarterdeck. For a long time he stood at the rail, his mind in a whirl of strange emptiness. He could not give the order to make sail, to leave her there alone, sinking slowly down to the ooze and the darkness.

But he could not keep his ship on station for ever and, finally, he ordered sail to be made and their course shaped for Barbados. He went down to his cabin, then, and sat quietly by himself, listening for the sound of his own heart beating, for the tiny murmur within that he would bear with him until his heart could speak no more.

Acknowledgements

I would like to thank all of my friends who read my manu-
scripts and offer their kind comments: Stephen Ariss, Don
Deese, Greg Janes, Doug Swanson, Chuck Bates, Carol
Shaben, Jack Moss, Brendan Russell and, my first and always
most trusted reader, my wife Karen. I want to thank Rob
Margolis, who has advised me on all of Hayden's legal matters over the course of four books. I want to thank my friend,
the intrepid small-boat sailor Gil Mercier, for lending Hayden
his name when he is in France. One of my advisors passed
away this year – Lyman Coleman, who was the retired senior
padre of the Canadian Armed Forces. Lyman advised me on
all things religious in the Hayden books and had been a friend
for several decades. There is a little bit of Lyman in Mr Smosh,
and he will be missed by many. I want to thank my editors,
Alex Clarke and Sara Minnich, for all of their hard work and
insight, as well as the teams at Penguin USA and UK. I would
also like to thank my fantastic agents, Howard Morhaim and
Caspian Dennis.